PRAISE FOR WOLF'S MATE

"Wolf's Mate is powerful, compelling and intense."

— LINDA L. OLIPHANT, AMAZON REVIEWER

OMG!

— BOOKGYRL, AMAZON REVIEWER

A must read series for fans of fantasy.

— JEANIE JACKSON, AMAZON REVIEWER

WOLF'S MATE

GWEN RIVERS

ELEMENTS UNLEASHED MEDIA

WOLF' MATE

THE UNSEELIE COURT BOOK 3

Bound by Fate....

Nic Rutherford has a big problem. A magical problem. A classmate has unearthed a deadly secret and is using it to blackmail her. Will she be forced to kill an innocent to protect her supernatural life, including her boyfriend, Aiden? Can she live with herself if she uses her power to destroy a pure soul?

Forever Apart....

Aiden's been keeping secrets of his own. For a shot at vengeance against the woman who destroyed his family, Aiden has agreed to keep his mate in the dark. Though Nic is all he could ever want, the past stalks him with every beat of his heart. Will his silence cost Nic her life magic? Will he ever be enough for his mate?

One Final Chance to Save All....

Two selfish hearts must learn to beat as one. To trust and accept not only each other but themselves and destiny. For if Underhill is allowed to rise to power, the mortal realm will fall. *Ragnarök*—the end of the world is at hand.

WOLF'S MATE

PROLOGUE

Loki's Poem to Nic

Pretty dead girl
How will you die?
First fire, then water
And the stab of a lie.

Pretty dead girl
What will you gain?
Knowledge is power
Unless you're not sane.

Pretty dead girl

Third time will do it
The wolf at your bosom
Will be sure to see to it.

ISN'T THIS AWKWARD

I really don't want to kill the nice girl from my American History class.

Gretchen Hamill's life is just too damn sad. Her outgoing little sister is hosting the junior high event of the season—a massive sleepover not twenty yards away from where we are standing. Her mom, the supposed adult supervisor, is busy trying to recapture her misspent youth one glass of Chardonnay at a time. While smart and sweet, it's clear Gretchen doesn't fit in with the rest of her family. She's a plus size girl living in a size double zero world. I'm the closest thing she has to a friend. Cutting her life short would transform her unhappy existence into a tragic one.

Plus, there's the fact that she didn't do anything wrong. Curiosity killed the cat, but it shouldn't be the undoing of a teenage girl. Her tenacity and dedication will serve her well as an adult. One day she might cure cancer or reverse climate change. She's got the makings of a hero.

I, Nic Rutherford am the villain of the piece.

And Gretchen's got the evidence to prove it.

I stare down at the photos Aiden, my partner in crime,

had just handed over. The pictures will raise too many questions. Me, in a short skirt and slutty make-up going through the pockets of a corpse. A decent lawyer could argue that I didn't kill the man in question. Perhaps I was just a lowlife who'd stumbled across his body and gone through his pockets looking for money. Except Gretchen also has photocopies of my diary, which contain the dead man's driver's license, as well as the ID's of all my other victims.

And it stands to reason if she has the copies, she possesses the original as well. The fluffy diary with my unique and highly identifiable fingerprints all over it.

Fuck fuck fuckity fuck *fuck*.

Aiden stands a foot away, waiting for me to decide what to do. His hands are loose at his sides, his anger fully contained. Some guys act like monsters. Aiden actually has one trapped within him. I've seen the wicked claws punch through his fingertips like something out of a Marvel movie. His wolf is probably howling that he ought to *take care* of Gretchen in the classic mob boss sense of the phrase.

It's my call to make though. I'm his queen, an uncrowned queen, but still head honcho. For now, Aiden stands beside me looking sexy, still dressed in the black on black suit from our date. The male equivalent to my little black dress. His dark hair ruffles against his neck in the cold breeze while his leaf green eyes assess the threat. We look like two normal teenagers out on a special evening, not two magic wielding immortals contemplating murder.

"What are you?" Gretchen repeats her question.

She has compiled more than enough evidence to not only send me to prison, but to have me studied in a lab by scientists with questionable ethics. Maybe I've read too many physiological thrillers, but I can easily imagine being vivisected by creepy guys in white coats who want nothing more than to figure out what makes me tick.

And Gretchen's knowledge endangers more than me. She also has photos of Aiden. Maybe not as damning as mine, but someone somewhere would probably wonder at his ability to travel in the form of embers and shift into a wolf. Then there are the pictures of my aunts, Chloe and Addy, who literally hid the bodies of the perverts I'd offed after said perverts attacked me. My friends, Nahini and Freda and her daughter Jasmine, the teenage half-nymph at the slumber party inside. Plus, several other members of the Wild Hunt, the ethereal army from Underhill that is currently camping out at my farm. All their destinies hang in the balance.

I tighten my grip on the photos, not wanting them to slip from my grasp. Gretchen could have already turned these over to the authorities. The fact that she didn't tells me she's not interested in mortal justice. Which means there's still time to unfuck this situation.

Option A: I can step forward, place a kiss on her cheek and she'll fall to the ground, dead. It's how I kill, via the goodnight kiss. Through an odd twist of fate, my lips make me a weapon in human form. I can kind of control it, which is why Aiden is still around.

I don't like option A. For one thing, I have never murdered an innocent person before. I don't want Gretchen to be the first.

Plus, there are the logistics. I can't just leave her dead in her driveway wearing only her ugly nightgown that looks like her grandmother ordered it from the Sears catalog in 1978. That's just too cruel.

She might have told someone. The thought gives me pause. It makes sense she would've shared her insight in case she didn't return from confronting suspected murderers with preternatural abilities. But who would she confide in? Her parents? Her younger sister? Killing her might not stop the exposure, but instead, be the final nail in my coffin.

Then there is option B: Find out more. We need to know what she wants in exchange for her silence. I can always snuff her later if she backs me into a corner.

Slowly, I hand the pictures back over to her, then reach for Aiden's arm. It's a deliberate gesture, one intended to not only offer comfort to my wolf and myself but to humanize us in Gretchen's eyes. He stiffens but otherwise doesn't react. Good. I can talk to him telepathically when necessary, but I don't want the distraction of carrying on two conversations at once.

"I'm human," I say, deciding that tidbit is no more damning than what she already has on us. I speak only for myself since Aiden is the cursed son of a trickster god. I'm not sure what that makes him but summing it up for her would raise too many questions. Besides, this wasn't about divulging more secrets before I find out what she wants.

"But you're not entirely human." She points to the photos. "Right?"

"Until last spring I thought I was. I was born mortal." That I am no longer isn't relevant. Just with maybe a little extra thrown in.

"And the rest of them?" Gretchen shuffles the photos to one of Alric with a falcon on his arm.

He's a Spriggan, a type of fey who controls the birds and beasts of the Wild Hunt. Alric is beautiful, but no one who has seen him move would mistake him for human. "He's fey. They all are."

"Fey," Gretchen pushes her boxy glasses up her pert nose. I've never seen her wear glasses before. She probably uses contacts during the day. "As in fairies?"

I nod. "I know it sounds crazy, but yes. We come from a different world. A hidden realm called Underhill."

Her expression is inscrutable. "Hidden? Is that where you go when you disappear? Not doing more of…this?" She waves the pictures at me. The girl appears remarkably calm, considering we're discussing cold-blooded murder.

"That's right. I have obligations that take me back there sometimes."

Aiden makes a choking sound and I don't need to hear his voice in my head to know he's thinking *that's one way to put it.*

Gretchen appears to digest what I've told her. "So, what are you doing here? What do you want?"

Aiden squeezes my hand hard and projects a mental warning. *Tread carefully, sweetness.*

The affectionate nickname reminds me that I'm supposed to connect with her. Bonding with others has never come easy to me. I struggle for the right words. "Right now, we're talking to you."

"And before you came here?"

Good, an easy one. "We were on a date. Our first official date." One that had been going pretty well up until Gretchen's unexpected phone call.

"Oh." Her baby-fine dark hair is loose around her shoulders and hides the pink tinge in her cheeks. She looks young, even though she's the same age I am, almost seventeen, there's something vulnerable about her. Of course, she is mortal.

And breakable. It occurs to me that I might not be the biggest threat Gretchen is currently facing. The fey have remained hidden since the dawn of time, protected by the Veil, a web of spirits that cloak Underhill from Midgard, the mortal realm. But fairies do cross back and forth, drawn to rural places where they can manipulate and steal from humans without risking exposure or capture.

I take a hesitant step forward and hold out a hand, palm facing up. "May I ask you a question? Have you told anyone else about all this?"

Gretchen shakes her head. "No. I didn't think...." She trails off, her face flaming red.

"That anyone would believe you," Aiden finishes the thought for her and casts me a sideways glance. Without warning, he lunges for her.

"Aiden!" I bark. "Stop it!"

He doesn't though. A few hours ago, Aiden would have had no choice but to obey my command, immediately and without question. On our date, he'd finally taken the unbinding syrup that dissolved his oath of absolute obedience to me. After centuries of subservience, he's finally his own master.

Now, watching him feel up Gretchen, I wonder if maybe that wasn't a mistake. What the hell has gotten into my wolf?

"Ah-ha," he extracts a cell phone from the pocket of her flannel nightgown and pulverizes it with one hand.

"You were recording us?" Mental forehead smack. The possibility didn't even cross my mind. It should have. Gretchen must have gotten all these photos herself, shot them from a distance. Pictures could be doctored. Getting a taped confession, however, would cement her story.

I'd have been condemned with my own explanation.

Fury churns in my stomach and I take a step closer to Gretchen. "And what was the plan once you had my confession? Turn me over to the police? Sell what you had to some tabloid?"

"No," her light brown eyes round in fear. "Nothing like that."

I get right in her face, my deadly lips inches from her own. "Then what is it you want?"

"Nic," Aiden warns.

I ignore him. "What was the plan, once you gathered all this information?"

"I want to go with you," she gasps.

I blink. "Go with us?"

"To run away with you." She casts a forlorn look back at the house. "Find someplace better."

I blow out a frustrated breath. "Gretchen, Underhill isn't better. It's worse. There are all sorts of things that want to eat you, poison you, trap you, enslave you. There was no industrial revolution. Half the inhabitants are starving, illiterate and run around naked. Why do you think they come here to steal peanut butter and blankets?"

She licks her lips nervously. "I don't care. I want to see it for myself."

I make an exasperated sound and turn to Aiden, thinking *You explain it to her. Your social skills are better than mine and my patience is running thin.*

"My lady," he begins, his courtly manners rising to the fore. "What is it you're running from?"

Gretchen blinks, obviously trying to reconcile his politeness with the guy who'd frisked her a moment ago. "I'm not running from anything. I just want to see this place."

"Lies," Aiden taps the side of his nose and offers her an apologetic smile. "I can smell them. You have a comfortable life here, you are safe, loved. Why would you wish to give that up? To risk your life without cause?"

I see her eyes flash on the word loved and her lips press together, forming a tight seal. Stubborn, I never realized she has such a stubborn streak and my estimation of her rises when she says, "My reasons are my own."

"I'll make you a deal, Gretchen." I lift my chin, feeling more like a fey queen than ever. This is what the fey do, make bargains with foolish humans.

She turns to face me, chin up. "I'm listening."

So is Aiden. I can tell from the way he turns stiff, all the easy charm vanishing into thin air. *What are you up to, Nic?*

"Aiden and I will take you to the farm. To meet some of the others." I gesture to the pictures.

Her lips tilt up. "And if I can manage them, you'll take me to your home?"

"The farm is my home," I correct. "And the fey there—the Wild Hunt—are sworn to serve me. But if I bring you there, you have to promise to obey me. For your safety and theirs."

Gretchen studies me a moment, but I see the flare of excitement spark in her eyes. "What do you mean, obey?"

"You need to vow that you will never reveal your findings to another person. Not your family or friends or the authorities. And when I tell you something is too dangerous, you need to back off, instantly."

Nic. Aiden's mental voice is tinged with exasperation. *She can't just disappear. She'll be missed.*

Maybe, but if she stays here with her evidence and other fey find out, she'd be dead. I meet his gaze briefly. A muscle jumps in his jaw but he doesn't argue.

My focus shifts back to Gretchen. As queen of the Shadow Throne, I have the ability to tap into any fey powers from my subjects, including beguilement and compulsion. Problem is, my abilities don't come with instructions and I never know what exactly it is I am borrowing.

"Come with us," I hold out my hand and as I do a sharp gust of air from the north lifts my hair off the back of my neck. Air is my element and the crisp scents on the wind give me strength. "Let us show you who we really are, what we can do. And if I answer all your questions, you'll return my diary."

Behind her glasses, Gretchen's eyes are the size of duck eggs. Slowly, she reaches forward and takes my hand. Hers is warm and damp despite the chill night. I try not to sag in relief.

I decide to test her oath. Unlike the fey, mortals can tell lies. "Give Aiden those papers."

She frowns then holds out the stack of evidence.

Aiden holds the papers in one hand. There is a flare as his innate fire ignites the paper. Gretchen squeaks in surprise and leaps back, but the flame disappears as quickly as it had flared to life. Aiden opens his palm and ash trickles to the ground.

"Do you have the diary in a safe place? Somewhere that no one will find it accidentally?"

Her gaze darts from Aiden to me and then back. She nods but doesn't say more.

"Does your family know where you are?" I ask, sending another glance to the house.

Gretchen swallows and clears her throat. "I told them I was staying with my grandma. They never bother to check."

My head tips to the side as I take her in from a new angle. "And if you tell them you're going to move in there for a bit?"

A shrug. "They'll probably throw a party."

Yowch. "Then that's what you'll do. I'll go with you to pack your things."

"I already have a bag packed." She bends down by the rhododendron and extracts a small duffel.

"So sure of my answer?" I raise an eyebrow.

She shakes her head and looks down. "No. Just hopeful."

I can feel Aiden's sharp green gaze on me as I lead Gretchen to my battered pickup truck. I send him a level look and one mental word. *Later.*

This is a mistake. Mixing mortals and fey never turn out well.

I smolder at him a minute. *It's worked for you and me so far.*

His leaf green gaze turns soft and he runs one finger along my jawline. *That's because you're no longer human. You never really were one of them.*

I don't respond, don't tell him that in her own way,

11

Gretchen is just as much a misfit as I'd been. I've always known she was smart and capable, but I didn't realize *how* capable. She's followed me, spied on me, on a band of immortals, including the Fates. That takes massive amounts of both nerve and skill.

Mankind isn't known for dealing well with those who don't fit nicely into the prescribed mold. Especially teenagers. It's a communal flaw the fey take shameless advantage of at every opportunity. Like a lion stalking an injured gazelle, the forever young will prey on mortals who aren't part of the herd. Gretchen caught me in the act. Better I show her some small kindness and have her work for—rather than against—us.

Nic. The strain is clear even in Aiden's mind.

I hold out my hands, palms up so that the two rune marks, one a jagged and sideways A shape, the other a down-facing double arrow, are visible.

Time and resurrection. Souvenirs from the land beyond the Veil.

Instead of taking my hands as I'd intended, Aiden stares down at the markings. A muscle jumps at the side of his jaw.

"We can always kill her later," I say under my breath.

"You won't." A lock of shaggy hair falls across his forehead. "She isn't one of yours."

There's no talking to him when he's determined to brood.

Forking over Gretchen's bag, I murmur, "It'll be fine, promise," before scrambling up in the cab next to her and shutting the door in his skeptical face.

"I'll come to you later." Aiden tosses the duffel in the bed of the truck and then floats apart in a shower of sparks.

Gretchen gasps, even though she had a picture of Aiden and me in exactly that state. "How does he do that?"

"It's a gift, from his father." Loki, the trickster god.

She fingers a thin silver chain around her neck with a

cursive lowercase 'g' dangling from it. "Things must be very different…where you come from."

Our gazes lock and I shift into reverse. "Gretchen, you have no idea."

It's a silent ride through town and back to the farm where I live with my two aunts, Addy and Chloe. Addy has a veterinary practice at one end of the estate. Our home, along with the Wild Hunt's camp, is at the far side. I bypass the turnoff toward the clinic, the only part mortals of western North Carolina typically see and head up the gravel drive toward the farmhouse.

"So, does Aiden, like live here? With you?" Gretchen asks, once again fidgeting with her necklace.

"Sometimes, though he's building his own place." Something I'd only discovered a few hours ago. "He stops by regularly though."

She nods, accepting this and then asks, "Are all of the fey…like him?"

"Like him how?" We pass the barn which is lit from within and bursting with the sounds of fey revelry, heading instead to the gravel drive in front of our farmhouse.

I can't be sure in the dim interior but I think she's blushing. "You know, so… sweet."

A snort escapes. "Sweet? Aiden?" Of course, she's only seen his gallant side, not the tortured soul who blames himself for every loss he's endured over his endless existence. Not the vicious predator, the ruthless protector, the hot-blooded lover.

She nods. "Right, like he's actually listening when you talk. And he has this way of looking at a person, not like there's something wrong with her, but instead like she's unique. Special."

I park the truck and shut off the engine. "Aiden is one of a kind. But if you mean do the fey men respect women more than mortal males? Here they do." Out of self-preservation. The female of the species is deadlier. It's sensible to respect something that will merrily kill you.

She bites her lip, looking unsure.

"How long have you been following me?" I'm careful to pose the question in a neutral tone.

Even so, her head whips toward me. "About six months. Since right before Sarah's accident." She trails off, clearly not wanting to bring up my best friend's death.

I've made my peace with what happened to Sarah. Sort of. Feelings aren't my forte so I tend to ignore them. My interest lies more in the practical details than stopping to sort through a hopeless tangle of senseless emotion. "Was the rave the first time you saw what I can do?"

She nods. "I went to the warehouse that night."

I frown. "I don't remember seeing you there."

"I never made it inside." The charm on her necklace makes little *zip-zip* sounds as she tugs it back and forth along the length of the chain in a jerky maneuver. "I'd heard you two talking about going there at lunch and thought if I showed up at the same place, maybe we could hang out."

Gods. It took all my effort not to close my eyes and beat my head against the steering wheel for being so careless. "Then you saw me with Paul Anderson."

"Is he the man who followed you into that alley?"

"One and the same."

She takes a deep breath. "I saw him grab you and had my phone out to call for help. I thought he was attacking you."

"He was." All my victims had, male and female alike. Their last mistake.

14

She swallows audibly. "And then he just…fell. And you bent down and started going through his pockets. And I had my phone right there."

"So you took a picture." Of all the shit luck. "Okay. But you saw me in school the next day. I know you did."

That was the first day Aiden had shown up. I remember asking everyone around me if they knew him, including Gretchen.

"I was trying to figure it out. To get my head around what I'd seen. One second, he was attacking you and the next…the guy was dead. I thought maybe he'd had a stroke or heart failure or something. But the way you went through his pockets—you were so methodical. Like you'd done it before."

I had. More times than I can count on both rune-marked hands.

"I couldn't understand why you hadn't, I don't know, started screaming or run away maybe. And then there was no mention of the dead man in the papers. Nothing. I wondered if I'd imagined the whole thing. I'd almost convinced myself it hadn't really happened. But then there was the picture."

"So, you started following me." I blow out a sigh. Right after that encounter with the unfortunate Paul Anderson, my life had gone from occasionally strange to flat out bizarre. Gretchen couldn't have had better—or maybe worse—timing.

I shake my head. "Weren't you ever afraid? When you saw what I could do? Who was hanging around me?"

She scowls as if I've said something stupid. "Yeah, of course. But you were still you, most of the time. You just had this secret, like a superhero."

A snort escapes and I pop the door to the truck. "I'm no hero, Gretchen, believe me."

She scuttles down, flannel nightgown billowing in the

breeze. "You are though. You killed all those horrible things at the apartment complex."

"Valkyries," I supply and lower the tailgate to retrieve her bag.

Gretchen stops short. "Valkyries? They aren't fey, are they?"

"No," I grunt and toss the thing to her. Like Aiden, the Valkyries are something else. "They are servants of the Norse gods who walk battlefields and decide who lives and who dies. Left to their own devices, they are bitter, vengeful creatures with lousy hygiene."

"I heard that little queen," a voice hisses from the shadows.

I turn, shifting my sight to take in the spirit plane that exists on top of our own, the way skin lives on top of muscle. Ghosts, like that of the dead Valkyrie eavesdropping on us, are only visible some of the time. Without being tied to a corporeal body though, the spirits don't usually hold their mortal shape, more often traveling as mist or bits of fog. The spirit plane always shows me the shape of the soul though. Not that I need visual confirmation since I would know her hissing voice anywhere.

"Nightweaver," I greet the creature with a nod of my head. She isn't alone. Several of the other spirits tied to the Wild Hunt mill about with her, though none I recognize by name. "and company. This is Gretchen Hamill. She'll be staying with us for a while."

Gretchen gasps as the fog that rolls in around our feet begin to take a humanoid shape. Nightweaver's original form had been large and birdlike with murderous yellow eyes and she smelled of carrion. Being dead actually improves her, at least in my opinion.

The mortal girl steps back, eyes wide as the spirits circle around her like bandits circling a wagon train.

"Don't mind them." I push my way through one of the burly men wearing suspenders but no shirt. He disassembles then floats back together, none the worse for wear. "They're harmless, mostly."

It isn't a lie, at least with the mostly tacked on. Ninety-nine-point-nine percent of the time the dead souls tethered to the Wild Hunt do no more than skulk about like they are currently doing. They're a convenient way to send messages fast and untraceable and they round out the ranks without worrying about details like food, shelter, and weapons that living soldiers require. They don't need to sleep and must obey my orders and that of my third, Nahini. In the heat of battle, however, they are just as deadly as they were when they lived and breathed. Killers, culled by me in this life and my last to serve the Unseelie Court of Alba.

My court. Or it will be as soon as I get my ass in gear and reclaim it.

Taking Gretchen by the arm, I lead her away from the ghosts and over to the farmhouse. There'll be plenty of time to introduce her to the living fey in the morning. For now, I need to drop her off with someone I trust, and there are only five names on that particular list.

My aunts, Addy and Chloe, aka the Fates. Two of the three actual Fates from Greek Myth, also known as Norns by the Vikings. They've raised me since infancy and though they can be both strict and deadly, they are the most likely to understand why I've brought Gretchen to the farm.

Well, maybe *understand* isn't the right word. At least they both look human and won't try to trick her into a deadly bargain to eat her. Like me, Chloe and Addy aren't carnivores. The same can't be said for the Wild Hunt.

After unlatching the front door, I call out a greeting. Chloe is on the couch, her lower half lost under a massive knit blanket. Red gold curls spill like a molten river from a messy topknot. A trashy romance book with a bare-chested man and scantily clad woman entwined in a passionate embrace is in one hand, a glass of red wine in the other. She looks up at my entrance, smelling distinctly of strawberries and cream. "Nic! You're home early. That wolf didn't get handsy with you, did he? Or is it pawsy? I never know with shape changers."

"No, he didn't get anything with me." Though before Gretchen's call, I'd intended to get handsy with *him*. But hearing that wouldn't help Chloe sleep at night. I clear my throat and step aside to make room for Gretchen. "Something else came up."

Chloe's jaw drops open. The book falls from her hand, though she retains her grip on the wine. "Um, hi there. Sorry, we weren't expecting company." Chloe's golden eyes narrow on me.

"Gretchen Hamill, my aunt, Chloe," I say.

Gretchen clears her throat. "We've met, actually. At the clinic. You were there when I brought in my cat, Sassafras."

"Right." Chloe tosses the blanket aside and stands. "Nic, can I just speak with you in your room for a minute?"

Without waiting for my response, she stalks off. With an inward sigh, I shut the door and turn to Gretchen. "Just make yourself at home. There's food in the fridge, T.V. remote is on the mantel."

Gretchen sets her bag down on the bench seat next to my tattered backpack and nods, looking out of place and awkward.

I follow Chloe. The farmhouse had been gutted in the late nineties and redesigned with an open floor plan. Only Chloe and Addy's room up in the loft, the bathroom and my bedroom have actual doors.

Chloe paces the length of my room. Maybe it's my imagination, but I think I see blue and white sparks, like static electricity, coming from her fingertips. She rounds on me as soon as I shut the heavy oak door. "What the hell, Nic? Why is there a mortal girl here with no warning? And in that gods-awful nighty?"

"Not sure about the nighty." It didn't seem like the kind of garment one would wear to meet with a known killer outside of a cheesy horror movie. "And I didn't have a choice."

As succinctly as possible I fill her in on current events while simultaneously pulling on a pair of jeans under my dress. Denim and a hoodie aren't exactly queenly attire, but I'm not a decorative sort of queen.

"Blackmail?" All the fight drains out of Chloe and she lowers herself onto the edge of my bed. "You mean to tell me that shy girl with the posture of a mouse got the drop on you more than once?"

"Not just me. She has a photo of you doing your freaky swirly eye thing." I zip my red hoodie and then gesture to my own face with a circular motion to illustrate the point.

Chloe swears the same way she does everything else—with marked enthusiasm. "Addy's going to kill us both for being so sloppy."

"Where is Addy?" I perch on the end of the bed to pull on thick socks.

"At the clinic, catching up on inventory. She was too wigged out about you being on a date with Aiden, so I redirected her energies to some busywork."

"Good. Call her, tell her I'm home and encourage her to keep at it." I huff out a breath. "With any luck, she'll be there all night. Look, I need to go let Freda and Nahini know what's going on. Let's just keep the blackmail bit between us for now, okay?"

Aside from Aiden and my aunts, Freda and Nahini are the only other beings I trust fully. Freda is my First, commander of the Wild Hunt, second only to me. She's a buxom blonde badass warrior with a sadistic streak. Nahini, my third, is as deadly as she is beautiful, the most graceful killer that ever held a blade.

Chloe looks pained. "You know I can't lie to Addy."

I reach for my hiking boots. "You're not lying, you're just not telling her everything."

She casts me a sour look.

"The fewer people who know, the safer Gretchen will be. This is only temporary until I can figure out how to get the evidence back and ensure her silence in a non-lethal way."

She paces the small confines of my room. "Some of the fey know how to wipe memories from mortals. But the more memories she accumulates, the more risk in scrubbing her."

Boots laced, I dig my phone out from the tiny clutch purse Chloe had lent me. "What do you mean?"

She pauses by the window and looks out into the night. "Memories are funny. Anything can trigger them. Familiar scents, a noise, the way light filters through leaves. Each memory is unique to an individual so wiping them out isn't like erasing a straight line. More like unpicking threads from a knot."

I nod. "Nahini told me something similar when we were retracing my past."

"Right, so even if you cut the thread, memories that have significance have more than one way in. They can surface on the back of another memory." She shakes her head and cusses again.

I glance to my bookshelf, to where all my mythology and fairy tale information came from. "But the stories are littered with people who were taken by the fairies. You're saying they were lying?"

"No. When the fey take people, they put them in a pseudo trance, called a thrall. It's like being on a really strong medication that blurs the world around you. Everything takes on a dreamlike quality. The fey who can enthrall a mortal only do so for a year and a day. That way, they can release their thralls without having to manipulate their memories. But Gretchen was never enthralled. She will recall everything right up until this moment. There might not be a way to erase her memories without completely lobotomizing her."

It's my turn to swear, a string of curse words that make no sense and do little to make me feel better. "So much for the easy way out. Will you please keep an eye on her?"

After a pause, she nods once, this one much more reluctant. "Just hurry up. We're getting close to your birthday and there's much to do beforehand."

My birthday is October 31, Halloween or Samhain in the older places in the worlds. On that night I'm supposed to ride with the Wild Hunt across Midgard—the mortal lands—and cross the Veil into Underhill to reclaim the Shadow Throne. There I will rule the Unseelie Court until Beltane. At least that's how it worked in my last life.

"Any idea where Freda is?" I didn't ask about Nahini. She's been recovering from a horrific trauma and hasn't left her room.

Chloe undoes her bun and then retwists her hair. "In the bunkhouse, I'd imagine. Bard is putting on a show tonight. They invited me, but I wanted a little alone time."

I nod and plaster a smile on my face before opening the door. Gretchen is sitting at the very edge of the couch, obviously uncomfortable. Maybe it's just the scratchy looking nightgown.

"I need to go out for a few," I tell her.

She pops up like she has springs in her ass. "I'll come with you. Just let me get changed."

"I don't think—" I begin, but she snatches up her duffel

bag and heads into the bathroom before I can get the words out. The door shuts with a click.

"Determined, isn't she?" Chloe raises a red gold brow.

I eye the door and contemplate leaving without her. But with the tenacity she's demonstrated already, Gretchen will probably follow me out into the night with no idea where she's going or who might be hunting her.

In the end, I pace in front of the door and wait for her to emerge. Out of the corner of my eye, I catch sight of my reflection in the hall mirror and miss a step.

"What is it?" Chloe comes up to stand behind the strange dark-haired girl with my eyes.

"I'm still not used to it." I finger the dark locks, so different than my natural white blonde waves. Harmony, another refugee hiding at the farm, had helped me color it for a scheme.

She shrugs as if I'm being ridiculous. "Then dye it back until it grows out."

"It's not just my hair." I sink down onto the couch. "I'm one of the forever young."

Chloe picks up her wineglass and empties it with one gulp. "It's not so bad. You don't show the signs of age, won't get sick and wither away. You might live for hundreds of years…again. Many mortals would see that as a gift."

"Unlike Aiden." Somehow, I don't think my wolf looks at eternity as a blessing.

"Aiden." Always up for girl talk, Chloe lowers herself onto the seat next to me. "He's part of the problem, isn't he? Is it the age difference? His millennia and then some to your almost seventeen? Icky."

"It's not the age difference. If you add my two lives together I'm older than he is."

"So?" She raises an eyebrow.

"So, I have feelings for him. Physical ones. If Gretchen

hadn't called when she did, we might have…." Unable to say it, I wave my hand in a circular motion, to sum up.

"Done it?" My aunt supplies with a wide grin. "Do you need condoms? I have some."

I cast her a murderous look. "Don't laugh. This isn't easy for me to talk about, especially not with you. Wait, did you say you have condoms? Since when?" To my knowledge, my aunts don't date.

"I'll leave some in your room." Then as if just realizing what I'd said her scent shifts to roasted almonds. It's a smell I always associate with her affront. "And what's so wrong with me?"

"Other than the fact that you're my adopted guardian and up until a few weeks ago I thought of myself as asexual?"

She lifts one strawberry blond brow. "You'd rather talk to Addy?"

I shudder at the thought.

Chloe sighs. "You know what's wrong with your generation?"

"Which one?" I ask in a dry tone.

She ignores my quip. "You're all obsessed with labels and grouping yourselves like you're going to be sorted into bins of produce. At the end of the day, all being part of a group does is make it easier for marketers to sell you shit. Love is love. Let the haters screw around with the labels and just be who you are."

I stare at her. "But I've never had feelings for anyone before. I thought…maybe there was something wrong with me."

She makes a face. "You're talking to a woman who gets her jollies from trashy romance novels. Nic, sexual attraction is as unique as the person feeling it. It's like humor. Do you laugh at all of my jokes?"

"I would if they were funny."

23

"Smartass." Her tone is snide. "You laugh at the remarks that delight you. You feel an attraction for what attracts you. You're spending a lot of time trying to fight your feelings instead of embracing them. Don't you think you have enough battles already?"

Though I'm loathed to admit it, she has a point.

Chloe blinks, as if she's fighting sharp emotion. "As much as it galls me to admit it, Aiden is…special to you. Your feelings for him are different than anything you've experienced before, right?"

"Because of our history," I say.

She lets out an exasperated breath. "Because he accepts you as you are. That's all any of us want, really."

"There's just so much though. I mean I like him, I really like him, but there's all this mate stuff and it complicates everything."

Her eyes flash brighter. "Listen to me. Going on a date with him or doing anything more isn't promising him your forever. You are seventeen years old and you might live for centuries. The only person you need to worry about in the long run is you. If the wolf can't handle that, cut him loose."

"You'd like that if I broke up with him." I'm angry because I know she's right. She's hit the nail on the head. All the feelings I have for Aiden are so new. And every milestone has been filled with weight, significance.

"You want my advice?" Chloe arches one eyebrow.

"No, but don't let that stop you."

She ignores my sarcasm. "Keep it light. Easy-breezy lemon-squeezy. And speaking of squeezy, if you are planning to have sex, be safe."

If only it were so simple. Wolf meets serial killer, wolf can kiss serial killer, they live sappily ever after. But there are so many layers between us, around us, impacting us like a meteor shower. Our rocky past, my uncertain destiny, his stripped godhood. All his guilt and anger, my bevy of secrets, the fragile trust we are painstakingly building together stone by stone.

Then there is fact that the wolf who shares his skin views me as his mate. I have no idea what to do with that bizarre detail. What does the creature expect from me? Every now and then he sleeps on the foot of my bed, like a pet. But there are other times. Times when Aiden's green eyes flash with an unnatural hunger.

Times when I can sense him craving more.

And if somehow, we work our way through all of it, there's still freaking Ragnarök to contend with.

The end of the world is *such* a buzzkill.

"Gretchen," I call, unwilling to give in and brood over my train wreck of a love life. "We need to go."

"Just think about what I said," Chloe pats my arm.

Gretchen emerges looking even less comfortable than she had in the ugly nighty. Her black leggings are too tight around her chubby thighs, the sweater is gunmetal gray shapeless sack that does nothing to flatter her figure. The color makes her look sallow, like a girl going out after a long bout of illness. I'm no fashionista with my jeans and flannel wardrobe, but just looking at Gretchen makes me squirm in sympathetic discomfort.

Her honey brown eyes are bright though, sparkling with excitement. I keep my unflattering opinions to myself and lead the way.

Though the air is balmy, a sharp gust comes from the north, bringing with it the promise of cold, soaking rain. I just hope it holds off a little while longer. We pass the storage shed where the traitor, Isolde of the air sprites, is being held. There are no sounds coming from the shed, meaning Freda isn't currently questioning her. My second in command is relentless and I'm sure she'll have answers soon on how

Isolde managed to sneak *Seelenverkäufer* out of camp and into the hands of an enemy. The blade which reaps souls had belonged to me in my past life and had been in Freda's keeping since my untimely demise. My first had been brutal with her interrogation of the rogue fey. So far, she hasn't discovered who Isolde was working with.

"So why did you come to meet us in your nightgown?" I ask Gretchen in an effort to distract myself.

Gretchen shrugs. "If I wore something nicer like I was going out somewhere else, they might have gotten suspicious. Most of my clothes don't fit anyway."

"How come you don't have clothes that fit?" Gretchen's family lived in a mansion. I was fairly certain they could afford to buy her new clothes.

She swallows. "My mom wants me to lose weight so she buys stuff that's too small. She calls it motivation."

I call it sadistic, but I keep that to myself.

The barn is lit from within by hundreds of fairy lights. Not the battery-powered kind you can buy at a superstore, but actual bobbing bulbs of pulsing blue-white incandescence the color of skim milk. Though the decrepit space does have power, it is limited to a small generator that keeps the fridge and microwave running though neither is used often. The fey and technology don't mix well. Most of them resort to cooking over the large stone hearth or outside over smaller campfires.

The sound of rhythmic clapping greets us as we approach the building, along with the accompanying music. Some sort of stringed instrument, perhaps a fiddle or banjo—I'm tone-deaf and can't tell the difference—and a drum. I shoot a furtive glance at Gretchen. She appears nervous but not in thrall. The fey love music and use it to mesmerize mortals. I'll have to keep a close watch over her.

The hinges on the bunkhouse door groan when I pull it

open, but the boisterous song drowns out the noise. The bunks are up against the walls to make more room in the center of the space. The fey have formed a circle around whatever is in the middle, the living on the ground, some of the dead hanging out in the rafters, some incorporeal as mist, others holding their shapes. At five four, I'm barely shoulder height with most of the living warriors. Spotting Freda in this crowd won't be easy.

"Warriors and gentlefey, bodies and spirits." Bard's voice rings out over the clapping. I can't see the shapeshifter and have no idea what form he might be in but from his tone I can tell he's revving up for a show. "I welcome you to the revel. I welcome you, with a fairy tale."

Shouts of laughter. Fey humor, oy.

"Once upon a time there lived a young girl who kept a deadly secret. Though she was lonely, her aunts warned her to trust no one with her secret, not even her best friend. Then one day a wolf appears in the girl's village." At this, there is a flash followed by a howl.

"Did he...?" Gretchen is taller than I am and her eyes are wide." Did he just turn into a wolf?"

"Probably." Annoyed at my height deficit, I scramble up on a hay bale.

Another flash and Bard changes from a giant black wolf to his normal form of a sunrise colored, thin, hairless fey with no eyelids. "He is a clever wolf though and he is in disguise. The girl is the only one who knows he is really a wolf. And even though she knows she should be afraid of him, she is drawn to the wolf because he too has a deadly secret--he knows all of hers. From this life and the one she lived before, one where she was a powerful queen with powerful enemies."

Another flash and Bard becomes...me. At least the me I'd been before the dye job.

I start as I realize the "fairy tale,"—oh hardee har har, shifter— is actually a twisted version of my life. The wolf is Aiden, just like he'd been when I knew he didn't fit into my little world any better than I did.

Bard's storytelling magic bounces off the warped boards of the barn, trapping everyone in his web of intrigue. Still wearing his Nic suit, the shifter tosses his head so the white-blond hair billows like a banner then continues in my voice, "One day when the girl and her wolf go for a walk in the woods, they come across a group of hunters. The hunters have been ordered to capture the wolf by the queen. The girl and the wolf run away and hid in a magic tree where a wise giantess lives."

Another flash and the other Nic is replaced by Aiden's grandmother, Laufey. "The giantess teaches the girl about spells and magic and most importantly, that she can't hide and keep secrets forever. The girl decides she must face the queen to protect her wolf, her aunts and everyone in the village. But the wicked queen has captured her best friend. The girl cannot save them both so she must choose who lives and who dies."

Flash, and Bard transitions back to his resting form. He sweeps one long finger across the crowd, pausing for dramatic effect. "For she knows that secrets are deadliest when they are unleashed."

I've heard enough of my life filtered through the shifter for mass fey consumption. "Come on," I shout and grab Gretchen by the arm. "We need to get closer to the center."

But before we make it two steps, there is a scream. It is not a sound of fright but pure indignant fury. The massive barn door crashes against the wall, making dust from the exposed roof timbers stream down on fey heads. The reverberation echoes through the room, loud enough to disrupt the festivities.

"Where is she?" Freda bellows from behind me. Though once mortal, the official leader of the Wild Hunt has proven her ferocity to even the bloodthirsty fey, who cower before her quivering wrath. "Where is Isolde?"

"She's gone?" My throat goes dry at the question.

Freda's gaze meets mine. "And so is the Soul Reaper."

MISSING PIECES

*D*ead quiet accompanies Freda's announcement. I inhale slowly through my nose and try to keep my eye from twitching. This was not the sort of news I wanted broadcast to the entire camp. Not only did it undermine our authority, her announcement might have warned a potential traitor that we are onto him. Freda's infamous temper got the better of her.

I push my way through the crowd until I am standing before her. "You're telling me Isolde somehow managed to escape and took *Seelenverkäufer?*"

Seelenverkäufer, the Soul Reaper is the official weapon of the Wild Hunt. Whoever wields it has the ability to cross the Veil between the mortal world to the fey realm of Underhill without using an in-between, most of which are monitored by the fey courts under the hill.

To put it mildly, a missing *Seelenverkäufer* is bad news.

If Freda is surprised to find me here in the middle of the revel instead of on my date, she doesn't show it. "I double-checked her bonds myself after her latest interrogation.

There's no way she could have escaped on her own. Someone must have set her free."

"Line up," I command the fey soldiers in the room. "The First will do a headcount."

"First?" Gretchen asks as the soldiers make haste to follow my command.

With all the commotion I had forgotten her. "It's an honorific title because she is second in command of the Wild Hunt."

"So, who is first in command?" Gretchen's brows draw down.

"I am."

There is a surge of movement as the well-trained fey stand at attention. The Wild Hunt may have a reputation for causing chaos, but they know how to follow orders better than any mortal force.

Bard pushes his way through the crowd to me. The shapeshifter isn't a member of the Hunt and isn't under any obligation to obey my orders. He's more like a shape-changing mascot.

"Nahini isn't here," he says quietly. "Harmony and I tried to get her to come out, join the revel but she refused to leave her room."

"She didn't even acknowledge our presence." The seer's voice is accented with Latin spice.

I jump and then scowl at her pleased expression to my reaction. Her name is ironic as everything about the fey female sets my teeth on edge. Her purple skin and blatant sexuality, her underhanded jibes and especially the way she always seems to get the drop on me. The seer has helped me in order to help herself and though I don't exactly trust her, it's impossible not to admire her resourcefulness.

Freda finishes her scan of the rows. "Five missing, as well

as Alric, Nahini, Jasmine and your wolf. The Fates are also not present."

I know Freda's not accusing anyone, only being thorough. "Jasmine's across town at her sleepover. Chloe's at the house. She told me Addy is at the clinic. And up until an hour ago, Aiden was with me. I don't know about Alric though."

A tinge of red creeps up Freda's neck. "I can vouch for him."

Translation: they'd been taking advantage of Freda's daughter's absence by making the beast with two backs.

"Who was supposed to be guarding the prisoner?"

"I was, my queen." A fey male with pointed ears steps forward. Many of the fey have pointed ears but his are unusual as they include little tufts at the tips like a lynx. The fur twitches as he continues, "I made sure the door was secure and the iron padlock in place. I was only planning to be gone for one song—"

"Enough," Freda's tone is crisp. "Report to my tent in the morning for discipline."

Freda grew up in a poor Nordic village and centuries riding with The Wild Hunt has only sharpened her jagged edges. Discipline might mean anything from a whipping to days of forced fasting. I don't envy him.

The guard's ears droop a bit but he lifts his chin and nods. "As you command, First."

"The rest of you are dismissed," Freda barks.

There is no grumbling about the abrupt end to the entertainment. The fey file out, as fleet-footed as cats. Soon the barn echoes with the sound of silence.

Someone bumps into me from behind. Gretchen, who is trying to distance herself from Bard. I can't say that I blame her—Bard in his natural state is unsettling to behold. At nearly seven feet in height with skin the color of a brilliant sunrise, he is bald as an egg and prefers to go around in the raw. The shapeshifter can't seem to keep his unnerving lidless gaze off of the mortal girl.

"You too, shifter," Freda addresses him. "And you, seer."

"We don't answer to you, human." Harmony's chin juts up at a defiant angle. "We're members of her court."

Freda's skin tone goes from pale to mottled as her already boiling temper spikes.

"Last time I checked I hadn't officially selected a court," I counter, not liking the seer's tone.

Harmony's purple skin flushes lighter instead of darker with embarrassment. "Any monarch would count themselves lucky to have a seer and an entertainer as a part of her court. I just assumed you would name us."

"You know what they say about people who assume, right?" At her blank stare, I add, "It makes an ass out of you and me."

She scowls in apparent confusion. "How can it make a donkey—?"

"Never mind." I turn to face my First, not wanting to explain mortal idioms or puns to the seer. Humor isn't in my wheelhouse.

Freda's eyes blaze blue fire and she takes a menacing step forward. If I carry an active dislike for Harmony, it's nothing compared to Freda's utter disgust with the seer. For her part, Harmony hisses like a cat and crouches into a defensive stance.

I surge between the two women before they come to blows. "Enough," I command. "This isn't helping. Freda, go get Nahini. Tell her I need her."

My second-in-command exhales audibly, then, with a final glare promising a reckoning to the seer, storms out of the barn.

"You realize I could banish you if I chose?"

Harmony stares at me defiantly. "I'm entitled to my opinion."

I shake my head. "Just do everyone a favor and keep it to yourself."

"Who is this delightful morsel?" Bard's lidless eyes gleam with interest and the human girl flinches.

"Gretchen, this is Harmony and Bard. Apparently, they are two members of my court. Though that can *change*." I put special emphasis on the last word.

Harmony sniffs as though repelled by Gretchen's very presence, but Bard places a hand over his heart and bows.

"Enchanted to meet you," he murmurs.

"You have no eyelids," Gretchen stammers.

His grin is predatory as in his actor's voice he murmurs "The better to see you with, my dear. You are positively scrumptious."

Damn it, I do *not* need more fairy shenanigans right now. I don't have the patience for their politics on a good day. Aiden is right, I shouldn't have brought Gretchen here. Unlike the Wild Hunt, Bard and Harmony are free agents and aren't beholden to my commands. There's no way to tell if Bard is enamored with the mortal sexually or is hunting for a meal. With the fey, it's a toss of a coin but I wish he wouldn't use food descriptors.

I glance around, hunting for someone to escort Gretchen back to the house and into Chloe's care. But Freda is lighting a proverbial fire under Nahini and Aiden still hasn't appeared. I don't trust anyone else with her, at least not until they get used to her presence. From the expression on the seer's perfect face, she wouldn't turn a hair, no matter how Bard behaved toward the mortal.

At least the shifter's unnerving attention keeps Gretchen from asking too many questions. I see them there, in her intelligent eyes. Thank the gods she's smart enough to hold her tongue.

"I'm going to inspect the shed," I announce to them all.

"I'll come with you," Harmony says.

At my raised eyebrow she adds, "To help you see in the darkness."

Harmony is a seer first and foremost, gifted with foresight. The talent isn't inborn the way most of the fey abilities are. Rather it's a souvenir from a near-death experience. She also possesses the gift of fire. Like Aiden, she can utilize flames the same way I would wield a flashlight. Though I am working on learning how to handle all the different powers I can borrow from my Unseelie subjects, the last time I tried conjuring fire, I'd singed my eyebrows off.

"I'll come too," Gretchen adds hurriedly, obviously petrified at the thought of being left behind with Bard.

"I will join you as well." Bard's voice remains cool and smooth, that of a professionally trained thespian.

I don't respond, instead focusing on backtracking to the storage shed. I hadn't looked closely at it when we passed by not even half an hour ago, but I knew the door hadn't been hanging open that way. I would have noticed the creaking sound of the rusty hinges as it blew back and forth in the light autumn breeze.

"I left it open," Freda materializes out of the darkness and falls into step with me.

"Nahini?" I ask when I see that she is alone.

"She was sleeping," I see the worried frown on Freda's face. "I thought it best to leave her."

I nod in agreement. Nahini barely slept and hadn't spoken a word since returning from her last trip across the Veil into Underhill. To say her experience as a prisoner of a Seelie king had been horrific is an understatement. I have no idea what to do to help her recover. Whatever her experience, her normal resilience is nowhere to be found.

Harmony ignites a small ball of fire that floats about a foot above her hand like a miniature sun. I toss an arm up to protect my eyes, but the gesture is reflex. My night vision has always been good but my transition to one of the forever young kicked things up to a whole new level. Same with hearing and my sense of smell.

Which is how I pick up on the metallic scent. "Do you smell that?"

Freda and Gretchen shake their heads but Bard answers, "Blood."

"And lots of it." Harmony holds her fireball out and scans the small space. "I don't see it though. What sort of fey was she?"

"Half nymph," Freda responds. "The other half was human."

"Then the blood should be the same red color as a mortal's would be." Bard waves a hand and between one heartbeat and the next, transforms himself into a bloodhound.

"'Scuse me," he says as he brushes past Gretchen to enter the shed. She blinks but steps out of the way. The long ears drag on the ground as he sniffs, black nose twitching.

"Here," he lifts his head, his voice coming out of the dog even though the creature doesn't have the capacity for human speech. "It's soaked into the dirt floor. A lot of it."

I move to his side and bend down, pressing my bare palm into the space he indicated."

"Nic don't," Gretchen squeaks in protest. "The diseases."

"I can't catch them now." I lift my hand and study it in the light of Harmony's torch. "This is a lot of blood. Maybe a few gallons. Would she have been able to survive this?"

"Not if she was half-human," Freda sighs. "Though she

wouldn't visibly age, she has all the weaknesses of a mortal, including a limited lifespan and slow recovery from injuries."

The blood is making me a little dizzy. Gretchen had been right to warn me against touching it. Immortality may have gifted me immunity to disease, but it did nothing for my squeamishness. I wipe the appendage on a moth-eaten saddle blanket that the missing fey had been using as a bed and then frown as I hear the crinkle of paper.

I glance up and meet Freda's gaze. "Did you give her something to read?"

"Of course not."

I extract the crumpled note from beneath the blanket. One word is scrolled on it and the message chills me to the bone.

Tonight.

"Tonight?" Harmony asks. "What could it mean?"

My court, as I'm coming to think of them, have all gathered on the front porch of the farmhouse. Chloe, smelling of anxiety and licorice, Addy with dust and cobwebs coating her long braid and shoulders from her storeroom adventures. Bard back in his creepy resting shape, Freda and handsome blond Alric. Nahini and Aiden are still conspicuously absent and Gretchen has shut herself in my bedroom for the night. Smart girl.

"Obviously that whoever helped her escape was planning to do so tonight." Freda frowns at the seer.

"But something went wrong," Bard says. "They must have had a falling out, maybe over *Seelenverkäufer?*"

"Not necessarily," Addy murmurs. She'd shot me an indecipherable look when she'd seen Gretchen but she's all business now.

I nod, my thoughts traveling along the same wavelength. "Isolde might have wounded whoever entered the shed and he or she is the one who's down an enormous amount of blood."

"Or perhaps they staged the whole thing."

This last comes from the darkness and I smile in relief to see Aiden step up onto the porch. He too has changed into jeans and a long-sleeved black t-shirt that molds to his muscles. His leaf green gaze fixes on my face and I hear his voice in my head.

So much for a night off.

I glance away even as the knots in my chest ease a bit. Having him here makes the entire thing more manageable.

"Staged?" Bard, our resident thespian, frowns. "Why?"

I field that question, having already surmised what Aiden had meant. "If we think Isolde is dead, we won't go looking for her."

Aiden nods. "Which means they are probably close by, waiting for a chance to escape across the Veil."

In some places the fabric of souls that make up the Veil is stretched thin, making it easier for those who know how to cross. A little while ago, I tore a giant hole through the sucker but I know from firsthand experience that crossing through it is a bitch and a half.

"But they have *Seelenverkäufer.*" Freda points out. "They could cross wherever they want to with the sword."

We all consider that for a moment.

"That must mean the aim isn't just to cross," Chloe says slowly. "At least not right away."

Freda sets down a map of the nearby area she produces from the gods alone know where. She points with one hand. "The farm is here. We're assuming they are on foot since any human vehicle would have made noise and the sentries would have spied it."

"And all the Hunt's mounts are here," Alric adds. "Though I would have liked to see them try to steal one of our warhorses. We'd be picking up the pieces well after Samhain."

Freda nods once. "If that's the case they would only make it about three miles an hour over such rough terrain."

She draws a radius with her other hand around the farm. "I recommend we split into groups, start at the outer edges of the circle and work our way back in."

I get to my feet. "If we want answers, we need to find Isolde and whoever took the sword. Alric, do you have any hounds that can track Isolde?"

When he nods I point to him and Freda. "You two head east, away from town. Aiden and I will go the other direction." Aiden's nose can track as well as any dog and we would be less conspicuous than two fey and a pack of hounds heading into downtown.

"What about me?" Bard and Harmony say practically in unison.

Though the shifter could visibly pass for human in a pinch, Harmony's purple skin would attract unwanted attention from the residents of our small mountain town. "You two can search the farm and the nearby woods, but I want you to stick close. Call me if you see anything." This last is directed at Harmony, who nods once in understanding.

My courtiers trickle off and Addy has the discretion to wait until they are out of earshot before rounding on me. "And I suppose we're to babysit your newest mortal acquisition?"

I frown at her tone. I hadn't believed she'd be happy about Gretchen's arrival but snide isn't typically her style. "Look, I didn't have a choice."

"You could have killed her." The Fate's tone is matter-of-fact as she plucks a cobweb from her braid. "How do we know for sure that she hasn't shown the evidence you conveniently kept to the authorities? Damn it Nic, I told you this would happen!"

It clicked then. Addy had always hated that I'd kept the licenses of my victims, had given me a rash of shit whenever she discovered one missing. The killing of murderers, rapists and other deviants she didn't have a problem with but the trophies bothered her. In hindsight, keeping the journal had been stupid. I should never have been so foolish to give in to my craving for a physical reminder.

"Did you know this would happen?" I ask the goddess of foretelling.

She lets out a soul-deep sigh. "It doesn't matter now. Everything happens for a reason."

My lips part though I'm not sure what to say. Aiden takes my elbow. "We should go if we're going to make it to town and back by sunup."

I turn to my aunts. "I made Gretchen a promise and I intend to keep it. She's a good person and she doesn't deserve to die for her curiosity. I'm entrusting her to you two."

I can feel Addy's gaze boring into the back of my head as I walk away.

"She's worried about you," Aiden murmurs low.

She isn't the only one. "Do you mind if we check on Nahini before we go?"

"Of course." Aiden offers me his elbow in an endearing and old-fashioned gesture.

I take it and we make our way to the bunkhouse.

"Where did you go? I was expecting you to meet us here?"

"I have something in the works that I needed to check on."

I frown up at him. "Cryptic much?"

He glances down at me. "Sorry, it's a holdover from when I was a god. You can talk to one for an hour before you realize he's told you nothing. Loki is especially good at the doublespeak."

I don't miss that he didn't answer my question. Chloe's advice about easy-breezy lemon-squeezy keeps me silent.

The lights are on in the bunkhouse and several members of the Hunt who I don't know by name bow to me as I cross. "Your majesty."

"As you were." I try not to look as uncomfortable as I feel in their living space. It's kind of like walking through a fey locker room, with many of them wearing nothing more than their skin. Many of the fey don't wear clothing, though the Hunt dons armor when they ride. But somehow it's more intimate to see them lounging on bunks in the raw than striding across a training ring or dancing around a campfire.

Nahini's room is off the main corridor. Because of her rank, she has her own room with a door. Said door is open a crack but there's no light on inside.

"Do you wish me to wait here?" Aiden asks.

I nod. "Yeah, maybe you should."

"Don't tarry too long, sweet. The trail might grow cold."

"This will only take a minute." I slip through the open crack in the door and hold still for my eyes to adjust. I listen for any sound of breathing but hear nothing.

"Nahini?" I speak slowly in case she is still asleep.

There is no movement from the bed, no shifting.

I creep forward. A shaft of moonlight filters through the oak branches that have grown over the hole in the dilapidated roof. Most fey are uncomfortable sleeping indoors and prefer a natural canopy to a roof. Nahini is a turned mortal, like me, but never mentioned a preference.

She hasn't mentioned much since her last trip to Underhill.

I see the streaks of white in her hair first. It had appeared after the Seelie King, Wardon, had captured her and

41

condemned her to a trauma she hasn't yet spoken of, at least not to me. I haven't seen her since she regained consciousness. Her lids lift and I can tell she is looking at me, though she has yet to speak.

"I didn't mean to wake you."

"Lie," my third says.

I smile grimly. She always knows. "Don't tell anyone else that I can still do that."

"Only if you agree not to tell Freda I was feigning sleep when she came."

"Deal." There is nowhere to sit in the room so I remain standing. "Do you know what's going on?"

"My brother told me Soul Reaper is missing. I sent him and the Valkyrie to look for it."

Nahini's brother is one of the spirits tethered to the Wild Hunt.

My heart is in my throat. A week ago, I wouldn't have been able to imagine Nahini not going out to look for the sword herself, especially because *Seelenverkäufer* has power over spirits. Nahini's brother and the ghosts of the Wild Hunt mean everything to her. Yet she's still lying in bed.

"Is there anything I can do, for you, I mean?"

She turns away. "I fear I am broken irreparably. I must resign as your third."

Neither will be as you remember them. Harmony's prediction of what would happen to Aiden and Nahini under Wardon's ministrations has come to pass.

I don't have time to talk her down. Too much is at stake. But she needs help and tenderness isn't my MO.

I square my shoulders. "Resignation not accepted."

She starts. "Nic,"

"Get up, get dressed. You need to help with this search." Though I hate pushing her, Nahini is strong. I can't leave her to wallow in misery and action will at least distract her for a time.

I hope.

She is still for an endless moment. I wonder what I'll do if she outright refuses my command. Killing her is out of the question and I'm not good with the subtler reprimands. Maybe Jasmine can help. The half-fey girl has a devious mind for making the punishment fit the crime.

But finally, Nahini gets to her feet, without her typical fluid grace. She moves like an old woman rising from a sickbed, but her posture is ramrod straight as she draws herself to full military attention. "As you say, my Queen."

I nod crisply then return to where Aiden waits in the hall. His hearing is enhanced by his wolf's senses so I'm sure he heard every word.

And because he's Aiden, he says the right thing. "You did what you needed to do."

I lick my lips. "Do you think she'll be all right?"

Instead of answering, he takes my hand in his, raises it to his lips and I see him blurring around the edges, feel my own body coming apart as he shifts us from solid to sparks. The sensation unnerved me the first few times Aiden had done it, but now I savor the unique feeling. It's as if my soul is being set loose on the world, no longer hampered by physical confines or the laws of gravity. I close my eyes and summon the North Wind, using it to propel us closer to town.

All too soon we are on the outskirts of downtown, which isn't much more than a gas station, a hardware store, a hair-dresser and a diner along with a few other professional businesses in the office spaces above each. Several of the windows are boarded up, ventures that either went out of business or relocated to an area with a larger and more affluent customer base.

"That," I say, pointing at the defunct used bookstore,

"would be a stellar place to hide out, if one was in the market."

We cross the street and press our faces against the plate glass window. The books are long gone, but large dark shapes mound up in shadowy piles and draped with bedsheets and plastic. Furniture is most likely.

"No lights," Aiden murmurs.

"Fey live by the light of the sun and stars," I remind him. "One who's recently crossed over might not know about electricity." I blow out a frustrated breath. My instincts tell me our missing traitor is nearby. "I want to see what's going on in there, but breaking and entering doesn't seem smart."

Aiden studies the empty street. "There were some from Asgard who could detect power like that in Soul Reaper. I wish I knew how."

He doesn't speak of Asgard or its inhabitants very often. "Didn't you have any friends among the gods? Anyone that would have helped you escape or learn to control your wolf?"

His expression goes flat. "No."

I put a hand on his arm. Intentionally touching him is still a foreign sensation but I bully my way through it, for his sake. "I'm sorry, I didn't mean to pry."

"The past is done. I can get us in there." He chucks a thumb to the alley. "Shift to embers and go down the chimney, then unlock the door for you."

"Like Santa Claus?" I let my hand drop. He doesn't want to talk about his time as a god. Message received. *Keeping it light, Chloe.*

"Only sexier." He winks and in spite of the tense situation, I smile. That's something Aiden's taught me how to do—smile, laugh, enjoy myself. It's no wonder I'm falling for him.

Whatever's between us is more than simple curiosity. Being with Aiden, trusting him, makes me feel good. When he's not around, I miss his company. When he is, his presence snags my attention. It's like everyone else is in black and white and Aiden in vivid color. When I'm with him, for the first time in my life, I'm tempted to let everything else fade away.

Not smart when so many things want to kill me.

Aiden raises his face and then the transition takes him. Man to sparks in the span of a heartbeat. I call the air again, speeding him on his way. The sharp gust helps cool my flushed face.

Time and place, Nic. Keep your head in the game if you want to keep it on your shoulders.

It takes Aiden less than a minute from standing on the sidewalk beside me to unlocking the deadbolt. A little bell jingles as he opens the door. "That chimney is a disgrace. The next person who lit a fire in here would burn the place to the ground."

"I'll take it up with the town council," I murmur and push past him. Though it's dark out with only a sickle moon in the sky, the interior of the abandoned book shop is even more oppressive. The haphazard furniture is coated in a thick layer of greasy dust, the kind one would need a scrub brush and soap to combat. Some of the shelves have been tipped over and left as they fell.

We pick our way around the debris, careful not to over-balance the shelving units and send them crashing to the ground. I take a step, the toe of my sneaker connecting with something squishy. I squeak at the same time the mouse does and stumble back into Aiden. He pulls me tight into his chest, keeping me from landing hard on my ass.

"You okay?"

"Fine," I pant, embarrassed. "Don't tell anyone about that."

"What? That the big bad Unseelie queen is afraid of a mouse?" His tone is too innocent.

"I'd never live it down. The growing faint at the sight of blood thing is enough of a handicap."

"I've got your back, Nic."

Something in his tone causes me to jerk my head in his direction. Even though I can't see more than his leaf green eyes, which seem to glow in the dim room, I get the feeling that he's worried about something. Something more than our missing traitor and *Seelenverkäufer*.

Maybe I can ease his mind, even though words and I aren't always great together. "I know you do. You always have. I trust you, Aiden."

His lips part as though he's on the verge of saying something when there's a loud crash from the closed door in the rear of the building.

"What?" I ask.

Aiden is already in motion, putting himself physically between me and whatever might be back there.

A high-pitched keening sound erupts. Almost like it's another mouse. Only one in terrible agony.

"Aiden," I say but he vaults over a tumbled down bookshelf, transitioning into his wolf form in midair. He lands on soft paws, hackles up, ready to give hell to whatever lurks behind the door.

It creaks open on rusty hinges. Aiden doesn't growl, gives no warning before he leaps. The figure in the doorway is knocked down beneath his weight. I hurry forward to see whomever it is my wolf has pinned.

"You," I frown at the dark-haired stranger who I'd caught staring at me in the cafeteria a few days earlier. He'd been noteworthy simply because I knew every face in our dinky junior-senior high school.

"Me," his tone is cautious. The boy's eyes are closed. He swallows once and then opens his eyes. "May I get up?"

"No," I snap. He doesn't look fey but that doesn't mean

much. Most of the more powerful of the forever young possess glamour—the ability to change their appearance at will. Whatever resides under the handsome boy next door face could have engineered his cowlick, could be faking the slight tremor in his hands.

He looks again at the wolf and swallows hard.

"Don't meet his gaze," I snap. "He'll take that as a challenge. Just focus on me. Tell me who you are."

"Queen Nic-Nicneven," he stammers.

"That's my name."

Quit playing with him. Aiden's voice cautions in my mind. *And let me kill him.*

I don't answer the wolf because the brown-haired youth is speaking again.

"Queen Nicneven, heir to the Shadow Throne and the Unseelie Court of Alba. My name is Soladin and I'm here to help."

THE LAST MONARCH

"Soladin," I repeat the name. "As in King Soladin of the Seelie Court and ruler of the Green Throne?"

At his frantic nod, I mentally relay the orders to Aiden. *Let him up.*

The wolf looks at me over his shoulder.

"Let him up," I repeat the command out loud. He may no longer be compelled to obey me, but I am still his queen.

Slowly, the wolf removes one giant paw and then the other from the boy's chest. Soladin sits up and scrambles back, as though a few feet might provide some defense against the wolf's sharp teeth and claws.

I give the Seelie king a minute and study his appearance. The streetlight outside spills through the unshaded window and casts his profile in sharp relief. He's handsome, though nowhere near as good looking as Aiden. He's shorter, stockier, like a wrestler. His hair isn't artfully messy, it's just a mess. He looks overwhelmed as well as overexcited. To say he isn't what I'd been expecting as the last fey monarch is a massive understatement.

Both Brigit and Wardon had been larger than life, beings who commanded attention and received it in turn. Soladin appears so… ordinary. A little rumpled, a little dazed, though that might be due to Aiden's rough handling.

I rack my memory, hoping to find the bits Nahini had told me about the mysterious Lord of the Land. Not much was known about him, other than that he takes in refugees from other courts, specifically my court when Brigit sacked it. It was rumored that he'd been sired by the god Pan. As in I'll stick my prick in anything, because I can, Pan.

And Wardon, the psychotic Master of the Waves, feared him. That alone was reason enough to make me consider him as an ally.

"What exactly are you doing here, Soladin?" I put a hand on the wolf's head, letting the Seelie king of summer know that he was outmatched.

"Looking for you," he huffs the words out.

"Why did it take you so long to approach me?" I ask. "I noticed you in school on the first day."

"I wasn't sure who you were."

When I raise a skeptical brow he adds, "At least not until you gained immortality."

"How can you tell?" Even I'm not certain if Underhill made me immortal. Unlike most of the turned humans, I can still lie. And no one told me not to talk about what happened when I faced the immortal gauntlet.

"My gift," he touches his lips and smiles shyly.

The Kiss of Clarity. Where Wardon could drive a being mad and I can kill with a kiss, Soladin is able to help clear a struggling mind, ridding it of madness and overwhelm.

Maybe I should kiss him.

Aiden growls, and I jerk my head in his direction. Had he heard that thought?

Yes, the literal green-eyed monster thinks at me.

I blink, stunned that he'd be jealous of the fey before us. Not only is Soladin not my type—that is he's not Aiden—I'm having a hard time believing he is who he claims.

Could this soft-spoken guy really be the bastard son of the notorious god Pan? Wardon, the other Seelie king, had double rows of teeth, like a shark. Brigit had been beautiful and radiated feminine power. Soladin stutters and is in desperate need of a good barber.

Then again, I don't actually look like a garden variety serial killer. So much for appearances.

Aiden, still in his wolf form, hasn't taken his attention from the fey, though at least he's quit snarling at him.

"So. Like Brigit and Wardon, you heard the rumors that I'd been reincarnated and decided to spy on me?"

When he shakes his head frantically, I let out a huffy breath. "No? Then what are you doing here?"

"I wasn't. That is I'm not…," dark eyes, the color of rich loam, go wide. "I've handled this badly."

I wait and watch him flail. It's not in my nature to put others at ease or offer reassurances.

He takes a deep breath, shoots a tentative glace at the wolf and then turns his focus on me. "From what I've heard, Brigit and Wardon sent spies to observe you. I sent myself. I wanted to meet you. To work with you."

"Why?" Wardon had ambitions to become the supreme ruler of Underhill and then conquer the universe. Brigit had just wanted the competition dead. I wonder what motivates this fey leader.

He squeezes his eyes shut and admits, "I need help. The courts are falling apart. Every day more refugees spill across our borders from all three of the other courts, running from monsters and the war over Underhill. I can barely feed my own people and now minor skirmishes are breaking out over the few resources we possess. The Unseelie thrones sit empty and now Wardon is missing as well. Our people are frightened and I don't have what it takes to help them."

His tone grows stronger as he speaks, his words obviously heartfelt.

I school my features, not letting on how much his plea bothers me. *This is my fault.*

It's not. Aiden responds though I hadn't meant to project the thought to him. *You've been doing the best you can.*

"You still haven't said what it is you want from me," I focus on Soladin.

"Come back. Take up the Shadow Throne. It's almost your time. Help me restore order." His eyes are large, pleading.

"I plan to, come Samhain," I tell him. Even if he's not who he claims to be, I *want* word to spread that I'm coming for the Shadow Throne.

"There might not be anything to return to by then." His gaze drops away.

He's hiding something, Aiden thinks at me.

I agree with the assessment. "What aren't you telling us?"

When he doesn't respond right away Aiden lunges at him.

The fey scrambles away from the gleaming white teeth. "They are only rumors, I sent a squad to investigate but they haven't reported back."

"What sort of rumors?" I prompt.

"You won't believe me." He shakes his head from side to side, as though he doesn't believe whatever it is himself.

"In the last six months," I say slowly, "I've gone from being a teenage serial killer to a fey queen. I've crossed the Veil between worlds roundtrip not once, but twice. Believe me, my threshold for accepting outrageous and improbable things is high."

51

Aiden snorts and I clench my hand in the fur of his ruff to still him, unwilling to look away from the fey king.

Soladin studies me for a minute and then nods. "Though I haven't seen them myself, people claim the Draugar have returned."

There is silence for a full minute.

The dead are walking, Aiden mentally mutters, as though to himself. *Ragnarök approaches.*

"The Draugar? As in Viking zombies?"

Soladin nods. "Some say entire villages have been decimated."

An uneasy feeling is taking root in my stomach, flourishing in spite of the gut twisting acid. I'd been warned about resurrection and becoming Draugar. The spell or rather the rune that produced them is entrusted to a handful of people.

The Fates. A few gods. Underhill.

And me.

I exchange a silent glance with Aiden. If Soladin is who he claims to be and the rumors are true, we have a bigger problem than the infighting over the Unseelie Court to worry about.

"What is it you think I can do?" I ask Soladin.

"Bring your army to my lands. We need the might of the Wild Hunt. If we unite our forces and convince the Unseelie who hold the underground catacombs, we might stand a chance."

"But how do you kill something that is already dead?"

I extend a hand to Soladin. He hesitates for a moment and then takes it. Allows me to pull him to his feet, though he doesn't let go of my arm.

"Does this mean you'll return with me?" His brown eyes are wide, full of hope.

"I'll consider it." I'd be a fool to trust him, no matter how harmless he looks. "We have things to do here. Go back, do what you can, and I'll come soon." I try to pull my arm away but he holds on, his grip like a vice.

Soladin stares at me for an interminable amount of time. "I promised my people help. I won't return without you, Nicneven."

"You're going to have to," I snap. "Let go of me."

Aiden growls, the warning clear in the dangerous rumble. The Seelie king holds out his hand, there is a brilliant green flash. The charging wolf freezes in mid leap.

My lips part but no sound escapes. I've never witnessed Aiden immobilized so quickly, didn't think it possible. He'd been born a god. The kings and queens of Underhill looked like infants next to the abilities the gods possess.

Aiden?

No response. Not a hair twitch or a muscle shift or the flicker of an eyelash.

Aiden! Panic echoes in my empty mind. I can no longer feel the mental bridge that connects us. It's like he's not even on the other end.

"Is he...dead?" I don't realize I've asked the question until Soladin answers me.

"No. Just out of time."

"What?" I blink at him.

The boy holding me is shifting, growing larger. Taller. He expands upwards until his head brushes the ceiling. The fingers wrapped around my forearm extend, an extra knuckle on each digit until he can encircle my whole limb. When he speaks his voice is deeper even than Aiden's.

"I wish you had agreed to do this the easy way."

He raises his palm, the one that had frozen Aiden. Green light explodes across my field of vision and then I see no more.

❄

My lids crack open in an unfamiliar room. At first, I think it is fabric but as it moves in a breeze I see gaps and realize it is a series of silk threads, like those spun from a spider. The four posters holding it up are rough boughs about as thick around as my calf. The soft mattress molds to me like a lover, encouraging lingering. Outside the open window birds twitter and a gentle breeze stirs the white sheers. The air smells of damp wood and wet leaves. All the decorative bits I can see are made of exposed wood, giving me my first clue whose home I'm in.

Wardon, the Master of the Waves, had lived in a palace of sand and sea glass. It stands to reason that the Lord of Land would craft his home from his element as well.

My mouth is mossy as though I haven't brushed my teeth for a week. I sit up, only to discover I'm not alone.

"Where am I?" I croak to the stranger with the broad shoulders. His skin is the color of rich espresso and he turns from his place by the window, his face creasing naturally into a smile when he sees that I am awake. His irises are the color of polished citrine and tilted up at the corners, like those of a cat.

"My queen," he bows at the waist, a long intricate braid falling over one shoulder. His voice is the deepest I've ever heard. "You are in the Seelie king's private residence. I am his royal consort, Taj."

"M'kay." My limbs feel weak, drained, but I push past the fatigue. I'm forever young now. Eventually, I will recover. And this room, no matter how fine, is still a prison. I don't do prisons. "Tell your guy that the next time I see him, I'm going to kiss him with everything I've got."

My feet hit the oak floor but my knees buckle beneath my weight. It's as though my limbs have transmuted into cooked spaghetti. In spite of my threat, Taj is by my side to catch me before I faceplant onto the beautiful hardwood.

He guides me back to the bed, steadying me into an upright position. "Easy now. You're still a little disoriented from the crossing. Give your body the time it needs to catch up."

Though I understand his words, they make little sense. "Catch up with what? What crossing?"

"With time, of course." There's a pitcher of water and a glass sitting on the cherry nightstand. Taj moves to it, pours then wraps my shaking fingers around the full glass. "From what his highness said, he froze you before bringing you across the Veil. Said you were not exactly cooperative."

Soladin had kidnapped me. Dragged my frozen form across the Veil without my consent. If my arms had been less wobbly, I would have thrown the beverage at Taj. The last thing I was going to do was eat or drink anything offered to me by an opposing monarch's consort. Especially after the aforementioned monarch had just abducted me.

"You have to understand." Taj pulls a wooden stool over to my bedside. The thing looks spindly, as though it couldn't support his great weight. It holds though as he lowers himself onto it until we are at eye level. "Soladin needs support. His powers are great but Rodrick plans to sack the city and he has all the weight of the Unseelie Courts behind him. Soladin brought you here to save lives."

Rodrick is Alric's bastard of a father, a warmongering former consort to Queen Brigit who'd helped her overthrow me in my last life. Alric's half-sister was his puppet queen. From everything I'd heard about the fey male, I could understand the Seelie king's apprehension.

"Save lives. That's not really what I do." The fuzziness is gradually clearing from my head and I realize that Taj and I are alone in the white and wood bedroom. "Aiden. What did he do with my wolf?" Even as the words leave my lips I stretch my mind, searching for any sign of him in my mind.

"Take a drink," he coaxes.

"No," I say and then try to set the glass down. My hands shake and the liquid sloshes over the side. I see him study my rune marks but he doesn't comment. Taj takes the glass from me with a sigh, as though he's being forced to deal with a particularly difficult child.

A knock sounds and the heavy oak door swings inward. Soladin, looking the way I'd last seen him, peers around the corner. "Queen Nicneven, I'm glad to see you're awake."

"Where's Aiden?" My voice grows stronger, worry for my wolf shaking off the last of my fatigue.

Instead of answering, Soladin leans down and brushes a soft kiss on the other man's cheek. "Taj, give us a minute."

"She threatened to kiss you," his consort warns. "And she looks angry enough to do it."

"She's not my type."

"Next time, send me to handle the negotiations. Stealing people from across the Veil never ends well." With a final glance my way, Taj exits the room.

Soladin watches him go, a small smile on his lips.

"Stupid," I say.

"What?" The smile turns to a frown when he looks at me.

"You let me know where you keep your heart. Before, I was just planning to kill you. But it would hurt you more if I claimed Taj for the Wild Hunt."

"You won't hurt my consort," Soladin says with ease. "For the same reason, I didn't hurt yours. We are not enemies, Nicneven."

"You didn't hurt Aiden?" I ask. I needed to hear him say it. Fey can't lie, or at least most can't. Humans who make the leap to immortality are also unable to speak an untruth. Brigit could and I never found out why.

I can still lie like a rug. Aside from my deadly kiss, it's the best weapon in my arsenal.

Soladin lowers himself onto Taj's vacated stool if anything looking more awkward than the other man had. "No. Your wolf is unharmed. I left him behind in Midgard. He should be awake by now and will notify your courtiers that you are here. The Wild Hunt will cross and then we can ride out together to face the Draugar and the Unseelie army."

"Why can't you do to them what you did to us?" I gesture toward his hands. "Freeze them in place and kill them that way?"

"It's a limited power, one nearing its end. Even if I managed to slay Rodrick that way, the Unseelie are riled, leaderless. And there is still the Draugar."

"And what makes you think the Unseelie will listen to me?" I raise an eyebrow at him.

"You're their rightful queen. The fey respect the bloodlines."

"It didn't keep them from turning on me before." In my last life, Brigit had marched the Unseelie fey on my summer palace and sacked it, killing all who'd remained loyal.

"You command the Wild Hunt, the host all fey respect. Rumors of your return have spread like wildfire through the courts. If you rise up, there will be those who follow. Together we can bring peace to Underhill."

"Sounds like you have it all figured out." With great effort, I push myself off the mattress. This time my knees hold. "Except there's one problem. When you crossed our path, Aiden and I were out hunting for a traitor. A traitor who escaped with *Seelenverkäufer*. Without the Soul Reaper, the Hunt has no way to cross the Veil, except through a tear, which I've forbidden them from doing. It is treacherous and demands a toll of life to cross."

Beneath his tan, the Seelie king pales. "I...I...," There's no way to tell if his stutter had returned or he's simply in shock.

I nod miserably. "Even if they did cross, without the Soul Reaper in my possession, I can't stop the Draugar. Congrats, Soladin. You kidnapped me and made an enemy of an Unseelie queen for no reason at all."

BLOOD PRICE

THROUGH THE WOLF'S EYES

*S*he's gone. He can sense her absence, sense the man's distress even as his body crashes to the ground. Pain radiates from the shoulder that takes the brunt of the impact. Ignoring it, he rises and scents the air, seeking her unique fragrance of winter apples.

Nothing on the wind. Nothing through their bond. She is lost.

This is your fault, he snarls at the man. *You've been keeping secrets.*

The wolf knows better than to keep secrets from his mate but the man ignores his instincts. He overcomplicates things that should be simple. The wolf is in control now, his rage and hunger for vengeance against the one who took her keeps him in the foreground.

Let me help. I can track her in ways you cannot. For once the man puts his useless guilt aside. *Give me control and I will convince others to assist us. Her friends will want to find her, too.*

Blood price, the wolf demands. Nothing less will do. The one who would dare take his mate from him must pay with his life's blood.

Again, the man surprises him. *Blood price,* he agrees.

The wolf senses his conviction. After a moment he recedes. He is a patient hunter. He will wait.

Through the Man's Eyes

Aiden shifts as the wolf releases its grip on his body. He scans the deserted bookshop, noting the lack of blood or evidence of a struggle. His head swims, partly from the shift, but mostly because of the damn time spell. Judging from the condition of the store, Nic must have been affected as well.

My mate would have fought. Would have brought the roof down on the fey king's head. The wolf's voice is edged with both worry and pride. *Find her.*

Thank the gods she is no longer mortal. She would have been unconscious for days after being yanked so violently out of time. His own head throbbed with every beat of his heart. Time manipulation was not an ability he'd ever heard of a fey possessing, not even a monarch. Who had the Seelie king bartered with for such power?

Angrboda. The giantess had been swapping magic with Wardon. Why wouldn't she trade with Soladin as well?

He thinks the name at the same time as the wolf. With a destination set he shifts, not to fur but to fire, up out of the chimney and into the night sky.

Even with his body in sparks, he hunts for any sign of Nic, Soladin, or other members of the Wild Hunt. His senses are muted in this aspect but still, he knows he would sense her if she were close. But Soladin didn't want Nic in

Midgard. The Seelie king required her assistance across the Veil.

Aiden closes in on his destination, a hunter's blind a few miles from the farm. When it's in sight, he dives for the clearing. His heart, when it reforms in his chest, races.

If she's in Underhill then Underhill can get to her, manipulate her with her half-truths, harm her. Cold sweat forms at the thought of Pharaildis having access to her.

You should have told her. It's not the wolf's voice but guilt, his familiar companion, rising to torment him. Nic didn't have any warning, didn't know that the woman who had once been her mother is now bound to the fey realm of Underhill.

She doesn't know the atrocities she's engineered.

He'd left a pair of sweats in a plastic bag outside the door and pulls them on quickly. Not in any concern for his prisoner's comfort or his own. It made Nic uncomfortable when he displayed his body to others. Not to mention a naked male running through the woods drew mortal notice, something he couldn't afford. The thief that stole *Seelenverkäufer* is still out there somewhere.

He makes no sound as he races across the pine needles for the door to the hut, which is little more than a storage shed. There is no lock that anyone other than he can see, just a glamour over the structure. If anyone else were to enter the building all they would find would be an upside-down tin bucket that had been used as a makeshift seat and a couple of moth-eaten blankets. A mortal or even a fey of the Wild Hunt could walk right past Angrboda, even use the water pump she's chained to and never encounter her.

The giantess, still trapped in her human glamour, looks up when he flings the door open. It crashes against the wall with so much force that dust rains down from the roof. Her cold eyes peer out from behind a matted curtain of bloodred hair.

She looks innocent, a victim, and not at all like the mother of monsters who will bring about the end of the world.

"Wolfling," she greets him, her expression neutral. "What vexes you this fine eve?"

Aiden ignores her question as well as the smug tone. "Who has been trading magic with King Soladin?"

She leans back against the wall, chains rattling with her movements. "Why should I tell you anything, pup? You hold me prisoner when I tried to save you."

"More of your lies," he snarls and lets the wolf peer out through his eyes.

She doesn't flinch or change her story. "It's your choice to believe me or not."

He stares at her for an endless moment, the Hag of the Ironwood. His father's consort and mother of his half-siblings. He's hated her since he found them together in the woods, his father with the woman who wasn't his loyal, loving mother…

"You're more like them than you know." The giantess smiles and it is a sad sort of expression. "You always have been. My children didn't have your advantages, Váli. A pretty face to hide behind. The gods saw Fenrir for what he is, a predator, one who, if left unchecked, will destroy everything. And because of what he is he is trapped."

She sounds almost…sorry.

If she'd been anyone else, he might have felt bad for her. But she was the reason his father had strayed, the reason the life he'd known had been destroyed.

He stands before her, fists clenching, wanting to inflict the kind of hurt on her that she had on him. He should have killed her. Should have let Underhill kill her and told Nic the truth. Then she wouldn't be across the Veil and at the mercy of a madwoman.

Angrboda had traded magic with a power-mad Seelie king to capture him and he wanted to know why. He'd wanted vengeance, answers. A gods damned apology. Had traded Nic's justified faith in him for this sad woman who after days of imprisonment still insisted she had only wanted to do right by him?

If the price for his answers brought harm to his mate, he would never forgive himself. It was already a struggle to think logically past his guilt and need to protect her. He'd betrayed the fragile trust Nic had so carefully placed in his hands. Why hadn't he told her? Was he really so selfish?

If he lost her, if her life ended again, there would be no Brigit, no Unseelie Court and their machinations to blame. Logically, he knew the wolf had been mistaken. Nic would have been abducted whether or not he'd told her about Underhill.

But he could have prepared her better, told her who her mother is. Ignorance might see her ensnared. Or dead. And the knowledge that he could have prevented it would eat him alive.

He kneels before the giant and meets her gaze with his. "If you tell me who imbued Soladin with time magic, I'll let you go."

Her lips curl in a predatory smile. "Now which one of us is lying?"

Their standoff must end. Perhaps if he reveals why he is so motivated to find out anything useful about the Seelie king, she would relent. "Nic's been taken."

Her head jerks up. "Underhill has her?"

"Soladin took her, I don't know where but I can't sense her on this side of the Veil. I'm going after her, but I need to know who the Seelie king is bargaining with and what other magics he might possess."

"Not I." Angrboda rattles the chains again. "Set me free and I'll help you get her back."

"And why should I believe you?" He folds his arms over his chest.

"You bear my mark of debt, wolfling," she grunts in frustration. The chains tethering her also contain her magic, slowly siphoning it off, just as the Unseelie forged *Gleipnir* bound Fenrir. "I was trying to help you."

"By selling my mate to Wardon? He's mad."

She gets a mulish look in her eye. "Wardon is not mad, he's determined. I appreciated that about him."

"Right up to the moment when he tried to double-cross you."

She ignores that. "And I didn't know she was your mate. Only that she was the reincarnated Unseelie queen you'd dallied with. What are fey politics or politicians to us? No more than maggots. Annoying and disgusting, hardly worth notice."

"Careful, hag," he snarls a warning. Then reason surfaces. "If they are so unimportant, why were you bargaining with Wardon?"

She sniffs, looking more like a queen than a prisoner in chains. "Even maggots have their uses."

At his low growl, she switches tactics. "Wardon betrayed me and is incarcerated in the hall of giants. Without my assistance, he doesn't have enough magic to light a candle."

He narrows his eyes on her. "I only have your word to go on."

"My word should be enough," she snaps. "You have your reasons to despise me, reasons I even understand. But I never once deliberately set out to hurt you."

She lunges forward, clutching him by the ankle. "Listen to me, Váli. I could have handed you over when you came to the hall of giants. But I let you go. Ragnarök approaches and I can do nothing to protect my own offspring. I thought if I could keep you safe then maybe it would pay the blood debt."

The invisible marking on the inside of his arm tingles as he meets her steady gaze. The blood debt, the rune she'd marked him with so long ago. The memory of that night shoves its way to the forefront of his mind.

He'd been in human form for the first time since escaping the gods. Weakened by sorrow and starvation, he'd spied the tall figure draped in a silvery cloak. Had stayed still, hoping she was the angel of death, coming to claim him, to put him out of his misery.

Instead, she'd bent low over him and gripped his arm. Murmured something indecipherable. The marking had appeared, glowing as though she'd lit a fire under his skin.

"I'm sorry for what you've been through," she'd murmured. "For my part in it. And for your brother."

It wasn't until she'd spoken that he recognized her. This time when he jerked away, she let him go and left before he could go for her throat.

But her mark remained. Her vow to assist him whenever he needed it. In its own way, the rune was almost as powerful as his oath to Nic had been.

He recalled Nic's dismissal when he'd first approached her. Her stubborn refusal to allow him to help her in any way. Was he being just as short-sighted?

This is different, he tells himself. Nic didn't remember him or anything about their past together. She didn't trust him. Aiden knows exactly who the giantess is and what she's done to him.

Why Angrboda *couldn't* be trusted.

But she is right in one respect. The giantess had gone out of her way to not only not harm him, but to keep him safe. At great personal risk.

Perhaps she was telling the truth.

She rattles the chains again. "Like you, Soladin is the son

of a god. Pan possessed some minor abilities involving the slowing and speeding up of time because he ate a steady diet of bark from the Great Tree."

"Why would he do that?" From everything Aiden had heard, Pan was a god of beastly lusts and not much else. "The Great Tree is for time travel spells and enchantments. My grandmother and her lover are its custodians." He couldn't imagine Laufey handing bark from the sacred tree over to Pan.

"This was long before Laufey lived there when the Great Tree was known to all, respected by all. From what I've been told, Pan indulged in order to prolong his pleasure in bed. The original little blue pill."

Aiden raises a brow and she continues. "As well as to skip over boring political meetings. Most likely, his son learned how to manipulate time from him. Soladin might have a limited stash of the bark, but chances are it's near depleted."

He stares at her a moment, unwilling to trust her, unable to do anything else.

"Let me help you," Angrboda pleads. "I can't cross the Veil again but I can warn the Hunt. Don't lose time going back and forth. Pharaildis will manipulate her to suit her own ends."

She's right. The wolf is eager to get on with the search.

With a muttered oath, Aiden picks up a stray bit of metal. Holding it in his hands, he forges it into a key and then inserts it into the lock.

"If you betray me, betray her in *any* way, the last thing you see will be my teeth an instant before they rip out your throat," he vows.

She lifts her chin, shakes her unbound hair back from her face with a regal sort of dignity. She stands, her weeks-old clothing ripped and coated with dust, smelling none too pleasant but that doesn't seem to bother her. "I would expect nothing less, wolfling."

It's becoming more evident by the hour that the Seelie king has no idea what to do with me. Ever solicitous, Soladin has provided me with fine clothing, food, books-- items hard to come by under the hill. He's made flowers grow across my windowsill, fragrant blooms in every color of the rainbow. One morning I awoke to find an orange tree growing over my bed. I've accepted each offering without a word of thanks.

Thanks is too close to forgiveness for comfort.

He's tried to engage me in chitchat, a habit I abhor. He flinches when he meets my direct gaze across the table. At breakfast, he opened his mouth as though to pose a question, about the French toast invisible servants prepared especially for me. Or perhaps on my general comfort. All it took was one sharp sniff and he retreated like a kicked dog.

If I wasn't planning to plant him in the ground at my earliest convenience, I could almost feel sorry for him. Under different circumstances, I might have liked him. He and Taj both. But under different circumstances, I would have been a mortal teenage serial killer, not an immortal queen of the fey.

Earlier this morning I'd glanced up from a cantaloupe slice to see Taj patting his liege on the arm as though to console him from my frosty rebuff. Perhaps it's boredom but their relationship intrigues me. Though Taj's official rank is consort to the king which allows him certain privileges, he speaks his mind without hesitation, even if he disagrees with the Seelie king.

After witnessing the way the fey living around Wardon's estate groveled, and the lessons Nahini had told me of the authoritarian rule of the Unseelie courts, I was expecting something similar.

It appears my own court isn't the only one filled with independent thinkers.

Soladin always listens, no matter if the issue is the lack of kindling for the hearth or the ever-growing number of fey refugees seeking sanctuary within their borders. He considers the other male's words from every angle, never making a snap judgment. It might be some sort of act on their part but I am beginning to think that abducting me was probably the first and most likely the last impulsive act of Soladin's immortal life.

I stare out the window at the autumnal foliage. As with the servants, I have yet to spy any signs of the refugees. I have encountered no one in this place other than the two of them. It's as though they fear I might hurt someone innocent. As if I'm some kind of monster.

The fey other immortals fear.

I've nurtured their unease, coaxing it into full bloom. In their presence, I don't say much. I've never been a big talker anyhow so long silences don't bother me. During meals, I just sit quietly and observe them. Let Soladin wonder what I am plotting while I search for a way out.

I witness many things while I am sitting and watching them. Nothing pertaining to my escape plan. No, I witness personal things about them. The affection. Taj touches his king freely. Gripping his hand, putting an arm around the smaller fey's shoulder. They share looks laced with heat and promise at times, the emotion so intense that I can't help but feel a pang of…something.

It's not jealousy exactly. Envy perhaps for their easy relationship. Are they keeping it light? They seem content with one another. Of course, it is easy for Soladin to touch his lover. He doesn't have to worry about accidentally killing Taj with a kiss.

But if I'm honest it's more than that. Theirs is a relationship built on trust and mutual respect. Regardless of titles, it's clear that Soladin views his consort as an equal.

I wonder if they are mates if they could explain exactly what that is to me, but don't trust either of them enough to ask.

Tired of brooding in my room, I head for the door, the leaves of the orange tree rustling as I shut it behind myself.

Soladin's palace is designed like a beehive constructed of wood and leaf. Each compartment is connected by long echoing live wood hallways. I trail a finger over the knotty pine wall that connects my "guest suite" with the heart of the estate. The smooth boards pulse with something, though I can't tell if it's life or magic.

I turn into the atrium, an open area of flourishing plant life that connects the five hallways that stick out like spokes on a wheel. The left-hand corridor leads to the kitchens. The one on the right to the meeting room and library. The middle one is a straight path to the dining room, great room, and audience chamber. I have yet to explore the one adjacent to my own but I am fairly sure it's Soladin and Taj's private quarters.

Not in the mood to explore or intrude in their privacy, I study the atrium. Ivy snakes around tree trunks thicker than my torso. Overhead the autumn foliage blazes brilliantly in the sun. Pixie lights flit from branch to branch like glowing hummingbirds in search of the perfect red flower.

One zooms down to me, stops a centimeter from the end of my nose. So close I can make out her fine-boned features, her long golden hair. We stare at each other for a beat, then she casts me a lascivious wink and zips back to her tribe.

"Hey," I call up to her. "I want to ask you something."

There's collective giggling, then like a flock of birds, all the pixies zip-up out of the opened skylight.

There's no telling how long I've been here, how long I was unconscious or how much time has passed back on the farm. Time moves differently in Underhill, sometimes slower or faster than across the Veil.

I wonder if my birthday has come and gone, if Gretchen is still at the farm. If Nahini is talking and Freda is riding the Wild Hunt into the ground searching for me, the escaped nymph traitor and the Soul Reaper at the same time. If Harmony and Bard are still there or have moved on.

If Aiden is looking for me.

Scratch that last, I *know* Aiden is hunting for me. It's what he does. And loathe though I am to admit it, I hope he finds me soon. Since I'm having zero luck freeing myself.

Some people might love it here. The great stone hearths with roaring fires burning day and night filling the expansive rooms with light and warmth. Hearty meals served three times a day with the precision that would please a military officer. The finest linens I've ever slept on. Even a hot spring tub that the Seelie king invited me to use whenever I desire.

But a gilded cage is still a cage.

The doors and windows are sealed by magic. While it lets the air and light in from outside—and apparently pixies—when I tried to walk through, a grove of trees shot up and blocked my path. I'd spent an hour walking in what I believed to be a straight line only to end up back where I started.

"For our protection," Soladin said at our first breakfast when I asked about the barrier.

"Pass the butter." A vine grew out of nothing, wrapped around the butter dish and slithered across the table like a snake to fulfill Taj's request.

"Wardon used trolls," I comment, gaze locked on the vine.

The tip turned toward me as if it was tracking my every move,

"Wardon is an idiot," Taj stated in a droll tone. "One who misspent his magic and never saw to the practicalities. The forest barrier is much more elegant and won't turn on you at the first chance. Far more desirable."

Unless you were stuck within it. Gave a whole new meaning to lost in the woods.

I watch the doors sometimes, hoping to see how the spell works. Is it an enchantment or some sort of mystical talisman that makes the trees move out of the way for some and yet block the way for others? Soladin can't possibly be growing all the trees by hand every time I try to leave. But I have yet to catch anyone acknowledging the tree labyrinth. My questions remain unanswered.

I sit with my back propped against one twisted tree trunk. It's an odd variety, one I don't recognize. The broad flat leaves have a purplish hue, like the last kiss of twilight. Darker veins thread throughout like an old woman's hand. Hard to tell if that's an autumn embellishment or just it's typical coloring.

Maybe I could climb the tree and slip out through that open skylight the way the pixies had done. The top branches are about three feet from the edge of the glass dome. I've grown wings before to escape a sticky situation. But even as the thought emerges there is a scraping sound as a leafy moonroof grows to cover the hole.

"I wasn't really going to try it," I say aloud.

No response but the growth alone is proof I'm being monitored.

Like a rat in a maze.

My knee bounces rhythmically. My mood is on a carousel going from bored, too anxious, to angry and back to bored. I need to do something. Something like kill Soladin and Taj.

But my fear is that if I do, I'll never be able to leave this place. No one else will get in and I will be completely alone over the span of my immortal life and will go slowly mad.

"Looking for trouble?" Taj asks.

I look up to see him standing in the doorway. He's wearing an indigo-colored vest open over his bare chest and matching billowy pants. Nothing on his head, not even hair. He doesn't have hair anywhere I realize.

"It's genetic." Without asking, Taj sits beside me.

My eyebrows draw together. "What is?"

"The lack of hair. None of the fey of my lineage has hair. We're not technically mammals."

"Not mammals? Then what are you?"

One corner of his mouth kicks up. "I'm flora."

I blink. "You're a plant?"

"I'm a person, just one that feeds on sunlight." He tips his head back and lets the light of the sun pour over his face.

"But I've seen you eat."

One hairless eyebrow rises. "Have you?"

I open my mouth to say yes, of course, then shut it. He passes things to the king, always has a plate before him, but in all my watching I never saw him take a bite.

I tilt my head, studying him carefully, trying to see him as a vegetable instead of animal. There was nothing though, no indication at all.

"How did you know I was wondering about your hair?"

"You're not as mysterious as you think you are." He turns back to drink in the sunlight. "In fact, I find you easy to read."

"Oh yeah?" As comebacks went, it was incredibly weak.

His grin spreads, still facing the sun.

He's feeding, I realize with a shock. A freaking plant. Go figure.

I consider killing him yet again. One quick peck and he'd be nothing more than a sweet memory, his soul drifting back across the Veil to tell the Hunt exactly how to find me. The souls I claim are compelled to follow my orders.

Of course, I've never tried my goodnight kiss out on vegetation before. Would he wither? Dry up like a husk? Would his soul get gobbled up by the Veil instead of being tethered to me?

Hell, for all I know it might not even work.

But that isn't what stops me. I haven't killed Taj because the big man—plant—is not one of mine. He hasn't attacked me or tried to harm me in any way. It's Soladin who abducted me, Soladin who deserves my wrath. And while it might be effective to hurt Taj in order to hurt Soladin, I find I can't bring myself to do it.

I feel a little bit sorry for Soladin. Which is ridiculous. I don't feel sorry for anyone. Except for Gretchen. And now the Seelie king of the Green Throne. Did immortality turn my stone heart soft? There must be something really wrong with me since my pity only extends to those who've attempted to blackmail and abduct me. Fairy Stockholm Syndrome perhaps?

Yet just because I feel pity for them doesn't mean they are off the hook.

I don't get mad. I get even.

The Seelie king had been so distraught when he realized that instead of capturing an all-powerful Unseelie queen, he'd snagged a teenage serial killer who while forever young, was also mostly incompetent in all aspects of ruling, leading and stopping the undead.

Sucked to be him.

Perhaps the reason Taj is still alive and breathing has more to do with the man himself. I kind of like him, plant or no. He takes absolutely no shit from anyone, including his royal lover. There's a constant sparkle in his eye, as though he's planning something deliciously evil and can't wait to see how it all shakes out.

In an odd way, he reminds me of my former best friend, Sarah.

He's not at all pretentious. No embroidery or ornamentation decorates his clothing. He wears simple trousers that lace up the sides and a vest that laces down the front in a blue so deep it's almost purple. I'd donned similar garb, only mine is sage green, the only thing in my captive's room that wasn't a floofy princess dress. It's easier to escape in hunting attire than a corset.

"Well, I hate to interrupt your endless *will I or won't I kill him* debate," Taj says in a droll tone that makes me start. "But I thought you might like to join me for a ride around the city's border. Take in the sights, such as they are."

I stare at him a moment, eager for any chance to escape and trying to hide it. True, I have no supplies, no allies, no clue where in the ever-changing landscape of Underhill I am, but even if my jailers are courteous, I don't do incarceration.

I can't look too eager and rouse his suspicions. "Why should I?"

Taj tilts his head and surveys me. "If you need a reason other than you could use a little sun on that cavefish pale flesh? How about the pleasure of my company?"

"I don't take pleasure in other's company," I tell him.

He grins. "Not even your sexy beast of a consort?"

"We're keeping it light."

Taj raises one nonexistent eyebrow. "What does that mean?"

Damned if I know. I can deny my feelings for Aiden. Unlike the fey and the other humans turned forever young, I am not bound to honesty. But if I do lie about something so obvious, Taj might grow suspicious. And I'm too proficient at keeping secrets to let the cat out of the bag so soon.

He's been reading me. Learning my tells at the same time I've been studying Soladin. I need to be more careful with my expressions going forward.

Instead of lying, I do what the fey do, which is dodge a direct answer. "He serves his purpose."

"I'll bet he does." Taj stands and offers me a hand up. "Tell me about him while we ride."

I stare at the hand with suspicion. "Is that the price for this outing? Information on Aiden?"

"I'm being friendly."

"Fey aren't friendly."

"Maybe not in your court." He bobs the hand again.

After hesitating just long enough, I take it.

There is no spell, no obvious passkey, but with my arm in Taj's we exit through the door. The branches move as the trees shift back, out of the way, showing a clear path to the world beyond. Maybe Taj carries some talisman that allows him to pass through the labyrinth unhindered. Or, the answer I like least, the entrances and exits are somehow keyed to his DNA, like a magical identity scanner. My heart sinks at the possibility. If that's the case, there's no way I'm leaving the palace without one or the other of them.

Of course, I could always drag Soladin's corpse through with me.

Oblivious to my dark musings, Taj ushers me through the tunnels until we emerge on a vibrant hillside. The air is damp, as though it has just rained and there's a little chill in the air. The overhead leaves are mottled yellow, orange and red, as well as greens and browns, autumn on full display. Beneath it sits a wagon, not the ornate carriage I was expecting for the king's honored consort.

I inhale, holding the air in my lungs for a full count of five. My season approaches and something stirs within me. I used to think it was the urge to hunt, to take out the bad guys with my goodnight kiss. But now I know it's the gathering of power that proceeds Samhain. As the days grow shorter, I grow stronger, at least until the cycle ends at Beltane when the power transfers to the Fire Throne.

Which sits empty.

Hitched to the wagon is a mottled gray mare with a moonbeam mane. It's the same color my hair used to be, the color my roots are growing in. I move toward the horse and offer a hand, wishing I had an apple for her. She sniffs and then nuzzles her big nose into my palm. A sweet-tempered, gentle creature who doesn't look capable of much beyond a trot. There'll be no cutting her loose and riding hell-bent for freedom.

Though the sun is strong, the air is crisp. The temperature is somewhere in the fifties, a little too cool for my sleeveless top. A gust of wind carries a distinct chill. I shiver and gooseflesh rises on my exposed arms. My companion appears wholly unaffected.

"Put this on." Noticing my discomfort, Taj hands me a plain brown cloak with a hood. "It will keep you warm and shield your identity."

"A disguise?" I wrap the thing around my shoulders and put the hood up as he does the same with a much larger cloak. The garment is well made and provides much-needed warmth. "Who are we hiding from?"

"Not hiding so much as blending in." Taj climbs up into the wagon with ease and then extends a hand to me. "No telling what the common fey will do if they spy a royal in their midst."

I put one foot on the horizontal spokes of the wagon wheel and push off from the ground, using his grip to guide me into the wagon. Once we're both settled, the big man snaps the reins and with a whinny, the horse canters down the lane.

"So, Aiden," Taj prompts. "What's he like?"

I try to think of something to say about my wolf that will set the right tone. Is it better if Taj reports to his liege that my wolf should be feared? That he is loyal and fully devoted to me? That he'll be coming for me?

"Aiden is…." I trail off, wondering how to finish the thought. Wily? Loyal? Tricksy? He is all of those things and so much more. "He's complicated," I finish lamely.

Taj calls me out on the weak answer. "Come on, Nic. You can do better than that."

"Maybe if you tell me exactly what information you're hunting for I could better accommodate you," I snap

He shrugs. "I'm not hunting for anything. I want to get to know you, and Aiden too. I've heard so many stories about the two of you."

"You have?" Both my eyebrows go up.

"Of course. You're the ruthless Unseelie Queen and he was your consort for one hundred years. You died carrying his child and he sacrificed everything to bring you back. It's the sort of story legends are made of."

I had to admit to someone who didn't know the whole wretched tale, it *might* sound romantic. His words give me an idea of what to tell him. "Aiden says I'm his mate."

"Mate? Really? That's a rare bond."

"How rare?"

"Once every three or four hundred generations. No wonder he's so devoted to you."

"What do you know about mates?" I fish.

"Mostly that it's a primal connection. People, humans, the fey, we love here," he taps the side of his skull before placing a broad palm over his heart. "And here. But mates, ones who are fated, their love is connected to the soul. A heart might lie, a mind can deceive, but the soul is the root of all honesty. It is home to every scrap of self. Its light is pure and perfect.

To love on a soul-deep level is to be free of all deception, all trickery and to accept without hesitation or reservation."

Soul deep? I wasn't even sure if I *possess* a soul. Free of all deception? What did it say that my death was brought about by a lie?

"Does…," I clear my throat. "Does the connection of mates always go both ways?"

Taj casts me a sidelong look. "No, of course not. When a soul identifies its perfect match, it reaches for it. Many don't recognize the soul's cry. Even the ones who do might fear rejection too much to ever act on it. And so their soul goes unfulfilled.

"Loving is selfless. It's why mated pairs are so rare. It requires two souls willing to accept not only each other but everything about themselves as well. The good, the bad and the ugly. Most aren't strong enough to do that."

Myself included. Total acceptance didn't sound at all easy-breezy lemon-squeezy.

I swallow past the lump that had formed in my throat and reach for a topic, any topic just to change the subject. "What does the Green Throne look like? Is it actually green?"

He laughs. "Indeed it is. All vines and layers of leaves. You know the legend of the Thrones?"

No, but unwilling to admit my ignorance I respond with, "Bits and pieces."

Taj eyes me with a knowing look. "Each Throne is the final test for any powerful fey who wishes to rule. Only one who is invited by the Throne may sit upon it."

"And if you crash the party without an invite?" I raise a brow.

"The Throne will take care of it." There is a dangerous note in his voice.

"You mean the Thrones actually murder people?" Why

am I even surprised? This is Underhill, everything here is deadly.

Taj laughs. "It's just an old story, probably invented by the kings and queens to prevent anyone from trying to usurp power. What about the Shadow Throne? Is it really made of shadows?"

I shrug, though his story has unnerved me. "Having never seen the Shadow Throne,"—in my current life anyway—"I have no basis for comparison."

He makes a noise and contemplates the road ahead. I think about the monarchs and the Thrones as we bump along in the wagon. It's easier than thinking about what he told me about mates.

In many ways, Soladin is my direct opposite. He rules in the light, is most powerful during the summer solstice when my life force is drained. He surrounds himself with green and growing things. I command the darkness and ride through the air in pursuit of corrupt souls. He grows trees and gardens and sustains life whereas I steal it like a greedy thief. Long before I was an Unseelie queen, I was a danger, a thing that goes bump in the night. Someone to fear, like the beings in the Wild Hunt.

Then again, Brigit was supposed to be a healer, a saint according to some mortal tales. Wardon was Master of the Waves but couldn't master his desire for power.

Clearly, all the rumors aren't true.

"How long have you held your position?" I ask Taj. It's more than mere curiosity. The more I know about my captors, the better able I will be to manipulate them to my own ends.

The big man darts me an indecipherable look, then turns his attention back to the reins. "What have you heard?"

"Not a damn thing, considering you've kept me

sequestered like a monk." The only beings I saw, the pixies, disappeared before I could ask them for answers.

It's Taj's turn to sigh. "Soladin brought me to the palace fifteen years ago. He bought me from a brothel when I was twelve."

When I suck in a sharp breath, Taj shakes his head. "No, you misunderstand. He didn't want me that way, not then. He was fourteen, you see. I've only been his consort for the last five years."

I study him, this male-plant. "You were working in a brothel...when you were twelve?"

Taj nods, no shame evident in admitting to the ugliness of his past. "My kind are coveted by the fey. Many view us as foreign, exotic and even lucky. I was born there. I never knew my parents. Sometimes the impoverished fey, the ones who can barely feed themselves, sell infants to the brothels in and around the courts."

"That's terrible." Both the starvation and the repercussions.

"There are worse fates." Taj snaps the reins and the mare picks up her pace to a canter. "Some of the more power-hungry fey...dismember us. Break us down for parts."

I swallow hard.

"There are usually a couple of nursing mothers there, women with regular income, which is more than many of the farming communities have to offer. Not that I needed to nurse." He says this last part with a wry grin.

"So, if not for sex, why did Soladin buy you? For luck?" My lip curls up involuntarily at the thought of the fey purchasing one another like livestock for breeding or some sort of good luck charm.

But Taj shakes his head. "Though I was younger, I was a big lad for my age. My kind of fey typically are, since we make our own food with only time outside and clean water.

So I grew up strong even when food was scarce. Some might even say imposing. Soladin had been sick for many of his early years, his growth stunted. He hadn't ascended yet. Puberty is a dangerous time for fey rulers."

My eyebrows pull together. "How so?"

"It's when their powers start to manifest. Sharp emotion can cause a surge of uncontrolled magic and borrowing from other fey comes with the backlash from Underhill. Surely you've noticed, even living in Midgard?"

And here I thought it had been my ignorance that made controlling my abilities so difficult.

Taj smirks at the dumbstruck expression I allowed to take over my face before continuing. "With a ruler unable to wield magic, unable to defend him or herself, some of the more devious courtiers with claims to the Throne might try to usurp the monarch. It's happened, particularly with some of the less popular rulers. In the Seelie Courts, it's become common practice to have a stand-in. Better to have someone take a shot at a street urchin than the heir to the Throne, right? I still sometimes serve in that capacity outside the summer Seelie Court, with him posing as my servant. We've gained much information that way."

"You were the sacrificial fey?"

He shrugs. "I'm still here. There are very few things that can actually kill me. Fire, lack of water or sun. Maybe even a certain lady's sweet kiss."

Damn. Even as I schooled my features, I couldn't help mentally tipping my hat to the man. It was hard not to admire someone so insightful.

"Maybe later we'll find out just how resilient you are." I didn't mean for the words to sound so suggestive, they just fell that way from my poisonous lips.

He throws back his head and laughed. As though the

immortal queen with the toxic kiss threatening his life was the best joke he's ever heard.

"Doesn't that bother you?" It's probably a rude question, but I can't seem to stop myself from asking. "That your life is of less value than his?"

He shrugs. "Soladin doesn't think so. And if putting a target on my back allows him to interact with the people, to get to know them and to rule more effectively, I'll wear it."

I don't know if I could do that, allow one of the few beings I cared about to pretend to be me. "But the risk?"

He responds to my question with one of his own. "Have you ever risked your life for someone you love?"

I think of Sarah. "More than once."

At my nod, he goes on. "That's all this is. Soladin is a young ruler, one who craves neither the title he inherited nor the job that goes along with it. But just because he loathes his responsibilities, doesn't mean he'll refuse to help his people. It's my choice to assist him in figuring out how best to go about it."

If what Taj says is true, Soladin is a better leader than I'd been as Nicneven. My memories and flashbacks from my former life illustrated how much I'd hated the court, resented my role as a broodmare to the Unseelie. I'd gone off with Aiden or the Wild Hunt at every opportunity and neglected my subjects. The bitterness had consumed me.

The gray mare pulling the cart wheezes a bit as we plod up over the next of what seems like an unending series of rolling green hills and Taj eases her back to a slow trot. There are distinct bird sounds coming from the brilliant orange, yellow and red trees and I see squirrels scuttling with cheek pouches full of acorns. The scene is peaceful, serene, not at all what Soladin described of a war-torn land.

"Where are all the refugees?" I wonder if the Seelie king

had over-embellished the plight of his people for the sake of playing on my sympathy.

But Taj points to a hill not too far in the distance. "There. Only those favored by the crown can approach the palace— the courtiers. For anyone else, the trees will close in, stopping and redirecting them away from the seat of power. Don't you have something similar in the Unseelie Court?"

"I really don't know how things work there." It's not a lie. All I have are fragmented memories of my past life, puzzle pieces that leave huge gaps in my knowledge. Feelings trigger scenes from the past more than facts or details. Strong emotion carries them to the surface like an oily bubble in water. From what I've glimpsed, my winter stronghold is an empty, lonely place. And before Aiden had come, the only people who did show up were the hopeful lords who craved the power of being the queen's consort and members of the Wild Hunt.

Taj goes on. "It's a safeguard put in place back when the courts were established. So that no ruling king or queen would have to fend off a mob of unhappy fey should insurrection occur. The public can gather outside the gates, but never sack the home of the ruling monarch."

Which explains why Brigit had waited until I resided in my summer palace to move her army against me. "What makes the courtiers special?"

He looks surprised. "Bloodlines and magic. Along with the monarch's favor."

Which explains why Harmony assumed she and Bard would be appointed to my court. A seer and a shifter were almost as rare as Taj the plant-man.

Taj snaps the reins. "The strong are born to rule, to protect those weaker than themselves."

"And aren't they doing a bang-up job," I mutter as the cart crests the hill and I'm greeted by a swarming sea of fey.

Wings, antenna, skin, fur, and feathers every color of the rainbow greet my eyes. They all share an air of poverty, a cornered and wary look. Seeing so many of them gathered as close as possible to Soladin's home, two things become clear.

One, the king didn't misrepresent when he stated how bad the residents of Underhill were faring. And two, maybe the elitists who set up the court system were right to do it in the way they had. Because this many fey beings could swarm the palace like fire ants on a rotting stump, destroying everything in their path.

Three rulers down and Underhill is a powder keg. I pull the hood of my borrowed cloak up higher.

I don't want to be the match that sets them off.

THROUGH THE TEAR

THROUGH THE MAN'S EYES

*A*iden runs through the woods in his human form, checking the light in the predawn sky. He is unable to see the tear in the Veil of spirit that shields Underhill from the mortal realm, but still senses its presence as he draws near. He could have floated directly into it, but some instinct urges him to wait, to run and clear his head. Only reason would help him find Nic.

If he survives the crossing.

The Veil isn't sentient, even though it is comprised of souls that were once trees, plants, and animals. According to what Nic learned in the gauntlet, only the One True Queen could repair the tear.

There had always been two queens, one from Beltane to Samhain who wielded the powers of the Shadow Throne and the other of the Fire Throne. Until Brigit had shifted the balance. Now there weren't any Unseelie rulers, only hopeful contenders. Nic could wield the powers of the Unseelie and have been reincarnated from Nicneven. She'd passed through Underhill's gauntlet and been crowned by the Wild

Hunt. Her claim was by far the best. Yet in order to rule, she needed to sit upon the Shadow Throne, to bind herself to it. And the throne was deep within the Unseelie underground palace.

The fey respect power above all things. Nicneven had been the strongest, the fastest, the cleverest queen. She'd manipulated all around her, himself included. Nic Rutherford had killed people. Yet in many ways, she was more honest than the forever young, who could not lie. Her weapon of choice was going unnoticed, learning her enemy, luring them to her. She never played games with innocents, never pitted people against one another. She routinely went out of her way to help those she cared for-- Jasmine, Nahini, himself.

Of course, even if she did manage to get inside the underground palace, she had no idea how to repair the tear or even where to look. It would be nice if, just once, a prophecy came with some damn instructions.

He bursts from the trees, lungs heaving, gaze focusing upward. It's there directly over his head. As king of the Seelie, Soladin must have crossed directly to the heart of his court. If Aiden knew exactly where that in-between was located, he would cross there. But he didn't want to lose both time hunting for the crossing or the element of surprise. Without Nic's magic to shrink him down to size, a fairy ring wasn't an option and he didn't want to wait for midnight. Without *Seelenverkäufer*, the tear is the only way to cross into Underhill without alerting the courts to his presence.

He doesn't relish the trip though. For one thing, crossing through the rip in the Veil had nearly killed Nic. While he isn't worried about his own hide, getting his soul sucked out by the Veil that is struggling to repair itself, wouldn't help her.

"Just do it," he mutters, gaze glued on his destination,

feeling the pull of the tear between worlds like a giant vacuum trying to yank him free of the ground and gobble him up. "She needs you."

An engine rumbles in the distance. He frowns. That sounds distinctly like Nic's truck. But there is no way Angrboda could have made it to the farm and back already. No one would know where he is or what he intends.

Though he tells himself to press on, he can't seem to stop watching the truck approach. It is Nic's rundown vehicle, with a familiar mortal face behind the wheel.

"Aiden, wait!" she calls out of the window even as the vehicle fishtails to a stop.

He doesn't bother to stifle a groan. "Gretchen, what are you doing here?"

She scrambles down, slinging a familiar-looking backpack over one shoulder. "The seer told me I'd find you here. She said Nic would need this."

"Thanks." He takes Nic's bag from her outstretched hand, but she doesn't release her hold on the strap.

"I want to go with you."

"No." He's already shaking his head in denial. "Nic would never allow it."

"Nic isn't here." The mortal pushes her glasses up her freckled nose. "And I don't want to just sit around and wait for her to come back. Harmony said it might be awhile. She said time works differently in Underhill. That I might be an old woman before you return."

When he doesn't respond she pushes, "I can help."

"I don't see how," he says, not unkindly. "Human is a delicacy to many of those who reside beyond the Veil. Do you really want to be eaten?"

Her chin tilts up at a stubborn angle. "I don't want to be useless. Sitting and waiting in Nic's room is almost as bad as sitting and waiting in mine. Only now I know what I'm missing."

"Gretchen," he pauses and then swallows. The seer had sent Gretchen right to him, just as he was willing himself to depart. Though his belief in fate has been challenged on more than one occasion, part of him still believes that every-thing happens for a reason. Maybe not by design, but inten-tionally, to help future events unfold in a certain way. Anyone could have delivered the backpack, yet the mortal had been sent. What if Gretchen proves to be somehow crucial to helping him rescue Nic?

The mortal chews on her lower lip, as though hunting for the right words to convince him of the impossible, that she is up for the challenge. The next five words seal her fate. "Aiden, she's my friend, too."

Though his queen had lived spans of years, she had less than a handful of people she's claimed as a friend. And though a trip to Underhill might not be right for Gretchen, it *is* right for Gretchen to help his Nic.

If a soul needs to be sacrificed to the Veil, it could have his, but then Gretchen might make it through, bring the pack and whatever it contains that might mean life or death for his mate.

"All right. You take the pack and hold on to me as hard as you can." At her startled look he adds, "The crossing won't be easy. If we're separated, I'm counting on you to find her."

She nods, her honey-brown eyes shining with excitement.

He's done a poor job of explaining if she still looked so enthusiastic but there are no words to properly prepare her. The tear would wrench and pull her soul until either she passes into the fey realm or it is ripped from her body. Some things a person needs to experience for herself.

He holds out a hand and when the mortal girl places her

palm in his, he commands his magic to transmute them into sparks.

Gretchen isn't Nic. His mate held her own. The mortal girl clings to him, a yelp escaping a second before her mouth dissolves. He can sense her fear, of him and what his magic is doing to her, but there is a healthy dose of wonder and determination. Brave, foolish mortal. He makes a silent vow to do all he can to protect her.

The tear is growing stronger, like a gravity well. Instead of pulling matter though, it pulls souls. In their waterless form, its force is undeniable. They ascend and it takes an enormous amount of concentration to keep all their various pieces together. Like leaves in a current, they are sucked into the opening and into the in-between place.

The souls claw at him, not with hands but with will. Begging, demanding a sacrifice. The Veil grabs for them both, pulling and tugging, commanding them to join with the rest, to become part of the whole. There is no sense of individuality here. The Veil has many hands, scattered thoughts, echoes from what had come before, but only one purpose. To mend itself, to hide magic and Underhill from Midgard and those who dwell within.

Part of him wants to bend to its will, to belong somewhere. The wolf helps him resist. It sees the souls of the Veil not as a collective to join, like a pack, but that of the enemy, the thing keeping him from his mate.

Pain radiates through Aiden as the souls move from coaxing to claiming, no longer asking but demanding their due. If he had been solid he would have screamed. Beside him, Gretchen must have collapsed, her mortal brain shorted out by the sensation as Nic's had been.

Let her go. The wolf snarls. *Let it have her.*

No. The pounding noise, the bright lights, he's fading too. *I promised to protect her.*

We have a better chance of finding Nic. The wolf sounds logical, not the slavering beast he detests but a voice of reason. *If we are consumed, she will die anyway.*

And because he was a god, he could not die. Instead, he would be trapped in limbo, serving as part of the Veil forever.

He could no longer sense Gretchen at all. Had she let go of him? Could the wolf be right and she'd already been taken by the spirits of the Veil?

NO. Aiden bellows the word half a heartbeat before his strength gives out entirely.

A blinding white light erupts from somewhere nearby. It fills his every sense and he knows nothing more.

I scramble down from the cart, glad for the hood obscuring my face. The crush of the crowd is awful. I'm a small-town girl living in a lonely fey world. I'm not used to being surrounded like this. Bodies press together, some clothed but many without a stitch. The scents are overpowering. Food, stale sweat, the tang of woodsmoke from a bonfire. The air carries them all to me. Though the fey don't have a natural odor the way humans do, they often carry traces from their elements. But there's an overwhelming scent of hopelessness and from most a miasma of fear and anger.

Taj drops down by my side, his movements as graceful as a large cat.

"I'm not sure this is a good idea." I tug on my hood.

"We won't stay long," he mutters back and takes a large sack from the wagon bed. "Here."

I take the bundle and then ask, "What exactly are we looking for?"

He doesn't answer my question, instead saying, "Stay

close. No one here knows who I am or who I serve. Let's keep it that way."

Taj weaves his way through the meandering throng and I lengthen my stride to catch up with him. Only then does he respond to my earlier question. "We're bringing needed supplies."

"A drop in the bucket," I mutter as I study the size of the bags we're carrying.

His nonexistent eyebrows go up. "A little is better than nothing. Can you sense the edge of desperation here?"

I offer a grunt of acknowledgment and then look at our surroundings. Temporary shelters have been set up, tents formed from tree boughs and other crude structures made from natural debris. A hodgepodge of stone and wood and leaf. But there are far too many for the number of fey.

"What's in the bags?"

Taj nods to the bundle in my hands. "Blanket drop-off. For the neediest."

Blankets. Most likely from my world. But even my large parcel can't hold more than a few dozen, not nearly enough to go around. "How do you determine the neediest?"

"I don't." Taj moves to a stone hut that looks as though it had seen better days. There is no door, only a tangle of vines snaking over the threshold. He raps smartly on a stone beside the entrance. From inside there's the sound of a cough, followed by a groan from another direction. Is this a hospital of some sort?

The vines part of their own volition. Or perhaps they are separated by someone else's will, for a moment later a willowy woman emerges. She has gray-blue skin and silvery hair that falls loose behind pointed ears. She is naked, though she doesn't appear as disheveled as some of the others. As though her nudity is by choice rather than due to lack of resources.

"Taj," she greets my companion warmly in a musical lilt. "So good to see you."

"We brought blankets." He sets his own parcel which is twice the size of mine down and then reaches into a deep pocket of his robe. "And this."

Her silver eyes glisten with tears as she reaches for the vile. "Thank you. And thank Soladin for us."

"What else do you need, Mags?"

"Everything." She wipes her eyes. "Will you be coming in for a spell? The littluns will want to see you."

Taj looks down at me as though debating and then nods. "Yes, I think we will."

For the first time the fey woman—Mags apparently— turns her eerie gaze on me. All the warmth leaves her face as she assesses me from hood to hemline. Not that there is much to see beneath the baggy robe, but whatever she sees, she doesn't like.

"A turned mortal? Why would you bring one of her ilk here?"

I blink, surprised that she can tell what I am just by a glance. Her aggressive tone nettles. "None of your business."

Mags puts her hands on her hips. "If you wish to enter my house, it is."

"Ladies," Taj interjects and then holds out a dark hand toward the other woman. "Mags, she's with me. If that's not good enough we'll go and I'll come back another time."

It's clear that this Mags doesn't want me in her space and just as clear that she wants Taj to come inside. Another cough and she glances over her shoulder. When she returns her attention to us, it's obvious her mind is made up.

"All right. But I'll have my eye on you, girl."

"Something to look forward to," I offer an insincere smile. It fades the moment I cross through the door.

The room is dim, hardly any light passing through the

well-stacked stone. The air inside is musty and smells of sickness. And of death.

Rows and rows of beds are lined up in the space. The interior is much larger than the deceptively humble exterior indicates, almost fourteen feet across and at least twenty back. And every square inch of free floor space has a body crammed into it.

Small bodies. Child size bodies. All naked. Some even without a blanket, just curled up on the hard-packed dirt floor.

The neediest, Taj had said. This is some sort of orphanage. I would have frozen in place with shock, but he wraps his hand around my wrist and tows me forward.

Somehow a path clears before him as he heads for the far left corner of the space. There, three blankets are lined up as neat as can be. Three small bodies are tucked within them. The one on the right coughs as we approach. It's an awful hacking sort of sound and my chest tightens in sympathy. The one in the center shakes. The tremors are obviously uncontrollable.

Taj approaches, unfazed by the signs of illness. He lays his hand on the trembling fey's forehead and is rewarded with a small smile.

"You came back," the third child, a little girl judging by her long yellow hair, speaks.

Taj sinks to the floor, crossing his legs so as not to take up too much floor space. "I told you I would, little blossom. Now, would you care for a story?"

"The one about Queen Nicneven and the Valkyrie nest." The girl abandons her precious blanket so she can plop herself on Taj's lap. It's clear she is faring better than the two nearby.

I study them closely, note the similar pointed ears, the translucent skin and wonder if they are siblings. They perk up a bit at the mention of a story. Then her request sinks in.

Taj's eyes sparkle as he notes my reaction. "If that is your wish."

Other children scoot closer as he clears his throat and begins. "Once there was a fair queen of the Unseelie Court. Her name was Nicneven, which means—"

"Daughter of the little saint." A small boy, no more than six with large close-set eyes and long webbed fingers, interjects.

"That's right." Taj doesn't seem the least bit perturbed by the interruption. His voice is made for storytelling, his words carefully chosen to paint a picture. Even if that picture bears no resemblance to reality.

"Nicneven ruled from the mighty Shadow Throne of the Unseelie Court. As fearless as she was beautiful, the mighty queen rode out with the Wild Hunt, scouring the worlds for defective souls to bring to justice."

"With her deadly kiss!" The imp on his lap adds.

"That's right. For you see, on the day she was born, Underhill bestowed a gift on the future queen. She placed a single drop of water on the newborn babe's lips. Water from Hvergelmir, the poison spring that flows through the heart of Niflheim."

My heart thunders. Stories come from somewhere. While clearly this tale is being embellished, there might be a grain of truth in it. Could that fabled river really be the source of my goodnight kiss?

No, because if it was poisoned, I would have died. Taj isn't looking at me though and I have no way to tell if this part of his story is truth or creative license. The best ones are a blend of both.

Unaware of the bomb he's just dropped on me, Taj continues his story. "Nicneven was so beautiful, so strong, that the goddess Freya grew jealous of her. Freya, the embodiment of both beauty and battle and she who commands the Valkyries. She ordered the shield maidens to travel to Underhill and nest in the Onyx Mountain. The peak is black as night and higher than any mountain under the hill. It is rumored to suck all light from the stars in the sky around it, so dark that light seems to shy away from ever touching the jagged stone. It was there the Valkyries settled, high in the clouds above the Unseelie underground palace. The shield maidens would swoop down and capture any who dared to cross their territory, feeding on their flesh and leaving the bones at the foot of the mountain.

"Word spread about the monsters living in the cliff face. Only the bravest or the most foolish approached the mountain from above, preferring to come and go from the palace by the safety of the Unseelie catacombs. The Valkyries hadn't fed in some time. Hunger made them bold, had them straying farther afield to hunt. One day the queen was out in a nearby field when she heard a scream.

"The queen drew her mighty sword, *Seelenverkäufer*, and charged through the trees. Even without her horse, Nicneven was fleet of foot, swift as the Northwind. There she found a Valkyrie attacking a kit of about seven winters. Without hesitating, she leaped in the air, dragging the largest Valkyrie to the ground."

That's not how it happened. I'd been scouring my memory, looking for the story. The scene Taj was painting was heroic, but inaccurate. Their victim had been a full-grown male and he'd been dead when she—when I—had arrived on the scene. But he had been a member of my court, under my protection.

My hands clench into fists at the remembered the insult. No one steals from me.

"They fought and struggled, the great beast raking her

claws across the queen's unprotected body. But then Nicneven summoned a mighty gust of wind, and pinned the villain to a massive tree."

Taj softens his tone, making it sound more feminine and at the same time, deadly. "Too long have your greedy people preyed on mine. It ends today. Tell me where your nest is and I'll let you live."

I had serious doubts that I'd ever made such an offer, past life or not.

In his regular voice he continues, "The Valkyrie refused and Nicneven took her head. Her icy blue gaze turned upward, and she summoned her nymphs and the ghostly horde that rides with her, once again taking to the air with great shrieks that carried throughout the nine worlds. Up and up the Wild Hunt climbed, through icy rain and driving snow, thousands of feet to where the air grows thin. They took the creatures by surprise. The shield maidens are fierce fighters, but none can withstand the might of the Wild Hunt."

"She killed them all?" This from a boy with green scales over the left side of his face. He coughs, and I realize it's the same one who'd been under the blanket on the right when we first approached. At first glance, I'd thought the scales part of his fey genetics. The more I study them, the more likely they are a symptom of the sickness that plagues him.

All the children look weary and wrung out, so it's difficult to say if they are all sick with the same disease. Out of the corner of my eye, I see Mags in a shadowy alcove, mixing the contents of the vile Taj had provided her with into a large pitcher of liquid. Medicine perhaps?

"Yes. Nicneven destroyed the host of invading Valkyries. Then she commanded her fey leaders to deposit the remains at the door to Freya's temple as a warning to the goddess never to challenge her again."

I cringe at that last, remembering feeling smug about the

order. Nahini had cautioned against it, saying nothing good would come from baiting a goddess. But no, I just needed to put my mark on the kill, to show the love goddess who she'd been messing with. The wholesale slaughter of her creatures had been bad enough. Did I really need to rub Freya's nose in it?

Apparently, the goddess and I were on the outs. Probably I should cross her off the list of potential allies.

"Another!" The girl on Taj's lap pleads. I can't say I blame her. While not gifted with shape-changing, Taj's deep rumbling bass is almost as entrancing as Bard's out and out production.

He laughs and starts in on a new tale, this about Wardon the Wise—I snort aloud at that but no one pays me any mind.

It blows my mind, their response. I'm a hero to these children. Or at least, Nicneven was. I'd always thought of myself as a villain. Killing is wrong. So much of what I'd done had been rash and impulsive. I'd been driven by selfish motives, proving a point and staking a claim instead of protecting the people. Hearing the story made me realize that I was a hero and a good queen only compared to Brigit. I'd been trying to run away, to abandon these people. Heroes didn't turn their backs on those in need.

A hand lands on my shoulder. "Come with me, quickly," a soft voice whispers in my ear.

I look up just as the figure who'd touched me withdraws into the shadows.

Taj is engrossed in telling his tall tale to the young audience. He doesn't notice when I sidestep a few feet, then a few more. I glance around, but prickly Mags is nowhere in sight.

In the shadows, I find a door that stands ajar. After one final glance to be sure no one is looking in my direction, I ease through it.

The woman who'd come for me is waiting behind the

building. She smiles beneath her gray hood. The robe conceals her amazingly busty figure, the midnight spill of hair, the dark eyes. But beneath the hem, I see a set of silver anklets tethered together by a thin chain.

I take a deep breath and address the absolute last person I expect to see. "What are you doing here, Pharaildis?"

She tilts her head. "No hug for mother?"

THE TIES THAT BIND

I don't know if her suggestion is real or not, but I don't move any closer. My feelings about this woman, the one who gave birth to me and then turned me over to the Unseelie fey, are complicated.

"How did you know I was here?" I ask and then stare down at the silver chain, the mark of her imprisonment. "And why did Underhill let you come?"

"Underhill has a job for you." A noise from the side street causes her to look over her shoulder. She plucks at my robe. "Come, quickly, before that large brute realizes you've gone."

I shake free of her grasping fingers. "Taj isn't a brute."

She frowns. "Hasn't he been keeping you captive?"

"Well, yes, but it was mostly Soladin's fault." I have no idea why the urge to defend Taj arises in me. Just because he went out of his way to care for some sick orphans doesn't mean he's a good person.

Perhaps it's the way he's been treating me. Not like a captive or a queen but like a friend.

"Nic, people are either your allies or your enemies. It's time for you to decide. If you return to the Seelie king's stronghold, I won't be able to free you. Is that what you want?"

The thought of renewed imprisonment makes the decision for me. "Where are we going?"

She doesn't gloat. Instead, she leads me further from the rear door of the orphanage. "There are fey everywhere and their blood is hot. Keep your head down. Don't make eye contact with anyone. You don't want to be recognized."

Having already decided to stay hidden I simply nod.

She turns to look at me. "It was foolish of you to come back here alone."

Her words sting as though I'd gripped a nettle plant. "It's not like I was given much of a choice."

She stares at me a beat. "The fey are blaming the neglect and abandonment of the courts for the upheaval. If that crowd gets a good look at you, if they realize who you are, they won't hesitate to tear you, tear both of us, apart."

I'd felt the surging desperation, the spirit of the congregated fey when I'd followed Taj through the crowded streets. I don't doubt for a second that Pharaildis's assessment is correct.

"This way." She leads me out onto a side street that is little more than a dirt alley. The roads in Underhill aren't paved or even cobbled. The only light comes from the setting sun that is kissing the rooftop. Her jewel-toned robe is more noticeable than my borrowed brown one. I manage to follow her without rushing to keep up. If anything, the feeling of the crowd has grown more unsettled since our arrival. A fey male sporting rags that would fall apart if he ever tried to wash them stands at the center of a crowd.

"Queen Brigit is dead and the Unseelie are spilling across our borders in droves. Soladin sits holed up in his castle doing nothing. The change of seasons is almost upon us yet there is no sign of the Risen Queen or of Wardon. Where are the fey royals when their people need them most?"

All around him grumbles of agreement sound and I spy more than one nod of affirmation.

The grubby speaker pushes on. "For too long, the magic of the fey has resided with the kings and queens of the courts. They grow poison for their machinations, make deals with giants for power and use trolls as personal guards. Trolls that run amok, abusing those they are supposed to protect!"

Technically that had only been one king, Wardon. And he'd been spirited off by a giant. But I wasn't going to contradict the male. Not when the fey surrounding him are shouting their agreement. If this is the mood of the most stable court with the ruler who—despite his piss poor judgment—is doing his best, what is it like on the Unseelie side of things?

We are so hosed.

I glance quickly away, the instinct for self-preservation riding me hard. While I don't shove people aside, I find myself getting much closer than I wanted to be to the angry displaced masses. My goodnight kiss is a powerful weapon, but using it once drains me, even if I could force myself to kill these desperate creatures. There's no way I can take on a crowd of this size if they spot me.

It occurs to me why Taj chose the stories he did to tell the children. His tales of the noble kings and brave queens who defend their people. It's a small goodwill tour. Unfortunately, it seems like a cup of water against a forest fire.

Pharaildis winds her way through the streets like a snake slipping between leaves. Her stride is carefully measured, never seeming to hurry or draw notice. She slips between two fey females who are bickering over the price of eggs from a local stall and they don't glace at her at all.

It's almost like I'm the only one who can see her.

The speaker raises one knobby green fist in the air to punctuate his rhetorical questions. "Should we let the courtiers hole up in their protected lands, growing fat and hoarding all Underhill sees fit to provide while we suffer? Should we allow their edicts that protect the mortals stand?"

"No!" Answers a man as tall and broad as Taj with long red hair and creeping ivy tangled around his limbs. He isn't alone, just the closest one to me. I try to brush by him, but it's possible he's literally grown roots where he stands. I dodge to his left but can't see Pharaildis's purple robe anywhere.

I scan the crowd, hunting for her and instead spot a familiar pair of citrine colored eyes.

Taj witnesses my intent shakes his head slowly back and forth and mouths three words.

Don't do it.

I don't listen, don't bother hunting for my mother. I dive into the crowd at the farthest point from him.

"Don't be stupid," I grumble the words aloud, hoping against hope that Taj heeds them. "I'm not worth it."

But a glance over my shoulder reveals that the male has indeed decided to give chase. And since he's at least three times my size and is trying to cut a direct swath through the bodies, his passage is noticed.

"Hey," a female voice shouts loud enough to be heard over the crowd. "Watch it!"

Ahead of me, the bodies are thinning out and with a few hasty steps, I break free of the mass of fey. A cry of recognition goes up and I risk another glimpse over my shoulder, dreading what I'll see.

"It's him! King Soladin." A man's voice growls, deep and full of rage. The accent is like something out of a Dickens novel, from the streets of eighteenth-century London. "I done seen him on tour of the kingdom."

"No," I gasp and turn back around. The wall of bodies blocks my view of Taj. I know it's him though, recall what he said about standing in for Soladin from time to time.

A hand lands on my arm and I glance up into my mother's anxious face. "Nic, come on. While they're distracted."

"They'll kill him." There's no doubt in my mind.

"It's him or you. If you do anything to help him, if you reveal yourself in any way, they'll turn on you just as fast. Now let's *go*." She shouts the last word to be heard over the roar of the frenzied crowd.

I let her drag me several yards away. All the time my mind is whirling.

Whirling. Like the funnel of a tornado.

I've never called one on purpose before, only once by accident. But the wind isn't strong enough and my other abilities are too small scale. And if I set loose a tornado, people will get hurt. Innocent people might die.

Taj will die if I do nothing, of that I'm sure. Is his life worth more than possibly dozens of others?

No, but it's not just about Taj, is it? Killing will send this mob into a frenzy the same way blood would draw a great white shark. They will grow bolder once they have taken the first life, become less cautious. Fear and bloodlust will rule this last kingdom that teeters on the edge of chaos. After the first drop of fey blood is spilled, once that line is crossed, they will justify any action.

Once you kill, it marks you forever.

Perhaps this mob is the first ripple in the water. They will crash like a wave of death against not just the peaceful fey of Underhill, but also over the ignorant human population. There is a tear in the Veil, and if they choose to cross through it, some of them will die. But nowhere near as many as the unprepared mortals. Eventually, the human population will fight back, unleash the deadlier weapons in their arsenals.

Chemical, biological and nuclear warfare. The Earth will be their battleground, and those who live there caught in the crossfire.

"Nic, let's go."

I can see it all as though it's already happened. The end of life as we know it.

Ragnarök is coming. Aiden's words haunt me as do my visions of watching him die, torn apart by an army of the undead. Is this how it begins?

I owe nothing to the fey, no matter what anyone says. I've never had much regard for most mortals either. But to Freda and Nahini and Jasmine? To Aiden? The end of the world means the end of my friends as well.

Maybe, just maybe, I can stop it.

Decision made, I close my eyes.

"We must leave," Pharaildis tugs on my arm.

I shut her out and do my best to ignore the rage and shouts from the crowd as I call for the winds.

I focus, inhaling, feeling my element. The one that is my constant companion, the one that travels all the worlds, sees everything.

It rushes to heed my command, as though it had been waiting centuries for the call.

Through the Man's Eyes

War.

It's Nic's voice Aiden hears, the single word echoes inside his skull. It acts as an anchor, tethering him to consciousness. Agony accompanies awareness. Every inch of his human body is battered and bruised, every shift of muscle and bone pure torture.

"Hello?" A tentative female voice calls.

Calls from *below him?*

What happened? His memories are fragmented, like glass hurled upon a stone floor. Pain radiates from his head like a star gone supernova. Opening his eyes is pure torture, but he persists. He stares up at an unyielding sun, feels the shift of the breeze as it is drawn away from him as though lured by something.

Or someone.

Nic.

Pain he can ignore. Torture he will endure. But fear, fear for her will be the death of him. He shifts his weight, hearing a cracking sound, not within him, but outside.

"No, wait!" The voice that is not Nic's cries out. Too late, he realizes where he is, why parts of his body feel weightless, just as the branch holding him breaks under the strain.

The drop is too short for him to shift to embers but long enough to send a new wave of pain through his body.

His vision wavers as his head hits a particularly hard rock. Air rushes from his lungs on impact.

"Oh my God, Aiden! Are you all right?" It's the mortal, Gretchen, hovering over him, her hands flapping like disturbed birds. "I'm sorry! I shouldn't have called out to you."

He grunts one word just to get her to stop. The last of the trapped air escapes past his cracked lips. "M'kay."

She crouches down beside him. "What can I do?"

Be still a moment. But she isn't Nic to hear his thoughts and he can't manage much past a grunt.

"I thought you were dead." Even if he couldn't hear the fear in the girl's voice, the acrid scent of it clings to her like a cloak.

When the world around him finally stops spinning, he struggles upright. "I thought the same about you. What do you remember about the crossing?"

She pushes her glasses up her nose. "Nothing. One second, we were standing in the field and the next I was flat on my back, looking up at you like a deer strung up in a tree."

She is lying. The subtle scent of it overrides her fear. He is careful not to look at her, to study her the way he wants to. After spending as much time as he had with Nic, he's discovered that mortals lied for several reasons. To get out of trouble, to avoid discomfort, sometimes just for the sake of it. What does Gretchen think she stands to gain by lying to him regarding passing through the tear?

Perhaps nothing. He is essentially a stranger to her. One who'd been willing to kill her less than a day ago. While she couldn't hold a candle to Nic when it came to suspicion, he'd given her very little reason to trust him. Perhaps her instincts told her lying was the best course of action. He makes note of it, but doesn't call her on her lie.

"Sorry I scared you." He assesses the damage to his right shoulder, rotating it in small increments. Thankfully, it's bruised not broken. The elbow on the same arm oozes, the top layer of skin rubbed completely off. It stings but will heal.

The mortal appears agitated and he decides she needs a simple task to accomplish so she feels more in control. "Do me a favor and check Nic's backpack, see if the seer packed anything useful?"

"Of…of course." Gretchen hastily shrugs out of the canvas satchel and places it on the ground next to him. But when she reaches for the clasp, the bag starts to melt.

Gretchen scrambles back, tripping over him in her haste. He winces in pain but doesn't make a sound, his attention is on the backpack which no longer resembles a backpack, not as it grows arms and legs. Aiden makes an exasperated sound as the bag mutates into a familiar form. A form holding the real pack. "Bard. What are you doing here?"

The shifter ignores him. Instead, he reaches for Gretchen. "Forgive me, Lady. I didn't mean to frighten you."

His courtly manners are impeccable, yet the mortal doesn't seem to have heard him. "It was you the whole time?"

"A necessary disguise." Bard bows low, as though having just completed a performance. "The seer thought it best if I travel through the Veil incognito."

"Why?" Aiden scowls at the stowaway. When the shifter still doesn't look at him, he notes the scent of fear drifting off the girl again. *That's why.*

"Would it put you more at ease if I resemble one of your kind?" Without waiting for a response, Bard shifts once more, this time into Jim Harris, a student who'd graduated from Nic and Gretchen's school last semester. The resemblance is uncanny, right down to the faded jeans and letterman jacket. Blond hair, blue eyes, athletic but obviously mortal. The shifter's new disguise is seamless. Aiden wonders where Bard could have seen Jim because even his movements are a precise match to the boy he'd met briefly. Had he been spying on the human population? With his gifts, it would have been easy for him to sneak away from the farm at any chance.

A cold chill skitters down his back. Could Bard have been the one who set Isolde free? Perhaps he hadn't asked to cross the Veil with them, not because of Gretchen, but because he didn't want to risk Aiden saying no. Focusing his interest on the mortal girl might be a way for him to hide his true intentions.

If anything, Gretchen looks even more upset at seeing the shifter wearing a familiar face. She breaks eye contact, staring down at the ground.

"Give her a minute." Aiden pushes himself up and yanks Bard away, giving Gretchen some space to compose herself. "Why are you here?"

"According to Harmony, the queen has been taken. I thought it best that I come with you."

As a fey, Bard can't lie, but centuries of practice have made him proficient at truth-telling with a twist. After spending a lifetime with them, Aiden hears what Bard doesn't say as well as what he does. *According to Harmony* isn't the same as *the seer told me*. And he hadn't indicated that he was here to help Aiden and Gretchen on their mission.

Aiden weighs his options. Should he kill Bard? Nic had placed a small amount of her frugally kept trust in him. But circumstances and allegiances can change in the span of a mortal heartbeat. Bard's gaze slides to where Gretchen is dusting off the seat of her jeans. His interest in the girl is plain and though she's shown only fear toward Bard, killing the shifter for tagging along might be too much for the mortal to handle.

He could refuse to let Bard come with them. The shifter could change his shape but never his scent. To Aiden's keen nose, he always smelled of elderberry wine and rich spice, a memorable and unique combination. He'd been too distracted by his pressing need to find Nic to pick up on it earlier, but now he would be on alert.

Yet what if the shifter proves necessary? The seer told Gretchen to bring the pack, that Nic would require it. What if she'd meant Nic would need Bard's help?

His best bet was to keep his suspicions to himself, not to let the shifter know he was under surveillance. If Bard did have a secret agenda, Aiden would find out soon enough and deal with the male when he had evidence one way or the other.

Decided, he glances around for something to distract

Bard from the human. He studies the scorched landscape with a frown. In the region they've entered, the trees display no signs of leafy canopy, the ground no soft mossy carpet. The air is heavy with the scents of ash and death. Not old death like the blood vines of the Deadwood carry but new and tragic ends.

"Any idea where we are?" Aiden addresses his question to the shifter.

Bard, still in his Jim guise, moves to touch the tree Aiden had fallen from. It's little more than a blackened stalk that shoots up into the sky. "Judging by the size of what remains here, somewhere in the Great Golden Forest. About two days walk from Seelie Court lands."

Aiden frowns, not at the distance. He can probably travel that in sparks, even carrying the shifter and Gretchen. But could this charred husk be all that remains of the Great Golden Forrest? "A colony of wood nymphs protects that forest."

"I know." Bard's borrowed blue eyes look sorrowful. "If this is the Great Golden Forest, then that can only mean one thing."

"What's that?" Gretchen steps in to join the conversation. "Why do you both look so worried?"

"All the nymphs are dead." A new voice, thick with menace, hisses from behind them. "And they were delicious."

Aiden moves at the same time Bard does, both with the same goal in mind, to put himself between Gretchen and whatever could have snuck up on them unawares. Bard holds out his hands on either side, blocking the mortal's view, for which Aiden is grateful.

The creature, or rather what remains of what had once been a living breathing being, has sharply angled wings. Like a dragonfly, though the membrane covering them appears tattered, as though dozens of rocks had been hurled through the transparent skin. Its body is gaunt, skin hanging from bone as though the muscle underneath atrophied. Its eyes long gone, though the empty sockets stare at them as though it could still see. Perhaps the most disturbing part is its mouth. A great gray gap strung with leftover bits of decaying flesh and a few pointed teeth. Its jaw moves out of sync when it speaks as though it is lip-syncing.

A sprite, it had once been, or possibly a brownie. That was before it had died. Before whatever tainted magic had forced it from its grave and out onto the land of the living once more. As something else.

Draugar.

Soladin had been right. The dead are walking through Underhill.

"Will you be just as good when we devour you?" the dead thing asks.

Gretchen screams and it is only then Aiden realizes the creature isn't alone. More shamble out from the blackened tree trunks, beloved foliage the wood nymphs must have burned in the hope of stopping these monsters.

The fact that the Draugar stand here and there is no sign of the nymphs meant their plan had failed.

They are surrounded.

POWER OF THE UNSEELIE QUEEN

*T*he windstorm is unlike anything I've ever experienced. It comes from every direction, swooping in from every corner of Underhill, carrying the scents of far off lands and the people who dwell there, of sea and salt, ash and stone. But most of all of magic.

My hair whips into my eyes as a gale rushes by me, this one pulled from a nearby valley. Another gust shoves Pharaildis into me and would have sent us both sprawling if the North Wind, the strongest, sharpest and most sentient, didn't form a wall to keep me upright.

"What have you done?" Pharaildis yells to be heard over the roaring.

I wish I knew. This is different than any time I've ever summoned the wind or used any of my abilities before. I don't feel as though I'm controlling it. Air currents carry particles of sand and dust into fey eyes. A harsh gust blows clothing down the streets, knocking people into one another. The prevailing winds, pulled from their normal route, are stronger still, yanking the makeshift tents down, scattering personal belongings through the streets.

This isn't a tornado, sharp and focused. This is something else.

"Stop," my mother shouts. The North Wind surrounds us, acting as an invisible barrier from the airborne detritus that flies past, every bit of it a dangerous projectile. "Nic, you can't do this."

"Look," I point to the crowd, to the spot where I'd last caught sight of Taj. "It's working."

"Much good it will do him if he's dead," Pharaildis yells. "Stop this now, before you kill everyone in the region."

As though to punctuate her statement, I see a cart go rolling by, not on its wheels but end over end down the dirt road. Fey scatter in every direction, fleeing for the nearest shelter. Some are pushed down, and others trample them in their haste. Their instincts to preserve their own lives overcoming the mass hysteria that screams for royal blood.

An image of the children Taj had brought me to visit pops into my mind. This storm could tear down the structure protecting them. She's right, I need to call an end to this, now.

Closing my eyes, I reach out to touch the winds, to send them away.

Nothing happens.

"Nic!" Her voice is laced with an edge of panic.

"I'm trying," I grit while digging deeper, hunting for some hidden reserve, some untapped source of power that will help me stop the surging air. More people go down as the mass of bodies undulates like a giant beast.

My lips part as I take it all in. *I* did this. I brought this destruction down on them.

Air masses collide and thunder crashes. Rain sheets down, soaking the dusty street and turning it to mud in half a heartbeat. Tornadoes form, not the one funnel I'd envisioned but a baker's dozen. People scream in terror as their possessions, possibly all they own, are sucked up into the furious gale. Heavy moisture brought from the Trade Winds has a soaking rain dumping buckets of water down over everyone.

I must shut them out, need to silence the sounds of terror so I am not overwhelmed by the destruction. Or swamped by the horror that spreads through the fey like an airborne contagion. I did it, so I must be able to undo it.

My anger and fear summoned the winds. It hadn't been a request, more like an SOS. Somehow, I need to let them know the job here is done, that I no longer require them.

I put both rune-covered palms against the wall formed by the North Wind, the one I sense is more sentient than an element ought to be. Using my inner voice, the one I use to communicate with Aiden, I think one word.

Go.

There might have been a pause as it shifts around us.

"Go," I repeat the command out loud as well as letting it echo in my head. "You've done well, I am fine. Go back to where you belong."

A gust of air caresses my cheek. It's an odd sensation, although a comforting one, almost as though the wind needs reassurance that I truly will be all right. I scent snow-capped mountains and pine forests and then it is gone.

They are all gone, all the breezes from the tropics, gales from the mountain passes, the high- and low-pressure systems, all have dispersed leaving behind absolute destruction.

Fey are dead on the ground, bodies scattered everywhere. Large and small, glamour and magic having abandoned them along with life. There are at least twenty maybe more. Some are bleeding, others trampled until the breath of life left them and was snatched up by the raging winds. Their possessions are now detritus, littering the mud-caked street. A few groans here and there, but mostly there is death.

"Nic," Pharaildis says my name, her voice sure but shaky. "We need to go."

"I can't just leave them like this…." No matter that I want to turn my back on it, to forget what I've done. My heart hurts. These people weren't killers, they weren't souls I was claiming for the Hunt. They were hungry and scared. Desperate. I was supposed to protect them.

Instead, I'd stolen the little they had left.

"You can't help them. The Seelie courtiers will be upon us soon, to find out what happened here, along with King Soladin. If they discover you, we'll be right back where we started. If they don't execute you outright."

I stare down at my rune-marked hands, surprised to see they are shaking.

"Come with me," Pharaildis puts a reassuring arm around my shoulder. She's a little taller than I am and the weight of her limb is oddly comforting. I lean into her, allowing her to lead me away.

Even if a part of me will stay on that blood-soaked patch of ground forever.

Through the Man's Eyes

"Do you have a weapon?" Aiden commands his fire sword into his hand, wishing he'd brought something more substantial.

"No," Bard responds.

"Gretchen?" Aiden asks.

"You mean like a gun or something?" She shakes her head, her eyes huge. "All I had was in the pack…." She trails off and looks to Bard, who is still decked out as a Varsity football player.

The shifter picks up a blackened branch, about six feet in length.

Aiden scrutinizes the charred wood even as he keeps one eye on the Draugar. "That will crumble the second you touch anything with it."

Bard doesn't answer him verbally. Instead, there is a brilliant flash of light and the blackened bough transforms into a sharp-tipped spear. The shifter whirls it about expertly.

"Wow," Gretchen breathes and Bard flashes her a grin.

"Stay behind me," Aiden commands Gretchen as he and Bard do their best to shield her with their bodies and weapons, circling her like she's the nucleus of an atom. The Draugar aren't quick, but there are at least twelve of them, shuffling forward, intent on making the three of them into a meal.

Bard's spear has the longest reach and his aim is true. He plunges the newly sharpened end into the eye of one creature. It emits a startled screech and then continues its forward motion, pushing the point of the spear more firmly through its skull.

"We can't kill them," the shifter shouts.

"We can still break them." With a growl, Aiden launches forward.

He swings his fire sword in a mighty arc. Three heads roll. The bodies don't pause. Hands rise to grab a hold of him. He kicks out, knocking the one on the left into the other two. They go down like a stack of dominos. He slices again and cuts them through the torsos.

To his left, Bard changes tactics. He uses his spear more

like a club. He swings until he connects with a Druagar's ribcage. The bones shatter.

They fight on until all the dead are in pieces. Gretchen even picks up a branch to help. She isn't as effective but she manages to stall the creature heading for her long enough for Bard to impale it on a giant tree.

Even broken into pieces, the Druagar remain determined. Disconnected hands pull the upper bodies forward as the feet propel the lower half toward their targets. And in the distance, his wolf senses pick up on a disturbing sound. Like the creaking of old leather and scraping of dry bones.

"More on the way." Aiden releases his magic and the fire sword vanishes.

"How many more?" Bard kicks a scrabbling hand away from Gretchen.

Aiden takes in the scene. "Too many. We need to get the hell out of here."

Bard leaves his spear in the pinned creature and takes Gretchen's hand. "My lady, you have been impossibly brave. Now it is time for us to run." Then, without pausing, he hefts the mortal girl up over his shoulder. She lets out a startled squawk but doesn't protest as the shifter darts through the trees with her bouncing like a rolled-up rug. Aiden follows them down the hill.

He considers shifting to wolf or to sparks. From the air, he might get a better idea of where the Draugar are and the wolf can shred one of the undead faster than he can as a man. But being in the wolf's skin gives the creature a stronger hold on his body. With Nic gone and adrenaline pumping through his system after the fight, the beast could likely turn on friend as well as foe.

And as for the sparks, he doesn't want to leave Gretchen and Bard alone even that long. Not because of any outside danger. After watching the shifter fight, Aiden holds no doubt that Bard can protect himself. But because he still doesn't trust the male. No matter that the shifter appears protective of the mortal.

They emerge from what remains of the Great Golden Forest onto a purple and blue meadow, just as the sun sinks over the horizon. A pretty blue stream cuts its way lazily through the untouched valley. Tiny golden lights rise from the lush stalks to greet them.

He sniffs the air, trying to locate whatever it was that made all the fine hairs along his spine stand on end. Even with the peaceful scene before them, a haven after the burnt forest full of the dead, something isn't right. Underhill sets lures for the unwary.

His instincts, both man's and wolf's, scream *danger*.

"Wait," Aiden calls to the shifter when he reads the other male's intent to barge through the field to the burbling stream.

Bard frowns but at least he pauses. "What are those things?"

"Set Gretchen down," Aiden instructs. "Very gently."

Again, the shifter complies, sinking down and allowing the mortal girl to slide down until her sneakers rest on the dirt. Her hair has fallen free of the tie she'd had around it and her glasses are nowhere in sight.

"Are you all right?" Bard asks, obviously concerned.

She slaps at him, her cheeks red. "Next time ask before you pluck me like a flower."

The shifter grins, his borrowed façade's teeth flashing in the dim light. "Apologies my lady, I didn't mean to scare you. Allow me to retrieve you some water as an offering."

"No!" Aiden shouts. The warning comes a moment too late. There is a great crackling sound and the shifter is blasted back onto his rump. He bounces once and his head slams against the ground, eyes rolling back in his head.

Gretchen lunges for him and surprisingly, reaches his side a moment before Aiden. "What was that?"

"A protection spell." He nods to the valley. "This is the home of the will o' the-wisps, granted to them by the kings and queens of Underhill. They answer to no court, are a neutral zone of sort. Only those who have been granted permission by the creatures may enter."

Judging by her expression, Gretchen is only half listening. "I don't think he's breathing." Her fingers are nimble as she searches for the shifter's pulse. "I can't find a heartbeat."

"He might not have one." Aiden puts a hand on her shoulder. "Some fey do not."

"We need to treat him like he does." She shrugs out of his touch and performs CPR, counting along with the chest compressions that keep the shifter's heart pumping blood throughout his body.

"Who are you?" A small feminine voice, like the tinkling of silver bells, calls.

Since Gretchen is busy keeping Bard alive, Aiden rises and turns to face the floating blob of light. He strides closer, though stops well short of the edge of the field. "We are travelers who wish to pass through your valley. We were attacked by the undead but managed to escape them. We mean you no harm. Please, our friend is hurt. Can you help him?"

"He's dying," the soft, melodious voice says sadly. "His heart is not pure. Only those with pure hearts can cross into our valley."

"You're not going anywhere," Gretchen snarls. Her attention is on Bard but Aiden suspects the venom might be for the valley and those who inhabit it.

Her strength surprises him. He didn't think this soft, shy mortal had that sort of resilience in her. "It was an accident, he didn't know where he was, or that the spell would hurt him."

"His intentions were to take from us."

"Just water," Gretchen shouts, her movements growing more frantic. Bard's guise of Jim Harris fades back to his standard countenance, his skin going deathly pale. "Aiden, I think he's dying!"

"He's a member of Queen Nicneven's Unseelie Court," Aiden tries. "A shifter, an entertainer. His heart might not be pure but I am sure he meant no harm to any of you."

"The Risen Queen?" The wisp appears agitated and zips back to where the other balls of light congregate.

"No," Gretchen moans and Aiden races to her side. But it's too late. The mortal is crumpled over the shifter's chest, sobbing against the shifter as though her heart is breaking. "He's gone."

Helpless and panicked, Aiden sits by her side, watches her tears fall. She feels so much, this mortal girl. And unlike his Nic, she doesn't try to hide it.

As he watches Gretchen dissolve, a lump forms in his own throat. He didn't particularly like the shifter, didn't trust him at all. But he was Nic's—therefore Aiden's— responsibility. If only he'd spoken up sooner, warned the other male that something felt off.

He is pack. The image of a pack of wolves running across a snowy field flits into his mind. Eight wolves who morph into people. His own human appearance, Nic by his side. Then Gretchen, Freda and Jasmine, Nahini, Harmony and yes, even Bard. *He belonged to us.*

Aiden starts, the images throwing him. The wolf never mentioned a pack to him before, never claimed any other than Nic. There is no reasoning with the beast. Once its mind is set, it will not budge.

Our pack to help protect our mate. Another image of Nic before the beast recedes.

Along the path of their bond, he senses something. Her presence perhaps. But there are no images from her, no feelings at all. Or maybe he's just projecting his own numb state onto her and his Nic really isn't there at all.

"You claim he belongs to the Risen Queen? The new court made up of those beyond the Veil?" The will-o-the wisp lands on his shoulder. He moves his head so he can make out her tiny features. So close he sees long red hair and a small pert nose dotted with glowing freckles and enormous blue eyes. Her clothing looks like it's been made from flower petals. She's tiny and frail, hardly a match for even Gretchen. "Shifters are not usually part of any court."

"He belonged to us." Aiden stares down at the dead man, anger and regret twisting his insides. "His life is my responsibility."

The wisp flits up higher until she is positioned in the air between him and Gretchen. "All is not lost. He can still be saved."

"Not as one of those things." Gretchen's brown eyes are full of tears. "Those monsters?"

"No," the wisp agrees in her high voice. "They are abominations. Your companion is locked in a death curse, still alive, but trapped within his flesh. His body is still but his soul remains intact and will stay that way until the curse is completed—or reversed."

"How?" Aiden asks. "Not even a giant or a royal can break that sort of magic."

"The Hill holds the means."

Gretchen frowns. "The hill?"

"She means Underhill." Aiden studies Bard's inert form. "Underhill set the spell to protect this valley?"

"The valley is part of under the hill, and we are protected

by its lifeblood. The water that never sees the sun is the only way to reverse the death curse."

The water that never sees the sun. She must be referring to a stream or lake somewhere in the Unseelie catacombs.

"Then let's go find it." Gretchen wipes her eyes and shoulders her pack.

Aiden shakes his head. "No, you need to remain here."

"But—"

"I'll cover more ground without you. And one of us should stay to watch over Bard."

Gretchen pushes her glasses up her nose and nods. "Okay. I'll stay."

Aiden looks back at the wisp. "She is mortal. Do the old ways still hold?"

"They do." The wisp nods. "We will look after your mortal."

Aiden turns back to Gretchen. "The old ways promise safe passage for any mortal claimed by a court and taken under the hill for a year and a day. The fey can't hurt you, no matter whose court you enter."

"And those Draugar things?"

He shakes his head. "Are no longer under our control. You see them, you get inside that field under the wisp's protection. Got it?"

When the mortal stares down at the still form on the ground, he knows a moment's fear. But then she meets his gaze head-on. "I can't do anything for him if I'm dead, right?"

"Right. Be smart, stay safe. I'll return as soon as I'm able."

He is about to go when she reaches out a hand. "Hang on a second."

Aiden frowns as she starts rooting through Nic's tattered backpack and comes up with a silver flask.

"You'll need something to carry the water back with,

right?" Gretchen offers it to him. "I wondered why Harmony insisted I pack this."

Because the seer knew what would happen. Aiden takes the flask and puts it in his back pocket. "Be cautious, Gretchen. Nic will skin me alive if anything happens to you."

She smiles, probably because she believes him to be jesting.

He changes into his sparks form and floats, up high above the will-o-the-wisp valley. Higher until he can no longer make out individual trees, just a sea of green forest in front of him and the scorched ground behind. Unwilling to get caught in the same trap that snared Bard, he steers south of the glade, toward the jagged peaks that crown the heart of the Unseelie power. Only through the crystal palace can he enter the catacombs and once there….

One thing at a time. It is an expression Nic mutters when she practices with Freda and Nahini. He supposes it is to remind herself that the future doesn't matter if she slips up in the present.

He'll do whatever he must to help his mate's court.

His pack is worth the risk.

DISCOVERIES

I lose track of our surroundings. My mind is foggy from the trauma of the last few days. Though I've never gone into shock before, as I look down at my blood-less, trembling fingers I am certain that's what I am experi-encing. The image of those dead fey bodies scattered about like straw on a barn floor chases me as we flee from Soladin's valley. If we ever stop walking, I feel certain the tremors would spread and shake my entire body until it fell to pieces.

Pharaildis says nothing. She moves like a wraith, almost gliding over the ground. Needing something to focus on other than all of those dead fey, my mind seizes on her, her grace and endurance. She never stumbles or slips or even appears to put a foot wrong. When the path slopes up, she easily uses her hands to help pull herself up. She doesn't look back at me once. Leaves me to stew in my regrets.

So I stew.

It's the smell that brings me back to the present. The strong odor of sulfur permeates my morose thoughts. I frown and glance around, surprised to find that we are on a narrow path that twists between jagged red rocks.

"Where are we?" I ask my mother.

She pauses to turn back to me, the first time she's looked my way in hours. "Near where I brought you last time."

"The heart of Underhill?" I pant. It's been hours since breakfast. I'm hot and sweaty and disheveled.

Not a strand of her dark hair is out of place.

At her nod, I ask, "Why didn't you just poof us over here the way you did before?"

She laughs a little, the sound like tinkling bells. "Silly, you were dead before."

"Right," I mutter. "Somehow I keep forgetting that."

Probably because the entire experience had been surreal.

I study her perfect visage. "So, are you taking me to see Underhill?"

Her eyes are as clear blue as a mountain lake. "Yes. She is going to protect you." She resumes walking.

"Protect me from what?" I quicken my steps to catch up with her longer stride.

"The fey." The words are spoken low, almost too low for me to hear. "They court Underhill's wrath if they enter the catacombs."

The wrath of Underhill did not sound like a fun time. Having never met the fey realm in person, I have no idea what she's like, or what crawled up her ass and died. Since my mother was bound in service to her though, I decide to phrase the question a bit more tactfully.

"Does Underhill have something to do with the Draugar? Or the spreading of poison from the Desolate Realm?"

She ignores my question. It could be because the passage up is growing steeper and she's winded from the climb, but she's shown zero signs of exertion. I decide to leave her to it. After all, she's wearing ankle shackles, pretty though they might be.

I'll get answers soon enough.

We crest the hill just as the sun begins its final descent below the horizon line. My mother sits on a large boulder and retrieves a canteen from the folds of her purple robe. She offers it to me first. I enjoy the water that is still somehow cold despite hours in her pocket.

After drinking my fill, I scan the area. It's flat enough and there are plenty of dry branches to use to build a fire. "Are we stopping for the night?"

At her nod, I set off toward the tree line, ignoring my own sore muscles. The climb was deceptively rigorous. But just like me, Pharaildis hasn't uttered a single complaint.

Family trait?

Physically we couldn't be more different. I study her surreptitiously as I collect the firewood. She's curvy where I am lean, tall where I barely top five foot four inches. Her hair fades into the twilight, where mine typically shines as pale as moonlight. I want my organic color back, wonder if I can put in a request with Underhill to restore my natural color without the unfortunate awkward root growth phase.

And how ludicrous to be worrying about my hair when my long-lost mother is sitting a few feet away?

I only have her word to go on that she truly is my mother. She's offered no evidence, told me very little about herself. So why do I, a natural skeptic, actually believe her?

Because of the connection. It's a real thing, something I can feel, sense, accept. Similar to the way I reacted when I met Aiden, there's just something...right about being in her presence.

As if we belong together.

It's been a while since I've been camping, though I do remember some of the basics. I make a little teepee with the sticks and stuff some dried leaves in for kindling. Then I roll another stick back and forth between my palms in a rapid motion atop a dry piece of bark. The runes add a flash of darkness to the whirling motion. A little smoke emerges from the connection point, but no sparks.

Aiden, I think. *I could really use some fire magic right about now.*

With Aiden around, there would be no need for sticks or the blisters that were forming on my rune-marked palms. He could snap his fingers and the fire would spring to life.

I indulge in a brief fantasy of him, wielding *Seelenverkäufer*, cutting a tear in the Veil right to me. He'd be wearing his customary grin and tell me that all the fey from the campsite were fine. The traitor has been captured, my court put back to rights, the Draugar vanquished. Oh, and while I was daydreaming, all my homework would be done for the rest of high school. He'd take me in his arms and….

"I'm going to find something for us to eat." My mother, who'd been watching me struggle with the fire, stands, shaking out her skirts.

"M'kay," I mumble, trying to hide the flush on my face. *One thing at a time, Nic.*

While I work on the fire, she heads into the trees, emerging soon after with a nest of large eggs in one hand and a handful of bright purple berries in the other.

"Dinner," she smiles and hands me her treasures.

I study the eggs and wonder how to go about preparing them with no cookware or utensils.

Pharaildis arches one brow. "You're the Unseelie queen, Nic. Borrow magic for whatever you need."

"I don't want to pay Underhill's price," I say.

She sighs, as though I've tossed a wet blanket over her fun and then there is a flash, and a cast-iron skillet appears in her hand.

She hands it to me and I study her. "You don't look like you had to pay the price."

"Because I didn't." Another flash and she is holding two plates, a spatula, two forks, and even a salt shaker.

"Is this some kind of storeroom thing, like the giants have?" I ask.

She shakes her head. "As a servant of Underhill, I can tap directly into her magic. There are no bargains, no games."

"Games," I repeat the word. "Is that really how she sees it?"

Pharaildis hands me the salt. "What's life without a little spice?"

I set the skillet on a flat stone next to the fire, then crack the eggs into it. The yolks are an almost orange-yellow color, like duck eggs. I don't ask where she got them, just add some salt and then dole out half to her, keeping the rest for myself.

We eat in awkward silence. I don't know what her problem is, but I can't figure out what to say.

I want to know how she got into her current predicament, bound to serve Underhill for eternity. I crave to find out more about her. Where she came from, maybe even who my father had been.

I yearn to know what she thinks of me when compared to Nicneven, the fey queen she'd given birth to centuries before. I know she feels…something for me. Is it love? Instinct? Why else would she have helped me escape?

"Tell me about the women who raised you." Her tone is commanding, not one I'd expect from a servant.

"Chloe and Addy? What do you want to know?" Odd, why would she want to hear about them instead of me? I try to ignore the hurt that her questions aren't focused my way.

"Were they good parents?" There's an odd note in her voice that I can't quite place.

"I guess it depends on who you ask. Probably not by human standards." They had hidden my serial killer tendencies, something most mortals would find abhorrent. "They always had my back."

Her blue eyes search my face. "They never told you who you were? That it is your destiny to rule the Unseelie Court once more?"

I'd had some time to mull over that exact question. "I'm not even out of high school. I think they would have, eventually. When the time came."

But it hadn't been time that had pushed me down this road. It had been Sarah's death, and Aiden's arrival and that of the Wild Hunt.

Full dark set in while we ate and with a wave of her hand, the dirty dishes vanish into nothingness.

Pharaildis holds up one hand and a glowing ball of blue-white light appears within it, like a mini-moon.

"That's very cool."

"Fey light." She tosses it to me and I catch it. It is weightless. I can barely perceive that I am holding anything. The light turns my skin translucent. I try closing my hand around it, but find I can't.

I hand it back to her and dare a personal question. "How did you come to be here?"

The light reflects back at me in her clear eyes as she cradles the fey light. Her expression is distant, almost sad. "It's a long story."

"Do you have someplace to be?" I snipe, tired of non-answers from old creatures who like to shroud themselves in mystique.

The light winks out. She stands from the rock and then stretches out on a flat piece of ground a few feet away. "Get some rest, Nic. All will be revealed to you, soon."

She wants to play the woman of mystery card? Fine. "Then if you don't want to tell me about you, tell me about Underhill."

There's a catch in her breath as she asks. "What do you want to know?"

"You said she plays games. That's what the whole trade thing is about. Power for a price, magic that can be punished or rewarded. Why does she do that?"

There's a pause. "She's lonely, bored, restless. The fey don't appreciate her, won't respect her any more than the mortals do their world. All sentient beings in all the worlds have one trait in common—their total lack of appreciation for what they have. All they can see is what they want next. Underhill's bargains can be fun for her to watch, but she is also trying to teach the power-hungry fey a lesson."

"So, Underhill is teaching them to appreciate her?" She made it sound as if the fey realm were both a spoiled child and an authoritarian mother.

"Underhill does what she does to survive," Pharaildis snaps. "If she didn't parcel out the magic, make the fey think twice about whether or not they actually *need* a spell, they would have burned through the source of power long before you were born."

"Which time?" I quip.

She resumes her stretched-out position. "I'm glad to see you have a sense of humor, Nic. You're going to need it."

Through the Man's Eyes

Aiden enters the underground castle the way he had the very first time he'd sought out Nicneven. Like the mortal myth of Santa Claus, he drifts down the chimney of the great throne room.

Still connected only by magic, he hovers for a moment as

a smattering of sparks. It wouldn't do to be recognized. The space looks exactly as the last time he'd seen it.

On a raised dais on the far left, facing the fireplace sits the Fire Throne. He's seen that chair on fire, flames licking out and around it, blazing with heat and the very spark of life.

The room stands empty. Aiden coalesces into his human aspect in front of the great mantel as fast as his magic allows. Lightheaded from his whirlwind recombination, he staggers, placing one hand against the great stone edifice for balance.

When had he last eaten? The picnic with Nic. It feels like a lifetime ago.

His original plan had been to head directly into the tunnel that led to the catacombs, but he'd been expending a lot of magic. He wouldn't do Bard or Gretchen any good if he burnt out before contacting Underhill.

Deciding, he moves soundlessly through the receiving room, doing his best not to look at the platform on the North wall. Still, his eyes gravitate to the chair, the sinister twin to its fiery sister. Spotlit in a shaft of moonlight streaming in through an octagonal window, the Shadow Throne had endured all of Brigit's efforts to destroy it. Her rage had proven ineffective against the seat. She'd hurled fire, ice, water, and boulders at her rival's seat. On one memorable night in a fit of characteristic temper, she'd taken an ax to the thing.

There isn't a mark on its gleaming ebony surface.

For its part, the chair seemed to grow stronger and more sinister with each attempt. The twisted blackened wood sucked all the light from anything nearby until it created a sort of permanent haze around itself. As though it really was made from the shadows and madness.

Without a queen to sit on it year after year, the air pressure around the throne has shifted. Almost as though the unspent magic builds upon itself. Being near it now makes all the small hairs rise along the back of his neck. His impression is that The Shadow Throne is not just a symbol of power, it *is* power waiting to be unleashed. The wolf's hackles rise as he looks at it and something sentient stares back. Holding him in thrall, the same way its mistress does.

Like his Nic, the Shadow Throne waits for its moment to strike.

Aiden shakes himself and tears his gaze from the eerie object, focusing on his next step and the next and the one after that.

He reaches the alcove between the receiving room and the banquet chamber and turns left, toward the servant stairs. Much like the gods he'd grown up with, the Unseelie fey are narcissistic by nature. Never focusing on much beyond the end of their noses. With Brigit defeated, it is unlikely anyone will recognize him as the queen's consort but he still doesn't want to risk drawing too much attention. He takes the servant's passage to the kitchen, where he is even less likely to be recognized.

The servant corridors wind through the castle like tunnels in an anthill. Fitting since the fey who built them resemble the insects in question to a startling degree. Stronger by nature and lacking even the most basic magic, the tunneling fey swore obedience to the Unseelie Court in exchange for room and board. Since their hive-mind works well as a team, they make a solid ground force as well as exceptional builders.

Brigit had deemed fey incapable of wielding magic, "as expendable as the mortals." She'd turned the tunneling fey out, claiming there was no longer any need for them.

When he'd first come to the court, the tunnels had been flawless. Every brick and stone intact, the mortar reinforced as needed. Now the stones are crumbling in sections, the curved tunnel ceiling held in place by rustic beams instead of the carefully orchestrated pressure, even caving in in spots.

One such spot sits directly across from the strategy room. Aiden hears the voices well before he reaches the opening. He ducks behind the pile of rubble when he recognizes Rodrick's clipped tones.

Alric's Spriggan father never smiled. He was a grim male who'd been Brigit's consort for many years. Their union had produced a daughter, Alric's half-sister and a potential heir to the Fire Throne.

Peeking up from his hiding place, he takes a brief inventory of the room. A long stone table hadn't fared as well as the Shadow Throne, its top thick with char. Rodrick is seated in a cushioned chair at the head of the table, a spot typically reserved for the ruling queen. Three others were in the room, two male Spriggans and a small female. Only the girl's face was fully visible from his vantage and she had the same flowing blond hair and gold-flecked brown eyes as Alric.

"But father," the girl, who looked to be about Jasmine's age, pleads. Her voice is low, and lyrical, with an Eastern European lilt. "I want to go home with you. I don't like to be here alone. Please, take me with you."

Alric's sister, Brigit's natural-born daughter, looks as though a stiff breeze could blow her away. She seems impossibly young.

"I said no," Rodrick's fist slams down on the tabletop, emphasizing the final word. Unlike her, the lord's accent is as clipped as an aristocrat. "You will do as I say, Rowena."

Tears fill her big brown eyes but she nods. "Yes, father."

"You are dismissed." Rodrick waves her off.

Defeated, the girl slips from the room, shoulders slumped. For a possible heir to fire, she demonstrates none of her own. In fact, Aiden can easily picture her taming wild beasts with her brother.

The remaining fey wait until the door clicks shut behind her.

"Stupid chit had it coming." The smaller of the two Spriggans is first to speak. "Sneaking off all the time."

Rodrick turns frosty gray eyes on the other male. "That is your future queen, so if I were you, Leif, I'd modify my tone."

Alric had said his sister was unlike their father. Judging from what he'd just witnessed that is a massive understatement. With the fey, appearances are often deceiving.

Rodrick gets to his feet and begins to pace the length of the room. Aiden ducks down lower behind the caved-in stonework, ready to shift into his fire form if the steps draw too near his hiding place.

"What are we even doing here?" The other brother's voice is thick, as though forming the sentence took an enormous amount of effort.

Rodrick halts feet from the collapsed wall and then rounds on his son. "We are here so your sister can claim her rightful place as queen of the Unseelie Court."

"Just have her sit on the stupid chair already." The older brother flops down in a chair.

Rodrick smacks his palms on the table. "And what if the Fire Throne rejects her? What if it *kills* her? Use your head, Kef. It's that useless lump on top of your equally useless carcass."

Aiden frowns. He had never heard that the thrones could kill hopeful kings and queens. But here Rodrick is acting as if that is a real possibility.

"Besides," Rodrick continues. "If we wait long enough, the lone Seelie king will be desperate to cede power. He is surrounded on all sides, his feeble magic unable to protect his own people from the Draugar. If we wait long enough, we'll rule both courts unhindered."

It takes all his effort for Aiden not to suck in a breath.

Ceding power across court lines had only happened once, long before Nicneven's time. The resulting disaster was why the fey rule the courts in groups of four. So that no one ruler grew too powerful and tipped the balance to one side or the other.

But Brigit's attack on Nic had changed everything. With only one ruler of the Unseelie Court, the balance has already been disrupted. With Brigit removed both sides of the court were up for grabs. And with Wardon held captive by Angrboda....

Rodrick is right. King Soladin has no relief in sight.

"What about the Risen Queen?" the first son, Lief, asks. "She might try to claim both Thrones."

Rodrick makes a dismissive sound. "Nicneven has always been a reluctant ruler at best. She cares only for the Wild Hunt. And with my operative working to dismantle the Hunt from within, I'll make sure she doesn't cross into Underhill again."

Isolde. Rodrick doesn't know that his spy is dead and that Soladin had kidnapped Nic. Even if he had a second spy, the traitor hadn't used the Soul Reaper to cross back over and deliver the news that the Risen Queen has disappeared.

A knock sounds on the door.

"Enter," Rodrick bellows.

"Milords," a servant addresses him with a cockney accent. "Your horses stand ready."

He listens to the men depart. Though he longs to follow them, perhaps even beat them to their destination, he made a promise to Gretchen. Rodrick will have to wait.

Aiden waits until their footsteps recede to continue down the hall. If nothing else, he's taking away several valuable tidbits from eavesdropping. Rodrick is more ambitious than anyone gave him credit for, craving not just one throne, but all four. He has a daughter with the right bloodlines and yet he is waiting for something before placing her on the Fire Throne. Wardon had wanted to marry into Nic's court, but the Unseelie lord is willing to destroy them all as long as he controls whoever is left.

Aiden reaches the kitchen unhindered. Servants bustle about, each intent on their own duties and don't pay attention to a stranger in their midst. He manages to snag bread, cheese, and fruit before he feels the tap on his shoulder.

Expecting one of the cooks, he prepares a lie even as he turns.

The goddess standing before him smiles, sending chills right to his heart. "Hello, Váli."

THE HEART OF THE HILL

I've discovered something important about my mother.

I don't like her. At all.

If she wasn't the only thing standing between me and wandering aimlessly through the barren wastelands of Underhill, I would tell her to kiss off.

Or maybe kiss her myself.

It had started this morning. I'd opened my eyes to find her staring at me. Not all that unusual, considering she'd never had the chance to see me sleep. Not as an infant, a toddler, a prepubescent. Not as a fey nor a mortal. But something in her stare hadn't been at all motherly. Not that I'm an expert, but in her shoes, I would look on my progeny with curiosity, tenderness or maybe even wistfulness. But Pharaildis had been studying me as if she were looking for something, some sort of trait, and her drawn eyebrows indicated that she wasn't finding it. Her scrutiny made my skin crawl.

"What?" I'd barked, unnerved.

"You look like him."

Her words sent a cold chill through me. "My father, you mean?"

At her nod, I sat up, ready to receive the answers I'd been longing for and simultaneously dreading. The puzzle pieces that when connected, equaled me.

But instead of a heart to heart, she stood and shook out her skirts. "We best get moving. Underhill is waiting."

I hid my disappointment and dusted off my own rumpled clothes before following her down the slope of the hill.

I'd been hoping once she grew more comfortable with me, she'd volunteer some info. About herself, my father, how she came to be a prisoner. But the woman's lips are locked tighter than the Federal Reserve. She hadn't offered a single personal detail. She is even more miserly with information than I am.

For the second time in my existence, she's come to me. Because she wants something? What? Each step sans conversation adds to my unease until I'm ready to explode.

Giving people the benefit of the doubt doesn't come naturally to me. I am judge, jury and, when need be, executioner. If she'd been anyone else, I would confront her, demand some answers. More information about the mysterious Underhill and how she came to be in her service. What sorts of abilities could she tap into? The terms of her imprisonment. Who my father had been, what their relationship had been like? Had he been fey, an immortal? When had she found out about my death and subsequent resurrection?

But I held my tongue and all the anger that seethed inside me like a knot of serpents found a new target—me. Why not just ask? Am I afraid she'll take offense and abandon me forever this time? Do I really expect that staying quiet will make her like me more?

And do I really care if she likes me at all?

Being with Pharaildis shines a spotlight on something

ugly in me. A shadowed alcove I've kept hidden from the outside world and myself. It's been tucked away deeper than my penchant for killing, behind my fey heritage even.

I, Nic Rutherford, the teenage serial killer turned immortal queen, am incredibly insecure.

Just thinking it brings a sneer to my face. But when my mother turns, I wipe the expression away and offer her a tight-lip smile. She looks away without smiling back and the useless fretting doubles inside me, like a flock of disturbed bats trying to escape a cave-in.

This woman is a part of me. Helped to create me. I don't like her, yet I want her to like me. How ridiculous is that?

My gaze falls to the delicate chain around her ankles. She's a criminal. Did something so heinous she got her pregnant carcass tossed in the immortal pokey. Had her *child* taken away from her.

I frown. And that child became queen. Why would the fey want the half-blood issue of a human prisoner to rule one of their powerful courts? But that was precisely what they'd done.

I remember the expression on her face, the tone of her voice. *You look like him.* Whatever had been between them, that sour note told me that their relationship hadn't ended well.

The sun rises higher in the east and sweat slides down the back of my neck, making my hair stick unpleasantly to my scalp. I can feel blisters forming on my feet. In spite of all my training with Freda, all this slogging is taking its toll. The brown robe is tucked beneath one arm and I wear the vest and pants from Soladin's court. I upend the canteen over my lips, but I finished the last of the water hours ago.

Pharaildis, looking cool and fresh as though she were standing on a frozen pond in midwinter, points to the left.

"There's a small stream over that rise. We can stop for a drink."

Sure enough, a small mountain spring burbles happily down the hill. I kneel beside it and slurp several mouthfuls before whipping my vest off so I am left in my bra and the linen pants. Using the shirt as a cloth, I drench it in the cool water then use it to clean the perspiration from my skin.

Downstream, my companion slides off her gauzy slippers and pulls up her skirts before soaking her chained feet in the icy stream.

"Aren't you thirsty?" I ask between more greedy gulps.

"I no longer suffer thirst. Nor hunger, fatigue, nor lust." Her gaze is far away, attention on something I cannot see. "No urges of the flesh at all."

"But I saw you eat. Last night."

"I need food, though I never suffer from pangs when I am forced to do without." Her focus is still on the horizon.

"That must be nice." No wonder she looks so cool when I'm a hot mess. How many times have my very human feelings, the needs of my body, gotten in the way of something I wanted? How many times did I wish to be numb? It would have made my life *so* much easier.

She faces me and when she speaks, her voice is flat. "It's a hell from which there is no surcease. Without desire, there is no satiation. No fulfillment. Each day as long and pointless as the ones before and the endless expanse after."

Though she claims to feel nothing, her eyes are burning blue fire.

My lips part, but before I can think of something appropriate to say, she extracts her feet from the stream, replaces her shoes and then stands ready. I take one more sip of water, refill my canteen, and then tie my saturated shirt over my shoulders.

Spending time with her also illustrates the relationship I

have with my aunts. True, they aren't overly demonstrative. The Fates aren't big huggers and for most of my life, even a peck on the cheek was a nonstarter. But Chloe would have been plaguing me with questions, barely pausing to draw breath. She'd dish out celebrity gossip, horoscopes and all sorts of other nonsense as well as prying into my relationship with Aiden. And although Addy can be terse, I always know her actions are calculated to do what is best for me.

Pharaildis has her own agenda. And whatever it is, she keeps it to herself.

Maybe she's just not used to talking. My inner voice pipes up. *Maybe she doesn't know what to say.*

Shut up, self, I snarl in my head. The excuses have grown tedious. The woman gave me life, she owes me nothing, I owe her nothing. I should just walk away.

Yet every time I try to do exactly that, my gaze returns to the chain around her ankles. In spite of her own captivity, she came to that village and helped me escape. Okay, maybe I *do* owe her something. I should stick with her and at least find out if I can set her free.

For all her personal defects, she is a good guide. She has proven herself knowledgeable about every source of water, every plant Underhill provides. My stomach rumbles once and she returns with a fistful of edible flowers, nuts or berries. Every time the canteen goes dry, we are in spitting distance of a fresh stream. For a prisoner garbed in silks, she's one hell of an outdoorswoman.

The sun is sinking over a black arch of stone on the western horizon when she stops.

I am panting, out of breath once more, and gasp. "Why are we stopping?"

"We're here."

Frowning, I glance around. "Where's here?" The

surrounding landscape looks no different to me, just more scrubby bushes and dusty rocks.

All at once a feeling sweeps over me, one of unfathomable grief.

I stagger. "What…?"

Pharaildis raises her right hand and the foreign emotion dulls from a Tsunami to a gently lapping wave. "Do you feel them?"

Them?

She points to the arch with her other hand. "You see that? It used to be a settlement. The very first immortal settlement. I remember when it was constructed."

I frown. "You were here for that?"

At her nod, I do some quick calculations. Some of the immortals I've met are thousands of years old. And she remembered this place before they'd come? Exactly how old is she?

She turns to me, blue eyes bright in the low light. "In the beginning, this was a land of magic, of possibility. A dream plane that mortals could touch only through the deepest part of the unconscious. That's where true power resides, deep within mortal imagining. If one could dream it into existence, here it came to be, sprung to life. It was raw, wild untapped. There were those who gathered here, those who were powerless within their mortal bodies, the old, the sick, the weak. All helpless, trapped in their own flesh, used and abused, neglected and forgotten. Every night they would congregate here, at the heart of the hill and experience unbridled freedom, limitless, endless power. Deeper than the ocean, stronger than the wind. Then the fey came and trapped them." She spits the last words.

My lips part. "Trapped them? How?"

"Through trickery, mostly. It is the way of the fair folk, to take what they can, whenever they want. Freya's get have knowledge of the world, of magic. They proposed trades, promising the mortal visitors endless life here if they would only cede some lands. Not all agreed. Some had loved ones back beyond the Veil. But many accepted, lured by the thought of forever freedom, endless possibility."

Her focus was not on the arch, but something beyond it that only she could see. "The fey delivered on their promise, binding the souls to the winds, the sea, the ground, the fire, and even the shadows. Trapping the souls within those elements allowed the fey to control them. The mortal souls couldn't fight, couldn't return back across the Veil to their flesh. Without the soul, the body breaks down and without the anchor, the soul loses the core of self. What makes you Nic, that's found deep within, the part of you to be most protected. Everywhere you look, in every leaf, every stone, even the blackened husk of this village, the essence of those noble dreamers live on. If you can call such an existence life."

"Is that what happened to you?"

She shakes her head. "My imprisonment is different. It came after."

"But you were one of the ones who used to visit here? You know those souls." The tone of her voice, the way her hands clench into fists….

She doesn't deny it.

What she is describing, sick people who'd craved independence, a sense of power over themselves being duped into serving the fey….

"Can they be freed?"

Pharaildis stares out over the landscape. "Even if there was a way to free them, their mortal bodies have long since turned to ash. There's nowhere for the scraps of souls to go."

My heartbeat increases. "What about the Veil? Could they go there?"

She looks at me then. "I suppose it's possible. But if the dreamers go on, the magic goes with them."

"So?" Magic hadn't been a whole lot of help to the fey, keeping those who could wield it lording it over the ones who couldn't, forcing a master-slave society onto the beings who dwelled here. "Look, I made a mess when I took Brigit out. Tore a hole in the Veil, exposed humanity to the fey and the other creatures who live here. Now you're telling me there are trapped souls who need to move on. It's the perfect solution."

She tilts her head, studying me. "You're a queen. Without magic, how will you regain the Shadow Throne?"

"I don't care about the Shadow Throne or about magic." I'm desperate to convince her of this.

The sun dips below the horizon. "Magic is power. The Shadow Throne is power."

"I'm not interested in power," I say.

She narrows her eyes at me then turns and enters the darkened entrance to the cave without another word.

So much for mother-daughter bonding.

Through the Man's Eyes

Aiden picks up her scent so he knows the female figure before him is truly the goddess he hasn't seen in a millennium. "What are you doing here, Freya?"

Her hand touches his arm. One second the scents and smells of the palace kitchens surround them, the next they are on a hillside with the sun setting at their backs.

"Where have you taken me?" he snarls. Close, he'd been *so* close to finding the catacombs.

The goddess ignores his ire. "Aren't you happy to see me?" She holds out her supple arms, her expression expectant.

"Why would I be? You turned your back on me long ago." He can clearly recall the last time he'd seen the goddess. Seen her walking away from him, unable to meet his questioning gaze as he, his mother and Nari were led down into the bowels of the world.

She lowers her arms, her infamous temper flickering in her green irises. "The All-father commanded no one help you. What could I do?"

"And you want to stand there and pretend that you never disobeyed him? If you'd truly cared about me, you would have found a way to stop it." Her long ago betrayal was scarred tissue, hardened and mostly forgotten over the centuries. The memory of a single hurt buried beneath a life-time of them.

"Is that why you never sought me out after it happened? Did you think I'd abandoned you?" She lifts her pointed chin. "I waited for you to come to me to have your curse lifted."

"Why assume I would come to you? I went into hiding after what the gods did to my father...my family. Why could *you* not seek me out?" How many nights had he hidden in crags of rocks and snarls of roots? Exhausted from battling for control over the wolf's instincts, riddled with guilt and grief over Nari. Cold, hungry, struggling. How many times had he prayed Freya would find him and offer him comfort?

"I am a goddess of Asgard." Her pride gets the best of her. "What would you have me do? Your brother was dead, the gods stood united against Loki."

"You could have looked for me."

"Skathi told me you'd been transfigured into a ravening

beast. How was I to know there was any of the man left?" But she wouldn't hold his gaze.

He stares at her flawless profile for an endless moment. There it is, all the explanation he would ever get from her. This goddess he'd adored, the creator of the fey, had abandoned him in his darkest hour. And she wasn't even sorry.

Didn't you have any friends among the gods? Nic had asked him. *Anyone that would have helped you escape or learn to control your wolf?*

No. Freya didn't care about him, she never had. He'd been her temporary plaything, a toy she'd discarded when he'd broken. He'd been young and naïve to believe her regard for him went any deeper. To imagine she could love anyone but herself.

"I was your lover until you discarded me like trash. But in the end what do titles matter? We will all burn together come Ragnarök."

She flinches, but recovers quickly. "We still have time. The worlds may not need to burn."

"The dead are already walking." One of the signs that herald the approach of Ragnarök.

Her cat eyes burn into him like coals. "The dead are just a weapon in her arsenal."

He shivers as the sun slips below the tree line. "Angrboda?" Had he made a horrible mistake by releasing the giantess?

"The mother of monsters?" the goddess scoffs. "She can't control her own brood. No, it is Underhill who resurrects the dead who slaughter my children in droves. You must stop her."

"Underhill?" Aiden frowns. "That makes no sense. She's been a prisoner since before the fey dwelt in these lands. Her powers are vast but they do not include raising the dead." Unless....

His chest tightens as he recalls Nic's story of the Gauntlet. The rune marks etched like brands on her palms. She'd been sure she'd died and her friend Sarah had shown her how to reverse time and come back. Yet Underhill had bragged that she'd shown Nic how to reverse the flow of time. Had the fey realm disguised herself as her daughter's dead friend?

Aiden eyes the goddess and voices his suspicion. "Pharaildis has control over runes."

Freya nods. "Brigit, that silly chit, taught her. Approached the spider in her web as though she herself wouldn't be ensnared. She underestimated Pharaildis, as so many have done. She is older than the fey and none outside of Asgard knew she's birthed one of their precious queens." The goddess's tone is full of contempt.

Aiden takes a deep breath. "What did Brigit ask for in exchange?"

"She bargained with Underhill so she could lie. But the realm is crafty. In return, Brigit revealed the god's magical language to their greatest enemy."

"Why would the gods care? Pharaildis is mortal, not fey. Even if she can wield the power of runes, she can't bring about the end of the world. Why do you fear her?"

It was the wrong thing to say. Freya's cat eyes blaze with ethereal blue light, reminding him he isn't just facing the goddess of love and beauty, but a battle maven as well.

"I am a goddess of Asgard, one of the great Vanir tribe. I do not *fear* anything, not even the end of the worlds."

Nothing would be gained from antagonizing her. Instead, he asks, "What can I do about Underhill? I can't stand against her. She knows my true name."

Váli Sigynjarson. She'd said it to him when he'd traded his silence for Angrboda's life. Naming a thing gave one power over it. He couldn't attack Underhill with magic or set his wolf upon her because she had true named him.

"You need not stand against her. Find what you seek."

Riddles. Gods damned gods and their gods damned riddles. "I seek many things. Maybe you could narrow it down for me?"

"Nicneven is the key. She commands the Wild Hunt, wields the Soul Reaper. Find her and you will have everything you need to defeat the Draugar army. Stop them and you stop Ragnarök. Or at least delay it a little while."

"Do you know who took *Seelenverkäufer*?"

A single nod.

"Tell me."

Her smile is even more dazzling than the sunset at her back. "I will when you come to the tree of gloaming with her. Fair well, Váli."

He mutters several explicit oaths under his breath. Her laugh rings in his ears. He sucks in a great lungful of air for patience and that's when he scents her.

Nic. She's nearby.

"Praise be," he mutters to the spot where Freya had been standing moments ago. If the goddess who had abandoned him helps him find his mate, will he forgive her past treachery?

Aiden vows he will. Sucking in a deep breath of her winter apple scent, he follows it down into the cavern at his back.

I'm coming Nic. Hold on.

Pharaildis stops so suddenly I slam into her back.

We'd been slogging down switchbacks inside the pitch-black cave with nothing but a glowing ball of fey light illuminating the treacherous path. How long had we been walking through the winding blackness? Hours? Days?

It's cold inside the cave. Not a mild chill or even a frosty bite like that carried by the North Wind, but a soul deep sucking kind of frigidity. The sort of frozen agony that leaches all the warmth from a body and burrows into the pit of the soul.

Between that and my weary feet, I can barely hold a thought. My blisters have blisters. Each step is a misery. I've been so focused on my next footfall and making sure I don't stumble down into the yawning darkness that I'd lost track of where my mother stood until we collided.

Her skin feels no warmer than the icy cavern walls. I wonder if that's part of her imprisonment curse—to be cold even if she never feels its effects. My teeth chatter as I ask, "Why are we stopping? Are we…wherever we're supposed to be?"

If this is our destination it appears no different than the last ten thousand steps.

"Someone's breached my wards." Her gaze is distracted. In the blue-white light, I can tell her eyes have gone unfocused.

"Your wards?" An idea is bouncing around inside my skull, one I wish I could dismiss. It sounds crazy, it feels idiotic to even consider.

But it won't go away.

Slowly, she pivots and points. "We're almost there."

"Where?" My heart is pounding. "Where are you taking me?"

"To the Heart of the Hill. The true seat of power in Underhill."

"And is she waiting there?" I press. "Waiting to see me? To meet me in person?"

No answer other than her soft footfalls as she presses on.

My apprehension is growing like invasive weeds in a garden. When she'd told me the story about the trapped souls bound to serve the fey, I'd blundered ahead, wanting to do whatever I could to help free them. To free her. But the long downward slog had chipped away at my resolve. Too many unanswered questions lay between us. Why was Pharaildis corporeal when the North Wind wasn't? What made her imprisonment different?

The fey light winks out. I stop. The darkness surrounding us is darker than a starless night, darker even than the depths of space. It is total, complete, unending.

I can feel its power even before I see the first rune. Hear the first groan.

The odd markings pulse in the wall on the far side of the chamber, a twisted F. Then another that looks like a scraggly pine tree, a sideways E. One by one they light up as though in greeting. *Welcome,* they seem to say. *We are here to serve.*

I look around the now glowing cavern. Directly ahead of us a stone bridge juts up, ascending to a dais. And on that dais sits a throne seemingly carved from the bedrock itself.

Beneath the small rock dais that the throne perches upon, a milky pale liquid eddies around, like a moat. Though it shimmers with an iridescent light.

I lick suddenly dry lips. "I've seen this place before, in one of my dreams."

"Not dreams," Pharaildis corrects. "Visions."

"The throne is empty." I swallow past the lump in my throat. "I thought you said Underhill would be here."

"She is." Her voice is even as she stares at the dais. As though she wills it into being, blue light erupts. Not the soft glow of fey light, but blue flames, jagged and wild. They lick upwards forming what I realize are the bars of a cage.

I gasp as something shifts within the cage and I hear another pained groan. Whatever is in there is being slowly roasted alive.

"Who is that?" I ask in horror. "It can't be...Underhill?"

"Of course not," Pharaildis laughs. It isn't a pleasant sound.

No. I don't want to believe it. Don't want to accept it. But my suspicion is blossoming into certainty. "Why would I, the daughter of a prisoner, be gifted with the power to rule the Unseelie Court?"

She turns to look at me, her eyes as bottomless as the pit. "Ask your other question, Nicneven. The one you really wish to have confirmed."

My lips part but the words won't come. I don't want to hear this, don't want to know.

She doesn't give me a choice though. Her hands bunch in her still perfect skirts and she crosses the narrow bridge to the dais. She turns and then lowers herself onto the throne, the silver chain catching a glint from the runes, the shadows in the firelight throbbing like eerie heartbeats as though this place is alive.

"Yes, my daughter. I am Underhill." Her lips curve up in a predatory smile. "And you are here to help free me."

FATED OR MATED

"*P*lease," the unfortunate creature wheezes from within the cage. I hear him hiss in pain and one too thin and filth encrusted arm braves the fire bars. It's riddled with pinkened mottled flesh, like what appears in the wake of burns. "Have pity on me, great lady."

That small smirk stays on her ethereal face. "Ask my daughter for pity, Wardon. See how much you'll receive after how you tried to blackmail her."

"Wardon?" My feet are planted to the spot as though they've grown roots. The missing Seelie king. Too much, it's too much to believe that my mother, *my* mother, who I thought was an innocent prisoner has taken one of the most powerful beings I've ever seen.

"Please." Wardon turns his focus to me. Though I didn't know him well, he looks nothing like the tall, proud being I remember. His gray skin flakes off in spots as he reaches through the bars beseechingly. "Nicneven, please. Release me."

"And where will you go, Master of the Waves?" Pharaildis —Underhill asks. "Your kingdom is overrun by the dead."

She waves her hand and the liquid surrounding her throne like a moat rises into the air. It shimmers as though lit from within by invisible stars. She moves her hand in a circular motion, creating a mirror.

Images appear within it. I recognize Wardon's sea glass and sand estate, even though it's in ruins. There is no sign of life in the busy square out front, no trolls guarding the courtyard, no fishermen hawking their wares. Debris is scattered everywhere, wooden benches overturned. And in the distance a huge plume of smoke billows into the sky.

"The few who are left," she tells him, "have gotten into the habit of burning their dead."

"No." Wardon makes a pained sound.

"You see, Nicneven, each court has its own way of dealing with the dead. The Seelie have never burned bodies before, it's considered a violation to the gifts of water and earth. Each of his subjects who picks up a torch instead of a shovel is stripping the magic from his mantle. They are essentially throwing their lot in with the Unseelie, who burn bodies and scatter them to the winds."

No wonder Wardon appears so pale hasn't managed to free himself when she was gone. With no subjects to draw power from, the Master of the Waves is master of nothing.

The bars of his prison blaze, the same color as her eyes. Wardon retreats into the cage but there is nowhere for him to go. More of his flesh falls from his bones as the ragged scraps of clothing he wears catches fire. He screams and it's a more horrific sound than any I've ever heard.

Underhill laughs.

I've killed people. Wardon is a villain who would use blackmail and the darkest means to protect his own power. Yet he is still a fey king. This torture, this agony she's intentionally inflicting on him is too much for even me to witness.

"Stop," I order through the mirror still showing the awful scene. "Stop hurting him."

She tilts her head. "This doesn't please you?"

"Please me?" I stare at her blank face. "Why would it please me to see him suffer?"

"After all the suffering he and his kind have caused? Wardon is your enemy. He tried to blackmail you into marrying him. He had your lover tortured and replaced him with a fake to deceive you. He imprisoned your Second and forced her to drown repeatedly for days. Does she not still suffer from that experience?"

Nahini. The shock of white in her hair. Her unnerving silence. As though all the life, all the will to go on had been drained from her. I watch as the flesh on Wardon's arm begins to melt, as the scent of burning meat fills the cavern.

Seeing me wavering, she pushes. "In your last life, he helped Brigit kill you. Don't you want vengeance?"

Maybe once I would have. An eye for an eye, a hurt for a hurt. Back before I'd understood that protecting the weak was about more than picking off those who would prey on them.

"There is enough suffering going on in the worlds without adding to it. You told him to ask me for leniency. He did. And I want it to end."

Her gaze bores a hole into me. Her eyes narrow, as though I've presented her with an unexpected variable. I lift my chin and stand my ground.

She raises one hand and the flames disappear. The liquid from the mirror dissolves into droplets and returns to the moat.

"Let him go." I don't hold any hope that she'll do as I ask but I want to see how far I can push her. Perhaps she'll let me bind him to the Wild Hunt, though I don't know if my power will extend over another fey royal.

To my surprise, the cage lowers to the stone floor beside me. Underhill rises from her throne and strides across the bridge. I keep one eye on her as she approaches me, the other on Wardon who is on his hands and knees, weeping.

She thrusts a hand through the bars and drops something. It clatters to the bottom of the cage.

A dagger.

"Give it to me," she orders him.

Wardon shakes his head frantically.

Her face is hard, unyielding as she points at the fallen dagger. "Give it to me or I'll kill you and take it."

A sob escapes Wardon's throat. His body, the charred mass of it shakes in fear and pain. He's unrecognizable. His shimmering silver scales have burned to ash. A mortal would have been dead after such treatment.

Underhill waits, her expression unmoved by the pitiful sight.

Slowly, so slowly, he reaches one hand down. Two of his fingers have been burned to nubs but he manages to wrap what's left of his hand around the hilt. Just as slowly, he brings it up until the tip hovers just above his heart.

Was she going to force him to take his own life before our eyes?

"Please," he begs, the blade shaking wildly with his spasms. "It's all I have left."

"Do it," Underhill demands. Her voice is infused with power.

I can't breathe, can't move. I feel as though I've detached from my own body and am floating several yards above their heads as I watch the horror unfold.

A single teardrop slips down the great Seelie king's charred face. With a hoarse cry, Wardon plunges the dagger into his own chest.

Through the Man's Eyes

Underhill knows he's here.

Aiden can sense her feelers skittering over him even as he hears her voice from up ahead. He hears Nic's too but his wolf doesn't relax a hair, sensing the great predator circling his mate. In the heart of the hill, Pharaildis can be everywhere and nowhere at once.

She knows he's coming, wants him to come. Though he would never have told Freya, the goddess is smart to keep a weather eye on the imprisoned mortal who wields far too much magic.

He moves along at a steady pace through the bowels of her world. The wolf can see without magic and he is conserving all his strength for battle. He does not wish to fight her. Underhill is treacherous and wily, but her reach is limited to the fey realm. She can't extend herself beyond its borders.

He keeps one eye peeled for any source of water, water that has gone untouched by sunlight but so far has found nothing.

His mate's scent is growing stronger. Almost in reach. He takes a corner so fast one foot misses the narrow ledge and his arms pinwheel to keep him from flying off into the abyss. His heart thunders in his chest. Careful, he must be more careful. Nic's life, Bard and Gretchen's lives all depend on his success.

For them, he must not fail.

If he can collect Nic, can get her back across the Veil,

Underhill won't be able to wrap her tentacles any tighter around his mate.

I should have told her. Guilt, his old companion, surfaces but he ruthlessly shoves it down. Now is not the time for second guessing himself.

There is a cry of pain and an involuntary snarl rips from his throat. Though through the bond, he can sense that Nic remains unhurt.

Who is being tormented?

Rage bubbles inside him when he realizes that his young mate is being forced to witness Underhill's vengeance. The mad old creature kept Wardon as a prisoner. Has been torturing him endlessly trying to get him to give her…something. He doesn't know what the precious object is. Occasionally Nic has sent him vivid images, but their connection is muted by the power of the fey realm.

We will protect her. Set her free. The wolf is adamant. *Whatever the cost.*

The darkness engulfs him completely as he descends deeper into the heart of the hill. A soft glow from up ahead makes him pause.

"Come out, wolfling," Underhill calls. "No need to skulk like a whipped dog."

His wolf curls up a lip, his hackles are all standing on end. *Be wary.*

Aiden. It's Nic, shouting in his head the way his brave mate would never do aloud. Her mental voice wiggles with emotion. *Aiden she's insane.*

Don't panic, he tells her.

She forced Wardon to stab himself.

I know. Nic, do you trust me?

No hesitation, not even a moment passes before she responds. *With my life.*

He is so proud of her. She's come so far from the prickly,

suspicious teenager she'd been when they first met. *I have a plan. Just play along.*

He takes a step out into the open archway and beholds the scene. Slumped in a cage made of some sort of glittering metal that smells of smoke and magic, is the Master of the Waves. His skin, what little remains of it underneath the blackened flesh, is the color of old death. Like the Draugar. Yet in spite of the dagger hilt sticking out of his chest, he is alive. His webbed fingers are wrapped around the thing as though he means to pull it free. His eyes are dull, almost devoid of life yet a spark remains.

Magic. It's his water magic that's keeping him alive. But even a royal kept in such a weak condition can die. Nicneven had.

"There you are. This is a moment that deserves an audience." Underhill nods to him. "So glad you could join us. Aren't we, daughter?"

Nic. Where is she?

He scans the cavern. There. He spies her on the far side of the cage. Nic, wearing travel stained fashions of the Green Throne but otherwise unhurt. And behind her sits a dark pool of water. So deep down beneath the surface that he is sure, the sun has never touched it. Everything he needs is a few steps away. The wolf prowls close, ready to shred any obstacle. Including her mother if necessary.

Nic's eyes round and she turns away as Wardon pulls on the knife, not to extract it but to *cut deeper?*

Blue blood gushes from the wound and spills down the front of the fey's ruined body. Underhill watches with an avid gaze. Almost to herself, she mutters, "Almost there...."

Aiden barely keeps from retching. "What is he doing?"

Pharaildis turns to face Nic. "Have you ever heard the expression *cut out his heart and gift it to her?*"

"That's just a saying." Nic's voice is thin but still strong like a steel wire pulled taut. "No one can live without a heart."

"A fey can. They are born heartless after all, in the image of the gods they are cast from."

Aiden frowns. He's never heard that before.

Wardon makes a gurgling sound. The dagger clatters to the floor. His trembling hand reaches into the gaping wound and he extracts something that pulses with a glowing blue-green light. His eyes are closed, his skin a horrible ashen hue.

Underhill bends down. Her long, white fingers wrap around the king's limp wrist while her other hand pulls the object free.

"A heart, you see is more than just a muscle. It has taken me centuries to understand. The giants hoard their knowledge, their understanding. It wasn't until you, my dear daughter," she points the hand holding Wardon's heart at Nic, "that I learned the truth."

"What truth?" Aiden asks. He doesn't care especially. He just wants to distract her so she will move away from Nic.

Come toward me, he thinks to his mate. *While she isn't watching you.*

She nods once. Message received.

Pharaildis faces him and Nic slips out from behind her. "I have you to thank, wolfling. You not only resurrected my daughter, you showed me what I was missing. The key I'd been searching for."

Aiden scowls as Nic veers closer to the cage. Closer to her mother. "What key?"

Caught up in her storytelling, Pharaildis continues, "I watched you take her body to Laufey, saw you collect the dead heart from your butchered brother and at that moment, I understood. It is the heart that holds all the power, for gods, fey and everything in between.

"The reason the fey royals are so powerful is that they

have filled their empty chests with all the combined powers of those they rule. Like little tokens given to one's sovereign, those powers form a heart. And in order to wield the power of all those souls the ancient fey bound to the elements, to summon them at will, one needs the heart of a royal."

"I don't understand," he says as Nic takes another step out from behind Pharaildis. She bends to scoop up the fallen dagger.

No, Aiden thinks at her.

She ignores him.

Desperate, he asks Underhill, "You want his magic?"

"I have his magic." She holds her bloody trophy aloft. "His and Brigit's both. And that's close enough, Nicneven."

Nic freezes with the dagger raised in her hand.

Her mother glances over her shoulder and makes a *tsking* sound. "And here I thought we were...what is the modern expression? Bonding?"

Nic's gaze darts to him in a panic.

Keep her talking. Aiden moves a step closer. To her, the water, everything he needs. *I'll come to you.*

Nic inhales, still clutching the dagger. "I thought you wanted to release all the souls into the Veil? To heal the rift?"

Pharaildis laughs at that. "No, that's what *you* said. Silly girl. I want to remove the Veil entirely." She snaps her fingers and a glass cabinet appears. Inside is a glowing red object on an orange and gold velvet cushion. Three other cushions sit empty beside it. One gray with blue thread, one green with brown thread and one black with silver thread.

He moves quickly, not to Nic, but to the edge of the black water. He reaches into his pocket and extracts the small flask Gretchen had given him.

Underhill places Wardon's heart on the gray and blue pillow and then snaps again. The cabinet vanishes. Aiden bends down, dipping the mouth of the flask below the waterline.

"Brigit was first. She came to me, desperate to seek you out. Unknowing of our relationship she offered me anything if I could enable her to lie. She was as good a test as any to see if my theory proved correct."

"But Brigit still had her abilities," Nic says. "I saw her."

"She could touch them, use them, but she no longer owned them. It was only because I allowed it. From the day she handed me her heart, she was powerless."

Nic's grip tightens on the dagger. He sees the hurt and confusion on her face. Her mother, the one person in the world who was supposed to protect her, had allowed her greatest enemy, the woman who'd killed her once, to nearly destroy her.

Kin or no kin, we will taste this female's blood, the wolf promises her. The flask is full and he carefully screws the cap back on and stows it in his pocket. All he needs to do is get to Nic, touch her and they can rise like embers from the room.

Leaving the water behind.

He curses himself for a fool. They can't just evaporate into sparks. His magic removes all the water from their bodies and anything they carry. If he changes to embers, the water he just collected will vanish. They'll have to find another way around Underhill.

"Why?" Nic breathes. "Why do this?"

Underhill blinks as though the question startles her. She gestures to the seat above her underground river. "I rule all. Yet I rule nothing. This throne is my prison. Wouldn't you do anything in your power to free yourself, daughter?"

"You can't have Nic's heart," Aiden snarls.

One corner of her mouth curls up. "Who says I want it?"

Nic's hands ball into fists. "Then what do you want?"

"I need the two of you to do me a little favor."

"And if we refuse?" Nic asks.

As though lifted by a great wind, Wardon is whisked from the cage. Invisible hands grab hold of Aiden. He struggles, trying to fight the grip. Nothing. He wants to shift, but if he does the water will be lost and Bard along with it.

Underhill plucks him like a leaf and throws him inside the recently vacated cage.

She refocuses on Nic. "If you refuse, you get to watch him suffer until you agree. You, my daughter, have a soft mortal heart, regardless of its origins. You couldn't even bear to watch me play with Wardon. What do you think will happen once I set loose on your consort?"

"He's not my consort." Nic stares at her, unblinking, with hatred in her blue gaze. "He's my friend."

His own heart swells as it always does when she verbally claims him. "I can withstand fire. I come from a line of fire," Aiden tells her, tells both of them.

"Yes, but now, I have other talents." Pharaildis smiles a horrible smile.

She steps closer, looking so much like the Nicneven he'd known. Sensual and selfish. Behind her, Nic's eyes widen in alarm.

"Don't," she pleads.

His lips part to tell his mate he'll be alright, that he can withstand any torment.

Underhill strikes like a snake, pressing her cold lips to his. He's so shocked he doesn't withdraw.

And deep within the darkest part of Aiden's mind, the place where thousands of years' worth of secrets, guilt, and sorrow have been stored, cracks open like an egg.

I have no idea what madness feels like for Aiden, but watching him writhe as though my mother is stabbing at him with a thousand blades is the most horrific thing I've ever seen. His hands grab fistfuls of his dark hair, yanking and pulling as though he can physically remove whatever is torturing him from his brain. I watch in horror as his nails morph into claws. Where they connect with his skin, blood trickles out like tiny waterfalls. His eyes bulge, and all around him, mini flames erupt.

It's as though his powers are being torn from him.

That seems to panic him even more. Why didn't he just shift to sparks and disappear out of the cage? Knowing Aiden, he has a reason and I'm betting it has something to do with that flask of water he filled out of Underhill's moat.

If he won't shift, it's up to me to get him free.

"Let him go." I grip her arm and pull her away, needing to put myself between my mother and Aiden.

"Silly creature," Pharaildis shakes me off as though I'm a fly. "You only have one option, Nicneven. Return with Soladin and have him bestow your wolf with the kiss of clarity."

The thought of leaving Aiden as he is doubled up in her cage….

"Undo it," I say, my eyes on him.

"I can't undo it any more than you can undo death."

Deep in my chest, there's pure agony. It's as though I can feel his anguish in my bones. I feel as though I'm being rent in two, as though part of me is being shredded under sharp claws.

Taj's words return to me on a phantom breeze. *When a soul identifies its perfect match, it reaches for it. Many don't recognize the soul's cry.*

In a horrid flash, I understand. Mate. This is what it

means to be his mate, to suffer as he does. The willingness to trade anything to spare him.

Aiden twists and falls to his back. The noise he makes, it's too hoarse to be called a scream. If grief has a sound, it is the one emanating from his throat.

I have to end this, have to set him free. No matter what. Tears well but I blink them back, not wanting to show any more weakness. "There has to be a way."

"I can tuck the madness away for a time," she offers.

Another blood-curdling scream from Aiden.

I swallow. "Do it."

"Agree to do my bidding."

Wordlessly I nod.

Pharaildis raises a hand and clenches her fingers into a tight fist. The fires wink out, the claws retract, though the blood still streams from half a dozen gouges. Aiden's body goes limp, a puppet with his strings cut. I run to him and the cage fades away as though it had never been there. I fall to my knees next to him, checking his pulse, his breathing.

He's alive, just unconscious.

There is a white streak in Aiden's hair. Just like the one that had appeared in Nahini's ebony locks after Wardon had condemned her to drown again and again.

The Kiss of Madness. Death, by contrast, seems almost merciful.

"It won't last long." My mother moves closer and I look up into her beautiful, terrible face. "Madness won't be held in check for more than a few days. You will bring Soladin to me."

"That's it?"

"It's not as easy as you might think to extract a ruling monarch from his seat of power. Angrboda only managed it with this one," she waves to indicate Wardon's limp form, "because he made a bargain with her and then tried to renege. Use every skill in your arsenal. But remember, I want him alive."

Because she wants his heart and the Kiss of Clarity. Underhill already possesses half of the fey powers. What will happen when she has all of them?

Undoubtedly, once I secure Soladin for her, she'll force me to cut my heart out as well.

"You will leave immediately," Pharaildis says.

I remind myself not to blink or show any other sign of surprise or relief. "You're allowing Aiden to come with me?"

"Yes." Her poker face is better than mine. There is no way to tell what she's thinking, why she'll allow Aiden to leave.

No way could I carry Aiden up all those switchbacks. "He needs time to recover."

"He'll have it." Her eyes narrow. "You're going to need his abilities. Don't try to cross the Veil or the madness will claim him once more." Bloodred lips curve up in a smile. "And next time, I won't stop with just a splinter in his mind. I'll shred it to pieces."

With a wave of her hand, Underhill and her surroundings, vanish.

GOT ANYMORE BRIGHT IDEAS

*I*t takes a moment to realize it isn't Underhill who vanished but Aiden and me who've been removed from her lair. Though I'm still kneeling on stone with his head in my lap, the night sky twinkles above me and a cool breeze kisses my face.

I shudder at the display of her power. Because Pharaildis is the fairy hill, there are no repercussions for her wielding magic straight from the source. She's had eons to learn what magical rules can be bent, which can be broken, and the best way to use them. She may be a prisoner but we're on her turf. How am I supposed to fight that sort of power?

"Aiden." I stroke his cheek. It's rough with stubble. He doesn't stir but the warmth of his skin is reassuring.

A groan sounds from my right. My head snaps up and I see Wardon, still looking like a blackened shrimp. She released him as well now that she got what she wanted.

"Are you all right?" It's hard to keep the hard edge out of my voice as I address the Master of the Waves.

"I'll live," he says, sounding as though that's a punishment of its own.

"How long have you been down there?" Only a day passed on the farm, but time moves differently under the hill.

He shakes his head. Gone is the once proud monarch who'd tried to blackmail me into marriage. My crustacean image is spot-on because, without his glowing gray skin, he is a shell of a man.

He'd held out for as long as he could. The gods alone knew what sort of torture Angrboda had put him through before Underhill had taken custody of him.

"Help me," Wardon reaches out toward me with one hand.

"With what?" Seeing the streak of white in Aiden's hair glowing in the moonlight reminds me of the matching one on Nahini's head and how my badass third had been suffering because of him.

"I need to go home." He struggles upright. "To get back to my court."

"Oh, boo hoo, poor powerless Wardon," I snap. "Sorry pal, but that's a no on the RSVP to your pity party. Maybe, if you had been less of a megalomaniacal asshat and hadn't tortured my friends, I'd feel an iota of sympathy for you."

"Nic?" The voice comes from the region of my lap.

I look down to see Aiden's leaf green eyes staring up. He doesn't appear to be tracking though. His pupils are dilated and the whites of his eyes are bloodshot. He looks like he just came off a weeklong bender.

Or escaped from an insane asylum.

"Hey, I'm right here." I don't do the tenderness thing well at all, but instinct guides me to stroke his cheek. "We're out of there. You're going to be fine."

He shakes his head back and forth and I can't tell if he's denying my reassurance that he is going to be fine or trying to shake off the shadows that have crept into his mind.

He gasps and a golden ring appears around his irises. The wolf is rising.

"No." Beads of perspiration form on Aiden's forehead and his hands clench into fists. "Stay back."

He's fighting off the wolf, I realize. Trying to keep the beast locked down. And the wolf, confused and scared, is reacting to Aiden's mental anguish. It rises to protect them. To protect me.

His mate.

"Wardon." I keep my tone level. "If you want to die, stick around. Because if Aiden loses his hold on the wolf, there's a good chance he'll eat you."

There is a rustling and the sound of feet. Wardon may be down, but the former Master of the Waves isn't out yet.

"Okay big guy," I say to the wolf. "Just you and me."

The golden halo in Aiden's eyes grows brighter. The wolf is winning.

"Aiden," I say slowly. "Let him out."

"No," he exhales through his teeth.

"Let him out. The harder you fight him, the harder he struggles. You know he won't hurt me."

His breaths are shallow, pain-filled pants. He breathes, "I'm sorry."

Then there is a flash.

I stay perfectly still as the large black wolf rises up where Aiden had just been. His eyes are the familiar green ringed with gold. Cast with the night sky behind him, he is only a menacing shape in the darkness.

I lower my eyes to the ground. My heartrate has sped up. Just seeing the wolf evokes a primal fear response. It can sense fear and my fear, in particular, could set it on a killing spree. Blanking my mind, I focus on my own breathing. On radiating a sense of serenity and peace.

The wolf sniffs once. Its head whips to the side and I can feel him tense, ready to spring. He doesn't growl, which is more unnerving. A growl is a warning. This creature is set to kill.

An image flashes into my mind, through our bond. Wardon as the wolf last saw him, on a seaside cliff with water spraying up around him.

Alric had once showed me how the hounds he cared for in the Hunt thought in images instead of words. They associated experiences of sound and feel and scent. It is how they perceive their world. Body language and experience are everything. I've talked to Aiden's wolf before, but I get the sense that this is simpler for him.

"No," I reach out, careful not to touch him. I made that mistake before. The wolf values my life but isn't afraid to use pain to teach me a lesson. "It's all right. He can't hurt us."

The words do nothing.

So, I think the picture at him. Wardon, handing his heart over to Underhill. Wardon, begging me to help him. Wardon, blackened, beaten and bowed. Every image communicates the same message. He is no longer a threat.

The wolf turns to face me. He sniffs at me and then, to my shock, lowers himself to the ground.

I exhale wearily. "Okay, now that we have that settled, can I have Aiden back?"

The wolf shifts so his side is pressed up against me. The message is clear. He is here for the duration.

Too tired to plan or scheme or even think, I stretch out on the ground beside him. "Later then."

He turns his head and a breeze ruffles his dark fur. He is poised, on alert and will eliminate any threat.

Another image pops into my head. One of me sleeping in my bed, back on the farm. He is there on the foot of the bed, his eyes open and watchful. Again, his meaning is clear. Sleep, and I will protect you while you rest.

When exhaustion rolls over me, I give in to it.

Through the Wolf's Eyes

His mate is hurting. Though he smells no blood on her he can sense her despair. It is the man's fault. The weak, foolish man who lied to her. He wanted something more than his own contentment and the survival of his mate. The wolf knows better. The wolf no longer wishes to share the man's skin.

The man is broken now, broken and hiding. His pain and fear for her is what called the wolf forth.

The wind ruffles his fur. It comes from the North, carrying the scent of snow. Her season approaches. She needs the wolf more than the man. The man is just flesh that looks like her. He does not understand her, cannot protect her.

The wolf will stay. For her. Forever.

Sunlight jabs through my closed eyelids like a thousand hot pokers. I keep them closed as I sit up and take stock of my myriad of aches and pains. The good news, my blisters have healed overnight. Becoming one of the forever young does come with certain perks.

The bad news, I'm parched as well as ravenously hungry and feel like I spent an uncomfortable night sleeping on the side of an exposed mountain. Which I did.

"Aiden?" His name comes out as a croak between my cracked lips.

There is no answer and I use one arm to shade my eyes before lifting a lid to see if he's still asleep.

The green and gold irises of the wolf look back at me, unblinking.

"You're still not Aiden?" I was sure he would have come back by now. "I thought the two of you worked out an…understanding."

Still no reply.

I try to send him a mental picture of Aiden, drawing the lines of his face in my mind and projecting them to the wolf along with my sense of urgency.

I need his help. Aiden knows things about Underhill and the fey that I don't. His insight would be invaluable.

The wolf's head swivels to the left and his right ear twitches once. I suppose that's the only answer I'm likely to get.

"Okay then." I push up from the ground, careful not to make any abrupt motions. "We should get going."

Aiden in wolf form is like an overgrown dog, with a mischievous personality. The wolf as a wolf is an entirely different animal. He doesn't play pranks. Sudden movement or anything that he perceives as a threat could set him off on a killing spree.

I feel as though I'm carrying a live bomb through the fey lands.

My stomach growls and the wolf rises to his feet in one graceful move and trots off.

"Hey," I call. "Wait a minute."

He stops, turns his head and flattens his ears. Again, there's no growl, only silent menace emanating from him. His body language sends the message. *Stay.*

"But," I protest.

He turns and resumes his trot until his black shape melds with the shadows of the scrubby pines.

I kick a rock. It goes sailing up into the air in the direction Wardon ran the night before. Damn stubborn wolf. I couldn't just sit here all day. Even if mommy dearest isn't observing me right now, she would check in. What would she do if it looked like I was frittering the day away in this meadow? If I didn't bring Soladin to her in a timely manner?

I didn't have time to play dominance games with Aiden's wolf.

A small stream runs at a sharp incline that made an almost mini waterfall. Cupping my hands under it, I drink, uncaring of the sediment or even some awful parasite swimming in the liquid. Without Aiden or my backpack, I have no way to distill it. It is cool and clear as it slides down my parched throat. Enjoying the feel of it, I strip down to my skin and stand beneath the spill, letting the small rush of water and gravity wash away the grime of the last few days.

Stalling while waiting for the wolf to return, I pluck my clothes and rinse them out in the water by my feet, then lay them on a flat rock in the direct sun. Now I have two things to wait for, dry clothes and the wolf.

Naked as a nymph, I decide to explore. Some berries grow on a scraggly bush that juts from a crag in the rock face. I don't know if they are poisonous, though they look exactly like some Pharaildis had given me.

Underhill, not Pharaildis. She's the land I'm standing on, holds dominion over the world around me. I feel like such an idiot. Here I thought she was some sort of intrepid outdoors woman, able to track and find things when we needed them. When all along, she really just used magic to get the fey realm to offer up whatever she wanted.

The same way she made me offer up what she wanted by torturing Aiden.

Stay focused, Nic. It's my own voice giving the pep talk, but the advice is sound.

To make sure the berries are truly safe, I collect one and sample it as a litmus test. The taste is a little sour, as though it hasn't fully ripened even though it is tinted a brilliant violet hue. I swallow. Wait. Nothing changes. I eat a few more. No stomach cramps, dizziness or other unfortunate side effects. Satisfied, I glut myself on the berries until the bush is picked clean.

The angle of the shadows shifts as the sun makes its way across the bright blue sky. In Underhill, it must be roughly nine in the morning. I glance back to the tree line just in time to see Aiden trotting out of the trees, a brace of dead rabbits swinging from his jaws.

"Oh no," I say when he drops his kill at my feet in obvious offering. "I don't eat corpses, pal. I just make 'em."

He tilts his head and waits. The poor dead things stare sightlessly up at me, the blood on their fur the same dark color as the berries had left on my fingers. My stomach turns over. It might be the vengeance of the berries, but I doubt it.

He sends me an image of me tearing into the meat raw the way he would. I barely stifle the urge to retch.

This is not something I have the ability to communicate with him. In the wolf's mind, he brought me a completely acceptable breakfast and he won't understand that I'd rather scavenge for seeds, nuts, and berries than have him slaughter innocent animals. To him, I must look ungrateful and wasteful.

"You go ahead and eat." I step back and gesture at his offering. "I'm okay."

His ears prick.

I take another step, and that's all the encouragement he needs. I turn back to the waterfall, to avoid the grisly sight. Though the sounds of wet tearing will haunt me.

At least the bunnies didn't die in vain.

I sit down beside my drying clothes and pop my feet into

the cool water. Maybe I should feel uncomfortable being naked in front of him, but the wolf doesn't look at me that way. Not the way Aiden always did.

That scares me more than anything else. What if the madness has driven Aiden into permanent hiding? What if he never comes back? I struggle to sort through all that has happened. Through her coronary extractions, Underhill has the powers of two of the four fey royals. She can wield fire and water. Can access the kiss of life and the kiss of madness. She could have insisted I cut out my own heart in exchange for Aiden, but she hadn't. Why?

"Aiden," I try again when the wolf comes up beside me at the stream. "I need to talk to Aiden."

He ignores my request and bends over the stream to drink. I yank my feet out of the water so they aren't coated with the slick blood being washed from his muzzle.

"Has he gone around the bend?" I ask the wolf. "Would you let me know if he's checked out permanently?

He sits beside me, leans into me, as though offering comfort.

I huff out a breath. "Okay, well, if he does show up, I'd appreciate it if you tell him I've been looking for him."

With that, I get to my feet and scramble into what is left of my clothes. "Any idea how to get back to Soladin?"

The wolf stands and heads back toward the trees. Hoping he knows where he's going, I follow.

Something metallic reflects the early morning rays. The flask Aiden had filled. Instinct tells me I shouldn't drink it, that the water inside isn't meant for me. I pick it up and tuck it in the waistband of my jeans.

I am a fool to follow a wolf. Not only does he set a grueling pace—one I almost have to jog to keep up with—but by midday, I'm sure we are heading in a different direction than the one I'd come. For one thing, the sun is directly ahead of us, shining directly through a copse of birch trees. We'd had our backs to the sun in the morning the day before. Then too, the terrain looks very different. Less craggy hills and streams, more meadows and ponds.

My newly healed feet are getting that same old soreness again, a fresh crop of blisters springing to life. The wolf trots on, unaware that I'm struggling to keep up. Though training with Freda has made me strong, I can't go mile after mile, day after day on a handful of berries. I'd been planning to hunt around for some sort of tree nuts to add some protein to the mix, but I was afraid I'd lose sight of my companion.

Doubts plague me as our endless trek wears on. What if I was wrong and the wolf hadn't sent me those images? I might have conjured them myself. I've been through a great deal lately. It is entirely possible my mind has snapped like a dried-out rubber band that's been stretched one time too many.

My sense of direction isn't stellar in the human realm, never mind in Underhill where everything is constantly in flux. Where it rearranges itself to my mother's will, I suppose. And if I can't reason with the wolf, we're both screwed.

"Hey, slow up a minute." I bend at the waist, trying to catch my breath.

He looks over one shoulder, green eyes piercing.

"Are you sure we're going to the Seelie Court?" I gesture with one hand. "None of this looks familiar to me."

Another image appears in my mind. It's so vivid, that I blink, feeling as though I've been shifted to an entirely different landscape.

A purple blue meadow, with glowing golden balls of light flitting over the top. Gretchen, on her knees crying over Bard's still form.

It vanishes as quickly as it came.

There is a feeling associated with the image too. One of belongingness, protectiveness, loyalty.

Of pack.

I fall to my knees. "Wait a second. Are you telling me they are here? That this really happened?"

The wolf turns his head back to the trail he's been cutting through the dried grass stalks. Up ahead I see a gap in the mountains.

"Is that where we're going? To where Gretchen and Bard are?"

He turns back to face me, his expression neutral, but I get the sense that he's impatient.

"Aiden, what the hell?" Never in my wildest imaginings would I have thought he'd bring Gretchen across the Veil with him. And was Bard dead? Or just knocked out? How long have they been there?

If the wolf has any answers, he doesn't share them. After assessing me he sets off once more in an easy lope.

Ignoring my discomfort, I break into a jog beside him.

The sun is at its zenith when we stumble through the pass, sweating and half starved. Up ahead is the meadow from my vision, cast in blue and purple as though it is surrounded by a protective bubble of dusk.

And an army of the dead.

"Oh shit," I breathe, when I spot Gretchen, dragging Bard over the colorcast line from the brown and gold of autumn and into the glowing field of hazy twilight. "I need to get down there."

But before I can take more than a step, the wolf is in my way. His teeth pull back from his fangs.

When I try to move around him, he snaps at me. I hold up my hands, rune marks facing him in a defensive measure. I can't command the wolf but perhaps I can reason with him.

"We need to help them. I know it's dangerous, but we can't just leave them there."

Assured that I won't go anywhere, I see the wolf turn back to survey the scene below us. His posture is poised, ready, but there's also something else. It's as if he's willing himself to do a difficult task.

I repeat his name again even though I know I'm not addressing a man. I need to get through to him so I can help Bard and Gretchen.

"We need to shift to sparks," I tell the wolf. "Aiden needs to shift us. It's the only way we can get past them."

A warning growl. He doesn't like my plan.

"There's no other way. I can't borrow magic from the Unseelie, not with Underhill watching my every move." Though she hadn't given us a timeline, I was fairly certain she'd be displeased with our detour right into the dead clutches of the Draugar.

I shift to the side and he responds with another snap. Straightening my shoulders, I stare him down. I won't let him bully me away, not when Bard and Gretchen are at risk. My only choice is to reach him. "Please. I need to help them. They're my court."

Pack, he thinks at me.

The word feels foreign and familiar at once. I see the flare of indecision in his green eyes.

"Let him out," I push the wolf. "Let him do this. For me. We need Aiden."

Through the Wolf's Eyes

The wolf stares at his mate, unsure. He knows her. Knows she is foolish and that she will put herself in harm's way. The ones down there might be his pack but one is as good as dead already. The other is not worth their lives.

A wolf may die but the pack must survive.

A sensible mate would understand. Would accept his wisdom. But his mate is different, other. Within him the man writhes, fighting to get to the surface, to take control. His useless words and images that fill the space between them, dark matter that forms a bridge between one flesh and another. But four catch his attention.

I have a plan.

The wolf looks again at his proud and stubborn mate. The man lied to her. But she will die if he doesn't allow the man to the surface. He cannot let that happen.

He drinks in her image, her scent. And recedes.

Through the Man's Eyes

Aiden struggles up, sensing the wolf's turmoil and Nic's presence. He's in the wolf's body, so he focuses all his efforts on shifting.

It hurts. The wolf doesn't help him the way it did the night before. He senses the beast prowling restlessly, eager to seize control. It's harder for the beast to take over from the two-legged form.

"Aiden?" Nic's voice helps him focus.

Touch me. He thinks the words at her. *Help me focus.*

Her hand rests gently on the crown of his head and provides the anchor he needs. He pushes through the pain that the fire usually protects him from. It's a horrible transition, like the very first, the one the gods forced on him.

He is shaking by the end of it, his limbs weak from the strain. If he moves, he'll collapse into a useless heap.

"Flask," he rasps.

She reaches into the back of her pants and, thank the gods, she has it.

She unscrews the cap and sniffs. Then wrinkles her nose. "This is from Underhill's moat. I saw you fill it."

He nods, unable to form the words to explain.

"Do you want to drink it?"

"Just a little." He has no proof the water will be any real protection from the meadow's death curse. Yet if he is going to take the risk, he wants to stack the odds in his favor. He won't do Gretchen or Bard any good by succumbing to the curse himself.

Nic holds it to his lips and tips it back. He takes a single small swallow. The water is crisp and cold, like freshly melted ice. The pain from his uncomfortable shift lessens but doesn't fade.

Nic screws the cap back on the flask. "Are you all right?"

He nods once and pushes to his feet. His knees feel rubbery. "You need to stay here."

Her eyebrows pull together. "What? Aiden, no."

"There isn't time. That can't come with me." He points to the flask, "If I try and carry that in sparks, the water will disappear and be replaced with the nearest water source. That's the only cure for Bard."

Nic stares at him a beat. "I don't like waiting behind."

"I know." He cups her cheek in his hand. "My fearless queen. Just this one time though, you must."

She lets out a breath. "Fine."

"I will be quick." He steps back and then shifts to sparks.

As he passes over the Draugar, he rains fire down on them. There are no screams as they burn, no fights for life. With no blood and very little water, they are turned to ash within moments. If he was at full strength, he could have burned them all. As it is, he only manages to destroy half a dozen, creating a small gap that the others fill within the space of two heartbeats.

Cursing his own weakness, Aiden crosses the twilight line that protects the will-o'-wisps and their meadow. The warding spell slows him. It's like swimming through a lake of honey. It's not sentient like the Veil, but more like a security checkpoint put on magical automation. He keeps himself focused on his task, to grab Gretchen and Bard and return to Nic.

Then he is before them and manifests on two legs once more.

Will-o'-wisps flit around his head, their tiny voices alarmed. The commotion draws Gretchen's attention from where she's wiping blood from the shifter's nose. The Draugar only ten feet away.

She scrambles up. "Do you have water?"

"Nic does." Aiden strides to her side and holds out a hand, which the little mortal takes. Crouching down he lays his other hand on Bard's shoulder.

"Don't forget us." The little red-haired wisp flies in front of him, her expression sad.

But before he can question her, Gretchen points with her free hand, "Look!"

A mountain is rising where he left Nic.

The ground beneath their feet shakes as a giant tremor surges across the land. Cracks split the ground. The mortal girl falls to her knees. Underhill is rearranging the landscape.

Right on top of this valley.

THE UNSEELIE COURTIERS

*T*he earthquake sends me sprawling. All the small hairs rise along the back of my neck as though someone is breathing on me. I hear the great roar first, as if the world itself is furious. Trees topple. And then the fissure appears. The ground juts up, impaling a few of the Draugar, like kababs. The dead flail, still trying to cross into the epicenter. Razor sharp rocks stab up into the sky, larger than any I'd ever seen, amassing into a vanguard of destruction.

The land is sentient in the same way the air currents are. It crumbles in places, surges together in others, reshaping itself. Then the peak emerges in the middle of what had been the valley. Not just a shift—a wall of wrath hell-bent on utter annihilation of the meadow and its inhabitants.

Within the span of a heartbeat, the entire thing will be sucked underground. It's the sort of power only Underhill can wield.

Crazy broad.

Underhill must be checking in. And judging from the size of that mountain, she isn't pleased with our progress.

"Stop!" I shriek uselessly at the land around me. More

trees topple, more of the dead are sucked down into the gorge. Whatever spell had protected that place from them is gone now. Eventually, they'll fill in the crevasse and walk over the other corpses to get to their target.

Pharaildis doesn't appear by my side and talk reasonably, either. I spin in a circle, looking for a surveillance system I know isn't here. My mother *is* the world around us, she's connected to it. There's nowhere we can hide.

But maybe I can fight back.

I thrust out a hand and call the winds, crying out to the souls trapped within them. Every breeze and air current rushes to me, led by the North Wind. My ears pop at the massive shifts in pressure. It's like being in freefall.

I aim for the Draugar surrounding the purple meadow and erect a barricade.

The dead halt even as the ground quakes.

I watch as my invisible soldiers batter the dead away from the formerly green meadow. Draugar are shoved back by invisible hands. They don't scream as they are tossed into the gap at the base of the mountain. It's a gruesome sight. The dead encircle the newly emerging summit, lifted by air currents then dropped face first onto the rocks where they shatter.

I concentrate the North Wind, my general, on keeping the mountain from growing any higher. It creates an invisible cage around the shifting land. I know I can't hold it though, it's like cupping sand between my palms. Eventually, some will slip free.

Sweat beads along my hairline. My fledgling powers are strong but they are no match for Underhill's experience at wielding magic.

Hurry, I think to Aiden. *I can't hold them back much longer.*

I see the sparks. Inside the wall of circling wind. Aiden's unique brand of magic carrying him up into the sky. Did he manage to connect with both Bard and Gretchen in time? Every muscle is taut with tension and my body shakes from the strain.

Little blobs of golden light follow in his wake as my winds falter and the mountain rises up and breaks through my barrier.

Within a heartbeat, the meadow is no more. The Draugar army is in tatters, dead sprawling across the ground like toy soldiers left to the mercy of the elements.

As suddenly as it began, the rumbling halts. Clouds form over the new peak and a drizzle of rain patters down on my flushed face.

I dismiss the winds one at a time. Just in case Underhill isn't done. But as the rainfall picks up and the land below us smolders, I know she's made her point.

The sparks are descending toward the tiny outcropping of rock. I reach out to the North Wind. "Thank you."

In answer, it lifts my hair off my face in a tender caress. Is that the wind or the soul trapped within it? I shiver at the touch and sense a presence. Old, almost ancient, but before I can ask any questions it's gone.

Gretchen forms first, her honey colored eyes the size of duck eggs. Then Bard at her feet and finally, Aiden.

"How...?" Gretchen begins but then shakes her head as her gaze fixes on me. "Nic. You're all right?"

I nod once and am surprised to see her relieved smile. It's just a flash though and then she asks, "Aiden said you have the water."

In all the commotion, I'd forgotten about the flask in my hand. "Here," I hand it over, relieved that I didn't drop it when I'd called the winds.

Gretchen snatches the flask from me and rushes to Bard's still form. I watch in awe as she tilts his head back, the gesture full of tenderness. She'd been so afraid of him when they'd first met. But obviously, things have changed.

"Are you all right?" Aiden's eyes are bloodshot, his chin unshaven. He leans against a rocky shelf as if its support is all that's holding him upright.

"That's what I should be asking you."

He takes my hand and laces his fingers through it. "I'm still here."

"And you're glad about that, right?"

He doesn't respond. His hand is hot in mine, his affinity for fire keeping him warm.

I have a million questions for him, but at Gretchen's sob, they all vanish.

"Why isn't it working?" The mortal drops the empty flask into a puddle.

"They said this would work!"

Aiden's throat bobs. "Maybe it wasn't enough." I can tell he's thinking about the sip he took earlier, wondering if that made the difference. "Maybe I took too long."

Not your fault. I think at him while running a hand down his arm. *You did everything you could.*

A muscle jumps in his jaw. He pulls back, rejecting the comfort of my touch. Always taking the weight of the world on his shoulders.

Gretchen's lower lip trembles. Helpless, I watch as a single tear rolls down her cheek. It caresses the contours of her face and lands in Bard's still open mouth.

And the shifter sucks in a great lungful of air. His cloudy eyes clear and he turns his head to face the mortal. "And I was supposed to retrieve refreshment for you."

Gretchen doesn't waste a second, she just throws herself on top of the shifter, clinging to him with all her strength. Bard appears just as lost as I am, but he returns the gesture.

"I thought you were dead," Gretchen sobs into his neck.

"I was." His gaze slides to me. "Mostly anyway. My queen, I see our rescue has at least been successful."

"Not exactly." I exhale wearily and turn to face Aiden, who appears no less grim. "We need to get out of here in case more Draugar come. Can you carry us?"

Aiden shakes his head. "Not all of you. But there's a place nearby. About an hour's walk."

Gretchen is helping Bard to sit up. "Do you think you can make it that far?"

He grimaces, but nods.

"I'll help him." Gretchen is already maneuvering herself beneath Bard's arm to act as a human crutch.

I move to take Aiden's hand to support him but he steps back. "I'll range ahead while you help them."

I open my mouth to protest, but he's already making his way back down the hill. Stung, I move to Bard's other side.

"Did you two have a fight or something?" Gretchen asks as we take our first collective steps.

"Not that I know of. We've barely spoken."

"He was lost without you, my queen," Bard says. "Beside himself with worry."

I roll my eyes. How ridiculous that the two of them just narrowly escaped death and yet they feel the need to reassure me about my boyfriend's feelings? "It's fine. We're in a hurry and he's the best fighter. It makes sense he should clear the way. None of us are at our best. We'll all feel better after a decent night's sleep."

They hurry to agree. What they don't know is that I can still lie.

Especially to myself.

Through the Man's Eyes

Aiden spies the ruined towers of the summer palace in the distance. The rain has chased them for the better part of the walk, leaving them all soaked to the skin. But now, the intense late afternoon sun breaks through the clouds and makes the stone seem to glow from within. It looks like a castle from a storybook, the white spires covered with climbing ivy. He half expects to see a prince galloping up over the hill on a white steed.

At least Brigit hadn't sacked the place.

His hands clench into fists at his sides. He hadn't been back here since Nicneven's death. And now they would be forced to spend the night.

"Hey." Nic appears beside him. Her hair hangs down in wet strands. The roots are growing in blond again, looking oddly fetching against the dark. She doesn't try to take his hand or touch him but he can scent her concern. "What's up with you?"

"Do you recognize this place?" He can't look at her, can't tear his focus away from the horrors of the past. *The blood. So much of it, an ocean of it. His mate's blood. That of their unborn child. It coats his hands. Stains his soul. Their deaths on his head.*

"Should I?" She turns her attention from him to the castle. A small frown causes the skin between her eyebrows to crease. She blinks, then shivers. "Oh."

That one word conveys a world of emotion. Shock, hurt, and perhaps a bit of curiosity.

"There isn't anywhere else." He curses his weakness, curses himself for not being stronger, unable to carry them all to safety. As if such a place even exists under the hill. "Nowhere nearby that will be safe from the Draugar."

Nowhere at all under the hill to escape her mother.

Nic inhales deeply. "It's one night. It'll be fine. Come on. Let's get the other's settled. Then we can talk."

He's having a hard time swallowing past the lump in his throat. Talk. In this place where they had betrayed each other so monstrously, now he would have to admit that he'd done so again, broken faith with her.

Will she send him away? Would he *let* her? And most importantly, will the wolf allow them to be separated?

The answer prowls under his skin. No, the beast will return to her side again and again. The only way she will be rid of him permanently is to execute him.

He won't beg for her forgiveness. He doesn't deserve to die in grace. His only request will be that she wait until she and the others are safely back at the farm, surrounded by her Wild Hunt.

Aiden helps Gretchen navigate Bard under a crumbling portcullis. The mortal's cheeks are rosy from her exertions, her eyes bright. He wonders if this is the sort of adventure she had in mind when she'd blackmailed Nic.

That seems like a lifetime ago.

Bard looks fairly well for a being who'd spent the better part of two days dying. His skin has regained some color and though his eyes are filled with pain, they seem otherwise clear.

They trail into the room, leaving puddles in their wake. They reek of smoke and exhaustion and fear, but their living smell is better than the scent of stale death in the palace.

Aiden scans the great hall. It's in total disarray. Tables and benches are turned on their side with trenchers of what, a lifetime ago may have been called food, still littering the long tables. Weeds sprout up through the cracks in the stone, some as high as his knee. The angle of the sun filters through the window, highlighting the bones of the fallen.

The Unseelie Court of Queen Nicneven. At least the ones who'd remained loyal to her.

He hears Nic swallow before she asks, "Brigit just left them all here to rot?"

"As a warning." His voice is flat, lifeless as the castle. "So that the rest of the courtiers wouldn't rebel against her."

He remembers them all. Fey were fey, and none among the dead had he called a friend. But they had been Nic's subjects, and loyalty to his mate went a long way with him. And with his wolf.

He moves to step away, to put some distance between them but Nic grabs his arm. "Did you hear that?"

"Hear what?" Gretchen asks as she comes up beside them.

Lines form between Nic's eyebrows. He listens, but hears only the mournful sigh of the wind.

Nic shakes her head. "Nothing, I guess."

"Not that I'm complaining, my queen," the shifter grunts. "But is there somewhere for me to lie down before I fall?"

She scans the space. "Not here. Any suggestions, Aiden?"

"Behind the kitchen, the servant's quarters. It's on this level." Because he couldn't bear the thought of going upstairs.

"Lead the way." Nic gestures.

They pass down the long corridor to the kitchen. There are no windows here, and without torches to light the way, it's very dark.

"Can you shine a little light around the place?" Nic asks.

He extends his right hand, the one not in contact with Bard and his flame leaps up, casting shadows across the cold stone.

"Take it," he tells Nic. "It won't burn you. Light, but no heat."

She frowns but reaches a hand forward as though to cup the flame. A small smile flits across her lips as the cold torch dances in her own palm. "How cool is this?"

Even wet and chilled to the bone, she makes his heart ache.

Aiden lights a second flame and they continue deeper into the castle.

While the summer palace had never been as grand as the royal seat, it could house and feed hundreds of fey at a time. Here too the room sits abandoned. A crusty cauldron still hangs over a long burned-out hearth fire. Mold spores from what had once been bread float through the air, looking for anything to consume.

"Damn. And here I was hoping there might be something edible left." Nic waves a hand and a soft breeze blows through the space, carrying the musty and closed-up scent away with it.

Aiden jerks his head to a sealed door beside the hearth. "Check in there."

Nic walks to the door, raises her cold torch high and yanks the panel aside.

The food inside looks as fresh as if it was collected earlier in the day. Ripe berries, wheels of cheese, baskets full of nuts. Jars of honey and syrups. Collections of vegetables, every color imaginable. Green, purple and orange shine bright in the low light. It's a symphony of color after the ashy waste of the rest of the palace.

"How is this possible?" Gretchen's eyes round at the sight. "Everything else is ruined."

"It's a preservation cabinet," Aiden explains. "This place was only in use half the year. The magic is meant to keep the food fresh when no one is in residence."

"Score," Gretchen shifts her weight. "Dibs on anything chocolate."

"You'll have to fight me for it." Nic's tone is teasing. She reaches inside the cabinet, grabs an empty basket, and starts loading it down with supplies.

With the mortal's help, Aiden maneuvers Bard through the space and into the pokey hallway beyond. The nearest door is closed and he takes Bard's full weight so Gretchen can reach for the knob.

On the other side is a small bedroom. Almost as small as the enchanted cabinet. There is a bed though, and a hearth, a tiny chest of drawers and even a window. No linens adorn the bare mattress, but Bard doesn't seem to mind as they help him to it.

He sags down and curls onto one side.

Gretchen shifts from foot to foot. "Are you all right?"

The shifter grunts and shuts his eyes.

Aiden places a hand on her shoulder. "He'll be fine. He just needs rest. You should eat."

"I am a little hungry," she confesses as though this is some sin.

It must be an understatement. Even if she has some of Nic's infamous protein bars in her pack, she had been without real food since they crossed the Veil. "Come on. We'll stay close enough that you can hear him if he calls out."

With a final lingering glance at the door, Gretchen allows him to steer her back to the kitchen.

Nic has been busy. Meats and cheese and vegetables have been pulled from the cabinet. A fresh pot sits atop the great hearthstone. There is no sign of the grimy cauldron. The flame he gifted her with flickers on the table beside her. The knife blade flashes as she chops carrots in a steady rhythm.

He'll never tire of seeing her cook. It's one of the many skills her mortal life taught her. One of the many reasons she's so different than the spoiled fey queen he'd been bound to obey.

She tenses, her head jerking up. She is hearing something, seeing something that the rest of them can't. He yearns to ask her about it, to offer her comfort.

"I'm making a vegetable soup," she announces louder than necessary, as though to banish the distraction. "Although, I think some actual fire would be helpful."

Taking the cue, he sets his own flame down on a scarred prep table and then summons a blaze for the hearth. Gretchen yelps.

"Don't worry," Nic looks up and gifts Aiden with one of her rare smiles. "You'll get used to him. I have."

There's something in her gaze as if she's trying to tell him something without words or images. A shared moment.

Gretchen shuffles over to check the pot. "Can I help?"

Nic nods. "There are all sorts of herbs in the pantry. Try to find something that looks and smells like basil. Oh, and salt. Soup isn't soup without a decent amount of salt."

He watches the two of them for a beat. His mate working in a space she'd probably never entered before. She's so strong, a survivor. And queenlier at this moment than she's ever been.

My mate provides. The wolf is filled with pride.

He turns away, his chest aching at the sight. "I'm going for some air."

Aiden can feel her eyes on him. She's trying to figure him out. He waits for her to say something, to demand an explanation either verbal or mental.

But there is only silence.

She turns back to her task and he slips from the room like an unwanted smell.

Better to keep his distance.

ACCEPTANCE

*J*hear the baby's plaintive wail again as I walk
through the desolate palace. Some primal instinct
is urging me to go, to find the child and offer it food or
comfort, whatever it needs just to get the sound to stop.

But the infant is beyond all mortal help. They all are.

The palace is haunted by the shades of the dead.

The Unseelie courtiers who had died here. Died in service
to me.

I recall Fern, Aiden's grandmother's significant other,
talking about how she had lost a daughter when the palace
was sacked all those centuries ago. I'd felt disconnected from
the events. After all, those were Nicneven's memories, not
my own. But it's one thing to hear about a tragedy
committed in a past life, another entirely to hear them. To
see them.

The servants carrying insubstantial trays or sweeping the
floors are oblivious to my presence. They aren't like the souls
tethered to the Wild Hunt. They can't interact with me. I
tried speaking with one, a kitchen maid scrubbing the floors
when Aiden and Gretchen had been distracted with Bard.

She hadn't paused in her chore. Hadn't turned a hair, not even when Gretchen walked through her and every cell in my body had started to buzz.

This isn't like soul walking, which Nahini had taught me to see the different planes of existence. These aren't fey anymore—their souls have moved on. What's left is like an echo. A shade of what had once been. Just a sliver of a memory paying homage to daily life.

Who had the baby belonged to? I can't recall.

Aiden is moving bodies.

I stand at the doorway, the tin mug full of vegetable soup meant for him in hand and watch him scoop up the remains of fey bones. Like me, his clothes and hair have dried, but probably also like me he is still cold in this musty damp tomb of a castle. He shows no sign of discomfort though as he carries them outside the building, and down the hill toward the tree line.

Setting his soup on a windowsill, I follow.

He is laying them out in a long line at the base of the trees. The sun is long gone, but the moon is up. Waxing and three quarters to full, its glow is more than enough for his wolf eyes and my fey ones. I study him as he bends down and places his latest collection of bones on the left end.

He bows his head, murmurs something too low for me to hear, and then turns.

Our eyes meet. It hits me again the way it had in the cave. Instant connection. My mate, the missing part of my soul. He's there. Right in front of me.

So why does he seem so far away?

For a moment he just stares at me, pain and longing written on his face. I want to go to him, but some instinct tells me not to. He's keeping his distance for a reason. As much as I want answers, I need to let him come to me when he's ready.

He looks away first, doesn't say anything. Even though I'm an idiot when it comes to emotions, it's obvious that he's avoiding me.

Why? With Aiden, it could be anything. He's prone to brood over events both past and present. Considering he has over a millennia of life experience and our current situation sucks on ice, that's a great deal of territory to cover.

Should I intervene or leave him to it?

He passes me and heads back up the hill without a word. After a moment, I follow.

I don't speak as he collects the next body, which is little more than a pile of bones and rags. I swallow. I've never liked dead things. Ironic, considering the number of deaths I've caused. Chloe and Addy have always handled the clean-up. These aren't fresh cadavers, though and dry old bones aren't as unsettling as a fresh corpse.

I move to the next one over. It's smaller, more delicately formed. Its bones are light and hollow and there are more than the standard four limbs. Arms and legs as well as long, graceful thin bones attach to the scapula. Wings, like a great bird.

A child. Not the baby.

"You don't have to," Aiden murmurs when he sees what I'm doing.

"Someone ought to. And I don't want you to have to handle such a task alone."

He stares at me and I wonder if he'll ask me to stop, tell me to go back to Gretchen and Bard. I see him swallow, then nod once.

We set to the grisly task.

The moon has moved across the sky by the time all the bodies are laid out under the stars. Aiden has said a few words in his indecipherable language over each one. A prayer, I realize, or maybe a blessing.

After the final one, he moves back to where I stand and raises his hand. Blue light leaps from his fingertips. I expect a great blazing inferno, but instead, the bones dissolve into ash.

It seems right to call the North Wind, who has been hanging around nearby since the fire earlier. As though it's guarding my flank. I reach out and tug it nearer. It gusts over the hill, past the castle, and down the slope. My unbound hair whips into my eyes and even Aiden's is tussled before it circles the heaps of ashes, gathering them up. The trees beyond moan at the passing, the limbs creaking. And then wind and the remains of the Unseelie courtiers are gone.

"I should have done that a long time ago." Aiden turns to face me. "Thank you for helping."

"They were my people, too. I was responsible for them." I reach for his hand needing a connection to the living. The baby is still wailing and I wish I was a different person, a good one who isn't afraid to shed a tear over the loss.

He pulls away. "Don't."

"Why not?" I swallow. "Did I do something wrong?"

He shakes his head. "No. I'm the one who's wronged you."

Ice forms in my stomach. "How?"

He looks away.

"Is this about Bard and Gretchen?" Aiden has a habit of blaming himself for other's misfortunes.

He shakes his head. "Though I don't entirely trust the shifter. It occurred to me that he might have taken *Seelenverkäufer* and killed the spy. He has the means."

"But why would he?" I ask.

He doesn't answer.

I think back to how Bard had helped us, how he'd entertained the Wild Hunt and requested only a place in my court. "Bard helped us when he didn't have to. I trust him."

Those leaf green eyes glance away. "You need to be careful about who you trust."

"Aiden," I step closer, close enough to touch. "Please, talk to me."

He is silent for a long moment. I see the muscle working in his jaw. "I knew all along that Underhill was your mother. I should have told you."

I'd suspected as much. Aiden is always cagey when it comes to doling out information. Is it because he wanted to keep me in the dark about certain unpleasant truths? "Why didn't you?"

He turns, his gaze bores into me. "She offered me a deal. After we crossed back to the mortal realm, she appeared to me. If I kept her identity to myself, she would give me Angrboda."

His father's mistress, the giantess who had ruined his life. I lick suddenly dry lips.

Aiden runs a hand through his hair. "I shouldn't have taken the deal."

There is a weird, squishy sensation in my stomach. "Why did you?"

He shifts his weight from one foot to the other, looking uneasy. "I knew the giantess was lending magic to Wardon and I wanted to know why. Usually, the giants keep well away from the courts."

"And that information mattered more to you than being honest with me?" My tone is flat.

He takes a step back. "No, of course not."

"Then why lie about something so important?"

He stares at me. "Because of them."

My eyebrows pull together. "Them?"

"Your aunts."

My lips part.

"Underhill and I have something in common. Our mutual

hatred for the fates and what they've done to us. You don't understand how powerful the Norns are, what they can do. It's why I left you with them when you were reborn. But...."

He trails off and I finish for him, "but you hate them just as much as she does."

His chest rises and falls as though he can't get enough air. "Believe me, Nic. I thought you would be safe. Underhill can't reach the mortal world. I didn't know you'd be dragged back across the Veil. Underhill is trapped here. I thought I'd have time to sort it all out."

He stares at the ground, shoulders rounding as though to ward off a blow. "I thought, if I had Angrboda as a prisoner, I could find out why she'd ruined my life."

My breath hitches. He may be older than the hill behind us, but at this moment, he has no more experience than I do.

He's as much of an idiot as I am.

"You think Angrboda ruined your life?"

A single nod. "Her and her children. If my father hadn't kept going off with her, hadn't sired such monsters, my family would never have been punished. I wouldn't have transformed, wouldn't have killed Nari. If not for Angrboda, there would be no wolf, no Ragnarök."

"That's a lot to lay at one person's feet."

He nods. "It's not just her. I know it's not, no matter what I want to believe. It's my father, too. But I can't get to him, can't punish him the way I want to."

"You mean the way you punish yourself?"

He whips his head up, his eyes flickering to the wolf's glow. "Don't."

"Aiden," I swallow. "I thought we were past this. I thought you were going to stop looking for trouble. Did you really want me to leave you there?"

His expression is... haunted. "No."

"I realized something when you were there when whatever she did was hurting you."

"What did you realize?"

I swallow. Why is this so hard to say? "Aiden, I'm not just your mate. You're mine, too."

His lips part on a puff of air.

I take a step closer, lace my fingers through his. "I didn't really understand it before, what that meant. What you were trying to tell me. It's not solely about your wolf, only in that he accepts this, accepts me, and his nature, right?"

His head bobs.

"The wolf accepts me as I am. Teenage serial killer resurrected queen and all. And when we were down there, when she was torturing you with madness, I understood. I accept everything you are, too."

I'm not sure what I expect. A smile, perhaps an exclamation of joy. Instead, he pulls out of my grip, runs a hand through his hair as though he's thinking of yanking the stuff out.

"Do you know what I saw when Underhill was torturing me with madness? Me killing you. Over and over, in a thousand different ways. The wolf losing control, shredding you to pieces the way he did to my brother. Wielding a knife to shove into your back, slipping poison into your food. Dropping you from a height. Smothering, drowning, burning. Each time you begged me not to do it and every time I couldn't stop. Over and over, I had no control of myself, no ability to change what was happening. I've watched you die, but there's something worse when I'm causing your demise."

"Aiden," I whisper. "It wasn't real."

"It *felt* real. That sick poem my father told you? Third time will do it. The wolf at your bosom will be sure to see to it. I'm fated to cause your death!" He swallows hard and his green eyes glisten as though he's willing back tears. "I already killed Nari. I can't kill you, too."

I shake my head. "You won't—"

He interrupts. "I've already betrayed you by not telling you about your mother. If you'd known who she is, she wouldn't have ensnared you."

"You don't know that. She's old, crafty. Addy likes to say where there's a will there's a way. Pharaildis has the strongest will I've ever encountered. She would have found a way."

His shoulders round inward. "Nic, you don't understand."

"Then help me to." I take his hand, risking him pulling away again. "I want to help you."

He doesn't withdraw. Exactly the opposite. Instead, he pulls me into his arms and rests his chin on the top of my head. "I love you."

Sorry, Chloe. We blew past easy-breezy lemon-squeezy in our last lifetime.

Mate. He's my mate. My heart pounds frantically. I want him the way I never believed to be possible. Not for me, the teen serial killer with abandonment issues. Not for me, the reincarnated Unseelie queen who had betrayed him so long ago. The lover he'd run from and then moved mountains to resurrect.

Aiden doesn't see titles, labels or power. He doesn't want anything from me. He only wants to be with me. To take whatever I can give.

And I want to give him everything.

I stand on my tiptoes and kiss him. It isn't a plan or a thought. This isn't the right time or the place. All I know is that he is mine and I am his.

He doesn't respond right away, his body stiff and hard as a rock wall. But I am insistent. My fingers thread into his dark hair and I press my body flush against his, my message unmistakable.

I want you. I think at him. *More than anything.*

I don't know if it's the words that tip the balance or just my insistence. He's held back, waited for me to be ready. Now I am.

His hands slide down my back and then he lifts me, pressing me back into a tree. His body finds the space between my legs, pinning me in place so he can kiss me more thoroughly. His mouth is hot, as he trails kisses from my lips down the side of my neck.

The sensations make my head swim. I have no experience with this, other than the handful of times Aiden has kissed me before. But then I was the one holding back. Now, my body, my heart, my mind, my soul, all recognize him for what he is.

Mate. My mate.

His hand pauses at the place on my waist where my top meets my pants. I can hear his questions in my mind. *Is this all right? Do you want me to stop?*

Our gazes lock. The current between us electrifies.

"Keep going." I breathe the words against his neck. "Please."

His lips curve up into a small smile. "How can I say no when you ask so nicely?"

A puff of air escapes my lips. "You can, you know. Say no."

He freezes. I could kick myself for ruining the moment.

"Nic," he says again in a completely different way.

"You have a choice," I tell him. "With me, you *always* have a choice. I don't ever want you to think I'm using you. You always have a choice with me."

His eyes burn emerald fire but he doesn't move. So much history, so much hurt between us. There are more good reasons to stop. Bard and Gretchen. The Draugar. We'd just cremated the dead. This is only a distraction, a temporary reprieve between running for our lives and expecting the worst. Madness. Death.

A distraction I need.

Mate. *My* mate.

Aiden is the one thing I won't run from anymore.

I listen but hear nothing from his thoughts. I swallow, trying to prepare myself for him to pull back, to set me away and shut me out.

He doesn't.

I gasp as his hot hand caresses up my side, his eyes flash on my own.

"I always want you," he leans in closer, until his lips graze that sensitive spot just below my ear. "Because it *is* you."

I know exactly what he means. I didn't know what it meant to want until he came into my life.

Our mouths meet again. Excitement fills me, a rush of molten heat that has nothing to do with magic. At least not fey magic or gods magic. Just good old-fashioned chemistry.

It feels inevitable. *We* are inevitable. Not because of some mystical connection. But because Aiden is brighter, more vivid, more real to me than anything, ever since he sat down across from me in the computer lab.

Somehow, he undoes the laces on my shirt until I am bare-breasted in the moonlight. He yanks his own dark t-shirt out of his waistband, then lays it out on a bed of moss before pressing me down on top of it. All the breath rushes from my lungs as our skin connects so intimately.

"Aiden." I can't stop myself from saying his name over and over, any more than I can stop my hands from skimming over the taut muscles of his arms and shoulders, down his back. It's as if speaking it, knowing that while all this is new for me, it's okay because it's still him. Still my Aiden. Wolf and all.

The soul I love.

His own hands aren't idle. He's exploring me leisurely, his touch almost reverent. Along my cheekbones, down the column of my throat, over my shoulders, breasts, belly...lower.

You're making me crazy. Speaking is beyond me. I can't pull in enough air to say a word.

You ain't seen nothing yet, the son of the trickster thinks as his hand works the laces of my pants open.

He isn't wrong.

I've felt these sensations before, but compared to his burning hot touch, my own curious fumbling is a breeze that is no match for a hurricane. I'm losing all track of myself. My identity is shattering and it scares me.

But I know him, those eyes the color of new spring leaves, the full lips that quirk up in a small, disbelieving smile. He is my anchor, the eye in the center of the hurricane. The sensations are both new and old, foreign and familiar. Overwhelming and not enough.

I don't want it to stop. Don't want him to stop.

My body shakes under the onslaught of need. I am poised on the edge as his fingers move deeper, leaf green eyes glowing brighter, brighter.

"I love you," he whispers again and that's all it takes to send me over. Past the Veil and all its colors, out into the universe where I burst apart in a shower of sparks.

Through the Man's Eyes

Aiden can't believe this is real. That she is real. His Nic, fantasy made flesh. She accepts him, all of him. He belongs to her.

It's not the way it was with Nicneven. Before she'd owned him, body and soul, and she knew it. Never missing an opportunity to remind him of it. She demanded his all and gave nothing of herself, ever the queen, always in control.

Her dark hair is fanned out around her head. Her eyes are closed, her lips parted. He leans down to steal one soft sweet kiss.

Her eyelids lift and the clear blue of them drink him in. She smiles, a little shyly and his chest swells.

How many times did he slam the door on this dream? The only person Nicneven loved was herself. And then when he finally met Nic again, she had been so cold.

A laugh escapes. Cold like a glacier over a volcano. There is nothing cold about the woman in his arms though.

Girl, not woman.

He stiffens at the thought. She's so young, so inexperienced.

He moves away, ignoring the urge to keep going, to strip her bare and…. No matter that his need thrums through him with every beat of his heart. He has to control himself.

"Don't stop." Those clear blue eyes flash. The burning intensity he sees there is hotter than any flame he's ever conjured.

"I don't…." He swallows, shakes his head. "We shouldn't."

"Why?"

The question takes him off guard. Nic had been so honest with him, telling him what she felt. He can be no less so.

"I don't want to rush you. You've never done this before and I…I've never done this right."

"When you say this, you mean sex?"

She's so blunt when she isn't being secretive. Like a two by four to the head.

He presses his forehead to hers, unable to stifle a grin. "Yes, I mean sex. This isn't the right time or place."

"Aiden, I want you. You want me. Don't do what you always do and overcomplicate the shit out of the situation."

A bark of laughter erupts. "I overcomplicate—?"

She breaks in with a kiss. Gods, it's the most incredible sensation of his life. er mouth on his, her fingers tunneling through his hair, to pull him back to her. Wicked fairy queen. He can't help but touch her more, exploring what feels like miles of smooth flesh.

She grows bolder. Her hands travel over his shoulders and down his back in a lazy sweep. The scent of her, the taste of her are designed to drive him completely out of his mind. He should push her away, put some distance between them. It's the right thing to do.

He moves back and she follows. Scrambles into his lap. Gone is the shy virgin. She's morphing into a hot-blooded temptress, boldly pressing herself against him. Her pants are still on, still undone, the barrier so feeble between them.

Her breath hitches. He feels the first press of intimate contact, him against her. Maybe Underhill did kill him. Maybe he's dead and this is some sort of afterlife reward. Hysterical laughter threatens. Reward for what? It's not like he's been good.

Her hips circle and then slide as she searches for a rhythm to please her. Sharp white teeth sink into his lower lip. Her winter apple scent grows heavier with her desire.

No male, mortal or immortal, could be expected to withstand such sweet torment.

His hands rest on her lush backside, urging her on. And then he feels the heat of touch on his own posterior. Which makes no sense. He's seated on the ground and her hands are on his shoulders.

The wolf surfaces and demands he take stock of the situation. But he scents no threat, nothing but him and her.

He turns to her to ask if she sensed anything amiss.

Her blue eyes fill with wonder as her finger drags down the side of his neck. "I can *feel* you. I mean, I felt me touching you."

"So did I." He pushes her hair over her shoulder and skims his fingertips down her side. He shivers as he experiences the contact as well.

"What's happening?" She presses her face into his, whispering directly into his ear. They shudder in unified pleasure.

"I have no idea." His thoughts are like shapes in the mist, slipping through his grasp. "It might have something to do with the mate bond."

"You don't know?"

"I've never experienced anything like this." If it had been difficult to stop exploring her before he knew how much pleasure she feels at his touch, it will take divine intervention to separate them now.

Every little caress sends a spiral of sensation through her. It's impossible not to imagine what it would feel like to be inside her.

"I don't have anything." Nic pants as her hips rock against him again with a desperate edge. "Protection, I mean."

"Neither do I." He grits his teeth. Gods, the *sensations*. He's never imagined anything like this. Pleasure so intense it's addictive.

"I don't want to stop." And she doesn't, fitting herself even more closely into contact with him.

A growl tears from his throat at the thought of being denied this ecstasy. She circles her hips again and he's lost. He lifts her up and presses her back against the nearest tree.

Her legs wrap around him, locking at the ankles as if she wants to hold him to her.

As if he would ever leave this. Leave her.

A hoarse gasp escapes as he feels the rough bark against her back, the hardness of himself as he shoves against her. She cries out, pleasure radiates through her. He claims her mouth and does it again, and again. The fit of her, even with the thin barriers of clothing between them, is perfect.

Her limbs begin to tremble and her nails dig into his shoulder blades. The small pain spurs him on and he moves faster, holds her tighter, delights in the waves of building pleasure inside her. She's desperate for this, for him.

"Touch me," she pants. "Like you did before."

He studies the position, her in only a scrap of unfastened leather, pinned against the tree. He tears the garment from her. Then Nic is in his arms. Naked.

Her hands are already on the fastening of his jeans. She reaches in, touching him for the first time and he nearly loses it. She wants him, she needs him...

Inside. She wants to feel him inside of her again. He wants that too. Just once.

Yet, in the shadow of the summer palace, the castle where she died still carrying his unborn child, he knows that dream is impossible.

Gripping both her wrists in one hand, he shifts so that he is only partly free of his pants. Enough to feel but not to risk.

He presses along her slowly. The angle is wrong for penetration but he can feel her heat, her ache. He wants to soothe her. To savor her.

To love her any way he can.

"Oh," she says the word on an exhale. Her eyes go wide at the intimate contact. Her lips form a small o as he uses himself to stroke her tender flesh. Sizzling contact. Her legs lock around him, her thigh muscles squeezing, squeezing...

The smallest movements create waves of sensation, the way her breasts flatten against his chest. Dear gods, the *connection*.

With their new link, he knows what she likes best, what will give her the most pleasure. And he needs to give her pleasure now before he disgraces himself.

"Nic," he pants. "I need to—,"

"I know." Her teeth sink into her lower lip before she adds, "I *feel* it."

His need as well as her own. He lifts her higher, moves closer, rocks faster. Building, building, building.

Over.

Her eyes squeeze shut and he takes her mouth, swallowing her cry. Her release triggers his own, a bolt of lightning scorches down his spine. The rush of heat almost makes his knees buckle. He leans harder into her to ride it out as their mutual pleasure creates a feedback loop that stretches on through eternity.

Gradually, he comes back to himself. Recognizes his surroundings. The cold night air on his bare skin, the way his fingers wrap protectively over her hip. He must protect her. Especially from himself.

"What's wrong?" Her eyes go wide. "Did I, do something wrong?"

He shakes his head. "Of course not."

"Then what happened?

He takes a deep breath and sets her down. "I need you to kill me."

MADNESS INCARNATE

I lay in the darkness of my old bedroom and listen to the ghost baby cry. Or rather, Nicneven's old bedroom. The one she—I—shared with Aiden. Like the cabinet downstairs, it has been preserved. No dust has settled in the hundreds of years since my death. That also means the bloodstains on the floor are as fresh as the day they'd been spilled.

My blood and the blood of our unborn child.

Easy-breezy lemon-squeezy? I laugh out loud at my own foolishness. Had I really expected that to work?

I'd cleaned the blood up with a towel, only gagging a few dozen times in the process, and tossed it in the unlit fireplace before lying down in the large canopy bed. Aiden wouldn't seek me out here. I doubted even the wolf would dare enter this space. Too much unpleasant history.

He loves me. The flaming bastard told me he *loves* me. And I'd felt it. Felt everything he did while he had me naked against that tree. I thought we were going to... that he wanted to make love.

But no, he gets me all worked up and in the next breath

asks me to kill him. As though requesting to borrow my truck for the night.

I was tempted to do it. I am that furious.

Were all guys such selfish asshats? Or just the one I've fallen for?

I've never wanted anyone the way I want Aiden. Even now the urge to go to him, to comfort him and let him soothe me, is strong. But I don't want to give in to the foreign impulse. I'm furious with him, not just about his asinine request, but because I'd thought we were on the same page. That he was going to get over his self-destructive streak.

How idiotically naïve of me.

Soul mate. Mated. Is Chloe right? Do those labels even matter when we keep hurting each other over and over again?

I flip onto my side and squeeze my eyes shut. Stupid ghost baby. Stupid mind showing me stupid Aiden at that moment after he'd told me to kill him.

My mouth had fallen open and I pushed back so I could see his face, see if he was making some awful joke. "What?"

"I've thought it through. It's the only way. If I'm already dead, Underhill can't use me as leverage against you." He swallowed and the gesture looked painful "Nic, I don't think I'm strong enough to battle my way back from the madness again. The wolf seized control too easily. My defenses were obliterated. Anything is better than that."

"But you'll be dead! Aiden, do you even hear yourself? Are you really going to tell me you've stayed alive all this time to just give up now?"

He shook his head "If you give me the goodnight kiss, I can become part of the Wild Hunt."

"And you'll still be dead!" I turned away, under the

pretense of retying my pants. Unwilling to let him see the tears forming in my eyes.

"Nic," he breathed my name like a prayer and cupped my shoulders. "Please try to understand."

"Don't okay? I just…I can't handle this right now. Not on top of everything."

"I didn't want to upset you."

"Upset?" I laugh, but there's no humor in it. "Did you even think about what killing you would do to me? You said your form of madness was to see yourself kill me and be unable to stop it. So how is it fair that you ask me to kill you?"

"I'm sorry I have to ask this of you. If there were some other way…but the wolf won't let me end my life. I've tried before."

I knew he had. "But why now?"

"I don't want to die." He gripped my hand and squeezed. "Maybe for the first time in my entire existence I have a reason to live. Because I've found you. But I can't watch you die. I'm not strong enough. And I will do *anything* to keep that fate from happening."

And what could I say to that? Not a damn thing. So I came here and cleaned up my own blood because even that was better than the alternative.

I would give anything to cross the Veil and be home with my aunts, if only for the night. To hear Chloe jabbering about celebrity gossip. To smell the roast squash and apple dish that Addy makes on cold autumn nights. The farm is home for me in a way I doubt any place under the hill could ever be.

When I think about the cold lair beneath the ground that my mother inhabits…is it any wonder she's a vindictive harpy?

Someone knocks on the door, breaking into my dark thoughts. "Nic?"

Gretchen.

I scrub at the tears staining my cheeks and call out, "Yeah?"

She pushes the door open. "Hey, are you all right?"

The old Nic, the one I'd been last spring would have shrugged off the question. All I can do is shake my head.

"Is it Aiden?"

I huff out a breath. "It's not always about Aiden." Even if he is a huge chunk of it.

She comes in and shuts the door behind her. "Do you want to talk about it?"

I stare at her. "Gretchen, one thing you're going to have to learn real fast is that I never want to talk about anything. Like ever."

She takes a hesitant half step forward, as though testing the temperature of a chilly lake. "Is that a fey thing?"

"It's a teenage serial killer thing."

She doesn't flinch as I expect her to. Instead, she takes another step. Her body language is tentative, unsure. But no doubt about it, the girl is ridiculously brave.

I don't have it in me to shut her down. I hunt around for something to say that isn't about me and settle on, "How's Bard?"

"Still asleep." She licks her lips. "I really like him."

"You mean as an individual or you want to have sex with him?"

"Nic." She blushes to the roots of her hair. "I can't believe you just asked me that!"

I shrug. "So? What's the big deal?"

She huffs out a breath as though I've exasperated her. "That's not...I mean it's too soon...I mean...." She trails off helplessly.

I study her reaction. Sarah had talked about sex in blunt, unapologetic turns. Then again, Sarah had been as much of an outcast as I am. The fey are blunt as well. They can't lie and while they are secretive about certain things, their sexual liaisons aren't one of them. But Gretchen is all a-flutter, like I crossed a personal line she didn't want to be breached.

"Sorry, I know my social skills are rough around the edges."

"No." She swallows and lifts her chin. "Don't apologize. That's the reason I liked you, you're so bold. Forthright."

I tilt my head to the side, wondering how she gets bold and forthright when every time I look in the mirror, I see a cold-blooded manipulator.

"May I ask you something personal?" She looks nervous as if I'll bite her head off just for making the request.

It seems only fair. "Go ahead."

"What does it feel like to know you can kill anyone?"

I jolt, wondering if Aiden had told her what he wants. "Why do you ask?"

She fidgets with the fraying edge of her jeans. "Ever since I saw you kill that man, the one outside the rave, the one who wanted to rape you, I've wondered what you were feeling."

Paul Anderson. "I wasn't feeling anything at the time."

She tilts her head. "And now?"

"Now, that I understand what I am, what I can do, it's different." I study her posture. "Honestly? It's scary as hell."

"But you're so powerful. Not just because you can kill bad people, but because you have all these abilities. Bard told me you can fight. And what you did earlier with the wind…." She shakes her head.

"Gretchen," I say slowly. "Just because I can kill people doesn't mean I should. I've always worried about hurting the wrong person. Someone who doesn't deserve it. And one thing that I've learned over the past few months, there's always someone stronger, who knows more and can do more. The only thing magic has done is to make me a target."

"For your mother?"

When I raise an eyebrow, she smiles sheepishly. "Harmony told me."

I flop back on the bed. "Of course she did."

There is a shift of the mattress then Gretchen lays beside me. "There's something we have in common. Both our mothers are nuts."

I turn to look at her. "Gretchen, my mother is an ancient prisoner who is willing to torture to get me to do exactly as she says and probably plans to rip my heart out. Literally."

She shrugs. "And mine is an emotional blackmailer and borderline alcoholic trapped in a loveless marriage who likes to blame me because I don't live up to her standard of beauty. Same disease, different stage."

She has a point. I picture Gretchen's mother with her perfectly manicured hands clutching a wineglass for dear life. "Maybe I should get my mom a crate of Chardonnay to mellow her the fuck out."

Gretchen's whole body begins shaking. Tears trickle from the corners of her eyes. "Did you just tell a joke?"

"It happens from time to time."

She laughs harder. It's a good sound, happiness set free. I smile as I listen to it.

"Wait 'til I tell Bard. I doubt he'll believe me."

I roll onto my side. "What do you like about him?"

Her dark eyebrows pull down as she considers. "It's weird, I didn't like him at first. I mean, I just met him a few days ago. He's kind of scary looking and sort of odd. But then when he was dying, I felt like something in me was being shredded. I couldn't stand to watch him suffer."

Again, I hear Taj's words in my mind. *Many don't recognize the soul's cry. Even the ones who do might fear rejection too much to ever act on it.*

Could Gretchen and Bard be mates? Was that why he'd

risked returning to Underhill to protect her? And what if Aiden is right? If Bard might have been the one to take *Seelenverkäufer*? Should I warn Gretchen so she didn't let herself fall too hard for a would-be traitor?

Would a warning have stopped me from falling for Aiden?

A headache was forming at the base of my skull. This is why I don't do feelings.

"What do you know about him?" She sits up, tucking her feet beneath her.

I raise an eyebrow and almost tell her I don't do girl talk. But her face is so bright and hopeful. She's held up better in Underhill than I'd believed possible. So, I make a stab at it. Because really, anything is better than brooding about Aiden or how I had been murdered in this very room.

"I don't know him well," I begin. "We met a few weeks ago. And that's weeks in Underhill time…."

I awake in the darkened bedchamber, a feeling of unease crawling along the back of my neck. Beside me, Gretchen snores softly. I get out of bed and move to the window, checking for Draugar or any other sign of a threat.

Nothing, just a soft breeze stirring the tops of the evergreens.

The hairs stand up on my arms. My instincts clang like the late bell at school. There is danger, I feel it, even if I don't know where it's coming from.

I debate waking Gretchen. We might need to run. But in the end, I leave her where she is. No sense freaking her out if I'm wrong. I can always send Aiden to snag her. If I can fall asleep in this room after cleaning up my own death blood, he can damn well set foot in it to retrieve the mortal under our protection.

My sneakers make little scuffing sounds as I move quickly through the stone corridors, Aiden's heatless flame held out in front to light my way. I head down the spiral stairway to the great hall. The mug with Aiden's soup is gone. Either he ate it or Gretchen took care of it before she came to find me.

"Aiden," I call out.

It is the green-eyed wolf who pads out of the shadows. I don't know if he transformed after our argument or because he also senses a threat. He tilts his head at me, as though asking a question.

I hear no voice, but answer as if he'd spoken. "I'm not sure. I just have this feeling."

A crash sounds from the kitchen.

"Bard!" I shout as Aiden darts ahead.

We find the shifter crouching on a kitchen counter, his teeth bared at a figure standing backlit in the hallway. Aiden tenses to spring, his own lip curling up in a warning snarl.

"You," I breathe. "You're like a bad penny."

Wardon takes a single step out of the shadows with his hands up in front of him. He appears a little better than when he ran off. "Please, hear me out."

I glare at him. "Give me one good reason why we should?"

"Because I can help."

I cross my arms over my chest. "How? You have no magic."

He flinches at my blunt reminder. "But I have knowledge. I'm the oldest living fey royal. I have known Underhill the longest. That should be worth something to you."

Aiden crouches lower, silent and in position to spring. I

have half a mind to command him to tear the Seelie king's throat out and be done with it.

"And what do you want in return?" I raise an eyebrow. "You can't tell me you're doing this out of the goodness of your ink-black heart."

His gaze is on the wolf but at my question, it moves back to me. "All I've ever wanted was the power to protect my people. The Draugar are killing them in scores. If I help you destroy the Draugar, I will have served my purpose and can fade away at peace to make room for the next Master or Mistress of the Waves."

"That's a hell of a turnaround for a guy who was colluding with giants and trolls."

He holds my stare, his eyes still clear despite his wretched appearance. "I haven't been a perfect ruler. Neither were you."

Aiden takes a menacing step forward.

Wardon flinches but holds my gaze. "You said you plan to be better for the sake of your court. If you can change, Nicneven, why can't I?"

I study him. He appears in earnest. Is it possible that torture and torment forged Wardon into a better being?

What do you think? I ask Aiden.

He growls low. Answer enough.

"Don't trust him." Bard is still perched on the edge of the counter.

"Don't worry, I won't." But he might come in useful. "Bard, go upstairs and wake Gretchen."

The shifter hops down into a bow. "Yes, my queen."

Wardon tracks Bard's departure. "What did you offer him to secure such loyalty?"

I blow out a breath. "Not everything is a bargain or an advantage. Bard is with us because he chooses to be here. Same with Harmony. Maybe if you'd treated your people better, they wouldn't have all abandoned you to Angrboda's tender mercies."

The Master of the Waves appears skeptical, then his eyes go to where Aiden is transforming back into a man at my side.

We wait in tense silence for him to regain his composure.

"Your consort is looking a little worse for wear," Wardon smirks. "You should take better care of him."

I ignore the jibe and put a hand on Aiden's arm before he can rise to the bait. "Was Underhill telling the truth? Is Soladin's kiss the only way to cure the Kiss of Madness?"

Wardon nods once. "Sadly, yes. Each court, both Seelie and Unseelie, balance each other out. In your court death presides half the year while the other celebrates life. So it is with madness and clarity. I could control the rate of madness, but never reverse its effects."

"Is there anywhere we can go where Underhill can't spy on us?" I ask.

Wardon shakes his head. "Underhill can see everything, but she can't see everything at once."

"Is there any way to know when she's tracking us?" Like if she is watching the Nic, Wardon and Aiden show right now.

"Use your minions as sentinels."

I frown. "My minions?"

He huffs out a sigh as though I am a slow pupil. "Your spirits, the ones of the air. They will notify you of when you are being observed. There is nowhere they cannot go, even underground."

I close my eyes and hunt the way Nahini taught me, feeling for it with my mind. There is nothing for a time and then the air in the kitchen changes. It becomes cooler as if someone left a window open. The North Wind.

"Well?" Wardon's tone carries a note of impatience.

I think to it, the same way I do with Aiden. *Is she watching us?*

The pressure shifts so that my ears pop as the wind rushes out and then back into the room. It doesn't speak, doesn't send images like Aiden's wolf but there is a feeling. If I had to put a name to the emotion, I would call it grim satisfaction.

"She's not watching now."

"Underhill controls the Draugar," Aiden says. "She used runes to create them so why did she burn them up earlier?"

"She created the Draugar but she can't control them," Wardon replies as Bard returns with a sleepy-eyed Gretchen in tow.

"How do we stop them?" Aiden asks.

Wardon casts me a level look and I answer, "With *Seelenverkäufer.*"

Bard, Gretchen, and Aiden turn to face me, all wearing identical expressions of surprise. I hurry to explain, "That's why Soladin kidnapped me. He wanted to convince me to use the Wild Hunt and the Soul Reaper to destroy the Draugar."

"King Soladin will help us." Bard nods with surety and casts Wardon a censorious look. "Unlike some rulers, he actually does what is best for his people."

Wardon glares at the shifter but remains silent.

"There might be a bit of a problem with that." I tuck some hair behind my ear and shift my weight from foot to foot.

"What?" Gretchen asks.

"I sort of annihilated one of his villages earlier."

All four of them stare at me.

"Not on purpose," I say. "A mob was attacking his consort and I called the winds in to help. The people were already on the verge of a riot. I can't imagine he'll welcome me back with a smile."

Wardon leans against a table. Blackened scales flake off of him and flutter to the floor like autumn leaves. He doesn't appear to notice. "He still wants something from you. That's your way back in. Only you can command the souls of the Wild Hunt."

"But without the sword, I can't stop the Draugar."

Aiden clears his throat. "Then we need to find out who has the sword."

"Any ideas how?" I ask him.

He nods then thinks so only I can hear him. *But you aren't going to like it.*

POISON SPRING

"You're right," I say to Aiden as we trudge up the high hill just as the sun rises. "I don't like it."

In fact, there is no way on any side of the Veil I would like Aiden calling out for help from a goddess. Especially not a goddess who's already tried to kill me. "The tree of gloaming, really? That doesn't sound *at all* ominous."

"It sits on the borderland between the Seelie and Unseelie Courts and never grows or blooms. It exists in perpetual twilight."

"Why couldn't we just float up here?" I huff as the hillside grows steeper.

"My powers are…not working right." Aiden admits.

"Is it a side effect of the madness?" He looks pale, his hair unkempt. It's more than just strain.

"I'm not sure." He shakes his head. "Try not to worry about it."

Easier said than done. "Taj told the children a story about me baiting Freya. Did that actually happen?"

Aiden scrambles up the path like a sodding goat. He

reaches down a hand to assist me up to the summit. "That was before we met. But I believe that yes, it was mostly true."

I don't take his hand. "Great, so I'm going to meet a vindictive goddess who I challenged in my last life under the tree of gloaming. What could possibly go wrong?"

"I won't let her hurt you." Aiden's hand drops to his side.

I'm not really sure he can do anything to stop her but I am too focused on climbing to say anything. "I'm not afraid of Freya."

"Do us both a favor and don't tell her that." His tone is grim as he turns to face the tree. "She has an enormous ego, even for a goddess."

"You're forgetting, so do I." I flip my hair at him, striving for a light tone.

He flashes me a small smile but it doesn't reach his eyes. He starts pacing around the tree. Once, twice, three times. "We're here, damn you." I hear him mutter.

Grabbing him by the arm, I turn him to face me. "What aren't you telling me?"

He blinks as though I've surprised him. "What do you mean?"

Tilting my head to one side, I study him. "Are we ever going to talk about what happened?"

"Which part?" he toes the ground, looking more like a confused seventeen-year-old than an ageless demigod.

I cast him a level look. "All of it."

When he frowns. "I didn't mean…." He shakes his head and starts over. "Last night, I didn't intend for things to go so far."

"And is that why you asked me to kill you?"

"I'm a danger to you. I always have been. You died because of me and I…."

I get it then. "You're afraid."

His eyes meet mine and he doesn't deny it.

Taj's words. *Loving is selfless. It's why mated pairs are so rare. It requires two souls willing to accept not only each other but everything about themselves as well. The good, the bad and the ugly. Most aren't strong enough to do that.*

As I stare into Aiden's eyes, it hits me. Aiden's wolf has accepted me as his mate. But *Aiden* hasn't. He can't fully embrace me because he's never accepted himself. Never forgiven himself.

His self-loathing is keeping us apart.

I blow out a frustrated breath. "You know I'm new to this relationship stuff. But even I get that keeping things from the people you care about doesn't help establish trust."

He looks back to the black-limbed tree, then exhales. "I was with Freya. Before everything with my dad. And Nari."

I blink. "When you say with…?"

"We were lovers."

I blurt the question before I think better of it. "Did you love her?"

His brows pull together as though it pains him as much to say the words as it hurts me to hear them. "She was beautiful. And she made me feel good. I thought I did."

He'd been changed when he was seventeen-years-old. Freaking cradle robbing goddess. "I have no idea how to respond to this news."

He runs a hand through his already shaggy dark hair. "It's not news, it's ancient history. I never would have told you if you weren't going to meet her."

My temper snaps. "Seriously?"

"I never told you before."

I gesture back down the steep incline at the Summer Palace. "And look how well *that* turned out."

He blanches and I feel like a bully. "Okay, that was below the belt. Sorry."

When he doesn't say anything, I huff out a breath. "Cut me some slack. Like I said, I'm new to this."

He moves closer so that I catch a hint of his scent. It smells...different somehow. Less healthy than usual. But before I can puzzle out the thought he murmurs. "I'm just trying to do what's best for you."

"How about you let me decide what's best for me and you do what's best for you? In case no one's ever told you before, you are kind of a hot mess, Aiden."

A ghost of his usual playful smile. "So, you're saying you think I'm hot?"

No need to deny the obvious but I am done letting him distract me and restructure our conversations to hide from discomfort. He's about to get full throttle Nic, pissed-off and uncensored. No more keeping it light. Time to drop some truth bombs on his ass. "You're unhappy and full of self-loathing. Maybe you ought to fix that."

His grin fades away and he stares at me as though he's never seen me before. "It's not so simple."

"Actually, it is." This really isn't the time or place for this particular conversation, but if I wait until everything is perfect, I'll be holding my peace forever. So not my style. "Just figure out what makes you happy. Stop blaming yourself for all the shit that's gone wrong. You may have been born a god but that doesn't mean you can control everything. You've got to stop punishing yourself. Promise yourself that you'll do better, accept that you deserve better."

Even if it isn't me. I don't voice the last words, but I can't help but think them. I hope he doesn't hear them or scent the sadness that the thought of him ditching me brings.

His lips part as though he is about to say something more but there is a booming clap of thunder across the cloudless sky.

One second we are alone beneath the tree. A moment

later a man and a woman are standing on top of a hill beneath the twisted black branches. They are both tall, the man has to be at least six and a half feet and heavily muscled. He has a thick golden beard and gold-brown eyes. He's dressed in jeans and a fitted black sweater that shows off his rippling pectorals. The woman is only an inch or so shorter than her male companion. Her ruby red dress is obviously custom, fitted to the miles of curves she's showing off. Her hair is dark and piled up atop her head in a mass of curls. But the most striking thing about her is her eyes. Her irises are a frosty blue, the pupils shaped like those of a cat.

Cats, I recall, pulled Freya's chariot in the Norse legends.

"Thor." Aiden greets the man first. "What are you doing here?"

"Is that any way to greet your uncle, boy?" The man booms in a voice that makes the branches on the tree of gloaming shake. He chuckles, his bright blue eyes full of mirth.

"Uncle?" I ask.

"Honorary, not by blood." Aiden's expression is hard as stone.

Thor waves it off as though the technicalities are beneath him. "Now Váli, you know it had to be done. For the good of Asgard."

I can feel Aiden tense, and odder still, I sense his wolf prowling so close to the surface. As though he is looking for any reason to attack the blustering fool god who has dismissed his loss and suffering as an unfortunate side effect.

Aiden doesn't reply, just turns to face Freya, who is studying me for some reason.

I stare back, my heart racing. Lover. This goddess was Aiden's lover. After the night before I have a whole new understanding of what exactly their relationship might have entailed.

The thought makes my stomach flip over unpleasantly. It isn't jealousy, at least I don't think that's it. More disgust. He'd been so young when he'd been cast out of Asgard. What was the term Chloe had used regarding our age difference?

Icky.

The difference being experience, not age. He'd been a youth, she a goddess accustomed to worship. And from the little he'd said on the matter I get the impression that Aiden regrets the liaison bitterly.

Another adult who had screwed up royally, who'd let him down.

She's one of mine. I can sense it coming off her, the predator. Not Thor. Though he's a bit of a dupe, he's not inherently wicked but Freya....

Temptation claws at me, to kiss her, to kill her and bury her body under that damned tree. For hurting him and to keep her from hurting any others.

I level my gaze on her, deciding to let her set the tone. Better she doesn't know what I'm fantasizing about.

Silence. Thor shifts his weight, his thick blond eyebrows pulling together as though trying to puzzle something out. Or maybe hold a thought. Aiden is still as a statue by my side but I swear I can hear his heartbeat.

*I won't let her hurt you, h*e'd said to me. I would do everything in my power to ensure she wouldn't hurt him, either.

"You look different, Nicneven," Freya says at last.

It isn't a compliment so I feel no need to offer thanks. "Aiden tells me you know who has my sword."

Her plump red lips curve up. "I do."

"And what do you want in exchange for this information?" Because undoubtedly, she wants something.

"Your vow, Queen of the Unseelie. That you will kill Underhill and destroy the runes she possesses."

I stare at her a minute. "You're afraid of her."

I feel Aiden flinch mentally even though his body remains still. Even Thor seems to tense up.

Freya hisses, her cat eyes narrowing to slits as she snaps, "Watch yourself, little queen. I am a goddess of the Vanir tribe and one of the great warriors of Asgard."

"From the little I know about the gods of Asgard, you all seem uncommonly flawed."

Nic. Even Aiden's mental voice holds a warning.

But I don't give a shit. This goddess—who in my mind is little better than a child molester—wants something from me. So she can kill me. Big. Freaking. Deal.

"Tell me why you're bothering to enlist me to off Pharaildis. Why not send one of your many devoted worshipers? Someone who you actually like?"

"It is you who are fated to kill Underhill." Thor puffs up like a blowfish. "It is your destiny."

I offer him a tight smile. "I'm more of a make my own destiny kind of girl. Since I have an in with the Fates and all."

"Enough of your impudence." Freya's beautiful face flushes crimson. I can tell she wants to gank me in the worst way. The fact that she doesn't indicates she really does believe she needs me.

"Tell me how then." I switch tactics. "How do I kill the being that's inseparable from the land?"

Instead of answering, Freya turns to the males. "Leave us."

"What?" Thor's thick blond brows pull together. Judging from the god's reaction, this isn't part of the script he's been given.

Aiden puts his back to the goddess and turns his full attention on me. He's waiting. Though I don't mystically command his body anymore, I know he won't budge unless I tell him to go.

"Just a little girl talk." I force a tight smile.

He stares at me a long moment and then gestures for

Thor. "Come, uncle. Let me show you the Enrapturing River. Excellent fishing."

Thor still looks muddled but allows Aiden to haul him down the steep slope and toward the valley on the far side.

"You have quite a hold over Váli." Freya moves closer. "Or is it the wolf who is held captive?"

I have no intention of discussing my relationship with her. "His name is Aiden."

"For the Queen of the Shadow Throne, you have always been full of fire." Her tone indicates this isn't a trait she admires.

I recall the story Taj had told about the Nicneven of old taunting the cat-eyed goddess. "We're alone now, what is it you wanted to say?"

"Call your winds. Make sure her eyes are not upon us."

I almost make a crack about the all-powerful goddess not knowing if she's being spied on, but manage to hold my tongue. Instead, I close my eyes and reach out with my mind the way Nahini taught me. My hair is blown back as the North Wind comes out, in a burst of rippling current. It is excited, glad to be useful, to be near me.

I ask the wind spirit the same question I did earlier. *Is she watching us?*

It tugs at my clothes playfully as though giving me an all clear.

While she waits, Freya walks around me in a slow circle. The hem of her long ruby gown dragging across the ground like a pool of shimmering sunrise. Somehow, I doubt she has to worry about grass stains.

"We're unobserved," I tell her. Though I don't dismiss the wind, I encourage it to hold back a bit. Having it nearby is comforting.

She stops abruptly and looks at me. "Do you know why you have the Kiss of Death? Your goodnight kiss? Why though your immortal and mortal bodies have died you are still capable of killing with the merest brush of your lips?"

"It's tied to my heart," I say. "Like Soladin's Kiss of Clarity."

But Freya shakes her head. "No. The fey kings and queens do have power tied to their immortal hearts. But you are the strongest, have always been the strongest because of what Pharaildis did.

"In a land of ice and mist, the land of death we call Niflheim, there is a spring, *Hvergelmir*. Its waters are poison and all who would drink from it are condemned to die. Before you were born, Underhill drank that water, hoping it would end her misery and exile."

It's almost impossible for me not to react. Almost. But I can see by the intense way Freya is watching me that she's waiting for me to flinch, to show any sign of weakness.

If I didn't loathe the sadistic goddess with every fiber of my being, I might have. After all, it's not every day a girl learns her mother tried to end her life before it began.

If she is disappointed by my lack of response, she doesn't show it. Instead, she turns away. "Obviously, it didn't work. The terms of her imprisonment offer no hope of reprieve, not even death."

"But who is that strong?" Even as I ask the question, I feel the answer in my bones. "The Fates."

"Yes, your precious *aunties*," the goddess sneers. "All the Norns are cruel, but those three have always been utterly remorseless."

I think of Addy's patient hands as they stroke a sick dog. Chloe's ecstatic laugh when Jasmine tells her about the wonders of junior high. They've done awful things. But remorseless? The women I know aren't the ones Freya is talking about. They've been raising an accidental serial killer and doing their best to ensure that I don't get caught. That my gift is never unleashed on an innocent.

Which means whatever Pharaildis did to earn her punishment must be even worse than habitual killing.

I say none of this to Freya. There will be time later for me to sort through it all. "The toxin in my kiss, it's from the water in that spring? Not tied to Unseelie magic?"

"*Hvergelmir*. It is that poison that infects not just your heart but your soul as well. It was thought by some that having a creature with such power would prove useful." Her sniff of derision makes it clear that she hadn't been on board with that plan and resented having been overruled.

"Even if Pharaildis takes that blackened shriveled mass you call a heart, the poison in your soul will still compel you to end life. You are her greatest triumph, an unnatural abomination. A being born to kill. And she doesn't even know it."

I don't react at all. Not to her barely veiled insults or the news that I have legendary poison attached to my soul. My black heart pounds though. What can that possibly mean for Aiden, my mate?

Freya looks slightly disappointed that I don't come up swinging but she plods on. "Once she has Soladin's heart, Underhill will ask for yours. I want you to give it to her."

I raise a brow. "Give me one good reason why I should?"

The goddess holds out her hand and there is a brilliant flash of blue-white light, like a star going nova. I raise an arm to shield my eyes, but as quickly as it appeared, it disappears, leaving Freya holding a sword.

And not just any sword.

"You'll have to vow to me that you will if you want *Seelenverkäufer* back. You've been careless with her."

My hands clench into fists. With the Soul Reaper, I can go back to the farm, collect the Wild Hunt, do what Soladin had asked. Then a thought occurs. "You took the sword?"

"I did."

"Why?" And had she killed Isolde as well? Or was Aiden right, was the blood staged to make it look like the traitor had been slain?

"To keep the sword safe until the time came. Thor was correct when he told you your destiny is to destroy Underhill."

"You said she can't be killed, not even with water from *Hvergelmir*."

Freya holds the sword aloft. "Her body can't die, it's true. But with this, you can extract her soul. She'll be as good as dead."

I shiver at the thought. Could I really turn my mother into a vegetable, forever to be on life support? Even if she had tried to commit suicide, and by extension abort me, she is still the reason I'm here. "Extract her soul. And do what with it, exactly?"

Instead of answering the goddess asks a question of her own. "You've seen the chaos she's wrought on these lands. Pharaildis doesn't want to rule this world. She wants to destroy it and all the fey who reside here. And if she has all four hearts of all four rulers and a growing army of Draugar, she'll have everything she needs to decimate not just this realm but all the nine worlds. That much power can't be contained by one being. It threatens the very fabric of the universe. You need to give her what she wants, and then strike before she can."

I open my mouth but a gust of air pushes against my back. *Her gaze turns this way.*

"She's going to see us," I extend a hand to Freya. "Give me *Seelenverkäufer*."

She steps out of my reach. "Give me your vow."

I can lie. The goddess doesn't know that. But something deep inside tells me if I do fib just to get my hands on Soul

Reaper, I'll end up regretting it. "If she sees us scheming, I'll never get close enough."

The wind grows more frantic, whipping our clothes and hair.

"Now or never," I push.

Freya tosses me the sword and vanishes.

I don't hesitate to cut down in a wide stripe, parting the Veil between Underhill and the mortal realm.

I don't let myself look back down the slope toward Aiden before I step through.

Through the Man's Eyes

Nic's icy winter apple scent disappears.

Aiden turns away from where Thor wades up to his midriff in the stream to catch trout in his beefy fists to face the mountain. The wolf's voice in his head is insistent, even as he begins to dissolve back up the slope to where he left Nic with Freya.

Both have vanished.

His heart pounds. Did the goddess take Nic somewhere? To another realm? He knew he never should have left them alone. No good can come from leaving your new girlfriend and an ex-lover alone together, even if they don't possess godlike powers.

Then he sees it, the shimmering tear in the Veil as the souls bound to it scramble to repair the damage. A clean sharp slice large enough for only one weapon can make.

Seelenverkäufer.

The cut closes more slowly than it had before the massive tear in the Veil had come about. Not enough souls to repair all the damage.

Through the slice, he spies a familiar hilltop. It's his hill-top, the one where he'd planned to build a house.

And sprawled on the ground, where the remains of their interrupted picnic lay, is Nic, looking windblown and miserable.

Time has progressed in Midgard. The trees, just beginning to turn color when he crossed, are now leafless. How much time has passed?

He moves toward her instinctively but she holds up a hand. "You can't! The madness."

The wolf is urging him forward. The cut is closing. She's almost beyond reach.

His heartbeat is erratic. Not enough time to tell her what he needs to, to apologize for the night before, to say all the things she should hear.

Their gazes lock. "Nic, I—,"

She holds up the sword, her crystal blue eyes swimming with tears. "I'm coming back for you. Look after them. I love you."

The tear closes and she's gone.

He falls to his knees, a bellow ripping from his chest, half howl, half grief, his thoughts erratic, coming in bursts like that of machine gunfire.

Gone. She's gone.

She'd left him.

She *loves* him.

"Well well. I didn't think she'd do it. I underestimated her. Or overestimated your importance." A hand lands on his shoulder. "Come with me, wolfling."

He looks up into a face so similar to the Nicneven he'd first met that a sense of déjà vu washes over him.

But it is Underhill, not Nicneven who has come for him.

He bares his teeth and lunges for her, flaming sword

appearing in his hand. She is the reason he isn't with Nic. She caused this rift.

She laughs and the wave of madness swamps him. The wolf scrambles to take the upper hand. Aiden can't fight it. He crumples to the ground as he sees the wolf tearing her throat out, sees Nari's pale hand, hears his father laugh.

No. No.

Thud.

The last sound isn't coming from within his mind but from the world around him. The visions and the feelings back off, just as Thor appears.

"Come on boy, shake it off," the thunderer booms.

Underhill is sprawled face down in the mud. Thor's enormous hammer pins her to the ground.

"He's mine," she struggles, but the weight of the thing is clearly keeping her down.

"He is of the blood of Asgard." Thor steps forward. "You have no claim to him."

As if to punctuate his words, lightning flashes, hitting the tree of gloaming. "Give me your vow, creature, that you will no longer harm him and I will let you up."

"Never," Underhill spits.

Thor shrugs. "Then I guess you'll have to stay there. Shame. I liked that hammer."

He turns and begins to walk away.

Pharaildis claws at the ground, her hands ripping grass out by the roots as if she's trying to drag herself out from beneath the massive weight of Thor's hammer.

It doesn't so much as wobble on her back.

"Wait!" she cries.

Thor pivots on one heel. "Change of heart?"

"I vow," Underhill says grudgingly. "That I will do no further harm to Váli Sigynjarson."

"That's more like it." The thunderer beams and lifts his hand to call his hammer.

"No, wait!" Aiden gasps.

But it's too late.

The hammer returns to Thor's hand as though drawn by a powerful magnet. Underhill gives him a vicious smile and vanishes.

Aiden sags to the ground.

"Now now, boy. Why so glum? I've fixed your problem." Thor hauls him to his feet as though plucking a dandelion.

Aiden's head and heart are competing for which causes him the most pain. He doesn't bother to explain the way Pharaildis twisted her words. That her promise to cause no further harm only kept her from *actively* torturing him again. It would do nothing to mitigate the creeping madness that kept him on this side of the Veil or curtail the Draugar.

For a moment Aiden understands why his father had been tempted into betraying the gods of Asgard. Out of sheer frustration with their selfishness and stupidity. It excuses nothing Loki had done, yet he could relate.

"Now, where did Freya scurry off to? And your little dumpling is gone, too?" Thor frowns at the otherwise empty hilltop.

"She probably went back to the castle." His breathing is still erratic but he manages to point back to the summer palace where Bard, Gretchen, and Wardon are waiting.

I'll be back for you.

Nic, though immortal, could still lie as easily as he misdirects Thor. He wants her safe on the other side of the Veil. Safe with her aunts and the Hunt.

Thor clasps his shoulder hard enough to send him to his knees. "Well then, we best be off."

"We?" Aiden frowns up at the massive god.

233

"I thought I could stick around in case you run afoul of any more trouble."

He tries to think of some way to explain to Thor that being with the god is the greatest source of trouble he can run across. In the end, he decides there is no way to tell the thunderer to kiss off that won't enrage the short-tempered deity. "In that case, we should hurry."

Breathe. I tell myself as the tear in the Veil seals itself and I am once again cut off from Aiden. I've done harder things than this.

But not many.

I hadn't wanted to cross back over without him. Or to leave Bard or Gretchen behind. Wardon, I wouldn't lose any sleep over, but there is also Taj, Soladin and countless fey who are at the mercy of the Draugar.

At the mercy of my mother.

The merciless harpy.

I want to roll over in the leaves, to curl up like a pill bug, to sob. The things Freya had told me, the desperate look on Aiden's face as the tear shut. As he realized I was leaving him behind, were shredding my black heart.

Get up. The command comes from somewhere inside. *You need to get to the farm, to gather the Hunt. To go back there. No time to lose your shit.*

Slowly, I push up off the ground. *Seelenverkäufer* is still in one hand. The massive weight of the Soul Reaper grounds me, helps me to focus on what I need to do next.

Get back to the farm. Mobilize the Hunt. Talk to my aunts.

And then I will go back for Aiden.

As I take my first step toward home, leaves crunch under my feet.

I stare up in horror as I realize all the overhead branches are bare. The night we'd left, they'd just started to turn color. How long have I been gone?

A cold chill rushes up my back, stirs the fallen leaves, whipping them up into a frenzy as though imbibing them with new life. The North Wind. It feels different on this side of the Veil.

I reach out with my mind and try to communicate with it. But there is no deliberate response. I can scent snow and ice on it though. Winter is near. And in spite of going nonstop for days sans sleep and living on more than a cup of soup or a handful of berries, I feel stronger than I did.

My season.

Without Aiden to transport me mystically or any sort of conveyance, I'll have to travel on foot either by road or overland. The road is farther but less treacherous. I set out at a steady jog, the North Wind at my back and the Soul Reaper in my hand.

I don't make it a mile when gravel crunches under tires. I move to the side and am surprised to see my battered old pick-up, Addy behind the wheel.

And a smug-looking Harmony at her side.

"I knew you'd be here," the seer says as soon as I open the passenger's side door.

"Of course you did." I am glad to see her though, to see both of them. "How long have I been gone?"

"Fourteen months."

I flinch. "So long?"

"It could have been worse." Addy casts me a brief once over. "You're undamaged?"

That remains to be seen. "I'll do. How much do you know?"

"Freda and Nahini already have the Hunt mobilized." Addy maneuvers the truck around a hairpin turn. "They await your command."

I exhale and nod. "Aiden will go back to collect Bard and Gretchen and then head straight for Soladin's castle."

"The last royal standing," Harmony says. "Are you really going to give his heart to Underhill?"

I don't know. On the one hand, the Seelie king of the Green Throne had kidnapped me. On the other, I didn't want to encourage Underhill's scheme. "What do your visions tell you?" I ask.

She shakes her head. "Your path is fraught with choices, too many to see the outcomes clearly."

I turn to the Fate worse than death. "And you?"

Addy doesn't respond verbally but her knuckles turn white where she grips the steering wheel.

Not a good sign.

I blow out a breath. "All right, our first priority has to be protecting the fey from all the threats. From Underhill, the Draugar or the gods, all of it."

"You can use the Soul Reaper to embody the souls tethered to the Hunt into the Draugar," Harmony says.

But I shake my head. "Those souls are my responsibility. We don't know what will happen to them if we do embody them within the dead."

"And with the knowledge of the runes, Underhill will just make more," Addy adds.

The turn off to the farm comes into sight and the truck fishtails as my aunt accelerates up the drive. I see rows and rows of the Hunt lined up in the field. At the head, wearing her glittering armor like dragon scales is Nahini.

Jasmine, Freda and Chloe are standing on the porch steps. Chloe doesn't wait for the truck to roll to a stop before running to greet me.

"Nic!" She breathes my name and pulls me into a tight embrace. She is wearing a thick cream-colored sweater that comes down to her knees and smells of vanilla chai latte. "You've been gone too long."

I startle at the embrace—we aren't big huggers—but I ease into her hold.

Then another body slams into us in a desperate grip, this one lower down but just as fierce. Jasmine. I start at the changes fourteen months have wrought on her. She's several inches taller and looks less like a little girl and more like a young woman.

"I've missed you," she sniffles against my ruined clothing.

My throat closes up. Her easy affection is like nothing I've ever known. "I missed you too. We'll have to catch up as soon as we've got the chance."

"As soon as we get Aiden and the others back." She nods.

Behind us, the truck door slams. Jasmine jumps and flushes when a hand lands on her shoulder.

"Jazz, go get Nahini and Alric." Freda's tone brooks nononsense. The tone of the commander of the Wild Hunt.

"Yes, First."

"Good to see you, my queen." Freda bows. "The Hunt is ready to leave at your earliest convenience."

"We'll return immediately." I try to give her the sword but Freda puts up her hands.

"No, I am not worthy. Twice the Soul Reaper disappeared on my watch. The blade is entrusted to you as the commander of the Wild Hunt. It is you who must wield it."

Chloe puts a hand on my arm. "Nic, slow down. Eat a real meal, have a shower and strategize before you go tearing back across the Veil."

"She has a point, my queen." Alric comes to stand beside Freda. "The seer has told us much, but we need to know what you wish for us to do."

The urge to act, to get back to Aiden claws at me. But they have a point. It's not just our friends at risk but the entire fey population. I recall that the orphanage Taj brought me to. The children who'd been so enthralled with tales from the great queen Nicneven. Some of them had been Unseelie refugees, fleeing war and Druagar. I owe them some consideration.

"All right. Gather everyone vital to the house in fifteen minutes for a planning meeting. Tell the rest of the force to await our signal. We will be crossing the Veil tonight."

RETURN TO THE GREEN THRONE

THROUGH THE MAN'S EYES

*A*iden breathes a sigh of relief when he catches Gretchen's mortal scent as well as Bard's combination of elderberry wine and spice along with the weak dregs of the sea that cling to Wardon's person. The thought had plagued him all the way down the hill that Underhill might have gone for Nic's courtiers in retaliation for her leaving. With Thor at his side, he strides through the rear entrance, past the kale yard, and into the kitchen. Gretchen leaps up at his appearance. Her expression falls when she beholds his companion. "Who is this? Aiden, where's Nic?"

"She's getting help," Aiden says. It isn't a lie. Living with the fey had taught him that a twisted truth goes over better than a lie, especially to prevent panic. He doesn't want Gretchen to feel abandoned by her friend. Bad enough he does.

Part of him is still in shock. His mate crossed the Veil without telling him her plan. Circumstances had forced her hand, but she'd just...left him.

I'm coming back for you. Look after them. I love you.

He clears his throat, ignoring the stinging behind his eyes.

"We're going to meet up with her later. This is my…uncle, Thor."

Gretchen's scowl deepens, but Bard drops to one knee before the thunderer. "Most exalted one. We are humbled to be in your divine presence."

Wardon doesn't fall to the floor, but his lips part and he appears, well, thunderstruck.

"None of that, now." Thor, who enjoys worship as much as the next god but who adopts a more casual air in the company of his worshipers, helps the shifter to his feet. Bard is taller than Thor, but he's built on the wiry side, so he appears smaller.

The god settles himself at the counter and turns to the sole mortal. "Wench, fetch me ale and food."

Gretchen pushes her glasses up her freckled nose. "Are you talking to me?"

"Indeed I am." Thor slaps a meaty palm down so that the pans hanging from the beam in the ceiling rattle. "Be about it."

Instead of complying, Gretchen folds her arms across her chest. Aiden studies her a moment. She appears different than she had in Midgard. He's been so engulfed in his own worries that he didn't notice before. Her posture is straighter, as though she's learned to carry herself with dignity and her gaze brooks no nonsense.

The way she stares down her nose at Thor indicates trouble.

"First of all," she says to the god. "My name is Gretchen, not wench. And you forgot the magic word."

Thor's Cro-Magnon brow draws down in a scowl. "You require magic in exchange for ale?"

"I'll get the ale," Aiden interrupts before the god decides to smite the mortal for plaguing him with confusion. Then again, Gretchen looks about ready to headbutt the god. He turns to the enchanted pantry, extracts a jug of mead along with a round of cheese and a jar of pickles. A light snack for the thunder god. He'll have to make another trip if anyone else is hungry.

"Did you get the information we need?" Wardon moves to his side.

Aiden sets the food on the counter and tries not to flinch at the nearness of the Master of the Waves. His wolf remembers all too well how Wardon had treated them. But Nic had thought the defeated king might prove useful.

"I believe so." He'd been thinking it over on the journey back to the palace. He still has the madness to contend with and Soladin remains the only cure. Nic knew that, and Soladin's heart is the price Underhill demands. She would look for him there. "We need to find King Soladin."

Thor finishes the ale with a noisy gulp, belches, then slams the jug down on the floor, where the crockery shatters. Gretchen huffs out an exasperated sigh. Bard wraps his long fingers around her arm and she turns away.

"But does your queen have a plan?" Wardon pushes. "What of Underhill and the Draugar?"

"I have no answers for you." Aiden glares at Wardon, letting the wolf peek out through his eyes. "I have shared what I know. Come with us or go your own way, but do not plague me with questions."

Wardon pushes away from the table and stalks outside.

You're unhappy and full of self-loathing. Nic's words drift back to him as though she sent them on a sea breeze.

Did Wardon's outburst stem, not from a sense of entitlement but more because he blames himself for his failures. The same way Aiden did?

The thought is uncomfortable. He doesn't want to have empathy for the male who'd had his eye removed. Who'd ordered Nahini tortured until her thick dark hair started to turn white. Yet wasn't Nic always pushing him to look at the world differently? Challenging his long-held beliefs?

Her eyes, brimming with tears. *I'm coming back for you. Look after them. I love you.*

He was cursed with a wolf, teetering on the edge of a blade between sanity and madness. His own father foretold that he would be her doom.

And yet she claims she loves him.

My mate, the wolf thinks with pride.

How is it the destructive animal within him can accept that she will return his regard but the god—the man, cannot?

He is unhappy and full of self-loathing. But what could he do?

Again, that phantom response. *Maybe you ought to fix that.*

To distract himself, he returns to the pantry where he finds several empty sacks. He beckons the shifter over and hands one to him. "Fill this with as much food as you can. It's going to be a long journey with a hungry god in tow."

Bard places a hand on his shoulder. "I wanted to thank you, Aiden."

He blinks. "What for?"

The shifter holds his gaze. "You got that water for me, to heal me."

Unused to expressions of gratitude from the fey, Aiden turns back to his packing. "You're part of my mate's court. I do what I must for her."

"I am still in your debt," Bard says quietly. "No matter the reason."

Aiden does his best not to cringe. Having a powerful fey in one's debt is akin to having a wolf by the tail. Sooner or later, the beast will get free and then you're cornered.

We do not fear the fey or other wolves. His beast sneers.

But Aiden isn't so sanguine. "You owe me nothing, shifter.

But if you feel you do, then vow to me that you will never betray the Queen of the Shadow Throne."

Bard doesn't hesitate to put a hand over his heart. "I so swear it."

Not even a moment's pause in return for an immortal life of service. Much as Aiden had vowed so long ago. Would Nic be happy that she could trust the shifter completely?

If not, Aiden knows who she will blame.

He smiles and turns back to stocking supplies.

For better or worse, he's just secured her an immortal ally.

It's tempting to linger under the shower spray and dissolve like a pile of salt. I don't though. Instead, I scrub with my favorite herbal soap and a rough terrycloth to strip off the layers of grime that have collected on my bare skin over the course of my adventures in Underhill.

Once dried and dressed in a fresh sweatshirt, jeans and sturdy boots I move to the kitchen. Addy is seated at the table, hands folded in front of her. Chloe places a bowl of steaming vegetarian chili down before me and then returns to the stove to fill two more bowls.

No one else is in the house.

I pick up my spoon and twirl it in the middle of the bowl, displacing quinoa and beans to the outer edges. "She wants to kill you."

Neither one asks who she is. They know.

Setting the spoon down, I glance between them. "You imprisoned her there?"

"She imprisoned herself through her own actions." Chloe doesn't turn from the stove. "The same way Sissy condemned herself when she left you alone."

It's the same line my aunts fed me to help me live with my actions. *It's for the greater good. They brought it on themselves.* Is this also what they tell themselves so they can sleep at night?

Do I still believe it? Are we all just agents of fate, the executioners of justice?

No. I can't afford to think that way. Consequences have actions. That's why my mother is imprisoned. "What did she do?"

Chloe sets down her bowl. "Are you sure you're ready for this?"

At my nod, she and Addy exchange a glance and then Chloe takes a deep breath, as though steeling herself. "She called for your father's death."

"What?" Shock fills me to my core. I knew it had to be something horrific, but this? "Wait, you knew my father? Who was he?"

Addy leans back in her chair, her gaze level. "John the Baptist."

My mouth drops open. "A saint?"

"It's why the punishment was so severe. Pharaildis was young and beautiful. Influential. She asked for his head on a silver platter and her father gave it to her."

I remember the flash of hatred in her gaze. *You look like him.*

Nicneven. Daughter of the little saint.

"Why?" I whisper. I'm not sure what I'm asking. Why would she do such a thing Why didn't they tell me sooner?

"We don't deal in whys," Addy says briskly. "Only actions. And her actions required imprisonment."

"You need to eat, honey." Chloe smells of burnt sugar.

I pick up my spoon again and take a bite. The chili is delicious and flavorful, I'm sure but I might as well be eating sand for all the notice I take of it.

My aunts study me as they consume their own dinners. I

wonder what they are waiting for. Me to scream and carry on and rage that it isn't true.

How can it be true?

John the freaking Baptist.

I can't deal with this right now. Later, after I get Aiden back, I will try to make sense of the impossible.

When the bowl is empty, I pick up my napkin and tap it to my lips. "Can she? Kill you?"

"She wouldn't be the first to try." Addy pushes her dinner off to the side.

I twist the napkin in my fingers. "This is different though. She has unbelievable power over the land. And she wants to annihilate you."

Addy nods. "She's very angry. She's *always* been angry."

"Will she?" I find there's a lump in my throat. "If I don't kill her, will she be able to hurt you?"

Chloe sets her own spoon back in her bowl. How many meals have we shared at this table, exactly this way?

"We can't tell you that, Nic." Chloe puts a hand over mine. Her scent has changed to cumin and coriander, although that might be the chili. "We cannot influence you in any way."

"But you're my family." I stare down into the empty bowl, my stomach in knots. It's true, the women before me had suffered and sacrificed all for my benefit. They are more family than Underhill had ever been, mother or no.

"What do you think you should do?" Addy asks me gently.

"Whatever I have to for Aiden and the others. I promised to protect them."

"And that vow compels you to help, even though you can still lie?"

I open my mouth to say yes then snap it closed, another question snagging my attention. "Wait a second. How do you know I can still lie?"

Chloe smiles softly.

"It was you? I thought that Underhill...?" I shake my head.

"Underhill has no idea that you can tell falsehoods." Chloe puts a finger to her lips. "And neither does a certain goddess of love and beauty."

"But how? Why?" I'm starting to feel like a toddler who has gone too long without a nap and no one will answer her questions.

Addy smiles a bit. "We're still important in some circles. To some important people. Underhill can't lie, but she can mislead and she believes the same to be true about you. Perhaps you can use that to your advantage."

"And everything I was told about my goodnight kiss?" I glance between them. "Is that true too?"

Chloe nods. "It is. We don't know exactly who smuggled her that water from the tainted spring."

"Though we have our suspicions," Addy adds, her expression growing dark.

"But the spell we cast protected her life. She thought it was part of her punishment, but really we were only trying to save you from anything Underhill, in all her rage and despair might do."

"Why though?"

"That damned wolf isn't the only one who would risk everything to save you." Addy looks at me with the most forthright gaze I've ever seen. "We knew the great queen of the Unseelie would come from the hill herself. Even before we knew you as Nic, even before you were ours, we knew you were and always will be, destined for greatness."

I sit there, absorbing all they've told me when a knock sounds on the door. Freda.

"Are you ready?" Addy gets up, but instead of moving to let the Wild Hunt in, she places a hand on my shoulder in an uncharacteristic show of support.

I look up into her eyes, see they are swirling. A glance over to Chloe shows hers look the same.

The mighty Fates, whom even the gods fear.

"I don't have a choice, do I?"

"We all have choices. Every single day," Addy smiles softly. "And we believe you'll make the right one. Everything happens for a reason."

I put a hand over hers. Out of the two of them, Chloe is usually more demonstrative, so it means even more that Addy is offering up this kernel of belief in me. Not because she has the power to see the future, but because she is unflinching in her convictions.

"Thank you." I reach my free hand toward Chloe and squeeze her fingers. "Both of you. For everything."

They'd been protecting me before I was even born. Had taken me in and made me everything that I am. The good, the bad and every shade of gray in between.

I exhale and collect the dirty dishes, taking them to the sink. In my last life, I'd had servants to take care of such trivialities. In my last life, I'd been spoiled and selfishly short-sighted. Chloe and Addy made me stronger, better. They believe in me.

When the dishes are done I turn back to face my Fates. "Let them in."

While Addy goes to the door, I gesture to Chloe.

She takes me in her arms and hugs me tightly, murmuring in my ear, "You didn't take my advice, did you?"

I swallow and hug her back. We'd never been a family of huggers. "No, I didn't keep it light. He's mine, Chloe. I've never felt the way he makes me feel. And I can't imagine ever being with anyone else."

She lets me go, a sad smile on her lips. "Addy said you would. Just be prepared for what comes next."

I pick up on the note of warning in her voice. "Prepared for what, exactly?"

"I don't really know. Each mated pair is different." She exhales and pinches the bridge of her nose. "While only one of you acknowledged the mate tie, it didn't change. It was like a jacket hanging in a closet. Now that you've accepted him into your heart, you've empowered it to become more. Like a living thing, it will grow and change with you both, becoming what you both need. But it has needs that must be fed as well."

I thought about the way I had felt him when we'd touched and kissed. The overwhelming sensations that had taken both of us unaware.

"What if Aiden doesn't accept himself the way he's accepted me?" I ask. "What if he can't accept the connection going both ways?"

Chloe's expression is sad. "Then your bond will deteriorate. Love can't grow in poison soil."

The Green Throne is under siege.

Not from the Draugar, but a mob of angry fey. They swarm about just outside the tree line that separates the Seelie courtier's province from the fey. A few brave souls cross the line, only to have trees of all shapes and sizes spring up in their path, redirecting them away from the palace.

The mob's call is carried on the wind up to where the unearthly host spills from the temporary cut in the Veil. "Let us in. Let us in. Let us in!"

I stand in the stirrups of my mount, who Alric assures me is as sweet-tempered as I am sour. I've only been on horseback a few times, preferring Aiden's instant transportation or my battered old pick-up to a living creature that might decide to shake me off at a moment's notice.

Aiden. I think. *Where are you?*

There is no answer. He must be too far off. At least I hope that's the case, that Chloe's dire prediction about our bond collapsing isn't coming true.

"I did this." I clutch *Seelenverkäufer* tightly in my right hand.

"My queen?" Nahini comes up beside me.

"I caused this." Damn it, I knew I shouldn't have left the marketplace. Had Taj even made it out? "And now I need to make it right."

"Your orders, my queen?" This from Jasmine, who looks adorably badass in her golden breastplate. She is acting as the go-between for her mother who is riding at the rear of the procession.

Freda doesn't like my plan, partly because she won't be charging into battle at the head of the Hunt, but she is enough of a soldier that she accepted her orders without question or complaint.

"Tell your mother and Alric they are to proceed as ordered. Then come back immediately."

Jasmine nods and spurs her massive warhorse, who looks like he could eat mine for breakfast, to the back of the army.

"We could fly over them," Nahini suggests. "It would be safer."

I agree with her, it would be safer if we could just flit and fly above the crowd. But it also wouldn't be right. "Some of those people are Unseelie subjects. They are hungry and frightened and deserve to be heard."

"Soladin's courtiers should be out there." Nahini's lush lips thin with disapproval. "It is their job to keep the peace."

"I don't want the whole Hunt descending on the crowd," I tell her. "They've been through enough."

"What do you suggest?"

I study Nahini for a long moment. She's just as beautiful as ever, her dark gaze on the crowd below. Apparently ordering her out of bed had been the right thing to do.

"Have the ghosts follow us down. The rest of you, hold until I signal you!" I call out to my army.

My third nods and then turns in her saddle. The spirits of the Hunt pass out from between the ranks of the living and trail us down the hill.

Cries ring out as the fey see us approaching. I hold myself straight in the saddle, calling out to my friend the North Wind to come to my side. It responds right away, blowing my hair back off my shoulders, the dark locks tossed about like a banner.

"It's her! It's the Risen Queen!"

I send the wind forth to clear a path through the crowd to the tree line. Not a fierce one like before, no one gets tossed. But the intent is clear.

"Make way!" Another fey, a female with six bared breasts, calls out. "Make way for the Unseelie Queen!"

I nod at her once, acknowledging her.

Murmurs grow and a few brave souls dart forth, trying to touch me, or the Soul Reaper, but the ghost of the dead Valkyrie chases them off.

I feel like a fraud as I reach the middle. What can I say to these beings who have lost so much, who look at me with a mixture of adoration and hope on their faces?

Who am I to them but the reincarnated queen who'd once failed them?

I proceed to the first line of trees. Evergreens several stories high with a thick spread of branches interwoven like a net. Instead of pushing into them though, I turn my horse around in a circle so I am facing the fey. My heart thunders wildly. I hold the sword aloft. The ghosts swarm around me in an eerie mist. Nahini waits at the edge of the crowd, her watchful eyes hunting for any sign of threat to me.

Silence falls.

"You know this blade?" I ask the crowd.

There are some nods, a few murmurs.

I scan their faces, some dirty, others haggard, all weary. These people have been through hell. "This is *Seelenverkäufer*. The Soul Reaper. And I will use it to defeat the Draugar. I will use it to protect you as will King Soladin."

A ripple goes through the throng. A frisson of what might be hope.

I catch Nahini's eye and nod slightly. She dips her head. And thrusts her blade high. As orchestrated, the souls tethered to the Wild Hunt rise up high, encircling me. The North Wind whips my hair to and fro as the souls swirl in a whirlwind around the blade.

"I am Nicneven. I am the commander of the Wild Hunt. I am the Risen Queen!" When I'd envisioned this scene, I thought I'd feel like a snake oil salesman, making phony promises to these people. But the words come from a secret place deep in my soul. I mean them and they force their way out as though they'd been waiting inside me for just the right moment.

"I am the queen of the Shadow Throne and I will defeat the dead and send them back to their graves!"

Cheers erupt from the throng. Nahini nods once, a smile curving at the corners of her mouth. She'd helped me write the speech, knowing what the fey needed to hear to get behind me.

On cue, there is a gallop of hooves behind me. Two riders, wearing red-gold armor with skin like tree bark, emerge from the protection of the evergreens.

"Queen Nicneven," the larger of the two bows in his saddle. "King Soladin requires a word."

I bet he does. "I will be happy to meet with your king, as soon as you guide all of these people through the labyrinth."

Gasps and hopeful cries echo around me. They hadn't expected that I would champion their cause. Part of me wishes that I was their true-hearted defender. That I was there because being there was right.

But it is a stunt. A smokescreen that serves my purposes.

"Great Queen," the shorter rider hesitates as though hunting for the right words. "We have been ordered to escort you to the king."

Nahini had warned me that this moment would be critical. Across the battered dining table at the farmhouse, she'd held my gaze. "The mistake of your last reign was that you were out of touch with the needs of the common people. It is a flaw of many rulers, to distance themselves from the ones they preside over. To truly be their Risen Queen, you need their support."

And that meant knocking down the magical lines that kept them at arm's length from the ruling bodies.

"Let them through. They are our people and are in need."

Behind me, the fey resume their chanting. It's as though I've tossed kerosene on their fire. Their hope has been renewed. "Let us in. Let us in. Let us in!"

"Tell King Soladin," I say in my most even tone, making sure my voice carries above the din. "That either we all cross the labyrinth, or none of us will."

"It will take some time," the larger fey cautions.

I slip the sword into its sheath on my back and make a show of crossing my arms over my chest. "I'll wait."

Through the Man's Eyes

He picks up her scent first. Still miles off, across the craggy mountains which separate the Seelie and Unseelie lands. But he would know that winter apple scent anywhere.

Nic. His Nic.

It takes all his willpower not to ghost into embers and follow the scent to her side. He longs to take her in his arms, to hold her and assure himself that she is unharmed. Fear rises as well, because she's come back for him, and now Underhill once again has access to her.

But he promised to look after her courtiers and he can't carry them all. He glances back at the ragtag group. Gretchen lost her glasses at some point and her baby-fine hair sticks to her sweaty face. She might as well be carrying a neon sign that reads mortal.

Beside her, Bard appears to have recovered fully from his experience with the will 'o the wisps. He is near enough to the mortal that he can offer her a hand when necessary as well as guarding her back.

Thor strides along in front of them. One thing Aiden had forgotten about the thunderer, the god never complains, no matter how rigorous their path became. Though he expects regular meals, he will more than earn their keep if they come across any Draugar, or—gods forbid—Underhill.

Wardon appears just as gray and charred as ever like a fish left too long on a grill. But there is a fervent gleam in his eye, something Aiden doesn't like. What can the male be scheming?

He wants to tell them that he senses Nic, but keeps her nearby presence to himself. For one thing, he'd never informed them that she'd crossed the Veil. Then too, he wants to relish her scent without the interruption and interjection of his companions.

Her scent is stationary, meaning she's in one place, traveling very slowly or not at all. Good. The knowledge that she isn't moving away from him helps him keep the wolf at bay. Whatever her plan, the wolf would ruin it.

Brave, foolish mate.

She is all those things, at least to Aiden.

I love you.

He will never forget her face when she spoke those words. Aiden longs to hear her say them again, not because they are about to be separated or because she is afraid she won't have another chance, but because she means them.

Someone taps him on the shoulder. He starts when he realizes he was so lost in thought that the mortal managed to catch him unaware.

"What?" he snaps and then instantly regrets it when she recoils.

"I...I'm sorry." Gretchen takes a step back, bumping into the shifter. "I didn't mean to scare you."

She's an odd contradiction, this mortal blackmailer. She shows no fear of the god amongst them, but Aiden's short temper makes her quiver.

Of course, his Nic is also a contradiction. An insecure serial killer with a heart of gold.

He doesn't need to catch Bard's disapproving glare to know he screwed up. "It is I who should apologize. What is it you wish to speak to me about, fair maiden?"

Bard's scowl deepens, but Gretchen appears mollified. She takes a moment to compose herself, a habit he's noticed. The mortal doesn't speak without thoroughly considering how her words might be interpreted.

"You said that Underhill, Nic's mom, wants Soladin's heart. Assuming that's not a metaphor—"

"It isn't," Bard and Aiden say at the same time.

Her eyes widen but she pushes on. "How exactly is Nic going to convince him to give up his throne?"

"We don't know," Aiden says. "But I am sure she has a plan."

"I might sort of have one, too." Gretchen bites her lip.

"You have a plan?" Aiden raises one brow.

"My lady is as intelligent as she is beautiful." The shifter lifts Gretchen's hand to his lips. "Speak to us, so that we insignificant servants can bask in your greatness."

Aiden wonders if he sounds that ridiculous when laying on the charm.

Gretchen glances back to where Thor and Wardon are in conversation, about fishing of all things, and then refocuses on him. "You said she needs the hearts of the reigning fey nobles, correct? And that she already has two of them?"

"Wardon's and Brigit's, yes." Aiden lowers his voice.

Her eyes dart between the shifter and him. "What would happen if she didn't have them though?"

"I don't follow, sparrow," Bard says before Aiden can ask for more details.

"What if we steal the hearts before she can get Nic's or Soladin's. Then she'd be back to where she started."

"You want us to steal the hearts?" Both of Aiden's brows go up. "I don't think you understand, Gretchen. Underhill is the fey realm. She can see us, might be watching us even now."

"But what if she isn't?" the mortal pushes on. "What if she's watching *Keeping up with the Kardashians* and she doesn't know? Isn't it worth the risk?"

"It's not so simple, sweet." Bard lays a gentle three knuckled grip on her arm. "The hearts were given to her freely. This isn't a matter of mere possession of an object."

Instead of looking dissuaded, the mortal's face lights up. "Right, but just because Brigit and Wardon gave up their hearts, doesn't mean the new rulers will, especially not if we warn them."

Aiden stops walking, all his attention on the girl. "You're talking about crowning a new Master of the Waves and Mistress of the Hearth without Underhill's knowing?"

"Would it work?" Wardon has moved up beside them, his eyes fever bright. "Can we pass the power surreptitiously?"

"In all the songs, in all the stories," Bard heaves a breath. "It's never been attempted before. There's always fanfare, a feast of abundance when a new royal comes to power."

"That's not a no," Aiden points out. There's a feeling deep inside him, a feeling he can't identify.

If he didn't know better, he'd call it hope.

"What you're suggesting though is that we somehow secretly crown two new royals, one Seelie, one Unseelie," Wardon points out. Though he too appears intrigued. At the chance to name his successor? Or does he have something else planned?

"What does it take to crown a royal?" Aiden had never seen it done since he encountered Nicneven long after she'd assumed the throne.

He addresses the question to Wardon though it is Thor who answers. "The only requirement for a fey royal to take the power is to sit on the seat of power."

Wardon nods in confirmation. "I was told the Gray Throne held the power upon the death of the previous Master of the Waves. Since he had named me his heir, it was guaranteed but I didn't feel it until I took the throne."

Aiden studies the Seelie a moment. "Can you get your power back by resuming the seat on the throne?" Is that his angle?

But Wardon shakes his head. "I gave up my power."

Bard adds, "Once his heart of power has been relinquished, a royal cannot be re-crowned."

What did that mean for Nic, who had yet to sit on the Shadow Throne? What could it mean to her heart, the one he had gifted her so she might live once more if Underhill forced her to give it up?

"We need to rejoin the others," Aiden says.

But Wardon puts a hand on his arm. "Are you foolish enough to believe that Underhill is unaware of this loophole? We must take advantage of it now."

Aiden doesn't cringe from Wardon's touch, doesn't flinch at the dead skin which flakes off him to land at their feet. He simply raises his gaze and allows the wolf to take over his eyes.

Wardon releases him but persists, "I have already selected my heir."

"You?" Bard has no eyebrows, no facial hair at all, yet Aiden can still see the surprise written on the shifter's odd face. "I thought you planned to rule forever."

Wardon sniffs. "Even I had to come up with a contingency plan. One of my get with the consort Desdemona seems capable enough. It is him that I named. I should go to him, get him to the Gray Throne."

Aiden stares at the male for a moment. Wardon is too eager to escape when all he wanted was to slog along. Bard's confirmation that Wardon can't reclaim his heart or his power is one thing. But the wolf's instincts are screaming.

"No," Aiden says at once.

Wardon opens his mouth to protest but Aiden continues. "Not alone. I'll go with you."

"And I," Thor booms.

"Uncle, I need you to see my friends safe to the remaining Seelie king. You're the only being capable of defeating Underhill should she choose to attack. I need you to watch over them."

The thunderer frowns but though he has a noble heart, his ego is massive enough that the flattery wins him over. "But what of your affliction?"

"That's right," Gretchen points out. "Don't you need the Seelie king to lift your curse?" She touches her own lips, then blushes, most likely as she recalls that the cure for Underhill's Kiss of Madness is Soladin's Kiss of Clarity.

"I have time," he lies to the mortal, to them all. The truth is, he has no idea when the madness will descend again. Without Thor there to drive her off, Underhill can snap him up at a moment's notice. "I will take Wardon directly to his heir, then take the heir to the throne and meet up with you as soon as it's done. Time is of the essence."

"We should all go then," the mortal insists.

He steps closer and lowers his voice, taking her into his confidence. "I can travel faster with one. And you need to tell Nic of your plan as soon as you can."

She doesn't appear happy but allows Bard to lead her away.

Aiden turns to face Wardon. "Where?"

The former Master of the Waves points east. "To the site of my palace." There is no sadness in his face.

Aiden's instincts are screaming, but it is a good plan. A way to stall Underhill's expansion of power.

He manages to stifle his disgust as he takes Wardon's arm and turns them both to sparks.

You're unhappy and full of self-loathing. Nic had been right.

And it is past time I fix it.

Soladin doesn't look happy to see me.

Not that I expected him to roll out the red carpet, or whatever the Seelie equivalent is of the royal treatment. The Lord of the Land and I had gotten off on the wrong foot—what with the kidnapping and all—and after having decimated the shantytown that Taj had been holding together with a few blankets and a prayer, now I show up with the whole host of the Wild Hunt at my back. And I refuse to cross as a civilized royal ambassador should. Instead, I hold my ground and make demands of him and his people.

Demands that he can't refuse.

I see the children from Mag's orphanage at the edge of the crowd. What had happened to their shelter when my winds had attacked the village? Had they all made it out? I'd sent Freda back to the rubble of the makeshift gathering place to be sure we had all the living ready to cross over to safety when the time came.

Alric had sent the birds and hounds of the Wild Hunt out to survey the land. There was no sign of the Draugar within an hour's ride, but that didn't mean they aren't a threat to the unprotected fey.

Let us in. Let us in. Let us in. The chanting had died off but resumes at the appearance of the royal party. I hold up a hand. And they go silent like a bunch of preschoolers who learn they must be quiet before they receive a snack.

"Queen Nicneven." It is Taj who speaks. He rides a horse just as fine as his king, wearing much fancier garb than the last time I'd seen him. I scowl, remembering that Taj sometimes pretends to *be* Soladin, to take the target off his back while they are out in public.

Instead of addressing Soladin as king, I nod my head in acknowledgment. "I speak to you now on behalf of the Wild Hunt and all the fey under the hill. There is a great threat to all of us and I will do what I must to see it end."

Soladin's lips part. I can't read his expression. Is he surprised? Shocked? I'd told the idiot I would help if he just let me do what I needed to do. Of course, my guilt for calling the winds might have something to do with it.

I hold his gaze a moment before refocusing on Taj. "But

these people, our people need help. Guide them past the magic that keeps them out."

Taj looks pained. "The enchanted forest is our only defense. If the magic that protects this place is dismantled, there will be no shield for any of us to hide behind."

Nahini has ridden up beside me. I wish I could communicate with her the way I can with Aiden. Though perhaps I don't need to. She gives a slight nod.

He's fey. He must be telling the truth.

Shit. I hadn't thought about that. But I couldn't back down, not after I made the demand. Not with all the tired, dirty faces of the fey refugees gazing at me with a mixture of fear and hope.

The North Wind tugs at my hair, as if it's flirting with me, trying to get my attention. As though reminding me that it is still nearby.

I remember how it protected me from Underhill's attack, from the vicious gusts of the other winds. "If you allow them through the labyrinth, I can construct a barrier out of air."

"Will it hold?" This from Soladin himself.

I look into his dark eyes and see the hope there. Keeping these people at a distance hasn't been his choice. He's done it because he saw no other answer. Now that I am offering him a solution, he looks ready to leap on it.

But one of the courtiers behind him, a bulbous male with silver skin and a potbelly, makes an indignant spluttering noise. "But you can't possibly expect us to house all these...peasants."

"House and feed," Nahini speaks for me. I can tell by her tone she isn't a fan of Soladin's court. "Gods know you can afford it."

"Yes, but for how long?" another Seelie Courtier, a beautiful blue woman with the correct posture like she has a yardstick strapped to her backbone, asks. "The land is not as fruitful as it is in the spring and summer. The other Seelie king is late in taking over and it is rumored he has gone missing."

The other Seelie king is powerless. I think but don't say.

Potbelly guy, who looks sort of like a cartoon walrus, takes advantage of my silence. "The poison waters spread. We let them in now and soon we could all be starving together."

Taj turns to him with a glare. "You are far from starving, Gerhunt."

"I have children," the walrus—Gerhunt apparently, sputters. "And grandchildren to think of."

"There are children out here, too." Freda rides up beside me, a little girl with strawberry blonde hair seated on the saddle in front of her. "Children who have lost everything, including their innocence. Should they, the next hope of the forever young, also lose their lives because you don't wish to share?"

All eyes fall on her tiny passenger, who can't be more than three.

"I found her huddled in the shadow of a partially toppled wall. Did any of you bother to check and make sure the village had been evacuated?"

"There was no time!" the woman, her pretty face somehow less attractive every time she opens her mouth, protests. "They were at the border. And if you let them through, they will overrun us just as surely as the undead."

"It is your call, King Soladin." I stare at a fixed point between Soladin and Taj. I don't know what kind of identity and power games the Seelie king plays with his miserable courtiers, and I can't say I give a fuck. But I don't want to be viewed as a foreign invader here to take his throne either. Looking him in the eye at this moment could be viewed as a challenge. The choice must be his.

261

Because I need Soladin's help. And securing the refugees is only the first item on my punch list.

Taj shifts in his saddle and then turns to look at the Seelie courtiers. "I have heard your words and taken them under advisement. But Queen Nicneven is correct. We must stand together against the greater threat. Let them through."

A great cheer catches like a wave among the refugees, even as the courtiers splutter protests.

"I will not, however, compel you to take them inside your homes or share your stores, unless you choose to do so," Taj calls out. "Nor will I permit any acts of violence or theft against my people. If any of you commit such a crime, I will turn you over to Queen Nicneven for punishment."

Gee, thanks Taj. Still pissed off that I ran away from you, huh?

The shouts of protest die down at that. I stare at Taj who holds up a hand.

"Are we agreed?"

"On this matter, we are agreed." I nod.

Out of the corner of my eye, I watch as Soladin makes a crushing motion with one hand. To release the wards?

It must be, because moments later the trees part, creating a clear path through. I nod to Freda, who gallops across, the small girl's hair waving like a banner of hope. A heartbeat later, the rest of the refugees follow in a tide of immortal flesh.

Some of Soladin's courtiers, including the walrus and perfect posture bitch, turn tail and run as though being chased. Others reach into their saddlebags for provisions that they hand out to the children.

One hurdle down, I think as I watch the fey scurry to safety. *A million to go.*

Aiden, where the hell are you when I need you?

My only answer is the tug of the wind on my hair.

SCHEMING IS GOOD FOR THE SOUL

*a*iden releases the former Master of the Waves as soon as his hand reforms. Wardon smirks at his obvious disgust, but the fey's expression falls when his attention shifts to his former home.

"My palace." The two softly spoken words are filled with heartfelt despair. Probably the first genuine emotion Wardon has expressed, other than anger or fear.

His worst nightmare come to fruition. The loss of his power, his position, all he'd fought so hard to hold onto, has slipped through his fingers like so much sand on the beach.

Aiden almost feels sorry for him. Almost.

The castle has been completely washed away, nothing left of the sea glass spires. The shell-strewn courtyard is nothing but sharp fragments. Only a burning husk of driftwood flickers green where the troll barracks had once been.

Troll statues are scattered everywhere, their faces frozen in agony.

"When the giantess revoked her magic, the trolls no longer had any protection from the sun." Wardon reaches out a shaking hand and lays it against the statue that had once been a living being.

Having been tortured by trolls, Aiden doesn't experience the same sort of loss. But seeing the twisted expression on the stone creature's face makes him shudder. Whatever their crimes, they've paid for it.

"They destroyed everything." Wardon exhales as though his lungs are great balloons that have lost their ability to hold air. "It took me a century to perfect it."

"Castles can be rebuilt," Aiden tells him, not without sympathy. The craftsmanship had been exquisite and within the sea glass walls, Nic had turned to him in need for the first time. It was a memory he would always cherish. "But the dead can not be returned to life."

Except that Nic somehow had been. Twice.

His father's poem of a pretty dead girl. *Third time will do it. The wolf at your bosom will be sure to see to it.*

He stuffs the thought back into the dark recesses it came from. Not knowledge he felt comfortable contemplating in front of the scheming fey.

Wardon slumps. His head appears too heavy on his shoulders.

"Where do we go from here?" All the wolf's hackles are up.

"To the barrier island." Though his tone is thick, Wardon squares his shoulders.

Aiden barely stifles a flinch. "The same island where you had me tortured?"

Wardon's head bobs and he strides off to the west. "The very same. That won't be a problem for you will it, wolf?"

A low growl reverberates in his chest at the taunt but he doesn't let it escape. Rising to the fey's bait will only distract them. "If you tell me where we are going, I can use magic to get us there more quickly."

"Not every problem can be solved by magic," Wardon snaps.

"Says the fey that tried to solve all his problems by bartering magic with a giantess." The words were out before he could think better of them and he waves to the petrified trolls. "Remind me again how well that worked out."

"Judge me all you like, but I was a far better ruler than your precious Nicneven ever was. We both know it."

Aiden opens his mouth, then shut it again. Nicneven had been an incredible warrior, a born leader for the Wild Hunt and a selfish and embittered queen. She only wanted to bear his child—their child—so he or she could take her place on the throne.

But his Nic is different. She's both softer and colder, capable of great things. Unflinching in the face of human predators, fey and even the gods themselves.

I'm coming back for you. The Unseelie queen he'd first met never would have spoken words of love to him. Would never have made such a promise once she had escaped.

"I can see your thoughts, pup." Wardon sneers. "You think this Risen Queen is different? That she will defeat Underhill and drive the Draugar back to their graves, repair the tear in the Veil and set the people free? But ask yourself, what if she does?"

Aiden shakes his head. "I don't understand."

"What if she does all those things? Do you think she'll be content to molder in the Unseelie catacombs forever? To breed with the strongest fey noble as custom dictates?"

The word breed sets him off. Before he can consider his actions, Aiden grips Wardon by the throat and lifts the fey male off his feet by the neck. "She will end that custom. She has already said as much."

"She can lie," Wardon wheezes.

Aiden drops him to the ground. A chill rushes through his

body. It has nothing to do with the wind whipping off the ocean. At his feet, Wardon struggles to breathe around his partially collapsed windpipe. Aiden's heart pounds. He doesn't say a word, doesn't confirm or deny the accusation.

"It's true, isn't it?" Wardon gasps. "I heard her promise to do Underhill's bidding. She vowed it *immediately*, without setting boundaries or stipulations. She doesn't need to because her word is just as worthless as when she was mortal."

Kill him. The wolf is ready to tear the fey's throat out. Maybe that's what Wardon deserves—death, swift and final. *Before he can inform his heir.*

Nic wants this creature alive.

She doesn't know of the threat he poses, the danger to her rule. The wolf insists. Though the beast is not big on politics or royal machinations, he has an unerring sense for any danger to his mate.

And his solution is often murder.

Aiden glares down at the once-powerful being covered in sand and ash. "You will vow to me that you will never again speak those words. To anyone. If you don't give me your word, I will kill you."

Wardon's lips part.

"And before you say, Nicneven wants you alive, know that I will gladly take any punishment in exchange for protecting her interests. I am sure she will forgive me, in time."

He is sure of no such thing. Nic is a wild card, as unpredictable as her winds.

"The heir—," Wardon's eyes grow frantic.

Aiden shrugs. "It's not my concern. From what I can see from the funeral pyres, most of your remaining subjects are crossing to the Unseelie Courts."

Wardon's eyes dart back and forth and he nods once.

We still ought to kill him, the wolf pipes up. *It's not too late.*

Aiden nods once in return, ignoring his bloodthirsty counterpart. "Now, where are we going."

It isn't a question.

Wardon struggles to his feet, blood trickling down his neck from where the wolf's claws punched through Aiden's fingertips. "My hatchery."

The male isn't recovering. All of his injuries are stacking up like cordwood, taking their toll. Is his immortal essence fading now that his heart and all the associated powers are gone?

That would solve Aiden's dilemma.

Aiden gestures toward the caves. "After you."

For no particular reason other than needing a moment to myself, I climb the tree in Soladin's atrium. The Wild Hunt patrols the border, the dead on the outside of the former labyrinth, the living on the inside.

Down below the house with the interconnected log cabins, fey refuges set up in temporary shelters. I spy Jasmine's lithe form darting about. She's picked up two shadows, children from the home.

The home I'd decimated.

"I thought I'd find you here."

I look down to see Taj standing at the base of the tree.

"Am I needed?" It's a rhetorical question. Of course, I'm needed. I'm the Risen Fricking Queen.

It occurs to me that though I wasn't a fan of my former self, I'm starting to understand Queen Nicneven. Always needed, never wanted.

Not until Aiden.

"Not urgently." Though he doesn't smile, the consort's

eyes are kind. "I wanted to thank you. I know that you did what you did to save my life."

I don't accept his thanks. It seems like a betrayal to the ones who died. "How many."

"Thirty-seven casualties."

I close my eyes and lean my forehead against the rough bark.

There is a rustling of leaves and I crack one eyelid to see the large male climbing up the tree as well. I tense, ready to jump if he comes too close, but he settles on a branch about five feet below me.

He doesn't look up as he continues, "The people didn't recognize you, dressed as you were. The winds came so fast, they thought it was backlash from the tear in the Veil. So, you and I are the only ones who know."

"And Underhill," I point out. "That's who I went away with."

He makes a disgruntled sound, like the rumble of distant thunder. "I doubt she will care, since she's never cared about fey lives before."

Then I frown. "You didn't tell Soladin?"

Taj sighs. "No, I have not, which riddles me with guilt every hour."

"So why not just tell him?" I shake my head, not understanding.

"He had enough to worry about in the aftermath."

I don't know how to respond to that, so I don't.

"Why did you run?" he asks. "We were good to you, treated you with respect."

"You were keeping me against my will." Is it really that hard for him to understand? "That's not a situation I'm willing to tolerate."

He turns to stare up at me. "And, given the same set of circumstances, would you act the same way?"

My lips part to say no, of course not. I would find a way that wouldn't result in such a loss of innocent life.

But the words stick in my throat. I hadn't foreseen that fey would die, any more than I had foreseen who Pharaildis really was.

"Excuse me a minute. I need to go find someone." I scramble out of the tree and am running through the corridors before Taj can reply.

I find who I'm looking for in the palace kitchens, helping to prepare an evening meal for the refugees.

"Harmony," I gasp, out of breath from my mad dash.

She looks up, eyes frantic from where she is murdering a tomato with a dull blade. All the seeds are oozing out across the cutting board, the skin denting and warping in silent agony. "I don't know how to do this!"

I take pity on her and point to a vat of bubbling liquid hanging above the open fire. "Stir that before the pot scorches. I've got this."

She heaves out a relieved breath and picks up the wooden stirring spoon. "So, why did you come rushing in here?"

After wiping the blade clean on a rag, I hunt for a whetstone. "Because I just realized I can't see the future."

She casts me a perturbed look. "Why would you?"

"Um, because I died?" It feels a bit ridiculous to say out loud.

"Not all who have crossed over come back as a seer. Some come back altered, others are exactly the same. Others manifest different sorts of talents." Her thick eyebrows scrunch with concentration as she stirs the pot. "Am I doing this right?"

I give up on looking for a sharpening implement and instead grab another knife. "What is it?"

She shrugs.

"You're fine. If it looks like it'll boil over, push the arm there backward so the pot is no longer over the heat."

Her scowl deepens and she stirs with even more vigor. "I do not like chores here. They are easier on the farm."

As far as I know, Harmony hadn't lifted so much as a piece of paper on my farm, but I had been gone for a year. Who knows? She might have changed. Deciding to give her the benefit of the doubt, I say. "We're getting off the subject. Tell me about your gift."

"What is it you want to know?"

"Do you...see the dead?"

She tilt's her purple head to the side, jet hair streaming down her back. "What do you mean, see them?"

I point up to a high shelf where a fey spirit thumbs through the pages of a tattered book. "The ghosts. I see them."

Harmony looks in the direction I point, her purple face pulling tight in concentration. "You're saying there's a ghost here, right now?"

That answered my question. The spirit drifts lower, into our space and sticks out a forked tongue in concentration. She doesn't look up from her book though, not even when Harmony steps through her.

"Yes," I say. "Your gift. Maybe if you tell me how it works, I could better understand."

Her purple forehead wrinkles as she considers. "The term seer is a catch-all phrase. My gift doesn't allow me to see everything that will happen, or even everything that might happen. I just catch glimpses of possible paths. Like if you take the left-hand turn, then you will cross the river instead of the mountains. Only a few steps ahead."

I nod to show her that I follow.

"But seeing doesn't only go forward. There's this world and other realms of existence layered on top. Things normal people can't see. I once heard an old wise woman say that once a soul sets foot beyond the Veil, that foot acts as an anchor. It is in fact, what allows us to see more. Your last death must have connected you to the Veil and the souls trapped within it."

"But the Veil isn't here, right?"

"The Veil is everywhere and nowhere. Imagine a cloth draped over a table. Underhill is the table, the Veil is the cloth. If someone leaves a window open the cloth will flutter even if the table remains in place." She pauses and then says, "Tell me about the ghosts."

"They're different than the souls of the Hunt. They can't interact."

"And how about when you crossed the Veil?" The seer stares at me through the child's flickering outline. "Did you experience anything unusual?"

"Not while I held *Seelenverkäufer*." Looking through a spirit at her is unnerving and I refocus on the tomatoes. "Were you trying to dice these or slice them?"

"I was *trying* to make them smaller," she huffs.

Okay then. I go with slices, figuring it is easier to make extra cuts than make them too small. "What do you think that means? That I see these slivers of people I can't interact with, can't help."

The cry of a baby in the palace. The overwhelming feeling of grief at the heart of the hill.

Harmony gives up all pretense of cutting the tomatoes and lowers herself into a chair. "Not everything has to mean something, Nic."

But I shake my head. "It has to."

"Why?"

"It just does." I remember the story Underhill had told me, the sense of a presence an individuality in the North Wind. Originally, I planned to talk to Nahini or Freda, but they are both overloaded with their jobs. "Someone told me all the royal powers come from spirits tethered to elements. The fey trapped them and that's what causes magic in the realm."

The seer narrows her eyes on me. "Who told you this?"

I reach for another tomato. "It was just something I picked up."

"It's only an old legend."

"So are all fairy tales," I set the knife down, "and we're living in one."

She makes a derisive noise. "If that's the case let's skip ahead to the happily ever after."

No sense telling her that there will be no happily ever after. "Tell me about your relationship with Wardon."

I don't mistake her flinch at the name. "Why do you want to know?"

"Threat assessment. He's traveling with Aiden and the others."

She stands up and paces. "He's clever, ruthless, that you already know. But he can also be very caring. It was a side of him I saw only a handful of times in all my years at his court. Don't trust him."

"He's harmless. Underhill chemically castrated his magic."

She shakes her head. "You don't understand. Wardon without his magic is even more dangerous. Like a cornered animal, he will strike out in fear."

Aiden, I think into the echoing void. I want to talk to him, mind to mind, to reassure myself that he's all right and that I hadn't doomed them all when I'd crossed the Veil.

I offer a tight smile and wipe my hands on a rag. "I need to go clear my head before the next round of meetings begins."

She nods and looks at the neat pile of tomato slices. "For what it's worth, I think you handled the situation at the barrier well."

I raise an eyebrow. "Was that a compliment?"

A sneer crosses her pretty face. "Don't let it go to your head."

The ghost with the prehensile tongue turns another page.

I pause at the crumbled stone remains of what had been the orphanage. The North Wind is tagging along, tossing my hair about as if enticing me to play. I ignore it as I step over what used to be the roof. The building had been sturdy, but nothing could withstand the combined destructive forces of my winds.

Nothing and no one.

I crouch down and pick up a tiny rag doll from where it lies prone on a pile of debris.

It is soaked through with blood.

I swipe at the grittiness in my eyes. Damn it, why had I saved Taj?

"It's not your fault. None of it is."

Even if I hadn't recognized her voice, no one but Nahini could have moved so stealthily through the rubble. "It sort of is."

"You reacted to the situation in the only way you could."

The limp doll flops in my hands as I rise. "I could have let them kill Taj. Instead, I traded innocent lives for his."

Nahini isn't looking at me though. "And then an innocent man would have died."

"And how many innocents died instead?" The words are bitter on my tongue.

"How many lived because you brought them to safety?" she counters.

"You are not a soft queen, not a merciful queen. But you are a just queen, Nic."

"I didn't kill Wardon when I had the chance. Or let Aiden kill him."

Her dark gaze seems to spear me. "Why?"

"Because vengeance is yours." I reach up and touch one white streak through her dark hair. "And I wouldn't steal it from you."

"He wronged you as well."

I nod. I don't say what I'm thinking though. That Wardon hadn't permanently affected me.

She licks her lips. "He chained me in a cave offshore of his palace. And when the tide came in, it would come up over my head. I could feel myself choking, drowning, dying. The ghosts tried to lift me, but with the bindings, I couldn't escape. I'd lose consciousness and then I'd awake in the cave, still immortal, but knowing it was going to happen again and again."

I don't know what to say so I stay silent.

"For most of my life, I believed fear to be the enemy. It was fear I needed to overcome, to battle. But I was wrong. The anticipation is the greater threat. Knowing how it will hurt to hold your breath and feel sure that your lungs will burst. What drove me out of my senses wasn't the fear of pain, but when your body remembers it, responds to it in ways you can't control, no matter how hard you want to fight. The fear is a cobweb. The certainty, a thorny whip that lashes pieces off your soul. That's what makes a warrior helpless."

I think about Aiden's plea, that I should kill him because he was afraid he would betray me. Perhaps he'd spoken not out of fear, but because he possesses the morbid certainty Nahini spoke about.

"How did you bear it?" I ask her.

She smiles at me and though it is a little forced, it seems genuine. "I still am. One breath in, one breath out. One heartbeat at a time, one task at a time. You said you needed me."

"I do."

"That knowledge helps. Knowing that I am needed, wanted, of value, it helps me keep fighting. Even when I want to give up."

"You are one of the bravest people I have ever known," I tell her. "And I am glad to call you friend."

Her smile is much more heartfelt. "We should go back and make a plan to face the Draugar. Are you going to keep that?"

Glancing down, I'm surprised to see that I am still holding the doll. It is a gruesome reminder but unlike my driver's licenses, it isn't a trophy but a warning of what can happen even when I am trying to save lives. "Yes."

She doesn't comment as she falls into step alongside me. That's the beautiful part about Nahini. She doesn't feel the need to fill every silence with talk.

We stride up the same hill I traveled by cart down days ago in Underhill time. There is a small group cresting the opposite hill, heading toward the Seelie lands. At first glance, I think it's one of Freda's patrols but there are no hounds or birds, no horses. Just three beings on foot.

I recognize Bard first. Not a challenge since the being is nearly seven feet tall. He appears much recuperated from when I'd last seen him. Beside him is Gretchen, her hair blowing in the gusts from the North Wind. My heart sinks when I see the third is Thor.

No sign of Aiden.

As I point to them, they break into a run. All three of them at once, tearing down the hill.

"What the…?" I trail off as the hilltop they just vacated fills with bodies of the undead.

The Draugar have found us.

DEAD BUT NOT BURIED

THROUGH THE MAN'S EYES

*A*iden's cold flame flickers in Wardon's palm as they trudge through the cave tunnels. The wolf lurks close to the surface, uneasy at being back in the place where he'd been maimed.

Though it isn't the exact same cave, the similarities are unmistakable. The smell of salt, the lifeless wet rock worn smooth. It smells different though. The place where he was tortured reeked of blood and madness. This cave smells of… possibility. Even his keen nose can't narrow it down more than that. A hatchery Wardon had said. Where his heir waits.

They take another turn. Up ahead the tunnel widens into an underground lake. Bioluminescent plants hang from the ceiling but the lake looks like a pool of inky death, the water not reflecting them or the light from his fire.

Wardon gives him the flame and removes his tattered vest. "I need to go down to get him."

"Down?"

The fey nods to the lake. "Swim down. The hatchery is at the deepest part."

Aiden narrows his eyes. Does the male really expect him to cool his heels in this cave? "I'm coming with you."

"Fire and water don't mix, wolf. In fact, I wouldn't recommend even dipping a toe in. The water contains nullifying properties. The hatchery was designed to be protected from all the other courts so none but our own can access it." Wardon sneers at him. "Unless you're planning to grow gills, there's no way for you to breathe down there."

He doesn't like the thought of waiting for the Seelie to bring the new royal to the surface. Wardon could say anything to the child and Aiden wouldn't know.

"Give me your vow that you won't betray me."

"There's no time—"

Aiden seizes his arm again. "Make the time."

He would rather toss the fey's lifeless carcass into that lake to rot than risk Wardon ordering some underwater army to ambush him.

"Fine, I vow that neither I nor my heir will betray you this day. Good enough?"

He'd tagged the time limit on. Aiden isn't surprised. He really couldn't have expected much more. Wardon had been a ruler for a very long time and he wouldn't make openended bargains that he couldn't eventually wriggle his way out of.

He let's go of Wardon's arm and stands back. Wardon doesn't hesitate before striding into the water. His body forms no ripples, no wake trails him as he moves deeper into the eerie lake, striding then swimming out to the exact center. The fey ducks beneath the surface. A moment later, his webbed feet breech with nary a drop displaced and then he is gone from view.

The wolf paces within him, unsettled. Aiden is as well. He sniffs, picking up on that scent of possibility once again, trying to place it. It's a fecund sort of scent, sort of like that of a barn filled with fresh cut hey and foaling horses. But it's also wet, clammy and of the sea.

He longs to pace but forces his body to remain still, watching the spot where Wardon disappeared. He wouldn't betray Aiden, wouldn't be able to tell his heir that Nic could lie. Still, he's poised for any sort of trouble.

Time drags by slowly and the wolf grows more and more restless. What is Wardon doing down there?

*Nic. We need to get to Nic, t*he wolf insists.

He can leave. Shift to sparks right now and drift back to the hilltop where he'd left Gretchen, Bard, and Thor.

But he remains where he is.

Almost an hour passes when he hears it. Not from the lake but from behind. The shuffling of feet. Many pairs of feet.

Cursing himself silently, he scans the cavern for a place to hide. Seeing nothing, he shifts to sparks and drifts up toward the ceiling a moment before the first of the Draugar shuffles into view.

Followed by another. And another. Soon the mouth of the cavern is teeming with the dead all making slow shuffling progress toward the water's edge.

Aiden hovers, his incorporeal self still focused on the middle of the lake. What sort of mystical protections are on the lake?

And will they stop the Draugar?

His hopes fall when the first one breeches the surface, but it's rotting flesh seems impervious to whatever magic is in the lake. Do they know about the hatchery or is this place, this one cave among thousands, in their path?

Aiden has lived too long and seen too much to believe in coincidence.

Underhill must be controlling them. She's raised the damn things and set them loose on the fey, the beings she considers her enemies. Bringing the dead here the same way she brought them to wipe out Gretchen and Bard. Does she know what Wardon plans?

He contemplates dropping sparks down onto the Draugar —they burn easily enough—but there are too many. If they all catch fire at once, the flames will burn through the oxygen in minutes and anything alive in this place will suffocate.

And that won't keep her from sending more.

The second line reaches the water.

In a moment's time, he reforms into the man and braces himself as gravity takes hold. Sucking in as much air as he can, he plunges into the center of the lake.

Instant darkness greets him. His senses as a wolf are sharper than even those of a god but there is no light at all to aid him. Not a shimmer or a reflection. A stabbing sort of cold that threatens to explode through his every pore. Disoriented, he tries to dive deeper, but there is no way to see where he is, what lies beneath or how far down he must swim to reach the hatchery. He tries to light a flame, to see where he's going, but his magic doesn't obey. He reaches again, but his body and mind feel sluggish. Disconnected, as though they don't know how to function together.

Nullifying properties, Wardon had said.

He adjusts, his arms and legs, hoping he's now aiming for the surface. Air. He needs air and light.

His lungs ache, the oxygen he greedily gulped down almost used up. The need to breathe presses harder. A few bubbles escape his freezing lips. Then a few more.

I'm going to die. The sudden realization echoes through his skull.

Fight. The wolf tears and claws within him, helpless. There is no enemy to sunder, nothing the wolf can do. *You must fight.*

I wanted to die. Aiden kicks, desperate to breach the

surface. Better to face the entire host of Draugar than this suffocating endless night. His lungs are screaming now, burning as though he's swallowed his own sparks. *This is death.*

There is no peace. No better world waiting beyond. It all just…ends. All the suffering, but also all the good. He flashes back to the moment when Nicneven killed that farmer who had kept him chained. The terror in the male's eyes. The way his body jerked and fought for survival. What had that drunken bastard wanted to live for?

Nic is his. Has opened her guarded heart to him.

And he's about to plunge a dagger into it.

I love you. I'm coming back for you.

Aiden makes to kick again, but his limbs are too heavy. His head doesn't breach the surface. Deeper, he's swum deeper.

Too late! his mind screams as his lungs empty of the used-up air. The wolf doesn't bother with words as it bellows a mournful cry.

"Aiden," I stumble in my haste to cross over the boundary. My heart beats triple time from the race down the hill. "Where's Aiden?"

My mind screams out for him.

"Nic, the winds." Nahini ran right for the nearest horse and commandeered it from the fey noble. She rears it around and points it in the direction Gretchen, Bard and Thor are running. "You need to call the winds and shield this place."

It had seemed like such a good idea at the time. Call the wind to replace Soladin's tree labyrinth. Yet I hadn't held a barrier for more than a few minutes. And never one the size needed to protect everyone.

No time. I inhale and prepare to summon the winds.

Before I can, Nahini calls out a sharp command in a language I've never heard and the horse tears off, back out onto the field, past the living patrol of the Wild Hunt who are racing toward us.

My mind is a clusterfuck of tattered hopes. Aiden wouldn't have just left Gretchen and Bard on their own. He should be at the front of the line.

What if he didn't believe that I was coming back for him? What if he isn't alive?

"Nicneven," another mounted rider approaches me through the trees. Soladin. "You need to erect the barrier."

"Working on it." The calls must go out one at a time instead of all at once. Control, Underhill had said. I needed to develop control over my gift.

I look back to the hill, dark with animated corpses.

What if I hurt someone? What if Nahini and the others don't make it back in time?

We're out of options. I have no time for a multitude of doubts. The frightened people behind me need me to protect them. I have to do this right. And I can't screw it up again.

I take a deep breath and beckon the winds.

The air pressure shifts, slowly at first. An icy gust from the North Wind whips leaves up as well as a few stray items of clothing. Behind me, the refugees who lived through the last attack begin chanting. Praying.

"Let me go, too." Freda rushes to me, her winged helmet in place. She's eyeing Soladin's mottled mare as if anticipating how fast the animal can run.

"You'll never make it in time." I shake my head. If Nahini had consulted me first, I wouldn't have let her go either. Brave, foolish, heroic Nahini. She is halfway up the hill, charging for the three living beings.

The Draugar aren't running. They don't need to. There is

nowhere we can go. Like termites on a rotting stump, their fetid carcasses swarm over the lush green hills.

I can't stop them, can't stretch the wind barrier any farther than the tree line, not without compromising its integrity. My friends need to make it back to us.

I can't shield them yet, but maybe I can slow their pursuers down.

Mist rolls in, thin tendrils of wet air at first, then behind it a denser fog. Wet, heavy air surrounds the Draugar. It shifts with their shuffling progress, an opaque wall between the dead and my friends.

"Look," Soladin points. "What is he doing?"

His finger is jabbing toward Bard, who has scooped Gretchen up into his arms. There is a brilliant flash that bounces off the fog like a visual echo. One moment he's a long-limbed fey male, the next, he's a brilliant white stallion.

Even from this distance, Gretchen's body language betrays her surprise. But she tosses her arms around the horse's neck and hangs on. Somehow, in spite of the increased speed, Thor manages to keep up.

All around us, the winds are circling, circling, not solid, not yet. I don't know if I can undo the barrier once I've solidified it. Underhill still maintains a grip on the magic of the land. The more I use, the more I will expose myself to her. More murmured prayers, though there is no way to tell if the fey are more afraid of the dead or of my powers.

"Come on, come on," I hear Freda mutter. "They're going to make it."

Another wave of Draugar appears off to the right. Their approach was blocked by the hill. They move to cut off the four travelers.

"My queen," Alric rides up through the trees, the dead Valkyrie at his side. "There are more coming from the far side. They are almost to the tree line."

"It's a kill box," Freda breathes.

"Send the spirits of the Hunt out," I tell her. "Have them buy us as much time as you can."

She nods and swoops off.

Sweat runs down the side of my neck in spite of the wind. I stretch the fog down to the new threat, surrounding the Draugar.

"Alric," I say, my voice tight with strain. "Send out your birds. We need to know what sort of numbers we're dealing with."

The Spriggan nods and shuts his eyes, communing with his falcons.

Thunder rumbles. Lightning flashes. Thor stops and turns to face the Draugar, raising his fabled hammer high.

"What's he doing?" Freda asks.

And in a flash, I know.

Go. I command the North Wind.

It speeds off, rushing past Freda and I.

The god waits. Nahini reaches Bard and Gretchen and turns with them, guarding their flank, racing back toward us.

The thunderer's mighty hammer glints in a flash of lightning as my two air masses, wet fog, and icy North Wind collide. The moisture flash freezes in the embrace of the North Wind. Freezes the Druagar in their tracks, into a wall of frozen corpses.

As though it's what he's waiting for, Thor's hammer smashes it down.

The ground shakes. Though I'd been braced for it, I stumble into Freda. Nahini, standing in the stirrups and Bard and Gretchen beside her are tossed into the air. Air that I control. The North Wind holds the three in its embrace, carrying them over the frozen air mass.

The vibration of the impact splinters the frozen dead into glittering dust.

But not all of them.

Thor leaps high into the air and charges down the hill toward us like a heavily muscled freight train. He crosses over the semipermeable barrier of the wind at the same time as Nahini and Bard, still carrying a wide-eyed and disheveled Gretchen on his back.

I suck in another breath as the North Wind joins all the others swirling about the Seelie Court.

Protect us. I tell it, tell them all.

The air currents go still. Like someone has shut off a giant-sized fan. My hand trembles with fatigue as I reach for the new barrier. I lay my palm flat against the invisible wall of air.

Solid.

But how long will it hold?

I move first to Gretchen, who is sliding off Bard's back. Her feet touch the ground but her legs buckle. I catch her before she collapses entirely.

"You're all right," I tell her.

She's panting, her wispy hair loose about her shoulders.

Bard transitions back to his other form. "Aiden."

I grow cold at the name. "Where is he? Is he all right?"

"He was a few hours ago."

I let out a breath. Now it is Gretchen who is mostly holding me up.

"He took Wardon to find the new Master of the Waves," the mortal says. "We have a plan,"

Thor strides forth.

"Thank you for keeping my courtiers safe."

He nods once, though his gaze goes to the air barrier. "Will that hold?"

I don't know. But I don't want to admit the weakness, not in front of so many. "Alric. How many are there?"

The Spriggan turns his golden-brown eyes to me. "Too many to count."

"The wall of wind is holding," I say. "But no telling how long."

I sit at one end of the table in the Seelie conference room. Soladin faces me at the other end. Freda sits on my right. Nahini on the left with her brother and the Valkyrie spirit flanking her.

Taj, the only other Seelie representative, eyes the dead of the Hunt. "Your ghosts can pass through the barrier?"

I nod, though I don't offer an explanation. Not that I have one.

To Soladin's left, sits Thor. I'm not sure why the thunderer is included in the fey war counsel, other than that no one wanted to be the one to tell him he couldn't come.

"You want me to give my heart to Underhill?" Soladin says. "To sacrifice the last Seelie ruler and the only hope for our court?"

Not until after he kissed Aiden, whenever my wolf shows up. But I keep that to myself. "*I* don't want you to. But it's what she wants. All of our hearts to set herself free from her imprisonment."

"This cannot be allowed." Thor slams one meaty fist on the live oak table until I'm sure it will fracture. "With the powers of the fey, Underhill could challenge the gods. Even the Fates."

"I agree," Taj nods. "Personal considerations aside, it seems counterproductive to give Pharaildis what she wants. You said she blames the fey for her imprisonment. What's to stop her from destroying all of us?"

My kiss of death, which according to my frenemy goddess,

will still work. "Listen, Gretchen's plan is solid. We let Pharaildis think we're giving up, ask for a deal. Give her our hearts. But at the same time, our replacements will ascend their thrones, and the magic will transfer to them. Just a little bait and switch."

"I see two problems with that," Soladin says. "First of all, we have no way of knowing if Wardon has found his replacement. And second, what of the other Unseelie seat?"

"Alric," I call and the Spriggan steps forward. "Do you believe your sister will want to be the new Mistress of the Hearth?"

"She will, but you realize you'll be handing the throne to my father."

I let out a sigh. "There are no perfect solutions here. Get a message to her. She will need to ascend at the same time as the rest of us."

"The rest of us?" Taj tilt's his head to the side.

"I have yet to ascend. She'll take your heart then bring me to the Unseelie palace, to sit on the Shadow Throne. That's when all the other courts must be ready to take their powers back."

"The timing must be precise," Freda leans forward, hands clasped on the table. "Alric will get his sister the message and you know of your plan. Have you chosen an heir?"

"I have." Soladin places a hand on Taj's who starts.

"Me?"

"Our goals and dreams are the same, are they not? What is the difference if I am king with you as my consort or the reverse is true?"

Taj's lips part. "The Seelie Courtiers will never accept me."

"Then that is their loss," I say. "Besides, the people already adore you, already believe you to be their king."

"The same people who tried to tear me apart a few days ago?"

"Keep them fed, give them what they need to rebuild," Nahini advises.

Soladin squeezes his hand. "You are easy to love. Let them see that."

I see Taj swallow, then nod. "If that is your wish."

Thor scowls though. "That is only three of the thrones. What of the other Seelie king?"

Nahini turns to me. "Have you heard from Aiden?"

I shake my head. "Not a word. It's like there's something blocking our connection."

Freda scowls. "Without a direct line of communication, we can't tell him of the plan."

"For all we know," Alric adds, "Wardon's heir has already ascended."

"Then Underhill will be heading right to them." I look around the table. "Perhaps that's where we should intercept her."

Soladin scrubs a hand over his face. "It's a shaky plan, at best."

I hold his dark brown gaze. "It's the only one we've got."

"What of the Draugar?" Thor asks. "How will you get past them?"

"With this." I draw *Seelenverkäufer* and lay it on the table. "We're crossing the Veil to exit and reenter the realm."

All eyes are on the Soul Reaper.

"Two days from now, at midnight," I say to the table. "That's our deadline. Agreed?"

"Agreed." Soladin nods. There is a scraping of chairs as the room clears.

I close my eyes, reaching out for Aiden.

And find nothing.

Please be okay. I think. Gods, I will do anything to see his green eyes sparkle in the sun, hear his laugh just one more time.

"Are you all right?" I glance up to see Soladin watching me intently. We are the only two left in the room.

"I'm fine," I lie.

He tips his head to the side. "I'm sure he's all right."

"Thanks." I hold his gaze. "I want you to do something for me."

One dark eyebrow lifts. "Something other than sacrificing my heart, my powers, and my throne?"

"When you put it like that it sounds bad."

He pushes back from the table and moves to look out the window. "You saved all those people when I couldn't seem to find a way. You're risking all your people as well as your throne to help us. So yes, name your request and I'll do everything in my power to make it so."

"I want you to abolish the breeding laws for the royals."

His large dark eyes grow even larger. "Abolish. I can't do that. Not without the consent of the others."

"What others? I haven't ascended. Brigit is dead, Wardon has been dethroned." I continue before he can protest. "Right now, you are the only crowned royal. You don't need anyone else's agreement to make it law."

"A temporary technicality. The heir is supposed to be blood of the first fey."

"I've spoken with Freya herself. She doesn't care." Not that the goddess said as much, but considering she didn't give a flying rat's ass about the fate of the fey, it is a solid assumption.

Soladin's thick eyebrows pull down into a v. I can see him teetering on the edge. Time to shove him over. "You named Taj as your replacement and he is not of your blood. If this works and Taj becomes Lord of the Land, do you really want to share him with one of those piranha courtiers for the sake of some archaic breeding rule?"

He lets out a long-suffering sigh. "You are more dangerous than I ever could have believed."

He has no idea. "Is that a yes?"

A steady exhale. "One condition, that you forgive me for abducting you."

"Agreed." I let out the breath I've been holding. After getting to my feet, I move to his side and extend a hand. He looks down at it.

"Where I come from, it's customary to shake hands when you've reached a mutually beneficial agreement."

He takes my hand slowly and I mold my palm to his, adding light pressure.

"Thank you, Nic."

I smile, but it fades as a tightness builds in my chest. I let go of his hand and lean against the wall. My knees have gone weak.

"What is it?"

"Aiden." I look into the Seelie king's concerned face as my vision blurs. "He's dying."

HOW BADLY DO YOU WANT IT

THROUGH THE MAN'S EYES

*N*othing.
Nothing.
Nothing.

Aiden doesn't know how long he floats in the void. There is no light, no sound, no feeling. No dead friends or relatives, no tunnel of light. It's enough to drive one mad. There is no peace. No ease.

Nothing.

No color, no scent, no sensation.

Empty.

His wolf is gone. Not silent. Not buried deep down. Vanished as though the beast never was, leaving him bereft.

This was what he'd wanted. To be rid of the beast, the monster that had killed his baby brother. But without it who is he? What is he?

And he knows fear. If he had a heart it would burst from the lack of sensation. If he stays in this place long enough, he will dissolve into nothingness as well.

Nic.

He clings to her memory, to the remembered texture of

her hand in his, her winter apple scent. The feeling of her in his mind.

Nothing.

He is nothing.

Has always been nothing.

Will always be nothing.

Doesn't deserve her.

Can't live without her.

The wolf could protect her. He can do….

He is….Who is he?

Nothing. No one. Floating.

Above him lights. The Veil. It wants him, it pulls at him, demanding he come and make it whole. Death is all he's ever known. The end. Ragnarök is coming, the end to everything. And he is prepared. Impatient.

He expected to die. Awaited it. He never lived.

Until her.

Words. *I love you. I will come back for you.*

Not him.

Not the beast.

Both.

She came back to him once. She will do it again.

And he must be there. For her. For her, he would…live.

The Veil awaits. But he fights. Because he wants her. More than he has ever wanted anything.

And because he deserves to be happy. *We deserve peace. Not nothing.*

So he resists, he holds on to her image, her essence. His Nic. His mate.

Sensation so sharp it pulls him back, back into the body he's all but abandoned.

Burning in his lungs. Blackness everywhere.

Sharp fingernails digging into his calf, dragging him down.

Draugar. Aiden kicks out, still without air, desperate.

The claws in his ankle dig deeper, his captor dragging him down, down. His immortality brought him back. And so long as he has a body to return to, he will drown over and over and come back over and over.

Because life could be worth living. Not for Nic. Not even for Nari. But because he wants to live.

To be free. To be happy. To know peace.

Fight. His wolf is back, struggling, fighting inside him. Not against him but with him.

Below him there is a glimmer of light, fracturing the blackness of the water. It grows larger and larger as he is pulled toward it. He can see the pale hand holding him now.

Wardon.

The former Master of the Waves drags him in through a tunnel. A glass door slides shut behind them, sealing them in. The floor beneath them is made of the same thick glass as well but filled with holes. With the outside water blocked, the water drains through the small openings down into a pool below. Just in time, as Aiden is about to suck in another lungful.

Air greets him and he coughs and chokes, spitting up water.

"What in all the gods' names are you doing?" Wardon barks. "Trying to get yourself killed?"

If Aiden had any breath he would have laughed.

"Fool wolf. I should have left you to drown."

Aiden coughs. Gods, it feels good to breathe. A simple pleasure he will never take for granted again.

Wardon makes a sound of disgust and turns. He places his palm against the glass door that separates this section from the rest of the brilliant white city.

For it is a city, a Seelie stronghold. Not just a hatchery but a civilization. Buried deep inside this black lake.

Wardon yanks him up by the arm. "Come on. And I vow, if you tell another living soul about this place, I will find a way to end your sorry existence."

"What happened to you?" For the first time, Aiden realizes that Wardon looks...better. His skin no longer appears to be flaking off to ash, his posture is straight, his eyes clear. As though he has been restored.

"All of my best healers reside here." Wardon gestures toward the glass catwalk.

"Where...?" Aiden does his best to wipe the water out of his eyes as he shambles after Wardon. "Where are we?"

"The heart of my power, where the water fey dwell."

Aiden had heard rumors about a separate Seelie city devoted to the water fey, but even his wildest imaginings hadn't conjured something so spectacular. Everywhere he looks there is light, movement. Life abounds at the deepest pit of the black lake.

Outside the glass walls, kelpies and merfolk swim with dolphins and schools of brightly colored fish. Within the space, fey every color of the rainbow stroll with easy grace, as though they don't know that the world above their heads is burning.

"I thought you said this was your hatchery?" Aiden glances around.

"My hatchery is located within the city. The safest place for them, until they ascend." He eyes Aiden. "Many of the beings here have never seen anything that is not a water creature. Try to keep that beast of yours in check."

Aiden nods, still too stunned to reply.

They make their way through the glass city. Half of it is filled with water, where the water-bound fey swim as though traveling on a sidewalk. Several of the rooms are split down the middle, some with air, some full of water.

"This is incredible." Aiden studies Wardon, for the first time glad he didn't kill the fey king.

"Not all of my people can breathe air and water alike. For centuries, the water Seelie were forced to live separately from the rest of the court, their interaction minimal, and their voices unheard in the court. Your Nicneven changed all that."

"Nic?"

But Wardon shakes his head. "When her Unseelie attacked my fishing villages and killed my people, I saw the vulnerability in our court. We are stronger as a whole when we are invested in the wellbeing of all. I built this place so the water fey could live and work together."

"How many?"

"At last count, we have about twenty-five thousand who call this place home." Wardon looks proud, as well he should. "Some breathe only air. Some breathe only water. But they are connected here in a way they have never been before."

They pass what looks to be a schoolroom. A small green fey with an enormous dorsal fin presses a book up to a glass wall, showing something to the three jellyfish-like beings on the other side. The city is like a giant fishbowl.

"They're learning together?"

"Science, mathematics, languages other than their own. Some of the more advanced students are studying engineering, agriculture, and economics."

Aiden looks at Wardon, trying to reconcile the madman who had him tortured by trolls with the mind behind this underwater utopia. "This must have taken you centuries."

"Almost three from inception to reality." There is a gleam in the former king's eye. "A skilled and knowledgeable population is a strong population."

Aiden shakes his head. Maybe he'd done it for the wrong reasons, out of fear and hate, and no doubt he'd gone about it in despicable ways, but the Master of the Waves was the first fey ruler to bring his people out of the dark ages.

Between Angrboda and Pharaildis, he had certainly paid for his crimes.

"What of Underhill? Does she know of this place?" Aiden couldn't imagine Nic's mother being complacent with the advances the Seelie Court was making here.

Wardon shakes his head. "I don't think so. I sold my soul to the giants for enough magic to keep this place hidden under a refracting spell. Only one from the city can escort someone new to it. Underhill took so much pleasure in showing me the destruction of my castle. If she knew about this place, I'm sure she would try to destroy it."

"The cave was full of Draugar," Aiden says. "That's why I risked the water, even in spite of your warning."

Wardon hisses. "Then we're stuck here until they are gone."

"Nic." Someone is slapping the side of my face, a strike punctuating each word. "Nic, wake up."

Smack. Smack. *SMACK.*

My eyelids crack and I throw up a hand in defense. My head is pounding and the jostling isn't helping. "Stop."

Freda reels her hand back. She and Alric stand over me, wearing identical expressions of concern. Behind them, Soladin hovers like a mother hen.

"I'm fine," I tell them and struggle to a sitting position.

"You said Aiden was dead," the Seelie king says.

I flinch as it comes back to me, that all-consuming wave of…nothing. As if something crucial vanished. Instinct takes over and I stretch out, not with my body, but with my mind.

He's there. Still not accessible like before but at least I can feel him.

"Whatever's going on just sped up our timeline," I say as Freda helps me to my feet. "Alric, can you get a message to your sister in the Unseelie catacombs?"

The Spriggan nods. "I'll deliver it myself."

"I'll go as well," Freda hands me a cup of water.

I down it greedily and then wipe my mouth on my sleeve. "No, I need you here, to defend the fey with Taj and half the Hunt in case the air shield fails."

"Nic," she protests. "You might need us to guard your flank."

"Thousands of lives are at risk from the Draugar, including your daughter's. I trust the Hunt and only the Hunt with you as their leader to guard them."

"What about you?"

"I'll take Nahini and the ghosts. We'll make do and if I need backup, I'll send one of the ghosts to fetch you."

Freda's lush lips form a tight line but she doesn't push any harder. A good thing too because once we're gone there will be no leaving the protection of the air barrier. At least not for the living.

Because I'm taking *Seelenverkäufer* with me.

"Soladin, tell Nahini I will meet her in the Enchanted Forest in one hour," I tell Freda before turning to her Spriggan. "Alric, you have animals on the outside, right?"

"A few hounds and birds of prey," the Spriggan nods.

"If you run into any trouble, send your fastest ones to me and to the shield. Freda, post a lookout. Our efforts must be as coordinated as possible. King Soladin, time to say your goodbyes."

His dark eyes are troubled, but he nods. "I will fulfill my vow to you. My last act as Lord of the Land."

To abolish the consort rule and the law of blood. So that

if I ever do have a child, it will be because I want one, not as a measure of fey politics.

Me, as a mother is enough of a stretch without adding magic to the mix.

I thank him and then turn to the hallway, looking for the person I need.

She is seated in the great hall in front of a roaring fire. The temperature has dropped down into the forties and I can smell frost on the breath of the North Wind. Soon it will be too cold for the refugees to sleep outside.

I need to save the world before then.

"Gretchen?" I ask.

She looks up from the book she was reading.

"I need your help." Quickly, I explain to her my backup plan.

Her eyes go round as duck eggs as she listens, but when I'm finished she scrambles upright. "Me?"

"Unless you've had enough adventure." I hold *Seelenverkäufer* out. "I can send you back to the farm. Chloe and Addy are standing by to drive you home."

She looks at the sword for a long moment. I can't read her face at all. It's gone utterly blank. In a soft voice, she asks as though terrified of the answer, "You said a year has passed back home?"

"Maybe more by now."

Her teeth sink into her lower lip. "Do they...miss me do you think?"

I don't know how to answer that. They *should* miss her. There ought to be posters of her face all over town. I hadn't been back long enough to check. But do I believe her fat-shaming, wine-swilling maternal unit actually misses her?

In the end, I go with the only truth I feel comfortable uttering. "I'm sure your sister does."

She nods, accepting that. "I've missed so much of their

lives already. But if you're right and over a year has passed, I'm legally an adult. It's time to make my own choices."

I scowl and consider her logic. Chronologically, we're still sixteen. I am also one of the forever young, frozen now into immortality. I will always be sixteen. But given that October 31 has come and gone, not once but twice, legally, I am an adult. Gretchen has been in Underhill for a handful of days, but the way time moves here is different than in Midgard, so she too has reached the age of majority.

What makes an adult? A date on a calendar? Irrelevant in our case. Life experience? Gods know we've had more than our share. The ability to make hard choices?

She's doing that right now.

"I want to stay here, to help you."

I turn to her. "Since you're sticking around, I have something for you to do."

Her eyes sparkle with excitement. "Am I going to be a courtier, like Bard and Harmony?"

"Better."

I pace the area in front of the fireplace as I outline my plan. Plan is too generous a word for this harebrained scheme I've concocted. Her eyes grow wider and wider until I'm surprised they remain in her skull.

"It's just a backup plan," I conclude. "In case everything goes to shit."

She licks her lips and repeats, "Backup plan," in a faint voice.

"If you don't want to, I can find someone else." It's a lie. There is no one else.

She takes a deep breath then claps her hands on her knees and gets to her feet. "I'll do it. But only if I have to."

I take her in, this brave mortal who is so smart and completely out of her mind. "Then let's go save the world."

The Wild Hunt gathers at the edge of the tree line to see us off. On the left of a small pond, Freda, Jasmine, and Thor stand at the head of the living ranks. The fearless men and women under my command are prepared to defend what is left of Underhill's fey population for the rest of their lives.

On the right, Nahini, Bard, Gretchen, and Soladin surrounded by the ranks of the Draugar. Five lives and countless disembodied souls against the multitude of the dead.

Taj stands flanked on either side by Seelie Courtiers and refugees. Faces are bleak as they stare at us, their protectors and only line of defense.

"Midnight," is all he says to me.

"I'll take care of him," I say and move off so he can say a private goodbye to Soladin. Even if Underhill is listening, she won't know what that one crucial word means. Midnight, the time for the heirs to step forward and steal the fey power back from Pharaildis. It's the message we must get to Wardon's heir and the same one Alric carries to his sister in the Unseelie palace.

Our entire plan relies on precise timing. And of course, crossing the Veil twice is the difference between the upcoming midnight and one a century from now.

If that happens the citizens will all be dead, either because the shield falls or because they starve within it, and with them, the entire realm lost.

Including Aiden.

Casually as I am able, I sidle over to Thor. Aiden's "uncle" might have a few insights that will help.

He looks down at me, both literally and figuratively. "What is it, little queen? Have you come to your senses?"

He means, am I about to fall to my knees and beg him to

come with us. But I shake my head. "The people here need you to *guide* them."

He harrumphs but I can tell he is pleased by my lie, even if he would prefer to be in the thick of the action. The only thing the fey here need is his very large hammer in the event my shield of winds fails.

"Is there any way you know of to cross the Veil without losing time?"

Thor studies me for a long moment. "Time is not something even a god can control. It passes for us, as it does for you and for the mortals of Midgard. Not even the Norns can stop its steady march."

Disappointment swells in my chest. "That's what I thought."

"However," Thor's thick blond eyebrows pull together, in what I assume is his thinking face. To me, he appears constipated. "There is a prophecy. That when a sacrifice is made time in all the realms will move in tandem."

"What sort of sacrifice?"

"That I cannot say, only that it must be given selflessly in an in-between."

Perfect. "Okay, thanks for that."

"Battle well, little queen."

I move over to where Nahini holds the reins of my horse.

"Did you want to address the crowd?" she prompts. Ever my teacher, trying to help me win over the people.

I shake my head. "Either we will succeed and they will live free of Underhill or we will all die. We know it and so do they. No pep talk will change that."

She doesn't argue and as soon as I am settled on horseback, she turns to her own mount, dragon scale armor glittering in the midday sun.

I raise *Seelenverkäufer*. In one smooth, slashing motion I cut a tear in the fabric of the Veil. Through the gap, I can see our farmhouse, near the spot we had crossed. It is night there. Then, stowing the sword, I nod to Nahini. She rides through, followed by the souls of the Hunt.

I follow, with Gretchen and Soladin, and the shifter brings up the rear. We gallop hard up the hill, then launch, high up into the air. The sound of hooves is replaced with the silence of the late night as we pass above the farmhouse where no lights are on. I wish we could stop in and see Chloe and Addy, but there is no time. It is passing with every beat of my heart.

"Gretchen!" Bard calls out.

I turn to see the mortal swaying in her saddle. Her face is the color of chalk.

"Are you all right?" I ask her.

She blinks as though waking from a long nap. Then starts and throws her arms around her steed's neck. I'm about to order her and Bard to return to the ground when I see the shifter launch himself in midair from his saddle to hers. I hear him call out. "Don't worry, little sparrow. I've got you."

She turns to look up at him and his smile is tender as he gazes down.

Wind tugs at my braid, my clothes, and I can see Nahini's black and white mane being tossed about like a banner as she rides even higher, up above the clouds so we won't be spotted from the ground.

Even climbing in altitude, we move steadily towards the tear, the place where we had crossed into the Seelie Court. I hear a gasp and look over to see Gretchen's face flushed with delight. I can't help but smile back, in spite of my awareness of the clock. I am glad she chose to stay with us.

My friend.

"How long until we get there?" Bard asks.

"Five minutes, maybe ten."

"And we'll come out right where we want to?" Gretchen chews at a hangnail.

"Yes." Underhill can move the fey land in whichever way she sees fit. But since the tear happened above Wardon's lands, crossing through it will bring us out in his lands, no matter how mommy dearest redecorates.

Below us, smoke from chimneys curls up into the night. All the people in our podunk town going about their dinky little lives, never guessing for a second the danger they are in.

I feel it before I see it, the pull of the rip. It's gotten stronger than I ever could have believed, like the force of a collapsing star, yanking and tugging on me. Not on my clothes or hair like the wind, but on my soul.

It happens in the span of a heartbeat. One moment, Nahini is in the saddle, heading toward the tear as fast as her mount can carry her. The next, she is plummeting to the ground. The riderless horse whinnies, as though it senses the loss of her weight but it doesn't deter from its frantic gallop onward.

I spur my own horse down after Nahini. Blood pounds in my ears and my heart is in my throat. I won't make it in time, can do nothing but watch her splatter on the ground like a water balloon.

Then the Valkyrie soul, Nightweaver, snatches her up less than ten feet from the ground. The spirit materialized from nowhere and arrived just in time to keep my second from becoming nothing but a smear on the pretty hilltop.

"Thank you," I hear Nahini say to the dead Valkyrie as Nightweaver places her on the ground.

The spirit nods once, then disperses into a mist.

"What the hell happened?" I yank hard on the reins and my horse rears up alongside my fallen second.

She shakes her head, braids clattering together at the motion. "I'm not sure. Where's Hassan?"

Above, we hear a scream, not from a person but that of an animal. We look up in time to see Nahini's black stallion being torn apart in midair. I switch my vision to the soul plane so I can see the tear. It's changed in size and color from the last time I viewed it.

Blood rains down as the poor creature is sundered like the horse is being put through a paper shredder. I barely stifle the urge to vomit.

"Holy shit," I breathe.

We take a few steps back so we don't get horse remains on us. I feel a little dizzy, not a fan of blood and guts. Poor Hassan.

Nahini's face has paled to the color of ashes as she whispers, "That fall just saved my life."

Though I am a novice at offering comfort, it feels natural to put a hand on her shoulder. "Are you okay?"

She nods slowly, as if she is checking in with all her systems, making sure everything is still functioning. Her dark eyes are solemn. "I am whole, though I feel like a piece of me is missing. Hassan was a loyal companion, right to the end. Alric trained him well."

We both stare at the place where the horse had died while the rest of our party gathers around us.

"It's grown too large, the Veil too tattered. There is no way to safely cross through it," Soladin says.

"This will have to be close enough." I remove *Seelenverkäufer* from its sheath and am about to order Nahini into the saddle behind me when I see the robed figure with the bloodred hair.

Angrboda.

"Did you do this?" I shout across the twenty feet between where she stands and where we do. "Did you cause her to fall?"

"I saved her life," the giantess responds.

That might be. I would hate to think of Nahini suffering the same fate as her poor horse.

"Stay here," I order my party. "I want to talk to her."

Nahini looks as if she is about to argue, but I send my horse galloping down the hill before she can protest.

Angrboda doesn't budge from her spot on the hilltop as I near her. "The tear has grown unstable."

"Yeah, I caught that. Were you waiting here for us?"

She nods once. "I knew sooner or later you would try to cross."

I study her clothes, which look tattered and torn. Jeans with rips too ragged for designer methods and a jacket that had probably once been black but had faded to a charcoal color. Her feet are encased in battered ballet flats that are completely inappropriate for the rugged terrain. Here in Midgard, her glamour is in place and she merely looks like a tall, buxom redhead. Not the giantess I know her to be.

"Aiden let you go. Why are you still here?"

"As long as Underhill reigns I cannot return to the castle of the giants or even set foot in the fey realm."

"But why go out of your way for us?"

She stares at me, her expression unreadable. "Because of my son. I beg you, queen of the Unseelie, not to kill him."

I start. "Your son?"

She nods once. "Fenrir."

"Pretty sure I've never met him."

Her gaze is penetrating, eerie. "I have a debt to Váli and for his sake, I will not kill you in spite of the threat you pose one of my blood. Fenrir is destined to die at Ragnarök, at the hands of the All-Father who imprisoned him in *Gleipnir*, the chain that cannot be broken."

I don't have time for this. We might already be out of time. "Listen, if that's his destiny, then I don't know why you would think I would off him."

"Because he has done as his father bid and wronged you. Unconscionably so. And you are Nicneven, the Unseelie queen of the Shadow Throne. You do not tolerate disloyalty."

"I need to go." I am about to kick my steed into a trot but quick as a striking snake, Angrboda grabs my ankle.

"Your word, fey queen. You will not kill him."

I can lie. She doesn't know it any more than Freya did. My lips part to tell her whatever she wants to hear, but then I stare at her face. The face of a mother, separated from her offspring. And I hear the cry of the ghost baby.

"I promise."

She nods once and releases me. "Then I wish you luck with your endeavor."

"Will we be too late?" I'm not sure what prompts me to ask, but the giants wield some of the strongest magic, outside of the gods or the Norns. She might be able to help me, or at least tell me if I'll be in time. "To save them?"

"You mean to save him?" Her expression is neutral. "Your mate?"

I just stare her down, unwilling to admit anything.

"It is your destiny to save the fey," she offers. "To be worthy of his trust."

"How though?" The giants know magic better than any other race under the hill. "How can I stop an enemy that is already dead?"

"You need to replace what is missing."

"Can you be more specific?"

She shakes her head. "Remember your promise, Queen of the Shadow Throne."

I turn away from her. A fey queen cannot lie, a turned immortal cannot lie. Not so sure about a giant. I can lie, but my word must be solid. I must be trustworthy. For Aiden's sake as well as my own.

I just hope I don't live to regret it.

FRENEMIES

THROUGH THE WOLF'S EYES

"There must be another way out." Aiden paces the confines of the medical center, casting bleak looks out at the water as though it is what is keeping him trapped. Wardon reclines in a glass chair behind him while one of his healers works on buffing the last of his burned scales. All of the Seelie fey medics flinch every time Aiden turns their way, as though fearful that the big bad wolf is about to lose his shit.

They are right to worry.

"I've already told you, there isn't." Wardon is reading a report one of his aquatic minions delivered him. "The cave is completely surrounded by at least a thousand Draugar."

"What kind of idiot only has one exit to his underwater lair?" Aiden pivots sharply, glaring at Wardon. The wolf is restless and not just because he's trapped underwater. He can't sense Nic, can't feel her at all.

"None of that in front of the heir." Soon after they'd arrived, Wardon had sent one of the white-clad minions to go get his heir.

It was taking too long. Everything was taking too long.

I love you. I'm coming back for you.

And if he didn't clear a path, she would get herself killed. He knew it deep in his bones because it's exactly what he would do if she were the one stuck down here.

She would die. Trying to save him. That accursed rhyme was stuck in his head and with no room for the wolf to run, he had nothing to do but think. *Pretty dead girl. Third time will do it. The wolf at your bosom will be sure to see to it.*

What if she didn't die because he hurt her but because she got herself killed trying to save him?

A man could go insane thinking about this. If the madness didn't drive him there first.

"Wolf," Wardon snaps. "You need to get yourself under control or so help me, I will find another magic suppressing collar for you to wear."

"Try it," Aiden snarls.

Wardon huffs out a breath. "No, because that will only give you the excuse you are looking for to rip me to pieces."

He isn't wrong.

Aiden moves to the glass wall and stares out at the lake. He'd died in that black water. He was sure of it. The barrage of medical tests the staff had performed showed no sign of anything other than perfect health and the traces of madness that were even now expanding within him. But he'd felt the disconnect between himself and the wolf. Had felt the loss of self.

So, what power had brought him back here? What gifted him enough time for Wardon to save him and drag him to this underwater prison?

It wasn't his wolf, nor his father's fire magic that had saved him. He doubted Freya would have bestirred herself, and Underhill, the only other being powerful enough to keep a soul out of the hands of the Veil wanted him dead.

He stills. Not the only other being. There were two

others. Two others who were powerful enough to look out for his Nic.

The Norns.

Aiden scowls at his reflection in the glass. The same Norns who had allowed the gods to transform him into a wolf. The same ones who had almost killed his grandmother for helping him resurrect Nicneven. The same beings who'd destroyed their own sister for tampering with Nic's fate.

Who had raised her, protected and loved her for her entire life.

Could it be that they saved him...for her?

He lets out a weary exhale. Too much introspection, not enough action. "Do you have a vehicle? Something that can take me to the surface?" If he wasn't in the water his magic should work.

But Wardon shakes his head. "Nothing like that."

"Then how did you get all of this stuff down here?" Aiden gestures toward the high-tech medical equipment scattered about the glass room.

"My magic mostly," Wardon sighs and glances down at his long fingers as though he misses the feel of the powers between his hands. "Though some of it came through an in-between."

Aiden stops in midstride and turns. An in-between, or bolt hole, allows one to cross through the Veil that separates Underhill and Midgard. "Is it still open?"

Wardon blinks his large eyes at him. "Of course, but I don't see how going to the mortal plane will help."

"We leave here and then return through the Tear in the Veil. It's open not a day's walk from your palace. Bring your heir and we'll have him on the Gray Throne by sundown tomorrow."

Wardon shakes his head. "The Tear? You *must* be jesting.

Even if the in-between drops you off anywhere near it I would never—"

"Father!" Wardon is cut off abruptly as a small pink and gold-skinned fey boy runs for him. He scoops the boy, who can't be more than six, up into his arms. "Jedda, my lad. Have you missed me?"

Aiden gapes as realization dawns. This child, this boy who looks no sturdier than dandelion fluff is Wardon's heir? The soon to be Master of the Waves doesn't even reach his father's naval. The child is not just his heir, but Wardon's son.

All Aiden's newly forming plans evanesce as quickly as they appeared. He would never bring a child through the Tear. Part of him is still surprised the mortal Gretchen had made it through.

"Who is he, father?" The boy, Jedda, looks to Aiden with curiosity.

"He is…." Wardon trails off.

Aiden folds his arms over his chest and waits.

"He is here to help us. Do you remember when I told you that someday you were going to have to do my job, to be Master of the Waves?"

At Jedda's nod, Wardon sets him down, then crouches beside him. "Well, that day is today. We need to get you to the Gray Throne."

"I'm ready." Jedda stands up straighter, his slim body quivering with excitement. "I have been reading all the books you told me to read. And I know all the realms of the sea."

Wardon's face tightens but he forces a smile.

Aiden studies the two of them, father and son. A pang goes through him. In another life, he might have a child born to rule. That had been Nicneven's plan, after all, to sire an heir to the Shadow Throne and free herself of her responsibilities. Wardon had been a ruler for a long time, but he had prepared himself for the day when Jedda was to rule one of the great fey courts in his place. If Nicneven had lived long enough to bring their child into the world, would Aiden have done half as well with his own son or daughter?

But if Nicneven had lived, he wouldn't have Nic.

For the first time, he wonders if all his suffering had been part of something larger than himself. Maybe not an organized plan, but is it possible that his trials have made him into who he is meant to be? That all of it has made him a better match for his Unseelie queen?

I love you. I'm coming back for you.

Aiden stands up, ready to announce he will go it alone when the glass beneath his feet trembles.

"What's that?" Jedda asks, his large eyes taking over half his face.

Wardon is already striding to the glass. His lips part.

"The water is changing."

Aiden moves to his side. Sure enough, the black water is being altered, almost like the inky blackness is being sucked out.

"Jedda, go find your mother," Wardon says.

"But—"

"Now," Wardon's tone is absolute. He may no longer be the Master of the Waves, but he's still the lad's sire.

Jedda moves to the door. It isn't fully closed behind him when Wardon turns to Aiden. "It's her. Underhill is here."

The glass structure rocks again, hard enough that Aiden's shoulder slams into the wall. "What's she doing?"

Outside the glass, water breathing fey flee in a wake of bubbles.

Wardon's tone is bleak. "She's raising the city."

"What did you see?" Nahini asks her brother's ghost as he emerges from the cave where she had sent him to spy.

They'd crossed the Veil onto a stretch of beach. Nic had felt a pull, like an invisible grappling hook, had anchored on her ribcage. Aiden is near.

And so are the dead.

We've ridden to the nearest hilltop, overlooking the sea caves and saw them streaming in from every direction. They don't move quickly but they don't have to. The animated corpses bottleneck at the mouth of a cave.

More than even surrounded Soladin's palace. More than I've imagined. Dead fey walking. I give up counting after five hundred.

"There are so many," Bard says what we are all thinking. "This is more than just an army. I see children in the mix."

Sure enough, there are small bent shapes, some on two legs, some on four. Even a crawling baby.

A shudder goes through me.

"But why?" Gretchen steps forward. "Why would she let this happen if she wants to rule?"

"Hatred," I say. "She hates the fey for trapping the dreamers and using them to empower this world. This is her revenge."

"She's doing what she's always intended to do," Bard's tone is full of horror. "She's annihilating the fey."

Nahini's brother doesn't speak aloud. Many of the ghosts don't, but Nahini nods as though he's communicated something to her. She turns to me, her expression grave. "Underhill is inside. She's working some sort of magic around an opaque body of water. It seems to be spelled because though the space is full of Draugar, they haven't tried to breach the surface."

"What about our spirits?" I ask.

But she shakes her head. "The ghosts can't breach the water either but they think there is something down there."

"Something or someone," I murmur.

Soladin moves to my side, his dark eyes wide as he takes in the scene. His shoulders slump. "There's no way we can fight our way past them all, even with your ghost soldiers."

"Maybe there's another way into the cave?" Nahini suggests.

"If there were, Aiden wouldn't still be in there."

My second's gaze turns assessing. "Can you speak to him?"

Slowly, I shake my head. "No, and even if I could, there's nothing I can say. He can't face Underhill's might on his own. If any of you have any ideas, I'm open to suggestions."

Bard shrugs. Nahini stares blankly and Soladin shifts his weight.

"Gretchen?" I turn to the lone mortal, hoping she will give me something—*anything*—to work with.

She stares at the ground. "She wants him, right?" She points to Soladin. "Tell her you have him but you'll only hand him over if she comes out to meet you. Then you can talk to her."

"And say what? In case you haven't noticed, we aren't exactly bosom buddies."

Gretchen does a palms-up gesture. "You asked for ideas, that's the only one I've got."

The Draugar are impassable, unbeatable. I could use my magic, but I have no idea what my threshold is. And magic that isn't attached to my goodnight kiss or calling the winds always, comes with a price. The kiss of death won't work on the dead and I can feel the tension in the winds still keeping Soladin's home barricaded from the dead. Any other magic that I borrowed would cost me. And Underhill sets the price.

I'd be tapped before I even reach Pharaildis. There's no getting past that many, not even if we had Thor's hammer.

I turn to Soladin. "Are you sure you want to do this? You know the cost?"

He gives me a tight smile. "It doesn't matter what she takes from me. Taj is the only one who holds my heart. There is one thing though that I need first."

"Demands, really?" I tilt my head to consider him. What will he ask me? I already made a vow to Angrboda, albeit one I don't entirely understand. Two might be overkill. Still, I say, "Go ahead."

"I need you to forgive me."

I blink, sure I heard him wrong.

"For abducting you. I was desperate for your help and I didn't want to risk—" he shakes his head, cutting himself off mid-sentence. "No, I won't make excuses."

"Soladin," I start and don't know how to finish.

"Long ago, when my father still ruled, I made myself a promise that I would not do as he did. Pan thought only of himself and neglected the needs of those around him, courtier and Seelie subjects alike. He was selfish and manipulative, preoccupied with his own pleasure. I vowed not to follow in his footsteps. And I kept that vow until the day I abducted you. I have done what you asked, but I still need the words."

My lips feel dry, as though they've been sealed shut. I can't move. Forgiveness isn't something I've ever had in me to offer. Not that anyone's ever asked it of me before. I've come to understand his actions, the desperate need which drove him. But can I not only say the words, *I forgive you* but, mean them too?

Aiden would forgive him. He'd released Angrboda and she, in turn, had saved Nahini. *Everything happens for a reason.*

Those are Addy's words and as the Fate of destinies, she knows what she's talking about.

The emotion in Soladin's dark brown eyes is heartbreaking. The Lord of the Land needs this from me and considering what he's about to give up, I can't hold this grudge any longer.

I put one hand on his shoulder and squeeze. "I would have done the same, or worse, in your place. So yes, I forgive you."

His lids lower and his head slumps forward, shoulders rounding. "Thank you."

Maybe in a different life, under different circumstances, we could have been friends. It's an odd thought, since I could count on one hand the number of actual friends I've ever had. Sarah. Freda and Nahini. The persistent Gretchen. And Aiden.

I don't think the Lord of the Land can hear my thoughts but he answers as though he heard them loud and clear. "Okay, let's get your wolf back."

I turn to Nahini. "Midnight."

"Midnight," Nahini's tone is grim but she's too well trained to object. She rides back to the ghosts to give them their orders.

Bard isn't so accepting of my plan. "What of Rodrick? He's not going to let us just waltz in there."

"One thing at a time." I study him for a beat. "Any advice on how to deal with him?"

The shifter fixes his lidless gaze on me. "Kill him fast, before he kills you."

"I'll see you all soon."

"Be careful." Worry tints Gretchen's golden eyes.

"I'll do my best."

I pull Bard aside and jerk my chin at the mortal. "Look out for her."

The shifter puts a hand over his heart. "It is my honor and pleasure to watch over the fair mortal as she has so done for me."

Soladin hands Nahini the reigns to his mount and climbs on behind me. I don't look back at my friends as I spur the horse and fly over the sand dunes. The ghosts fan out behind us like an ethereal cloak.

Some instinct tells me not to draw *Seelenverkäufer*. I tuck the blade beneath a saddle blanket, within easy reach. I don't know what sort of powers the Soul Reaper possesses against the dead, but one thing is clear. Pharaildis wants both of us alive. She can't harm the ghosts, but the rest of my people— my courtiers—she'll hurt, use them the same way she used Aiden in order to bend me to her will.

There is a small measure of satisfaction in knowing I have outfoxed her though. Even if she takes my heart, even if she kills me outright, she won't have the powers of all four royals.

I am expecting resistance. Instead, the Draugar part as though invisible hands have shoved them out of the way. Soladin's hands tighten around my waist. We pass by the dead fey. He says nothing, but his anxiety is palpable as the mindless creatures plaster themselves against the wet rock walls.

My mount's hooves ring out on the stone as we move deeper into Wardon's territory. The Draugar watch us with sightless eyes, some nothing more than empty sockets. They surround us on all sides but make no sounds, no breathing or shifting the way a living being might. They remind me of the lines the Dead of the Hunt formed the first time I saw them. Souls without bodies.

The Draugar are bodies without souls.

A jolt goes through me as I recall Angrboda's advice. *Replace what is missing.* Freya's bitter words. *It was thought by some that having a creature with such power would prove useful.*

"Soladin," I murmur his name as low as I can. Too bad we can't communicate mind to mind the way I do with Aiden. "You wanted me to bring the Wild Hunt to combat the Draugar. Why?"

He doesn't ask why I'm inquiring now. "The Hunt is unstoppable, the deadliest force under the hill. It was created by the first four royals to protect us in our time of greatest need."

"Were the dead souls always part of the Hunt?"

He shakes his head. "No, they were Queen Nicneven's—your—unique contribution."

I am a serial killer, a hunter of evil. I've tethered countless souls through my goodnight kiss in both my lives, swelled the ranks of the host with souls of killers.

Their numbers are legion, endless, unable to be destroyed.

Just like my mother's army.

What if the souls under my command don't fight the dead, but combine with them? Will the two broken halves make up a whole?

There is no time to test my theory. The rock tunnel opens up to a cavern. More Draugar skulk about the edge of a black lake. Something is just breaching the inky surface, something large.

"Ah, Nicneven, there you are." Pharaildis waves me over as though she's been holding a place in line for me. "Just in time, too."

"In time for what?" I ask as black water slides down the outer hull of a transparent *something*.

"The end of my imprisonment." Her blue eyes shine with triumph as more of the mammoth object appears. It looks like a building, or more, a series of buildings. People are visible inside the structure, looking like trapped ants in an upside-down test tube.

The water sloshes as more and more of it is revealed. A tip layer presses into the roof of the cavern but the building continues to rise. Glass shatters, cries ring out as the shards rain down on its inhabitants.

A city. An entire civilization buried beneath the water. A final shudder and the structure stills, floating like a large island in the middle of the lake.

So many. There are so many people scrambling around inside. I scan the faces of the fey, looking for a set of leaf green eyes. My heart lurches when I spy him at the window in the tallest building, the one with the top sheared off.

Aiden stares back, his hands press to the glass. I see his mouth form a single word.

My name.

Pharaildis stands there, surrounded by her reanimated army and looks from the Seelie king to me. "And the end of the fey way of life."

THE END

THROUGH THE MAN'S EYES

Nic? What are you doing? His heart thunders. She came back for him. Just as she promised she would.

And put herself in the line of fire.

Her eyes are on his and he's close enough to see her lids lower a moment as though in relief. *What does it look like? I'm saving your ass.*

Go to her. The wolf is ready to shift to sparks and materialize by Nic's side. Where he belongs. She is wearing armor and facing down her mother. But Wardon grabs him by the arm before he can go.

"The water is all that protected this place. Now that it is exposed it is no longer safe. Take Jedda." The fey male grips him hard, his bare feet crunching on the glass that had been the ceiling not even ten minutes before. "Take him to my former palace, to the Gray Throne."

Aiden stares at him blankly. "You want me to run?"

We do not run from danger. The wolf is adamant.

Wardon gestures to the small party on the land. "Nic and Soladin are both right there. She has all of the fey royals within her reach. Take Jedda, let him do what he was born to do, and then hide him until this is over. You're the only one can leave unimpeded."

Nic looks to him. Her beautiful blue eyes carve out a piece of his soul.

Wardon wants me to take his heir. He thinks to her. *Take him to the Gray Throne.*

Her expression doesn't change. Did she hear him?

Nic?

Where her voice echoed a moment ago there is only a great, howling space.

"She has a plan," Wardon's tone is desperate. "She has the dead of the Hunt and Soladin. She must have a plan."

"And what if I'm part of that plan?" Indecision tears at him like a vulture picking at roadkill. What if Nic was counting on him to be here? What if his leaving gets her killed?

Again.

But a new worry blooms inside him. What if his staying tips the balance and brings about the end of the world? She'd die anyway, everyone would.

"Wolf, I vow that I and everyone in this city will do everything in our power to help her but you are the only one who can make a real difference." The former Master of the Waves, the man who'd tortured him, falls to his knees. "Please, do this."

Two words echo in his mind, her voice like the touch of velvet. *Go. Midnight.*

He turns and runs for the corridor where Jedda had disappeared.

He finds the boy huddled in an alcove a few yards outside the infirmary. "Your father wants you to come with me."

"Where?" Jedda's eyes are huge in his thin face.

He prepares himself for the child to put up resistance as he tells him the truth. "I'm taking you to the Gray Throne."

The boy surprises him though. He untucks his small frame from the hiding place and reaches for Aiden's hand.

"Hang on." The second their skin connects they break into sparks. Jedda gasps a moment before his face dissolves and then they are floating up through the broken ceiling and out over the dead.

Though he is tempted to drop sparks onto the corpses, Aiden doesn't. Their exit will be most successful if it goes unnoticed by anyone.

He trusts Nic to keep herself alive and safe. He must do his job and get Jedda to safety.

They float out through the cave and up across the sky, sometimes crossing water, other times overland. He spies the remains of the Seelie glass castle. He does one pass, then another to make sure the place is as abandoned as it appears before setting them down in the former courtyard. Aiden is careful that they are still away from the smoldering remains of the dead.

They reform slowly. Jedda throws an arm up over his eyes to block out the intensity of the setting sun.

"Are you okay?" Aiden moves his body between the boy and the sunset, realizing how pale the child is, how unused to sunlight his eyes must be after living under the water and knowing only the glow of bioluminescence.

This is in all likelihood, his first sunset.

"Where are we?" Jedda scans the landscape.

"One of your father's estates." He glances around trying to get his bearings.

Aiden eyes the decimated troll barracks. Several of the creatures linger within, turned to stone in the light of day.

"What are we doing here?" Jedda is full of questions.

"Looking for the Gray Throne." He eyes the boy carefully. "Do you know where that is?"

Jedda shakes his head.

That would have been too easy. A sea bird cries out.

"What's that?" Jedda points.

Aiden realizes that not only has he been given the temporary guardianship of Wardon's son and heir, he is also responsible for his education about the world above the surface of the water. "A seagull."

"Oh, I've read about those." Jedda tilts his head, again shading his eyes as he watches the bird soar.

Standing out in the open isn't wise. Aiden takes the boy's hand and tugs him toward one of the standing structures. "Come on, we better start looking."

The sooner Jedda sat on the throne and became the new Master of the Waves, the sooner Aiden could get back to Nic.

Midnight, she had thought. What did that mean? Did she wish for him to return at midnight? Even if he found the Gray Throne by then, with no one to watch Jedda, he wouldn't be free to return. Yet it must mean something.

"What's that?" Jedda scampers off to crouch down beside a Hermit Crab.

At this rate, they'd be lucky if they found the throne before midnight.

I watch Aiden's sparks out of the corner of my eye. My mother is too busy studying Soladin shinny off the saddle to notice.

"What did she have to do to get you here?" Pharaildis asks.

Soladin, his arms still loosely bound shifts uneasily

behind me. "She told me it was the only way you would spare the fey."

"Spare the fey?" She looks smugly from him to me. "Did you really say that?"

"In a manner of speaking," I hedge.

She laughs and it isn't a pleasant sound. "My clever girl. I vow I will be as compassionate to the fey as they have been to the human dreamers who have ventured into this world. King Soladin, be a dear and create a bridge to the castle."

Soladin hesitates. "This isn't my season or my realm—"

"Do it," she snaps, "or I'll burn all of them inside that pretty glass sarcophagus while you watch."

I try to keep my face even as Soladin slithers without grace onto the cave floor. He staggers into a Draugar and his face drains of color. The dead fairy doesn't respond.

Underhill stares at the Lord of the Land with undisguised displeasure. "I grow weary of waiting."

He straightens up, adjusts his tunic, and then turns to face the water. His brows furrow in concentration. At first, there is nothing. Then the ground beneath us rumbles. My horse sidesteps uneasily, her eyes rolling and exposing the whites. I pat the great beast on the neck, doing my best to infuse some of Alric's Spriggan calm into my touch.

A land bridge forms, smoother than the walls or floor of the cave. It grows steadily upward toward the glass city. A final shake and it is done, the city looking for all the world like it had been designed in its current location at the end of a natural land bridge.

"After you." Underhill gestures Soladin out onto the Bridge. "You too, Nicneven. Off the horse and keep those ghosts right where they are. And your sword."

Replace what is missing. Is my theory correct?

My gaze flicks to Nightweaver and then to the Draugar

foot soldier closest to her. Silently, she drifts even closer. I dismount to cover the small movement.

Soladin and Underhill are already halfway across the land bridge by the time I catch up to them. The tip of the bridge ends inches in front of the tallest glass building, the one with the damaged roof.

Looking back at us through the transparent barrier is Wardon.

Pharaildis raises her voice until it rings through the cavern. "Come out, Wardon. And bring your little replacement with you."

He stares at her a beat, then, very deliberately gives her the finger.

I cough to cover my laugh.

"Break the glass," she commands the Lord of the Land. I wonder why she doesn't just take his heart so she can wield the power herself.

The Draugar don't move, don't blink or breathe as the cave rumbles again. I spread my feet wide for balance as the ground shifts enough to shatter the solid pane between Wardon and Underhill.

It is a delicate operation. Soladin's brow pinches from the concentrated effort. The bridge grows to a point and presses into the pane of glass. Cracks spiderweb out for a moment and then it shatters, leaving Wardon exposed and utterly defenseless.

"Soladin," he nods to the Lord of the Land as if they just ran into each other in the market.

"Wardon. I thought you were dead."

"Just out of commission."

A fireball forms in Underhill's palm. She pulls her arm back as though preparing to hurl the thing into the glass palace. "Bring him out now."

"Who?" The former Master of the Waves gives her a blank stare.

"Your heir."

"I don't know what you're talking about."

I have to give it to him. He has no magic and yet he stands there, looking for all the world like he's holding the winning hand of cards.

She studies him for an endless moment. Behind Wardon, a fey woman with skin so white it seems to glow, shifts beneath the desk where she's been hiding. The movement draws Underhill's gaze. Her smile turns predatory.

"Don't," I gasp, but it's too late.

The fireball sails through the air, straight at the fey woman. It's a direct hit and between one heartbeat and the next, her entire body is engulfed in flames. She shrieks and struggles, trying to get away from the fire, scrambling out into the open. Her screams echo through the entire cavern.

Wardon waves his hand then looks crestfallen when the water from his black lake doesn't respond. I too can do nothing. I can't call my winds from where they protect Soladin's people to help save this poor creature.

She staggers to the edge of the shattered glass wall and dives into the water. The flames sizzle out, steam rises into the air. Bubbles drift up from the surface. Then nothing. The silence is deafening.

A moment later, a black sphere the size of a Volkswagen lifts from the water. Underhill's arm is extended out, clearly controlling the thing. It moves to the bridge before us and then splashes down. Water runs off either edge of the land bridge and deposits the burnt corpse.

Wardon makes a sound and takes a step forward. The dead fey's eyelids flash open and she rises. There is no sign of the terror or agony she'd just experienced as she gets to her feet. She is utterly lifeless, brought back by magic. A Draugar.

Her hands reach out and wrap around Wardon's neck. Though she is half his size, she manages to lift him off the ground until his feet dangle helplessly in the air.

I can't move, can barely breathe. That easy. It was that easy for Underhill to transform one of the Seelie king's subjects and turn her into an obedient soldier for her army.

"Either you can give him to me," Underhill says, her voice calm and even, "or I will do the same to each and every one of your people one at a time."

Wardon makes a gurgling sound as though he's trying to speak.

Pharaildis's eyes narrow. "What was that?"

The Draugar's hands are like claws sinking into his neck. Rivulets of blue blood run down from where her fingernails puncture his skin.

"Gone." Somehow Wardon manages to laugh. It's more of a hysterical spluttering but his amusement shines in his eyes.

"That isn't possible." Pharaildis makes a sharp cutting motion and the Draugar releases her—its—grip. Wardon hits the ground like a sack of potatoes. "Nothing has escaped this cave since you came in."

"Nothing that you can control." Wardon grins.

She doesn't respond, asks him no more questions. Instead, the Draugar of the Seelie fey girl reaches for him, claws tearing and shredding.

"Stop!" I yell.

Madness must have taken over because he is laughing. We can see his insides and he's *laughing.*

"Nightweaver." It's now or never.

The ghost of the dead Valkyrie responds, diving right for the Draugar.

"No," Pharaildis's eyes are wide. "Stop her, Nicneven."

But I don't. The spirit dives into the body just as Wardon,

the former Master of the Waves and the last ruler of the Gray Throne, is eviscerated before my eyes.

Both bodies collapse onto the bridge, marionettes whose strings have been cut.

Underhill stares at me uncomprehendingly. "You would dare to defy me?"

Nightweaver emerges unscathed, a triumphant grin on her hideous bird face.

"What did you expect?" I gesture to Nightweaver to continue. She dives into the closest Draugar, a lithe fey male. I see her outline vanish and a second later, the body hits the ground in an awkward sprawl.

"That's not possible." Pharaildis gawks at the dead fey. "What did you do?"

I draw *Seelenverkäufer* and point it at her. "I set her free of your control. One less soldier in your army."

Behind us the dead surge into motion. Though the Draugar are formidable, there is no stopping the souls of my Wild Hunt.

Nightweaver dives into Wardon's body as all the murderous souls tethered to the Wild Hunt, do the same with the nearest Draugar, replacing what is missing, by tying flesh to spirit long enough to break the power of the runes and setting the dead free. The instant one corpse hits the ground the spirit rises up and moves to the next.

"You can't." Underhill's blue eyes are wild. "You must stop."

I level the blade at her. "I won't let you hurt them, not living and not the dead. They are mine to protect."

"I am your mother," she tries.

"She is?" It's Soladin who asks the question.

"Technically, she was Nicneven's mother."

His dark eyes narrow.

Pharaildis raises her hands. I expect her to unleash her

arsenal on me but instead, she closes in on Soladin. "You must help me stop her or she will destroy your entire court."

Large dark eyes shoot to me and I can see the many questions there.

"Don't listen to her," I tell him. "They are all safe behind my wall of wind."

"The winds are gone," Underhill's mouth curves up in a smug smile. "They drifted off the second you crossed the Veil."

"She's lying." I can still feel the air currents to the west, swirling in a protective circle around the Green Throne.

"Am I? It takes a liar to know one." Underhill is all sincerity as she faces the Seelie king. "Did she tell you she could lie?"

He doesn't answer, but his gaze crawls over me with accusation. Damn it, I should have told him of my relationship with her earlier.

As if sensing her advantage, Underhill presses, "She lied to you, told you she needed your help to overthrow me. But I am trying to save the fey. She's the one who wishes to destroy all of you."

"That's not true." I shake my head. "Soladin, think."

"She killed her own kind." Underhill jabs a finger to the ghosts who are embodying the Draugar one at a time. "Hunted them like animals, tricked them and trapped them into her service. The most powerful queen in fey history is a fully functioning liar."

"What of Wardon?" Soladin asks her. He appears to be listening to her. My stomach lurches with unease. Is the fey king actually buying her crap? Admittedly, I am not the best judge of character but I thought he understood who the enemy is here. "You stole his power."

"Wardon was unstable. Allowing him to linger would have been crueler than this end. "

"And what about the woman?" I push. "The innocent Seelie fey we just watched you burn and drown and transform unnaturally just to serve a point."

"She was no innocent. In fact, she was one of his courtiers. Check her quarters. She kept thralls, human slaves, to do her bidding."

She has an answer for everything. An answer Soladin appears to be swallowing whole.

Sensing her advantage, Underhill takes a small step forward. "You'd be a fool to trust her. To entrust your loved ones to her tender care. Remember, she's the one who brought the winds to the refugee camp. Don't you think it convenient that Nicneven decimates the village, bringing all those refugees to your doorstep and then has the miraculous answer on how to save everyone? You know Nicneven's reputation. She only thinks of herself."

She's good, all her arguments are sound, irrefutable.

"No one else has to die, Soladin. Stop her. She possesses the means to stop the Draugar. Isn't it curious that only now does she reveal them? How can you trust such a manipulative creature?"

"Is it true? You can still lie?" Soladin studies me, his expression unreadable. The fear is etched on his face. The backup plan will only work if Taj is alive if his people are still safe. If I am telling the truth.

"Yes," I tell him. "I can."

He stares at me for a long moment and then something collides with the back of my head.

I fall to the land bridge, right beside Wardon's body a single word, a command, lingering on my lips.

"Go."

Through the Man's Eyes

Aiden stumbles, his hand raising automatically to the back of his head as though a large rock struck him there. For a moment his vision tunnels, before returning to normal. His fingers probe the area but no lump forms.

"Are you okay?" Jedda blinks up at him, his small brow furrows.

"Yeah," Aiden lets his hand fall away. The pain fades until it is as if nothing happened. "It's nothing."

Nic. That strike had been to Nic's head. Like their intimate moments, Aiden is experiencing the world from her perspective.

His mind races. If she's been knocked unconscious, she's in danger. And without her to command them, the spirits of the Wild Hunt won't fight. She could be hurt, and Underhill might be here at any moment.

The sun has been down for hours. The moon has risen and glimmers on the rippling sea. His hands are scraped raw from moving debris. Though they have dug through the rubble of Wardon's sandcastle, inspected the remains of every chamber, there is no sign of the Gray Throne. It would take him a year of working night and day to complete this haphazard search. With Underhill about to descend on them, he needs to narrow it down. Fast.

"Jedda," he crouches down beside the boy. "Did your father ever say anything to you about where the Gray Throne was in his castle?

It isn't the first time Aiden's asked the question. And as he had all the other times, Jedda shakes his head.

"All he said is that it was well hidden in plain sight."

Aiden blows out a breath and murmurs, "That narrows it down."

"What?"

"Nothing." Frustrated, Aiden backs up. Well hidden in plain sight. The Unseelie Thrones shared the same space, within the castle. He thinks back to the meeting he'd overheard with Rodrick and his sons. The Spriggan might have been overcautious about the Thrones being able to kill. Then again, he'd been an Unseelie Courtier for centuries. What if they found the Gray Throne and the thing killed Jedda?

No, he couldn't dwell on that. Wardon wouldn't have sent the boy here if he thought the throne capable of harming him.

Aiden, he would have risked, but not his son and heir.

But why hadn't he given Aiden a hint? Paranoid and crafty, the Master of the Waves would have been hiding the Gray Throne, concealing its power as a sort of game.

"Hidden in plain sight." Aiden closes his eyes and tries to imagine the layout of the palace the way it had been. The study, the spiral stairs, the dining hall.

The dining hall.

He'd never been there but Nic had described a scene where the Master of the Waves lorded over the mahogany table and matching chairs. She'd noted it because the entire room had an entirely different feeling than the rest of the sandcastle.

His gaze falls on a heap of chairs on the far side of their rubbish zone. They appear to be constructed from gilt and wood. Several appear broken but one stands by itself, as though waiting....

Waiting in plain sight.

Wardon would have delighted in disguising his throne, presiding over every state dinner from the place.

Aiden lifts Jedda up in his arms and picks his way across the debris toward the chair. Something thrums within him. He doesn't know if it's the beating of his own overeager heart or a trace of magic.

"Do you hear that?" Jedda asks, eyes wide. "It sounds like an ocean current."

Aiden sets him down. "Where is it coming from?" he asks the lad.

The boy points directly to the chair. "It's inviting me to sit down."

"Do you want to sit there?" Aiden looks from the boy to the chair and back again. If the child says no, he won't force the issue. Jedda might not be ready for the power, might not understand what sitting on the throne means.

But Jedda nods. He's careful to pick his spindly legs up as he steps over the rubbish. He's too short to simply lower himself into the chair, so he scrambles up it, his feet hovering inches from the ground.

Aiden holds his breath. Waiting.

There is a sudden flash and then the chair changes. With Jedda still perched atop it, the thing morphs into a monstrosity of shells and driftwood and sleek, smooth stone. Jedda's eyes pale out and begin to glow. All the small hairs rise along Aiden's body, charged like the air around an electrical storm. Though the power is brand new and must be especially intense with it being in his season, he doesn't cry or scream. He doesn't make a single sound. Wardon really had been grooming him for this experience.

Aiden beholds the child sitting on the Gray Throne and bows. "Master of the Waves and ruler of the Gray Throne. It's good to meet you. Now, we need to get out of here, immediately."

"Where are we going?" Jedda hops down. The glow in his eyes fades.

"You," Aiden holds out a hand. "are going to cross the Veil. It's the only place I'm sure you'll be safe."

Jedda turns back to the chair and waves a hand. It returns to its mahogany and brocade state. "What about you?"

"I'll follow as soon as I'm able." Aiden gives him a tight smile and they evaporate into sparks.

I wake to a warm hand on my shoulder and another covering my mouth. I stare up into Soladin's dark eyes. Underhill, the Wild Hunt, and the Draugar are nowhere in sight.

"Don't scream," the Seelie king says. "There could be someone right outside the door."

I sit up and push his hand aside to feel the large lump at the back of my head. "You hit me with a rock," I accuse.

Soladin shrugs helplessly. "Sorry. It was the only thing I could think of to get us both out of there."

"No, you did right." I study our surroundings. The room is about twelve feet by ten feet with a firepit in the center. The floor is cold gray stone, and rough to the touch, and the walls look to be the same. No windows and only one door made from solid oak. Torches line the walls, casting the only visible light. It looks like something out of a Dark Ages film.

"Where are we? It looks sort of familiar."

"It should." The Seelie king shakes his head. "Never thought I would see the inside of the underground palace."

I let out a breath. The underground palace, the seat of power for the Unseelie. I knew she'd bring us here. She had to, otherwise, she wouldn't get my powers. "How long have I been out?"

"Not long. A few hours."

"Where is Pharaildis?" I am surprised she didn't prop my unconscious carcass on the Shadow Throne already.

Soladin gets to his feet and offers me a hand. "No idea. She deposited us here and locked us in."

"How very Flowers in the Attic," I grumble as I get to my feet. My head hurts, but I don't think I have a concussion.

"What?" Soladin appears confused.

I forget that he has never been human, he blends so well with them. "It's a book. A very screwed-up book about a mother who essentially locks her children in a bedroom so she can tart around."

The room is dark, none of the reflected light I recall from my memories of the dream palace. No bed, but there is what appears to be rows of spider thread woven hammocks hanging on one wall. "If I'm not mistaken this is the servant's quarters."

"How far from here to the throne room?" he asks.

"It's a few levels up, near the center front overlooking the underground lake. *Seelenverkäufer*?" I've finished my cursory inventory and come up a little too light.

Soladin shakes his head. "It disappeared before she could pick it up."

Dollars to doughnuts, it was in the hands of a grabby, cat-eyed goddess. Without that weapon, I can't cross the Veil or trap my mother's soul. "What about Wardon's glass city? Did she hurt the Seelie fey there?"

Soladin's eyes appear worried. "Not personally, but she took us out before I could retract the land bridge. Some of them might have enough magic to escape before the Draugar make it past that logjam of bodies, but without the ghosts, they will have to find another way out."

"At least she didn't set it on fire. Or drown them."

Soladin turns to face me and ducks down so he can murmur in my ear, "I don't think she can drown them. She tried to do something to the water but whatever it was, it didn't work."

"Aiden?"

The Lord of the Land nods. "I think your wolf got the heir to the Gray Throne and there is a new Master of the Waves."

I shove the mental image of Wardon's unseeing eyes out of my head. I hadn't liked him, part of me even considered him an enemy. But he'd fought as long and hard as he could for his people. I can respect that. "She probably knows you have someone waiting to snatch your power back to the Seelie Court if she tries to force you to give up your heart."

He nods. "The heir is going to be hunted to the ends of the realm."

"And Aiden can't cross to Midgard without losing his mind." I close my eyes, doing my level best to stave off the throbbing headache.

"How did she know about the heir?" Soladin asks.

My brows draw together. "What?"

"The heir. She knew about him. She sent the Draugar into the cave. Someone would have had to tell her."

"She could have seen…." I trail off with a frown. "All she would have seen was Aiden and Wardon going into the caves."

Soladin's eyes are grim. "Someone in the know must have told her. Someone we trusted."

Angrboda made me promise not to kill him, her son, Fenrir.

The wolf at your bosom will be sure to see to it.

At my bosom, someone close to me, a member of my inner circle.

Fenrir the wolf had infiltrated the Unseelie Courtiers.

The door creaks open and a tall gray-bearded fey who looks like a thinner, less kind version of Alric moves inside. "Well, well, Queen Nicneven I presume. You look…different."

The way he says it, with a slow sweep of my form, indicates that he finds me lacking. I give it right back to him, the slow, dismissive once over while I check for weaknesses. He has no weapons and Spriggan magic allows them to communicate with animals, so no need to worry about his magic.

I step forward and offer him a hand. When he reaches for it, I pull him in close and press my lips to his cheek.

Nothing happens.

I gape. This wasn't my doing. The magic of my goodnight kiss is intentional, I had to want my prey to die for it to work. And I definitely wanted this old letch to kick it. He is one of my souls, a remorseless killer and he should belong to the Wild Hunt.

He smirks at me and gestures to the thin chain hanging around my neck. "Lady Underhill saw to it that your magic was bound by *Gleipnir*. It contains all of your magic. It would be a waste of time for you to try to escape, but by all means, give it a shot if you are so motivated. I like playing with royalty."

I try to remove the chain, to call my ghosts, the wind. I try snatching the fire from the torch and transforming myself into a mouse. The harder I try, the faster my magic seems to drain away from me.

Rodrick nods as though he can see how hard I am fighting and my struggle pleases him. "I am to escort you both to the throne room for the trial."

"The trial?" Soladin's brows lift. "Which of us is supposed to be on trial?"

"Both of you. Well, all the fey really, but particularly the royals." Rodrick shoves me until I stumble forward.

"For what crime?" Soladin presses.

But Rodrick is done talking. He grips the Seelie king's arm with his left hand and the back of my neck with his right. With bruising force, he propels me onward.

The sensation of his hands on my flesh makes my skin crawl. I don't struggle. A trial against the fey, he'd said. Underhill is already set on our annihilation. Why bother with the farce?

Rodrick's shiny black boots tap out a steady rhythm, as

though his footfalls are heralding our arrival. Part of me can't believe I am finally in the underground palace. In the flesh. It appears dingier than it had during my flashbacks, more rundown. There are no fey servants, but ghosts abound. They drift through solid rock and mill about up at the high ceiling. Some look wounded, others appear hale, like the ghosts from the Hunt.

One in a ragged dress with dragonfly-like wings swoops down in my path and hovers not a foot from me. I stop short. She has no visible feet but I don't know if that is a reflection of her energy or a wound inflicted before she died. She opens a yawning toothless mouth and screams in my face. It is a mournful, wordless sound that sets my teeth on edge. This ghost knows who I am and unlike the spirits at the summer palace, she wants my attention.

I freeze, searching her face for anything familiar.

Rodrick doesn't give me a chance. When he notices I am no longer beside him he turns and reaches through her transparent body to yank me forward.

"Move," he barks.

I huff out a breath, still chilled from the ghostly contact. I know her eyes follow me down the hall.

"Where is everyone?" Soladin asks, though I'm not sure if he's talking to me or trying to distract Rodrick.

"Waiting." Rodrick's clipped tone sounds smug.

The stone wall and floors fade from dark gray to dove gray and then to cream and finally to moonstone white as we ascend the stairs. I can feel the power thrumming in the air of the throne room, like uneven pressure trying to equalize.

The room is full of fey. The forever young are packed in the cavernous space like sardines in a tin. The noise bounces off the high stone ceiling and cold hard floors. It's not happy sounds like a celebration, but low murmuring that throws off its own dark energy. The ones nearest to the doorway turn to catch a glimpse of us.

"Stand aside," a familiar voice rings out. Not Underhill, though I'd expected her. No, this comes from someone else.

And then I see it, the thing I'd been dreading and fighting for since Aiden first came back into my life.

The Shadow Throne.

Seated on top—its new queen—is Gretchen Hamill.

And right behind her, wearing a triumphant grin is my mother.

THE BEGINNING

"No," I breathe. "It can't be."

"Surprised?" Amused golden eyes assess me. "Why, you asked me to take the throne if anything were to happen to you."

That had been a fallback plan. In case everything went to hell. "It…accepted you? But you're not fey. You haven't been through the gauntlet."

"No, I'm not fey," Gretchen's tone is smug, so unlike the girl, I thought I was coming to know. "I'm something much better."

"Really, Nicneven. Haven't you figured it out yet?" Underhill, still in her purple robes, moves forward to stroke Gretchen's hair as one would touch a beloved golden retriever. "You suspected you had a second traitor. Didn't it strike you as odd that Isolde is slaughtered right when you bring Gretchen to the farm? A mortal tracked you, blackmailed you and you never once asked how she'd managed it."

I tip my head to the side to study Gretchen. "How could you have gotten to Isolde? I was with you the entire time."

One dark eyebrow arches up. "Were you?"

My mind is working furiously. I'd brought her to the farmhouse, gone into my room to change. Chloe had followed me. She'd been alone in the living room. The front door had been right there.

The Wild Hunt had been in the barn, watching Bard's performance. We'd heard nothing later when we'd passed the shed.

But that means Gretchen had sped out into the night, killed Isolde, hidden the body somehow and the Soul Reaper and then returned to the cottage in those few minutes.

No mortal could have done all that in so short a time.

I stare at her, the girl I'd come to think of as a friend. Again. I'd been betrayed by a friend again. This wasn't Gretchen, at least not the Gretchen I thought I knew.

"Where are the others?" The last I'd seen her, Gretchen had been with Bard and Nahini, heading for this palace as fast as their steeds would carry them.

Though I'd directed the question to Gretchen, it is Underhill who answers. "Why, right here."

She waves off to the side and I see a cage. Inside it, bound and gagged, are Nahini and Bard. It's not made of metal though, but of spirits. The Dead of the Hunt.

Who are now under Gretchen's control. Because she is seated on the Shadow Throne. She rules from it and they must obey her will.

I try to command them the way I had in the cave. They don't so much as twitch, not even Nahini's brother or Nightweaver.

Soladin sucks in a breath. Underhill controls the Draugar, Gretchen commands the spirits of the Wild Hunt. Two unstoppable armies with no way to combat either of them.

I stare at Gretchen, searching her face for answers. "Who are you?"

She pulls up her silver necklace. "Doesn't this look familiar, Nic?"

Only with my mother standing right beside her, only with the silver chain tethering her ankles glinting in the firelight from the great hearth does it register. The chain Gretchen always wears. As if she has to.

"Imprisonment?" I shake my head. "That doesn't make any sense. You crossed the Veil with us."

"There are different kinds of prisons." Golden eyes glow. "*Gleipnir* controls strength, binds the spirit to an unfamiliar land. Or an unappealing body."

Angrboda's plea swarms me. *He is destined to die at Ragnarök.*

Fenrir was bound in *Gleipnir*. By Odin. The wolf is trapped inside of Gretchen Hamill.

Loki's poem surfaces inside the yawning abyss in my mind.

Pretty dead girl
How will you die?
First fire, then water
And the stab of a lie.

Pretty dead girl
What will you gain?
Knowledge is power
Unless you're not sane.

Pretty dead girl
Third time will do it

The wolf at your bosom
Will be sure to see to it.

The wolf at my bosom was never Aiden's wolf. It was Gretchen. Or rather Fenrir trapped within Gretchen. I'd done it again, put my trust in the wrong person. Gretchen, who I'd been thinking of as my friend. I asked her to rule the fey if I couldn't stop Underhill.

And this whole time they'd been working together.

And according to the poem, I am fated to die a third and final time. Because of the wolf, I had kept too close. The wolf who wants to swallow the world.

"How long?" I ask Fenrir. "How long have you been possessing Gretchen?"

Underhill holds up a hand. "You can have all of your questions answered, Nicneven, but first tell us, where is your wolf going?"

"I don't know."

"You do," Gretchen—Fenrir snarls. "You do know. They communicate telepathically, mind to mind. She told me she could feel him die."

"I should have killed you when I had the chance," I snarl. Promise or no, lie or no, I will make up for that oversight at the next opportunity.

"Enough!" Underhill slams her hand down on a stone table. It cracks in half under her onslaught. All the living fey in the room jump back, trembling under her display. "He's here somewhere and the fey only have two strongholds left. How convenient that we have two unstoppable armies to annihilate them both. Rodrick, what time is it?"

"Almost midnight." Rodrick's hateful eyes gleam. "Just a few more minutes."

"No." The word slips from Soladin's lips.

"Oh yes, I know about your little scheme." Underhill strides down the stone steps from the throne.

With dread, I realize that Gretchen—Fenrir has betrayed more than me and the Unseelie Court. If Taj tries to sit on the Green Throne, assuming that Soladin's heart has been taken from his chest, that his power is up for grabs, the throne will destroy him. "Please, I beg of you. Taj is innocent."

"No fey is innocent!" My mother backhands him across the face. With his hands bound, he goes sprawling onto the floor. "You trapped all those souls, have held them to do your bidding." She kicks him viciously.

"Stop!" I shout at the same time as someone else does.

I toss my hair back in time to see...Aiden.

Run! I think at him.

He doesn't appear to hear me.

Aiden go, warn Taj! He'll die.

Not so much as a flicker of an eyelash to indicate that he heard me.

Our connection has been acting oddly, but this is different. Almost as though he *can't* hear me.

Or doesn't know our bond is there.

"Where is he?" Underhill focuses on this new target for her wrath. "Where is the heir?"

"The other Seelie king is safe across the Veil." It's Aiden's voice, Aiden's leaf green eyes. Yet the sense of something being wrong grows.

It's the way he's standing. Aiden carries himself lightly, on the balls of his feet, ready to act. But this figure holds himself up to his full height and peers down his nose at us.

And then there are the ghosts.

The mass of spirits is deliberately avoiding the Aiden look-alike, creating a soul-free circle several feet around him all the way up to the ceiling. They didn't do that at the summer palace. Several passed right through him.

The small hairs rise along the nape of my neck. Could it be a shifter? I turn my head slightly, to make sure Bard hasn't somehow escaped. No, he is still there within the prison of ghosts. Nahini catches my eye, her gaze insistent as though she's trying to communicate with me. She blinks down deliberately, then looks back up to me, then turns to Aiden. The message couldn't be clearer if she shouted in my ear.

View the soul plane.

I turn back to the Aiden imposter and switch my vision so I can see his soul. When I've viewed him in the past, Aiden has the spirit of a wolf as well as the man, both contained within his body.

This being's soul only has one life essence. But not only is it the wrong shape, it's the wrong color. Every creature I've met, human, fey, giant and even Underhill have a fuzzy blue outline that indicates their soul within his or her flesh. This being glows golden, like an autumn sunset. Only two creatures carry that sort of power in their aura. Power greater than even a cursed demigod.

The Fates.

Again, I study the rigid stance, the imperial way "Aiden" looks down his nose at my mother. The familiar derision that tugs up the corner of his—her, mouth. And I know which of my aunts has come to my rescue.

There's only one reason why Addy would come. She's foreseen my death and she's here to stop it. My protector, my champion, the woman who'd disposed of the bodies of my victims, who was always warning me to think through my actions. The one who is willing to trade her life for mine.

Because no matter what happens next, Chloe will have to abide by the law and kill Addy for stepping in where she doesn't belong.

That damned wolf isn't the only one who would risk everything to save you.

Dread pools in my stomach. Loki's poem about the silly dead girl is about to come true. And Addy has decided she would rather die than see that happen.

"Get him back here," Underhill hisses at the being she believes is Aiden. "Bring him to me now."

Addy folds her arms over her chest. "Not unless you release Nic."

The throne room has gone silent.

"You dare try to command me?" Underhill stares at the figure standing defiantly before her. "Have you forgotten who holds your leash?"

Aiden—Addy steps forward. "Nic is no longer an Unseelie queen. The Shadow Throne has been claimed. She's no threat to you. Release her into Midgard. Return her to the path she was on before."

"No," I shout. "I don't want to go back to that life. How could I?"

"Quiet," Addy almost ruins her disguise by snapping at me. "You don't have a choice."

We all have choices. Every single day.

Those had been her words, heartfelt.

"I won't go without you," I say to my aunt, to all of my loyal Unseelie courtiers. My family.

Addy had made her choice in coming here and interfering with the natural progression of fate. She will die either way. But they will have to drag me kicking and screaming from this place.

Underhill studies her a moment. "You will be forever separated from her. The madness will take hold of you if you cross the Veil. She will be banished, never to return."

Aiden's leaf green eyes, hiding Addy's soul, are steady on her. "At least I know she will live."

"Very well," Underhill nods and two of her guards grab me by the arms. "Nicneven, you are hereby banished from Underhill and my presence. If you return, you will be executed. Take her to the nearest in-between."

"No!" I shriek again and reach for the winds. Nothing, there is nothing there. *Gleipnir* has cut me off from my element as effectively as Gretchen-Fenrir has usurped my crown. Two Unseelie guards with skin the color and texture of dried moss, step forward and drag me by the arms kicking and screaming from the throne room.

"At least let me say goodbye!" I shout. Tears prick at my lids. I'm never going to see her again, my selfless aunt, my rock.

Gretchen snorts, but Underhill studies me. "Tell me who has the Soul Reaper."

"Freya, probably. She stole it before." I don't care if I'm giving away a goddess's great secret.

Underhill gestures with her hand. "Let her say goodbye to him."

The mossy guards release me and I stumble forward and fling myself into her arms. She still smells like Addy.

"Why?" I choke on a sob in her ear.

"Because it is my destiny." She pulls back and runs her fingers down the side of my face, more maternal than lover-like. "Embrace your fate, my girl. It has been my privilege to know you."

The tears roll unchecked. "Come with me."

She smiles and even though it's with Aiden's lips, I see Addy's face. "I might still do some good here before the end."

"Midnight, my liege," Rodrick says.

A distant clock tolls as the hour is at hand.

Bong. Bong. Bong.

Behind me there is a gasp, then a shriek. So focused on me, the guards moved away from the Seelie king.

Bong. Bong. Bong.

Soladin takes full advantage of their neglect. He reaches into his chest and removes his still-beating heart. Glowing green it lights up the cavern.

Bong. Bong. Bong.

"No!" Underhill rushes for him, her hands outstretched and grasping for her prize.

Bong. Bong. Bong.

The final chime sounds as she reaches him, but even as her hand closes around his wrist, the green light winks out.

Taj has taken his place on the Green Throne.

"Long live the king," Soladin rasps.

Murmurs fill the gallery, the Unseelie subjects growing restless.

Nahini grips the bars of her prison. Bard by her side. Soladin falls to the floor, laughing hysterically as tears of relief fill his eyes.

Underhill drops the dead heart to the ground. A ball of blue-green fire engulfs her hand. She rounds on me.

"You gave your word," Addy charges toward her, still wearing Aiden's face. "She is to go free. You can't hurt her."

Underhill huffs out a breath and then hurls her fireball at the fallen heart. Soladin rolls back as the magic engulfs the last little piece of him.

"I said I would return her to Midgard." My mother's smile is the stuff of nightmares. "To her life. Return her to the path she was on before. No magic, no crown. The bargain is struck."

She snaps her fingers and a door appears behind me. I whirl.

"Nic! Watch out!" Addy calls.

But she is too late. The mossy guards shove me through the doorway, through the in-between and onto a bridge.

The door slams shut behind me, closing me in darkness.

Through the Man's Eyes

"Angrboda!" Aiden shouts through the in-between where Underhill had shoved the giantess through. "The debt is paid!"

He'd waited until midnight to open the portal, the point where the Veil between worlds is thinnest. Underhill would be least able to track the crossing. Now he had to hope the Hag of the Ironwood hears his call. He couldn't just shove the boy through the portal with no one on the other side to help him acclimate to the mortal realm.

No matter how much he wants this task done.

Jedda lies curled up on a sand dune, fast asleep. The new Master of the Waves had struggled and fought when he learned that Aiden had no intention of returning him to the palace or his father. The child was brave and willing to fight for his people.

For his many faults, Wardon had been a good sire.

Aiden paces while he waits. He needs to get back to the cave, to Nic.

The portal opens and the figure with bloodred hair appears.

"Wolf," she nods. "What have you there?"

"The hope for the Seelie Court." He scoops the boy up, careful not to wake him. "I need you to watch him."

"Me?" Her brows draw down.

"I cannot cross, not without madness taking hold. The mortal realm would not stand a chance against my beast."

She still looks skeptical so he adds, "there is no one else I trust."

The giantess sucks in a breath and then steps forward arms outstretched.

The transfer is as careful as though he were handing her an egg twenty feet above a concrete floor. Both of their bodies in their respective realms, both of their arms in-between. He doesn't allow himself a chance to imagine what would become of Jedda if either of them didn't maintain a sure grip.

Angrboda steps back and looks down at the boy's sleeping face.

"Take him to the farm, to Nic's aunts. They will do whatever they can to help."

She looks up at him, her brow furrowing. "Then you haven't heard."

Dread coils in his stomach. "Heard what."

"The Shadow Throne has a new ruler."

"Nic?"

She shakes her head. "My son and your half-brother. He holds the mortal Gretchen in thrall."

Aiden staggers back and lands hard. Had he just made a mistake handing the giantess the child?

"I had no part in this scheme," she says. "Fenrir was trapped until your mortal girl crossed and he burrowed into her skin. Their life forces are joined."

Aiden remembers smelling the lie on Gretchen after they had crossed. He'd been so focused on Bard that he hadn't perceived the larger threat.

"There's more." Angrboda stares down at the child in her arms. "Fenrir plans to release Loki. I fear the end approaches."

Blood pounds in his veins. "I need to find Nic."

She turns away, but then looks back. "You are a better man than your father, a better mate to your Unseelie queen."

"She isn't a queen." He shakes his head. "Not with Fenrir holding the Shadow Throne."

Angrboda's lips curl up and he doesn't like the light in her eyes. "There are two Unseelie thrones, are there not?"

I cross the Veil about a mile from the farmhouse. A sickle moon hangs in the blue-black sky. I have no idea how much time has passed since I rode at the head of my Wild Hunt back to save the Green Throne.

I swallow hard. My Wild Hunt no longer. Gretchen's Wild Hunt. If Gretchen was ever a person, not just some sort of disguise for Fenrir all along.

This time there is no truck to pick me up. My feet seem to grow heavier with every step. Banished, I am banished from the fey realm. Risen queen no longer. Forever young, able to lie, but I have no weapons, no allies.

Addy is gone. Lost to me. Underhill will discover the deception in time. Soladin, Bard and Nahini are trapped in the underground palace. The ghosts obey Fenrir's command.

I need to do something. Banished or not, I must go back. Demand that Freya return *Seelenverkäufer* so I can cross undetected. Find Aiden and get him healed by Taj. Set them all free. I won't hesitate again to kill Underhill.

Why didn't you do it when you had the chance?

The first time in my life I'd shown mercy and look how it's turned out. Well no, technically Gretchen was the first time I'd shown mercy.

Note to self—showing mercy doesn't end well.

The farm is eerily quiet as I approach. No lights on in the house. Something strikes me as off. Even if it's late I would expect to see Chloe pacing anxiously in front of the hearth, waiting for me to return.

Did Addy tell her what she planned to do? Sickness passes

through me as I imagine breaking the news to Chloe that she now must kill her big sister.

Unless she is already on her way to do just that.

Snowflakes begin to fall as I mount the wooden steps. My heart is heavy, my mind distracted.

"Nic?" Chloe says from behind me. "What are you doing here?"

I turn and am immediately enveloped in the scent of cinnamon and sugar as she draws me to her and presses my face against her pink puffy jacket.

"I live here."

"You shouldn't have come back. It isn't safe." She glances around furtively.

It isn't like her to be so paranoid, but we have bigger problems. "Chloe, Underhill has Addy. You have to help me get her out."

She yanks on my arm, tugging me into the house. Once the door is shut behind us, she punches in the code. "You need to run before they come back. Pack as fast as you can. I'll keep watch."

"Before who comes back?"

"The FBI." Her green eyes lock on mine. "They have your diary, Nic. With your fingerprints on all the licenses. They know you killed Paul Anderson and that hiker in the woods. I played dumb but I don't think they believed me. Nic, they're coming for you. They were already here yesterday. The farm isn't safe anymore."

Dread coils in my stomach. "No."

The sound of gravel crunching under tires. Chloe whirls to the window. "It's them. Run!"

"Come with me."

She shakes her head. "I'll stall them."

"How?"

In answer, she moves to the side table and pulls out a pair of revolvers.

My blood chills. "They'll kill you."

"I can't die like that."

"Chloe," I beg, "please come with me."

"I will find you again." She checks the ammunition and cocks the hammers. "Go, before they know you're here."

I bolt for my bedroom, for the large window big enough to climb through. Blood pumps as true terror courses through me. The FBI. How many times had Addy warned me that they were watching? Not to keep the stupid licenses.

The screen hits the floor with a clatter even as someone starts hammering on the front door. "Open up, FBI!"

My feet hit the ground with a crunch. The tree line is about a hundred yards from the house. If I can just make it to the trees, I stand a better chance of keeping hidden.

The sound of gunshots breaks the still winter air. Chloe.

I hang onto what she said about being unable to die. She's a Fate, a Norn, a force greater than the gods or Underhill. She won't die.

I'm within touching distance of the hundred-year-old oak when more shots ring out. Snow flies up, bark splinters from the massive tree. Overhead, a single crow takes flight.

Something hits my shoulder hard enough to knock me off stride. The impact has me staggering forward. I've been shot.

Desperate, I reach the oak and try to meld with it in the way of a tree nymph. Nothing happens. My magic is gone. Snatched away by Underhill.

She dumped me back here, without magic.

I can't die, I'm immortal.

But a gunshot wound still hurts. And what's worse, the FBI is closing the distance.

I stumble on as the pain mounts, delayed by shock, the

bitter cold, seeps into my awareness. Another bullet buries into the back of my calf. I fall forward, my hands hitting the snow, the impact jarring my wounded shoulder. No!

They surround me in seconds, vultures circling roadkill. "Hands above your head."

Aiden! I call out with my mind. *Don't let them take me.*

But Aiden isn't here. My blood seeps into the snow, turning the virgin powder crimson. Chloe must be gone. I'm alone, abandoned and at their mercy.

"Hands behind your back." One of the men wearing an FBI jacket says.

There are too many for me to take out one at a time with my goodnight kiss. I consider letting them shoot me dead. I would rather die than be incarcerated. But how long will I stay dead? If I revive before they leave, there will be no way to keep them from taking me apart one piece at a time to see how I managed it.

Slowly, I move my hands into place. One steps forward, stowing his sidearm in a holster and extracting a pair of handcuffs.

And a leather mask with metal fastenings up the back. It has eyeholes and slits cut for my nose. But no opening for my mouth.

Terror racks me. They know about my goodnight kiss. About me. They came prepared.

"No." I struggle, but with my hands bound there isn't anything I can do as one man grips my short, dark hair and pulls it back. Another slips the mask into place.

The mask is zipped up and then they carry me back to one of their vehicles. I want to fight, but the more I struggle the harder it is to pull in a breath through the thin nose slits. Fearing I'll pass out, I hold still as they strap me down on a gurney.

The snow swirls down as the doors shut firmly behind me. In a few minutes, it'll be like I never existed.

To be concluded....

Need to know what happens next with Nic and Aiden? Buy Into the Fire *now.*

IT'S NOT MY WORDS THAT COUNT.
IT'S YOURS!

Please consider leaving an honest review for this book. Reviews help readers like you find books they enjoy, or warn them off from ones they won't. Reader reviews help the authors you love sell books and help them put money toward the next title. Even a sentence or two can mean the difference between a series that continues and one that flops. I found one of my favorite series from a two star review. So if you want more, tell the world.

Thank you for reading!

ABOUT THE AUTHOR

Gwen Rivers is the changeling of a *USA Today* bestselling mystery author. When not writing urban and rural fantasy with kickass heroines, you can find her poring over Norse mythology, dicing with the Fates, cavorting with werewolves or hunting for fairy wine in the deep, dark woods.

Find out what Gwen is working on now. Become a Patron today!